Better Left Forgotten

LISA HELEN GRAY

BOOK ONE IN
THE FORGOTTEN SERIES

Better Left Forgotten

Chapter One

CAITLYN

Gasping for breath, I shoot up in bed, sweat trickling down my neck and breastbone.

I know the nightmare wasn't real, yet the feeling coursing through my body is trying to tell me otherwise.

I swipe my thick, dark hair out of my face, my other hand gripping the bedsheets. I glance around my small room, trying to remind myself where I am.

It's dark out, yet I can hear people partying outside; the steady thump of the music shaking the walls.

When my daughter and I arrived at Cabin Lakes over three months ago, the place was quiet, practically free of any other people.

Not so much anymore.

Recently, the owners, Roy and Hayley, began to rent out the cabins once again. After being closed for construction for a long period of time, they couldn't afford to continue with no income.

I love it here. I love Roy and Hayley, who not only gave me a job, but help out with my daughter, Carrie-Ann. They're like surrogate parents to me, and grandparents to Carrie. Carrie has even started sleeping over on the nights I work, and she loves every minute of it.

Although I don't like our nights apart, I am enjoying working in the new bar/club that was finished a few weeks ago. It's the second part of my job here, and I prefer it to cleaning the cabins, even if I have to deal with a lot of drunken people. Now that the place is picking up, there are more people to deal with. It's also open to the public, so it isn't only paying guests who can use the restaurant and bar.

I guess I should have known my peace wouldn't last long.

Early this morning— yesterday morning now, I guess— a bunch of bikers turned up, and they didn't do it quietly. After working a night shift, I was stressed to be woken up by the revving of their engines. It was too much noise to handle for that time of the morning.

Carrie-Ann, on the other hand, loved it. She raced to the window, squealing with delight. She wanted to go and play, whereas I hated their presence and the disturbance of peace.

I just hope it's a weekend visit and they'll be gone by Monday morning.

Licking my dry lips, I decide to get up for a drink. My feet drag against the laminate flooring on my way to the kitchen, where I pull down a glass and pour myself some water. Gazing outside, my brows pinch together.

It isn't just a party going on out there. It seems like it's an orgy, and all the neighbouring towns have been invited.

There are men and women everywhere. Some are sprawled out on the grass, smoking and chatting with their group of friends; some are laughing uproariously; and some are dancing like they are in the middle of a packed-out club. It doesn't bother me. Hell, the sexual activities aren't bothering me. It's the music and the noise level.

There is no respect.

Nothing.

With a sigh, I head back to my room, hoping I can get at least a few more hours of sleep.

MY BLOOD IS BOILING. Each time the music or the noise level gets higher, the closer I come to exploding.

Two and a half hours I have been listening to this. Two and a half hours of trying to get back to sleep. I knew nearly an hour ago it was pointless, so I got my Kindle out, hoping I could tune it out with the words on the page.

Nope. I couldn't get past the first sentence without something happening outside, whether it was a loud bang, a squeal, or the music being turned up.

How my monkey hasn't woken up is beyond me, and I know I'm tempting fate by believing she'll stay asleep.

The bass of the next song has the few hanging pictures within the cabin shaking. Rolling over to my stomach, I shove my face into the pillow and scream.

I'm exhausted.

Nearly brought to tears by the lack of sleep, I let the anger burn through me. Throwing the sheet off, I jump out of bed and storm over to the dresser. I slip on my UGG kitten slippers, not really caring that I'm only wearing shorts and a thin tank top, before stomping through the cabin.

I jerk to a stop near the door, spotting a pair of scissors on the kitchen worktop. Leaning over, I snatch them up before leaving in a fury.

"Enough is enough," I grouch, as I storm across the grass, towards the sound system.

As I'm walking along, I notice the extension cable that leads to just the plug I'm after. I head over, ignoring the stares from the men around me. It isn't just the men curious and watching me. The women seem just as intrigued.

When I reach a group lying down on the grass, laughing and joking and talking about what 'Susan' did last week, I have to stop myself from yelling expletives at them for their rude and selfish behaviour. Instead, I glare, narrowing my eyes on each of them. When the whispers begin, I keep my head held high, not giving a shit what they're all thinking as I make my way towards the stereo.

I wrench the plug from its socket, and everything around me freezes— before it begins.

"What the fuck?"

"Who turned the music off?"

"What the fuck is she doing?"

"What is she wearing?"

I sniff, ignoring their comments and outrage. I lift the scissors, a small smile tugging at my lips. Peace is so close. Just as I'm about to snip that bloody plug, the hairs on the back of my neck stand on end.

I slowly tilt my head to the side and find a large, muscled male looming over me, his arms crossed over his chest.

My skin breaks out in goose bumps. Every fibre of my being is hyper aware of him.

I need a cold bucket of water tipped over me because every part of my body is beginning to heat.

He's… He's perfection. His dark hair is short but thick, and I can't help but imagine running my fingers through it.

He reminds me of a bad boy, with his ruggedly handsome appearance. I lick my lips as my gaze runs over his muscular physique. I've never liked muscle on a man before, but on him...

A sigh slips free as I gawk at his chest, the muscles tensing as I pass over them. His skin glistens, and a trickle of sweat drips down his muscles before disappearing beyond the low-hanging, baggy black shorts he's wearing. The urge to reach out with my tongue and lap up that trickle of sweat has me feeling like a thirsty nun in a desert.

I sway on my feet as I run my gaze back up, reaching his five o'clock shadow, then his lips. They are full, plump, and are pulled up into a smirk.

Slowly, I raise my gaze to his intense chestnut-coloured eyes. They're captivating, smouldering, but it's the amusement lurking in them that has me returning to the present.

Did he say something?

"Huh?"

"I said: I wouldn't do that if I were you, Kitten," he drawls.

I shake my head, trying to clear the fog, but it's useless when he's standing in front of me shirtless and looking all sexy as hell.

"W-what?"

His lips twitch. "Would you like five more minutes with my body, because I'm good with that."

I snap out of my lustful daze, trying to ignore the fact I know my face is flaming red. The heat is causing sweat to trickle down my temples.

"Put down the scissors," he says, his commanding tone making me shiver.

It's then I realise I'm holding the scissors up like a weapon in front of me. I place them down by my side yet remember why I'm out here.

I grit my teeth and straighten my shoulders. "I've had enough; it's three o'clock in the fucking morning. I have to be up in three hours— not that you would care. So, no, I will not put down the fucking scissors."

"Why don't you just put them down and I'll get you a drink, yeah?" he asks, his tone lower, more seductive.

I nearly sway at his persuading but shake my head, refusing to let him get to me. "No," I snap. "I gave you enough time to have your little party, but you've shown no respect for the people who actually have to work tomorrow, so I'm cutting you off myself."

I take the scissors to the plug, and as I lock gazes with him, something predatory and daring lurks in his eyes. With one hard snip, the plug falls free, and the sound of it landing on the floor is explosive.

When I drag my attention away from him, I notice everyone has dropped what they were doing to stare at our interaction. I ignore the gaping stares and turn around, picking my feet up once again to leave.

"My work here is done. Enjoy your night, boys," I call over my shoulder, as I take a slower stroll to my cabin, my legs shaking the entire way.

When I reach the front door of my home, my body jolts with fear as a hard, masculine body presses into the back of mine.

"You shouldn't have done that, Kitten," a voice whispers seductively into my ear.

My entire body is hypersensitive to his proximity, and I sway a little into him, like two magnets being drawn together.

Spinning around, I put distance between us. "Why? I have a daughter asleep in there, and I have to work in a few hours. I don't need to fucking listen to you lot partying all night."

Moving fast, he places his hands tightly on my waist. His touch on my bare skin, where my tank top has ridden up, causes a sensual, burning sensation, and once again, my cheeks burn. I harden my features, trying to pretend his touch doesn't affect me.

"Then why not fucking come and ask one of us to turn it down? I would have turned it down, or even turned it off, if you had asked me. Did you really need to cut the fucking plug?"

I narrow my eyes. "I made a point, didn't I? You won't be doing it again in a hurry."

When I try to push away so I can leave, his fingers tighten over my hips. He pulls me sharply against him, our bodies flush together. An involuntary shiver runs over me at the feel of his warm, hard body. My nipples pebble through the thin material of my tank top. I can feel them rubbing against the flimsy material.

My tongue slips out, running over my lip; my chest rising and falling as I stare into his chestnut eyes.

His gaze flickers from my chest to my face, and amusement tugs at his lips. I inwardly groan, mortified over my reaction to him.

He's a jerk. However, my body can't seem to get that memo.

My fingers and palms tingle as I place them on his chest, and I listen to him inhale sharply. For a moment, time stops, and all I can do is stare at where our skin touches. My fingers tense against the firm muscle on his chest, and I melt against him.

My torturous body.

"Let go," I demand, snapping out of my lust-filled state.

He smirks, and a shiver rolls over me. "No."

Glaring, I stomp my foot like a two-year-old. I don't care that it's immature. I don't care that it's embarrassing. I just hate/love my reaction to him.

I hate that he knows what the reaction was, like he can read my thoughts as well as my body.

"Oh, you made your point alright, Kitten. Will I do it again? No, because you cut the fucking plug," he growls, a disbelieving tone lacing his voice.

"Good," I bite out, trying to push him away. "Now let me go so I can finally get some sleep."

A sharp exhale of breath escapes me when he brings me closer, bringing his face down to mine. "This isn't over, Kitten. You owe me now, and I think I may just take my compensation while I'm here," he declares, his tone husky.

My head is screaming at me to run, to do something, but my body melts into him, relaxing into his deliciously hard chest.

My lids flicker closed when he's a breath away, but surprising me, he doesn't kiss me. Instead, he buries his face into the crook of my neck, inhaling.

His lips and breath tickling my neck has me biting back a moan. Desire courses through me. I can't believe my reaction.

This man is a stranger, someone I just met, and I'm letting him touch me.

Intimately.

It scares me. This egotistical, obnoxious man, who I don't really like all that much, is turning me on with a mere touch.

It isn't right, even if it feels it.

I've been bewitched; it's the only reasonable explanation.

"I can feel your pulse beating, Kitten," he whispers seductively, running his nose along my jaw. "Did you come over to cut my plug, just to get my attention? Because, baby, you have it."

My body tenses, and before I can argue, his lips crash down on mine. I try to fight him, to push him away, but once I get a taste, I want more.

I need more.

I find myself kissing him back with as much fire and passion as he is with me. My arms go around him, bringing him closer as he deepens the kiss.

What am I doing?

God, just shoot me now.

He pulls away, breaking the kiss and leaving me wobbling on shaky legs. I glance up, my lips swollen and bruised as I try to figure out what just happened. And why I'm missing his touch so badly.

I duck my head, too ashamed of my actions to even look at him a moment longer.

What was I thinking?

"You even purr like a kitten, Kitten," he murmurs, amusement lacing his tone.

The arrogant prick is laughing at me. I snap my head up, furious not just with him but with myself. I should have known better than to fall for soulful eyes and a hot body.

Although, I have never done this before.

"Well, this kitten has claws," I snap, jabbing him in the chest. "So, the next time you decide to maul me, you'll be wise enough to remember that."

I turn my back on him and reach for the handle. My fingers close around it, when a hand lands on my arm. He spins me around, and I slam into his chest.

His pupils dilate and his jaw clenches. "You wanted that as much as I did, Kitten. Maybe the next time you come over to cut a plug, *you'll* be wise enough to remember I'll be sticking my tongue somewhere other than your throat," he warns, his attention going to my lips.

I'm not a prude. I know exactly what he meant, and my body shivers in response. I squeeze my thighs together, trying to ease the ache pulsing between them.

I stare at him for a moment longer, my lips parted, unable to form any sort of comeback.

He steps back, giving me space for the first time since meeting him. A breeze blows over my damp skin, causing me to shiver.

My heart races as I turn to go inside, safely locking the door behind me. I hear him laughing and I grit my teeth, moving away from the door before I do something else stupid.

My back hits the wall, and I lean against it for support as I run my finger along the seam of my lips, still feeling his lips on mine.

I went out there to put a stop to the music, not to end up kissing the most pig-headed guy I've ever met. How I went from spitting mad to a puddle of goo is beyond me. I'm not even sure how it happened.

Talk about first impressions.

After taking a minute to pull myself together, I check all the windows and doors before heading into Carrie's room. She's sleeping soundly, her body curled around her pillow.

After leaving her door slightly ajar, I head to bed, flopping down onto my back and staring up at the ceiling. There is no way I can sleep now, not after that kiss. After him.

And all I need to deal with on no sleep is a four-year-old with energy like she is on speed and drinks Red Bull like it's water. But that's the way it's looking. She is talkative, mature for her age, and basically a smart arse. And I wouldn't change her. I just wish I had her energy and spirit.

Tomorrow, I will talk to Roy about our new guests. Because I don't want a repeat performance of tonight. I'll cut their electric next.

My lips still buzz from our kiss and peppermint fills my mouth. I don't even know his name, and I let him kiss me.

I growl, rolling to my side as I tuck my hands under my pillow. I'm not going to let him win.

It was a mistake.

A kiss.

Nothing more.

Chapter Two

CAGE

I STARE AT THE CLOSED DOOR, MY lips curling into a grin. She surprised me when she kissed me back. I thought she'd slap me, maybe knee me in the balls. Kissing me back hadn't crossed my mind. But I couldn't look at her a moment longer and not take those lips. She was hot, even in those ridiculous kitten slippers.

I adjust my dick in my shorts and step away from the door before I do what I promised I would do to her.

As I pass a group of people, I jerk my chin up. "Call it a night now, boys."

They groan but begin to pack up their things. I head back over to where they set up the sound system and the table filled with drinks.

Dante, my best friend since we were kids, looks up at my approach.

His brows pull together, disbelief written over his face. "What the fuck, brother? What was her problem? I can't even repair this, bro; I don't have a spare fucking plug with me."

"Mate, she's female," I reply, like that's answer enough. "And I'll get a new one."

He throws the plug down on the floor, just as a female sidles up to him, running a finger down his chest. He grins, before bending down and capturing her lips in a kiss. "Meet you in a bit, babe. I've got to clean this up."

She flutters her lashes. "Don't be long."

His dimples flash as he winks at her. "Promise."

"You're a pig."

He narrows his gaze. "She was sucking my dick when the music cut off."

"I told you to turn that shit off hours ago," I growl, a reminder of why I was even out on a run. "We aren't here to party."

He smirks, his eyes flashing. "Was it not worth it? I saw you tongue deep in that chick."

I smirk back. "Did you see her arse in those shorts? You'd have to be dead not to want that."

He chuckles, before sighing down at the broken music system. "Now I'm hard again and I've got no music."

"You need music to fuck?" I ask, arching an eyebrow because Dante is a whore.

Don't get me wrong, we have been working together for three years now, and he does his jobs, but sometimes, I wish he took life more seriously.

I own a construction business, along with a few motorcycle garages. My team also help out another friend of ours, Nate, who runs a security and private investigation company. Dante, however, is in between jobs. He doesn't need to work for me— he has talents of his own— but he chooses to.

When that dopey look crosses his face, I know something stupid is going to come out of his mouth.

"I like to fuck to the beat; heats things up and makes it interesting."

I roll my eyes. "Goodnight, Dante."

He salutes me before heading off in the direction the chick went.

I run a hand down my face before I head towards my cabin. When I got a call from Roy, an old friend of my dad's, saying he needed some work done after he had been fucked over, I jumped at the chance.

I thought it would be peaceful to be away from the shit storm of my life. I wanted to get away from it all.

Then we arrived and saw the mess Roy had been left with, and knew we were going to be here longer than expected. It sucks. Or it did— until that dark-haired, blue-eyed beauty with a nice set of tits and arse came marching over the green to cut off the plug. Now, things are finally starting to look up.

I push through my cabin door, heading straight to the bathroom. I need a shower, to wash away the sweat from my run.

My phone begins to ring on the side where I left it, and I head over, seeing my crazy ex-girlfriend's name flashing on the screen. I switch it off and move over to the shower, flicking it on.

We broke up eight months ago, and she isn't getting the memo. Then again, I should have known she'd pull this crap.

Things hadn't been good since I broke up with her the first time. Lou turned psycho on me. We had only been broken up for a few days when she came running to tell me she was pregnant. So, being the man my dad brought me up to be, I got back with her, wanting to be a father to my child. It didn't matter that I didn't love Lou. I knew I'd love my child.

And for some time, it was okay. It wasn't good, but it wasn't bad, not until some time had passed and my sister approached me. She wanted to know why Lou wasn't showing yet.

I'm a male; things like that don't register to me, so until Laura pointed it out, I didn't question it myself.

When I broached the subject with Lou the same night, she told me she had lost the baby and didn't know how to tell me. It was all tears and screeching as she told me. I believed every word that left her mouth; I had no reason not to trust her.

After that, I stayed out of obligation, out of sympathy. She was scared I'd leave her if she told me, and she was right; I would have. We had a deal when she told me she was pregnant. I told her we could try again if she changed her shit, stopped with the drugs and sleeping around. I was sick of it, sick of it all, but she was broken. Whether she admitted it or not, she was broken, and for some reason, she looked to me to fix it.

She put on quite the show and I soaked it all in. I was dealing with my own grief, and I let that cloud my judgement.

I let her pull the wool over my eyes. Still, as the days went by with no hospital appointments, or follow up appointments, I began to get paranoid.

I went through her phone, her emails, even her mail. There was nothing. Nothing about hospital appointments. But there was something else, something that had me searching the house like an officer doing a raid.

I close my eyes as the pain of that day hits me. The medicine cabinet was emptied all over the sink and worktop, and in my hand was her contraception pills, all taken, just like her messages said.

I lost my shit. I went into a fit of rage, smashing her phone against the wall and destroying all her stuff. I didn't even bother with bags for her clothes; instead, I threw it all over the front garden.

She had lied about being pregnant all along, conspiring with her mate on how to get me into bed so she could get pregnant for real. The bitch didn't even get through the door before I tore into her. I remember, at the time, wishing she were a bloke so I could punch the living shit out of her, but I'm not a woman beater, no matter what the crazy bitch had done and put me through.

It's why I was so glad Roy called about the job opportunity. She has hounded me every moment since, giving me shit and stalking me. I was hoping with some time down here, her crazy arse would find some other fucker to suck the soul out of.

The bathroom fills with steam as I slide the shorts off my body, picturing the sexy brunette from earlier.

I step in, the water scalding my skin as I put my back to the spray. I close my eyes, wondering what the hell she was thinking. She didn't know any of the men out there tonight, yet she strutted over the green like she owned every single one of them.

I had just run off the path to cut across the green during my run when I saw her. I paused, watching her tits bounce, her nipples hard through the thin tank. Then it was her arse.

After that, I unfroze, realising I wasn't the only one watching. The gleam in some of the guys' eyes made me want to commit murder, and I didn't know why.

It could be that a girl like her doesn't belong amongst rowdy, horny men.

But then I saw the scissors and where she was heading. It didn't take a genius to figure out what she was about to do, yet as my feet pulled me towards her, I couldn't take my eyes off her.

I didn't even care that she was wielding a pair of scissors. I just wanted to know who she was and get her into my bed.

And although I was very aware of her, it made me hard when she sensed me. It was like she could feel me; feel the dirty thoughts running through my mind. How I didn't bend her over the table there and then is beyond me, especially when the dirty minx ran her gaze all over me.

A grin teases at my lips as I think of how red her cheeks had gotten when she was caught ogling me. Not that I minded.

And then she went and surprised me further by cutting through the thin cord attached to the sound system. I was hard as a fucking rock. And pissed as fuck 'cause it was new.

Shell-shocked, I'd stood there like a plank, only coming out of my daze when the plug hit the floor. I would have laughed as I watched her arse strut off, but there was something about her that intrigued me. My feet moved on their own accord, following her.

I reach for my dick, clasping my hand around the large girth, pulling back as a groan slips free.

The globes of her arse shook as she walked off, and all I could picture was taking her from behind and smacking my hand across the pale cheek to make it red.

And her hair…

Another groan slips free, and I pump myself harder. She has the longest, wildest hair I have ever seen; the dark curls fall in waves, ending just above her round arse.

Fuck, what I would do to grab that in a fist while I slam inside her.

My balls tighten as I go over our encounter, never missing a detail. It wasn't just her body or her attitude that drew me to her. It was her piercing blue eyes that sparkled in the moonlight.

It was her luscious lips, ones I couldn't help but want wrapped around my dick.

Fuck, when she kissed me, she really kissed me.

And I kissed her like I was starving for oxygen. Why I didn't pull those tiny shorts down her legs and fuck her there, I don't know. It took tremendous strength not to.

The need to have her keeps building inside of me. It's strong, overwhelming, and as I rest my forehead against the tile, letting the spray hit my back, it's all I can think about.

If I see her again— and I wish I do— I'll fuck her. I'll have those sexy as fuck legs wrapped around me, my hands gripping that bouncy arse whilst her cunt squeezes my dick, if it's the last thing I do.

Imagining my lips wrapped around her tight little nipples, I explode, my cum spurting out in jets over the cream tile. I groan, stepping back and facing the spray. I find the temperature gauge, switching it down to the coolest temperature. I'm still hard, still wanting her.

I came here to get away from a woman; I don't need another one clouding my mind.

Still, fucking her won't be the problem.

It's knowing she doesn't seem like the one-night stand type that I have an issue with.

And even as the thought flitters through my mind, I have to wonder who is the one with the clinging issue. It's me thinking about her, fantasising about her.

"Fuck," I growl, slamming my fist against the tile.

I need to get laid.

Chapter Three

CAITLYN

Aﬀter getting a few hours' sleep, the chestnut-eyed guy is still on my mind. People always say things will look better in the morning, but it feels worse. I'm not only embarrassed by my behaviour, but I'm mortified. I kissed a complete stranger, and had he not pulled away, I'm certain I would have let him do more.

A lot of crazy stuff has happened in my twenty-one years of life, but never has a stranger kissed me with such passion, the likes of which I have never felt before.

I could still taste him when I woke up, and now, as I finish gathering my stuff together with Carrie-Ann running around me like a lunatic, I'm daydreaming about him.

Noticing Carrie still hasn't put her shoes on, I inwardly groan.

"Come on, Carrie, it's eight already and I need to drop you off with Hayley so I can get to work," I tell her, trying to keep my voice firm.

"Mummy," she whines, placing her fists on her hips. "Can't you just say you're sick so we can spend the whole day down at the lake? Please. I want to try out my new armbands that you got me."

"No, sweetie. I already told you I'd take you after work," I remind her. And I did. She loves the lake that's close by. It's more like a pond, and it's great for people who want to cool off or take a swim. It has a mini beach before you hit the water, which is great for picnics.

The weather has been hot of late, so midday is the best time to go down there. The water is always cool. Although I hate swimming, Carrie loves it, so I do it for her. It's late afternoon when the sun becomes too much, but it isn't like I can swap my shifts around. We need the money.

"But Mum," she cries.

"You know I need to work, Carrie, and it's not fair on Hayley or Roy if I pretend I'm sick just so you can go swimming. I promise we can go down there later."

She pouts, her shoulders sagging. "Okay. But just so you know, if I asked Roy and Hayley, they would let you come with me instead of working."

I smile, knowing they would let me if she asked. They probably would if *I* asked because that's how kind and generous they are. They've done so much for me, but I won't take advantage of their generosity.

I need the money though, just in case we have to leave quickly. And it always happens. I duck my head, not letting her see my expression. She's doing good here; she doesn't need to be reminded of any of the bad.

We were staying with an old family friend not so long ago. Tears gather in the back of my eyes as I remember the man we lost. He had been good to us— before he was murdered.

After his funeral, we left pretty much right away and kept driving from place to place, never staying for long. The last town wasn't working out so well, so when I saw a 'for hire' ad for Cabin Lakes, I took it.

Still, I was scared. I didn't want to lose anyone else. I didn't want anyone else to die.

But it seemed to be life, and I was petrified it would swallow me whole.

I rub my hand over her dark curls, smiling down at her. "That's because you're hard to say no to, sweetie."

She's beautiful, and is the spitting image of my sister, Courtney. They both have dark hair with springy curls, whereas mine is just long and wavy. They also have the same light blue eyes, where mine are a piercing royal blue. My dad used to say they looked like snake eyes— whatever that meant.

However, every time I look at Carrie, I see my sister; I see her smile, her eyes, and some days, Carrie even acts like her.

She's gone. Murdered. And each time I'm reminded of their similarities, it's a reminder she will never get to see her grow. She never got to see her first steps, hear her first word, and she never got to take her to her first day of school. She will miss it all.

It's been hard without Courtney, but every day I look at Carrie and the pain, the loss, lessens. Because having Carrie with me reminds me I have a part of Courtney with me.

She will never truly be gone.

I hold out my hand, and Carrie blinks up at me through those beautiful blue eyes before taking it, smiling widely. "Come on, let's go."

*** *** ***

We arrive on time and are greeted by Hayley on the steps leading to their front door.

"Hey, Caitlyn, heard you got in touch with your badass side last night," Hayley murmurs, her lips twitching.

Hayley is a middle-aged woman with a round figure, lovely short blonde hair, green eyes, and a smooth, gentle voice. She's so kind, generous and giving that it's a miracle someone like her even exists.

"Huh?" I ask, my forehead creasing.

She chuckles at my expression. "Cage Carter came around this morning, asking us if we knew who the firecracker was staying in cabin 4A. Roy asked him why, and he told us you cut the plug on their stereo last night."

Holy shit, he told on me. *That little dick.*

The blood drains from my face at her words. I'm grateful she's laughing and not giving me shit because I think I'd faint.

I grimace when I'm positive I'm not going to get fired. "It was early in the morning and they were blasting their music like no one's business," I explain defensively, yet keep my tone light. I bite my bottom lip, blinking up through my lashes. "Am I in trouble?"

She waves me off, her laughter turning into chuckles. "No, of course you're not. In fact, Cage laughed the whole time he told us, and from what he said, they were the ones in the wrong, not you," she tells me, and I instantly relax somewhat. "He also informed us they won't play music that loud or late again." She pauses, her lips twitching. "Not that they can play anything now."

My chuckle turns into laughter because hearing it from someone else is quite funny. And so unlike me.

Carrie had long run into their cottage as we were talking, which isn't surprising. She loves being here. It's a beautiful home, surrounded by beautiful land. Hayley takes care of her garden surrounding the cottage. Roy erected mini fences in the front and back so that Hayley has her own little patch to work with, while the gardeners Roy hired take care of all the other grass, weeds, and flowers. They own acres of land, so it must take some hard work to maintain the growing grass around us. I know Roy only bothers keeping the footpaths, picnic spots, and camping grounds clear of any weeds or overgrown grass. Everything else is neglected to the wild or dead, but that doesn't matter, because the place is stunningly beautiful, especially the views.

The scenery is breath-taking when the sun sets and the light is dim across the sky. If you're down by the lake, the way the light shines on the water gives it a soothing, almost intimate feel. Just thinking about it makes me smile.

"I am sorry," I tell her.

She reaches out, squeezing my shoulder. "Don't fret. It's fine."

I nod, then pull my bag higher over my shoulder. I have cabins to clean before the next flood of guests arrive. "Right, I should get going. Do you have the list?"

"Yes, here you go," she declares, handing me a clipboard with a list of cabins to clean and detailing who is in them. "We also need another favour. Tillie called in sick again this morning, so we need you for entertainment tonight, honey. We can pay you double for the inconvenience, and you can get off early. Is that okay?"

It's not okay. I hate being up on stage in front of all those people. But how can I say no when I need the money and they do so much for me?

Hayley caught me singing to Carrie one night at the front of our cabin. I strummed the strings to my guitar and sang whatever song came into my head. That night it happened to be 'I need a hero' by Bonnie Tyler, when Hayley came by. I sang it softer and slower than Bonnie. It also happened to be Hayley's favourite song. When I finally realised she was standing there, the song had finished and she stood on my cabin steps with tears in her eyes, staring at me in awe. She demanded I sing for the pub/club once every so often, but I refused, telling her I didn't feel comfortable. After much persuading, I agreed to do five songs one night, but they would have to hire someone if they wanted live entertainment all the time.

So, they did.

They hired Tillie a few weeks later, and ever since then, the girl has had more days off than I can count. She's a shy, timid young girl, but when she gets up on that stage, it's like she's a whole other person. She's so talented and gifted that I'm surprised she doesn't have other gigs.

"Yes, but I don't like it," I concede, letting out a breath. I'm praying I have time for a nap sometime today. "I'll be back before one to pick up Carrie. If you need me, call me. Okay?"

"Okay, girl, now off you go."

As THE DAY wears on, it's taking longer and longer to finish cleaning the cabins. And I know these are the men who arrived with Cage.

It feels weird knowing his name. I guess having him as a stranger kept me in denial about what happened. Now it's real. He's real.

Still, it seems his men don't know how to pick up after themselves, nor do any sort of cleaning. Their places are a mess, and as it's in my job description, I have to be the one to clean it all up. That includes cleaning up used condoms, emptying rubbish bags, and picking up wrappers along with empty beer cans off the floor.

When I arrive at the last cabin on my list, I stop just outside, looking up at the door. It's the one I've been avoiding like the plague all morning, putting it off till last.

Cage Carter's.

When I don't get an answer after knocking, I decide to let myself in. Entering, I call out, "Housekeeping." I wait for a minute, getting no answer.

Stepping further inside, I listen out for any other sounds indicating someone is here. Not hearing anything, I move forward, ready to get to work on the mess that's probably awaiting me.

Cage's cabin is the smallest one they have on site. It's the only cabin with one bedroom, which I'm thanking my lucky stars for right now. I just want to be in and out before he gets back. At this rate, I'll never get back to Carrie.

The men who were with Cage last night have obviously shared the other three cabins between them, as they sleep up to six people.

I'm surprised to find the place relatively tidy. The front living area only needs vacuuming and dusting, so I get to it, wishing I wasn't so on edge. I normally play music while I clean— it always makes it go faster— but I don't want to risk being caught unaware by him.

Not after last night.

After finishing up in the kitchen, I head down the hall to the bathroom as it's the one place that has taken me the longest in each cabin. At the end of the hall, there are two doors on either side of each other. One is for the bedroom and the other is for the bathroom, and from being in the cabin before, I know there's a door inside each of them for quicker access between rooms.

Leaving my cleaning supplies in the hallway next to the door, I enter the bathroom and come to a stop, my lips parting as I inhale sharply. My fingers clench around the door handle as my feet stay frozen to the floor. Cage Carter.

Naked.

Gloriously naked.

My gaze moves down his body, my eyes widening at his Donkey Kong hanging free. It twitches, and a whimper escapes me, my gaze shooting to his.

Holy shit!

"Oh, my God, I am so sorry," I screech, moving back and slamming the door shut behind me.

I lean against the door for support, but stumble backwards when it's suddenly pulled open. I fall on my backside, wincing at the sharp pain in my lower back.

I curse myself for not running for the front door when I had the chance. Now he's going to make my body react in weird ways and my head is going to get foggy and messed up.

I groan, straightening my back before looking up at Cage, who is standing above me wearing nothing but a towel and a cheesy grin. I'm just grateful he has on more than he did a minute ago, because I don't think my heart or nether regions could possibly take any more of… of all that is him.

"Can I help you?" he teases, holding his hand out to me.

Reluctantly, I place my hand in his, and the second I do, sparks fly through my entire body like electricity. My knees wobble and my grip tightens around his hand as he pulls me to my feet.

As soon as I'm on my feet, I pull my hand away, ignoring the tingles from his touch. I blush, ducking my head.

"I'm sorry. I called out, but when no one answered I assumed you weren't here," I admit.

I chance a glance and find him smirking instead of glaring. "It's no big deal. Shit happens."

No big deal? Has he seriously not noticed what a big *deal it is?* As those thoughts run through my mind, I can't help but look back down towards his package.

Embarrassingly, another squeak slips free. He's hard, and the damn thing is greeting me through the gap in the towel.

Holy shit, he has a hard-on.

"My eyes are up here, Kitten, but if you keep staring at me like that, then I'll let you take a closer look," he teases.

"What? I… I… I need to go," I stammer, and turn, rushing back down the hall.

"I thought you needed to clean up?" he yells, not hiding his amusement.

"I need to go," I grumble, more to myself than him.

My fingers are reaching for the handle on the door, when a set of hands land on my hips. I'm pulled back sharply into a hard chest, and I bite my bottom lip at the feel of his hardness pressing against my arse.

"Why are you leaving so soon?" he rasps.

My cheeks heat and I begin to tremble as his hands slowly run up my sides. How does he do this to me?

I fight the urge to push back against him.

"Let me go," I whisper, afraid he will hear the slight desperation in my voice.

He gently forces me to turn around, and I duck my head, unable to look at him. I gape, tensing when I get a birds-eye view of his erection.

Fuck!

Using his knuckles, he lifts my chin, forcing me to look at him. The second our gazes lock, it's like the walls I tried to put up fall away. He's all I can see. All I can smell.

He's a stranger, someone I only met last night, yet when I glance into his soulful eyes, it's like I've known him for a while. He doesn't feel like a stranger, not inside, and maybe that's why I'm not fighting him off, screaming at him to let me go, or why I'm not scared of him.

Because looking at him, I see something I can't decipher. I soften against him, trying not to think of the intensity shining back at me. If I did, I'd fall into his trap, the one where his lips are on mine again and I'm kissing him back.

"You need to let me go," I argue, my voice barely audible.

His lips pull up. "Is that what you want?"

Is it?

I don't know. Yet, he must see something in my expression because he leans forward, pressing his lips into the crook of my neck. I tilt my head back, closing my eyes at the sensation. It's a featherlight kiss, yet the blood in my veins begins to heat.

His fingers tighten around my waist and a moan slips free, and I feel his lips tug into a smile against my neck.

"God, you smell so good," he whispers, pressing another kiss just below my ear.

I grip his biceps when my legs threaten to give out. A 'hmmm' sound rumbles from the back of my throat when his tongue snakes out, licking up to my ear before he sucks my earlobe into his mouth.

What am I doing?

Why am I here?

When he pulls back, I sway towards him, drunk on lust. His pupils dilate as he scans my face, seconds before something changes. Something primal, exhilarating, charges the air between us. I'm not sure who kisses who first, me or him, but one minute we're staring at each other, and the next, my arms are around his neck while his arms wrap around me, bringing me flush against him as the kiss turns heated.

All thoughts of why I shouldn't be doing this fly out the window.

This is everything a kiss should be, everything I dreamed of. I don't know what kind of spell he has over me, but in this moment, I don't care. I just want him.

I hear the towel fall to the floor, and a small voice in the back of my head is telling me this needs to stop.

But it doesn't.

He grabs the back of my thighs and lifts me up, pressing my back against the door. He grinds against me, hitting the spot that has an embarrassing moan escaping me.

I'm so turned on, my body moves on its own, my hips grinding back, searching for friction to ease the ache.

The door vibrates behind my back, and it takes me a moment to realise someone is banging on it.

Humiliation flushes through me, and I pull back, breathing heavily. I open my mouth, but no words escape, not when I see he's just as turned on as me. His hair is a mess from where I ran my fingers through it.

The blood drains from my face when I realise what I was about to do.

With a stranger.

I have never reacted like this before; never felt such need and desire that I attacked someone like a crazy animal. I surrendered to him unapologetically, and a part of me, although scared, was excited by it. A thrill runs through me, and I wonder if this is what I have been missing: this connection.

His eyes bore into mine, making me feel vulnerable and open. I'm not sure I like it, especially when it feels like he can read my mind.

My body and mind are at war. I want to get down, to push him away, yet I'm frozen, willing deep down for him not to stop.

"What are you doing to me?" he rasps, watching me like I'm a new species.

"I was going to ask the same thing," I whisper back, unable to look away.

The banging on the door starts up again, startling me. I forgot about someone being outside. My eyes widen when a girl begins to shriek his name.

"Cage? Open the door."

Cage tenses, narrowing his eyes on the door behind me. The tension radiates off him, causing me to feel claustrophobic.

"Fuck," he growls.

"Um," I mumble, but trail off, not knowing what to say when he slowly slides me to my feet. I wobble a little on my feet and watch as he bends down to pick up his towel.

He was naked.

I was rubbing up against a naked man.

"Cage, I know you're in there. Open the fuck up, now," she screams, and I jerk at the venom in her voice.

"Wait here, Kitten. I'll go get rid of her," he orders, and I gape at him, wondering how he can function right now.

I slowly turn to the door, then back to him, finally finding my voice.

"I need to go. I need to pick up my daughter," I tell him. He pauses tying the towel around his waist, his brows shooting up to his hairline.

I'm used to this reaction, even from the same sex. I'm not sure if it's because I look really young, but it has been the same since I had her. She isn't biologically my daughter, but she is mine in every way that counts.

Only Roy and Hayley know this, and they know a part of my story. I missed out *a lot* and gave them a shorter version of it. It's for their own protection. The less people who know about my situation, the better. Everyone who has known what my secret is, or has tried to help me, have all died.

Although, I'm not sure why he is so surprised. I'm pretty certain I mentioned it last night.

"You have a daughter?" he asks, shaking his head, clearly not believing me.

"Yes," I snap. "Why do you think I went batshit crazy last night and cut the plug?"

He smirks, giving me a careless shrug. "I just thought you were batshit crazy, Kitten."

"Cage!" we hear screamed, right before a fist slams against the door.

I wipe the hair out of my face. What the hell am I doing here?

"I need to go," I tell him, but I'm wary about meeting whoever is on the other side of that door. I glance to it, biting my lip. There's no other way I can leave.

"Crazy bitch must have a tracking device on me," Cage mutters.

I snap my attention to him, my face paling. "What? You have a girlfriend? Oh my God! I let you… We… Oh God! We kissed. *Twice.*"

What the heck am I doing? I should have known. I didn't even ask. I open the door to make my escape, but a tall blonde woman steps right up to me before I can take a step out. I trip on my feet, slamming into Cage, who steadies me.

"Who the fuck are you?" she screams, pointing her finger in my face.

"Lou, you have two seconds to get out of her face before I move you out of it. Then you can get into your beatdown car and drive the fuck away," Cage warns her.

I gape at the anger pouring off her. I kissed her boyfriend. Tears gather in my eyes, and I push off Cage. This time, he doesn't stop me, and neither does she. I race down the steps, running away from both of them as I hear them arguing.

I should have known better. I don't need this kind of attention brought to me. It's only a matter of time before Robin knows where I am, unless he already does. Which wouldn't surprise me. He always seems to know where we are.

I can't form attachments, not any more than I have. And bringing this kind of attention to myself will more than likely get him to act.

Just as always.

I still have hope that my last plan worked, but only time will tell.

Chapter Four

CAGE

SHIT.

I watch Caitlyn run away and grit my teeth. I saw those tears before she left, and her expression told me what she was thinking.

I don't want whatever that was to end. Going after her isn't an option right now, but I want to. God, do I want to.

I narrow my gaze on the bitch in front of me, blocking her from entering the cabin.

How she has the nerve to show her face is beyond me.

"What the fuck are you doing here, Lou? You need to get it into your thick head that we. Are. Not. Together," I bite out, punctuating each word. "Do I need to get a restraining order against you?"

"Cage," she purrs, fluttering those fake eyelashes at me.

I put my hand up, my jaw clenching. "Don't," I warn her.

Just looking at the bitch is making my skin crawl. I want nothing more than to throw her arse over to her car. I don't want her here. I don't want to look at her. I came here to get away from her shit.

And Lou getting in Caitlyn's face like that still has me boiling with rage. I've never hurt a woman in my life, but when she got in her face, I wanted nothing more than to protect Caitlyn by any means necessary. And I don't understand it. There is just something about her that screams at me to protect. It shocks me, but then, I'm finding the little minx a surprise in all directions. But it isn't just that; it was the haunted look in her eyes. It was enough to undo any man. I didn't see it last night, but today, it was like a beacon, telling the world she has demons. Secrets.

And having a kid is one of them.

"Who is *she*?" Lou snarks, snapping me out of my thoughts.

I arch an eyebrow. "Nothing to do with you, so get out of here, *now*."

"No, Cage. We need to sort this out. We were good together; we can get that back, baby. Just let me show you. We can try for another baby. We can get married."

Shit the bed. She seriously has lost her mind.

"Are you seriously that far gone that you actually believe your own lies? I didn't want you when you lied about being pregnant; I didn't want you when I thought you were pregnant; and I certainly don't want you now. Now. Get. The. Fuck. Away. From. Me," I growl.

"No," she tells me, trying to step up to me, eyeing the towel like she can get access. She licks her lips when she looks back up. "We need this sorted out. Let me in. I'm willing to forgive you for whoever that skank was." She glances back down at my crotch, and I recoil, inwardly flinching. "I can make it up to you."

I reach across to the table by the door that has my wallet, keys, and phone scattered across it. Grabbing my phone, I dial Dante's number.

"What's up?" he answers.

"I need you to come and remove some rubbish from my door and toss it out," I tell him, keeping my gaze on Lou. Her expression hardens, her lips twisting into a snarl.

"Seriously? Clean up your own damn rubbish," he snaps.

"Dante, if I put my hands on Lou, I'm going to crush her. She's lost it, brother. She is standing here, seriously thinking we still have a chance," I tell him, and she glares at me, looking at me like I've lost *my* fucking mind.

I hear him exhale. "Okay, be there in two," he tells me, before the line goes dead.

"What did you do that for? You know Dante is going to poison you against me. He has never liked me."

"Seriously, Lou, are you even listening to me, or even yourself? You've lost your mind, girl. No way, in a million years, do I want *you*. I never did. Not after you cheated. You were easy as learning the ABC, so I took it while you were offering. You came willingly, and now we're done. Get that into your thick fucking head. You come on these premises again, and I'll call the police. You're banned from the property. If I see your face around here again, I'll make you wish you never met me. This is your last and final warning, Lou."

"It's because of *her*, isn't it?" she asks, with venom in her voice.

"God dammit, Lou!" I roar. "It's because of *you*! Only you! I can't stand you, and I haven't for a while. Now, get gone."

Dante comes jogging around the corner and doesn't make any small talk. He swings Lou up in his arms, throwing her over his shoulder. She kicks and screams as he jogs over to her car, blocking her path back to me when he puts her down.

I rush back down the hall to my room and throw on some clothes. When I'm back at the door, Dante is rubbing his mouth.

"She hit you?"

He grins, licking the blood from the corner of his mouth. "Bitch caught me with her ring."

"Sorry, mate."

He shrugs. "You know I love doing this shit. She gets angrier every time."

I shake my head in amusement as I grab my wallet, keys and phone. "Thanks for doing that. She's getting worse."

"Where you going off to in a hurry?"

I smirk. "Caitlyn was here before Lou ran her off."

He laughs, slapping his thigh. "No fucking way," he howls. "She cock-blocked you."

"I need to go, but I'll catch up with you later."

He waves me off and I race towards the direction of her cabin. She had been on my mind all night, and when I bumped into Roy this morning, I mentioned her.

He must have sensed my intentions because it got strained after that. As soon as Hayley went inside, he warned me not to hurt her.

From what Roy did mention about her, she hasn't been here long, and yet, she has somehow wormed her way into their life. Though I can totally picture her doing it. She has done it to me.

Luckily, things were left on a good note after I mentioned plans about building a new spa. Although reluctant at first, he finally agreed. On top of the new cabins, he is looking at filling this place up and finally having the room to house guests.

***

REACHING CAITLYN'S, I bang on the door with urgency. When no one answers, I make myself comfortable on one of the deckchairs, kicking my feet up on the railing while I wait. She has to come back at some point.

It isn't long until I hear two people giggling, and I look over the railing to find the source. Caitlyn is with a kid, walking hand in hand towards where I'm perched on the deck. Looking at them both, I feel my heart hammering in my chest.

I'm not sure what it is, or why I'm reacting like this. She's just a woman I want to fuck. But even as those words go through my mind, I know that isn't all I see when I look at her. And that fucking petrifies me.

"Let's go make some food to take down to the lake. You can get your swimming stuff ready while I go make it. Okay, baby?" Caitlyn tells the little girl, smiling with utter adoration at her.

Her daughter is beautiful. Her dark curls bounce with each step she takes. She must be around five or six. What strikes me is there isn't much resemblance, if any at all, between the two, and I have to wonder if she looks like her dad. She's tiny, a little peanut.

It's the little girl who spots me first. She jerks to a stop, before smiling wide and waving.

"Hello. Who are you?" she asks, her voice soft and welcoming.

Caitlyn stops searching through her bag and looks over at her daughter, then to me. Her face pales, and in a rush, she gently drags her daughter behind her. She squints through the blinding sun before I notice her visibly relax.

What the fuck was that about?

"Oh, Cage. Um, what are you doing here?" she asks, flustered.

The little girl peeks around her legs, grinning at me. I wink, before paying attention to her mum.

"I came to apologise for earlier. She's gone now. She's a crazy *ex-*girlfriend of mine who can't take the hint. I'm sorry for the way she behaved. She shouldn't have spoken to you like that," I tell her, my apology sincere.

I want to say more, but I know she wouldn't appreciate it in front of her daughter. I'm already struggling to keep my language in check around the little pea, who is still staring at me intently from behind her mum's legs.

"It's okay. You didn't need to come here for that," she replies, her voice low as she glances down at her daughter.

"What would you have liked me to come for, Kitten?" I tease.

Her entire neck and face redden, and I send her a knowing grin.

When she doesn't say anything, I struggle with what else to come up with. I rub the back of my neck. The need to impress her is overpowering. I've never really cared about what a chick thinks about me. With Caitlyn, it feels different. I want her to see me differently than others have.

And I'm not sure what that means.

"Mummy, who's he?" Pea asks, her dark lashes fluttering.

Interrupting before Caitlyn can say anything, I take the steps separating us and bend down until we are eye level. "I'm Cage. What's your name?"

"I'm Carrie-Ann, but you can call me Carrie," she tells me, nodding vigorously as she talks. "Would you like to come to the lake with us? I'm going swimming. I have new armbands and they have *Frozen* on them. You can borrow my Dora ones if you like. I don't wear them anymore."

I begin to grin at her enthusiasm, but it turns into laughter when I imagine her trying to get those things around my wrists, let alone my arms. Tilting my head up at Caitlyn, I see she's back to being pale, and it makes me laugh harder.

I ruffle Carrie's hair. "I'd love to come, but I'm okay on the Dora armbands. I'm more of a Batman or Spiderman armband kind of guy."

Her nose twitches. "Yeah, I guess," she mutters. "My Dora ones are better though."

Laughter spills out of Caitlyn, and not wanting to miss the chance to see it, I glance up, watching as her entire face lights up.

She is so bloody beautiful.

When she senses me watching, she tenses. "You don't have to

come with us, Cage," she assures me. "I'm sure you've got plenty to do."

I think about it for a moment, and although it would never have appealed to me before, I find I do want to go. I want to get to know her, to get to know both of them.

"No, I'm free actually. We don't start work till tomorrow morning, so I have the day to do what I please," I tell her, smirking when she gapes at me. "So, come on, ladies, let's get this show on the road."

"Yay," Carrie squeals, fists pumping the air.

"Yay," Caitlyn grumbles.

"What was that?" I ask, loving how uncomfortable she is right now. I glance down at Carrie, putting on my best frowny face. "Do you not want me to go?"

"Mum," Carrie whines. "Please."

"I said: yay," Caitlyn repeats, sounding much chirpier.

I smirk, trying not to laugh. "This is going to be so much fun."

"So much," Carrie agrees.

"Yay," Caitlyn mumbles, before pushing her key into the lock.

I glance down at her arse, praying like hell she wears a bikini. I can't wait to see more of that tight body.

I'VE MADE A new friend in Carrie; she hasn't left me alone since we left the cabin. I didn't even know kids could talk this much or be this open.

In fact, our friendship couldn't get any closer. She's up on my shoulders as we head down towards the lake, and twice now, she has let off some wind. The girl has no morals when it comes to being a lady.

When she lets off another, causing me to breathe in her contaminated air, I turn to Caitlyn, narrowing my eyes.

She glances away, chuckling under her breath. *I'm glad someone finds this amusing.*

"Whoops," Carrie cries, giggling to herself. She leans down, bringing her face next to mine. "Sorry, I had eggs and beans this morning. Miss Hayley says, 'Beans, beans, they're good for your heart. You eat too many, they make you fart'. It's so true, isn't it, Cage?"

Does she really need to ask me? I've had her arse vibrating on me for the last fifteen minutes.

"Hayley sure knows what she's talking about, Pea," I tell her, and when Caitlyn begins to laugh, I playfully nudge her, frowning.

"What?" she whispers.

"You know what," I grumble.

And although it isn't nice being shit on, I'm actually enjoying myself. At first, I found myself watching them interact. They're close, and Carrie is open and loud spoken. She's hilarious, especially when she keeps chatting about Caitlyn and the things she has done.

I don't think I've laughed this much in ages.

"Who's Pea?" Carrie asks after a minute.

"It's a nickname, sweetie," Caitlyn answers.

"Oh, you mean like the way he calls you Kitten, when you're not a cat?"

Caitlyn's lips twitch. "Just like that, sweetie."

"Yeah," Carrie suddenly screams, right next to my ear. I nearly trip over my own feet as I grimace, a slight dull ache throbbing in my head. "We're here. Mummy, can I go in the water?"

"Sure you can—once you've eaten all your lunch."

Carrie groans, resting her chin on my head. Reaching up, I lift her by her armpits then place her feet on the ground.

I stand back, feeling like I'm in the way as I watch both girls move effortlessly around the picnic bench, placing food, drinks, and plastic plates on the table.

Caitlyn pauses, holding one of the containers up and watching me with uncertainty. "What sandwiches do you want?"

I peer over at the containers, but they give no clue as to what is in them. "What have you got?"

She places another container on the table before pointing to each of them as she goes. "We have jam, ham, or cheese."

"I'll take the ham then, if that's okay?"

I rub the back of my neck as I slowly take a seat opposite them. I'm not sure why I'm suddenly nervous. I never get nervous. The only reason I can come up with is that this isn't something I have done before.

But it is something I pictured when I believed I was going to be a father. I imagined teaching my kids to play football or taking him or her swimming. I even pictured just this, going out on a picnic. But Lou was a bitch who thought she could play with my feelings.

Most blokes would be thrilled to find out they aren't going to be a dad with a woman they didn't like all that much. Me? I was devastated. Lou might not have been what I wanted, but I wanted a family. And although a part of me is glad I won't have to share custody with the crazy bitch, the image of 'what if' has stayed with me. For me, that child had been real, until it wasn't.

And now, as I watch mother and daughter laughing and joking over who gets to eat the cheese sandwich, those thoughts come flooding back.

This is how I pictured a family. This is what I had wanted.

Caitlyn beams as she hands me a plate of food. "Eat up, I made plenty."

Choked up, I take the plate from her, soaking in the warmth and love the two have flooding from them.

Yeah, I'm in deep shit.

She isn't who I thought she was. She isn't just some random girl. I knew this, sensed it, but witnessing it is something else. It means something else.

Chapter Five

CAITLYN

WHILST CARRIE AND I LAUGH about silly things and talk about what she did this morning at Hayley's, Cage remains relatively silent.

I still can't believe he's here; that he chose to be here. I'm hyper aware of him every time he moves. If I don't get my body's reaction to him under control, I'm afraid I'll give my feelings away in front of my daughter.

I cast another look at Cage from the corner of my eye when I feel his gaze burning into us once again. He's done it from the moment he sat down; staring at us openly like he's trying to figure us out.

I bite my lip, wondering if it's because we don't look alike. We have a few similarities, but none that would link us as mother and daughter. People see what they want to see, I suppose.

Carrie finishes off her juice, placing the rubbish in the bag. "Mummy, can we go and swim now?"

She has scoffed her food down within five seconds of it being on her plate. I chuckle at the crumbs all over her chest and the table.

I let out a sigh. "I suppose so," I tell her, grimacing at the squeal that escapes her mouth. I yawn as I reach over for the other bag. "Let's get your armbands on first then take off your shorts. You can keep your top on over your swimsuit. I don't want you getting burnt."

"This is so exciting," she cries, holding up her armbands. "Are you coming, Mummy? Come on, Cage, let's go."

"Okay, Pea, let's do it," Cage declares, surprising me. He has on some combat shorts with a black T-shirt. The black T-shirt against his skin makes him seem more tanned, and the muscles in his arms appear to bulge out more. I can't believe I'm going to be seeing him half naked again for the third time in the space of twelve hours.

Holy crap!

I whimper quietly when I watch him pull his T-shirt over his head. His ripped body tenses, and I can't help but sigh at the view.

God, he is so handsome.

"You coming, Kitten?" he asks, turning and grinning at me over his shoulder.

He caught me staring.

"Nope," I squeak.

I'm grateful I didn't change into my bikini. The thought of him seeing me half naked has me feeling fuzzy all over.

I've already experienced how he can make me feel with just a pair of leggings between us. Being around him with little to nothing on is a no-go. Even my shorts aren't enough, but it's hot and I don't want to look a disaster by sweating to death.

"Come on, Mummy, I'm four years old and I'm going in," she declares as a challenge.

"Yeah, Mummy, listen to the boss," Cage teases playfully.

"I don't have a swimsuit with me. I forgot to get changed," I lie, knowing full well I didn't get changed into one on purpose.

"That's okay. You can go in your top, like me," she states, pouting those lips at me.

Cage eyes my legs, his smouldering gaze burning into me. "That's a great idea, Pea."

Is he serious? I'm wearing a white tank top that will go see-through the second water touches it. He's got no chance.

"No, I'm fine watching from here," I tell them, as I watch him kick his trainers off.

"Nope, you're coming in," he demands lightly. "If I'm going in dressed, then so are you."

Carrie's head just bobs from side to side as she watches our interaction. She seems disappointed that I won't be joining her, and I feel terrible.

"I'm not going in. You two have fun," I tell them brightly, then turn away to get ready to pack up all the leftover food before the bees and ants come charging in.

I don't even make it to the empty crisp packet before I'm hauled into the air and over Cage's shoulder. The muscles ripple in his chiselled back as he walks towards the lake. Screaming, I pound on his back.

"Put me down," I demand, although I can't deny I love being in his arms.

"Let me go now or so help me God, I will kick you in your balls, Cage," I warn.

"Mummy, he doesn't have any balls with him," Carrie tells me, giggling behind her hand.

Cage chuckles underneath me and I smack his backside. God, he is infuriating.

"No, and he won't either when I've finished with him," I grumble, low enough so only Cage can hear.

His shoulders shake as he bursts out laughing, smacking me on my arse. I squeal, already planning my revenge.

"Don't you dare," I yell when I hear him hit the water, trudging through with me on his shoulders like I weigh nothing.

Waist deep in the water, I feel his hold over my legs loosen. I tense, already preparing for the worst, and try to grip onto him. It's useless. Seconds later, I'm sailing through the air, a scream tearing from my lips. I land in the cool water with a loud splash, submerging completely.

I splutter as I kick my feet, hitting the surface as I gasp for air. My ponytail comes loose, and my hair sticks to my face. I wipe it away, narrowing my gaze on him.

"You are so going to regret that," I growl, splashing water in his face.

His laughter only has me more frustrated. If I could pick up his muscled body and throw him underwater, I would gladly do it, but the hulk of a man is too much for me.

I hate that he has this much control, this much power. I met him early this morning, and yet he's acting like he's always been here, like he knows me better than I know myself.

And what's worse is he's making me happy.

The good kind of excitement never happens to me. Ever. It's a nice change from all the bad.

However, I don't want him to know that.

Ignoring me, he swims over to Carrie, and for the first time, I pull my attention away from him. Her arms flap in the water and she's out of breath as she tries to catch up to us.

Cage nabs her armband, pulling her into his arms, smiling. "You're such a good swimmer."

She pants out, her cheeks flushed. "I know. I love it."

Watching her in his arms has me frozen to the spot, treading water. She clings to him so easily, giving her trust so freely.

A sharp pain hits my chest. Carrie will never get to experience having a father; not really. She will never be loved, protected, or even get to call someone her daddy.

And it isn't because he's dead. It's because her dad is a murderous, sadistic bastard, who needs to be hanged.

She doesn't deserve that. She deserves someone who will treat her the way Cage is doing; the way he lets her cling to his shoulders even though you can clearly see she's strangling him. He doesn't care though.

Sadness hits me because she will never have that father figure. She isn't even safe from her own.

Like Carrie, I don't have my parents. My mum and dad passed away five years ago. They were both in a pile-up on the motorway and died at the scene. It was unexpected, hard, and it devastated me to lose them.

They were never blessed to know their granddaughter. They never got to hold her or learn her name. And my sister—Carrie's mum—died before Carrie's first birthday. She never got to see her through so many of her milestones. I'd do anything to have her back.

But what's worse than losing my family is knowing Carrie doesn't have them. She will never get to experience their love.

I never understood the world of sorrow until I lost the only people I ever loved. Some people go their whole lives never knowing the anguish of losing someone. Some people never get to experience the shit hand lady luck deals. Those are the people I envy. The ones who get a chance at living a normal life, who never see the cruel, the bad, or the downright devastating effects that some people can cause in the blink of an eye.

And Carrie's father was the cause for most of that in my life. He had caused so much pain, so much hurt, it was crippling.

But I'll die to keep her safe.

"What are you thinking about over there, Kitten?" Cage asks, waking me up from my daydream.

I shake away the depressing thoughts. This isn't the time, the day. Today is about fun, about laughter.

"Nothing," I assure him, forcing a smile before I tap on my bottom lip, eyeing him and then Carrie. "Now, I think it's someone else's turn to get dunked."

Cage grins at Carrie, who shakes her head, while screaming excitedly. Cage picks her up easily and throws her into the air, near to where I'm floating so I can grab her once she lands.

I LAUGH AT Cage's crestfallen expression as we head back to the cabin. After spending an hour swimming with them, I got out to dry and laid down on the beach. He's still pouting because I hadn't stripped down.

I have work in a few hours, so I want to get some of Carrie's schooling done before I take her back to Hayley's for the night.

Walking up the stairs of the cabin, I notice an envelope taped to the front door. It's not addressed anywhere, so it wasn't posted here; all it has on it is my name.

My brows bunch together because normally Roy and Hayley message me. I hear the sound of Carrie and Cage playing chase on the grass, so I leave them to it and pull the card down.

I turn it over, and my blood runs cold at the words. I stagger backwards, leaning against the stair railing.

Dearest Caitlyn, I hope you and my daughter are safe and well. Don't get used to it. I won't tolerate being blackmailed. Give me what I want, and I will leave you and the brat alone. Kind regards, R. x

I become unglued and scan the area, my heart beating wildly. I try to calm my breathing but it's pointless. The world spins, and I know I'm seconds from passing out. I grab the stair rail, using it for support.

I try to pull myself together. If he's here, if he's watching, I don't want him to see how scared I really am.

He's going to kill me and Carrie, no matter what I do. I thought keeping a hold of the information would bring me time and safety. I thought it would scare him away.

I was so wrong.

I fucked up, and now he's here.

A hand on my arm pulls me from my terror and I jump back, nearly falling down the stairs. Cage steadies me, his brows pulling together.

"Hey, are you okay?" he asks, running his hand up and down my arm. "What's happened?"

"I—"

When nothing else comes, he takes my hand. "Come and sit down," he offers, watching me closely as he pulls me over to the deck chair.

Fully snapping out of it, I stare at Cage and horror washes over me.

He isn't with Carrie.

I pull away from him, searching the area for her. My pulse beats rapidly when I don't spot her.

"Carrie! Carrie, where are you?" I yell, cupping my hands over my mouth. I turn back to Cage, sweat beading at my forehead. "Where is she?"

"Hey, calm down," he lightly demands, his brows pulled together. He points over to one of the trees. "She's behind the tree playing with that flea-infested tabby cat. What's wrong?"

I spot her run after the tabby cat, not moving far from the house.

I rub at my chest, wondering if this will ever end. I don't know what else I can do to keep us safe.

I won't leave Carrie in the hands of a monster. I won't leave her with no family.

"Right, breathe— in through your nose and out through your mouth. Slowly. That's it," he instructs, his hand on my chest.

I close my eyes, following his instructions, and ignore the card being pulled out of my hand. I can't think about that, not when I have Carrie to think of.

He knows I'm here. In fact, he probably knew we were here all along. He has connections everywhere.

My sister met Robin during a trip she did with some girlfriends. She called, telling me how she met this amazing man.

When she came home married to Robin, we were shocked, but we stood by her, wanting her to be happy. It wasn't until after my parents died that their marriage became strained, and he started acting weird.

At first, Courtney thought he was cheating, so she started following him. It all got crazy after that, like we were in some sort of action movie. It's a time I can't bear thinking about. I lost her because of that monster.

"Who is R? What does he want from you?" he asks, his voice hard as he looks on in concern.

"Nobody," I whisper.

"He's not *nobody,* Caitlyn. He's got you looking as pale as a ghost and panicking to the point you're about to pass out. What's going on? He's your ex; that much I can see. What I don't understand is why he is calling his own daughter a brat. You can talk to me. You can trust me."

"He's not my ex, Cage. He's a murderous prick," I snap, revolted at his assumption. I clamp my mouth shut when I realise I've said too much.

Shit!

"What?" he grinds out, staring at me in horror.

"Nothing, forget I said anything. Okay?" I demand, giving him a pointed look as I move to the stairs. I stop at the edge, turning to look at him. "Look, I need to get ready for work. Thanks for a great afternoon, but goodbye."

There's a burning sensation inside my chest. We had been having such a great afternoon. It was one of the best days I've had in such a long time. It hurts to know it's over.

He's an okay person from what I have made out, nothing like the man I thought he was when we first met. The way he played with Carrie, the way he laughed with her when she was being silly, it meant everything. Not only to me, but to her.

Then there was the way he looked at me; so intense, so... I don't know. It left me feeling like I was floating every time our gazes collided.

He has been charming, funny, kind, and compassionate, and is so easy-going it's hard not to like him. Every time we touched it was a beautiful torture, because I liked that he was touching me, yet whilst I was imagining ripping the rest of his clothes off, my daughter was only a few feet away.

It was kind of a mood killer.

And now he's being kind, showing concern over a matter that has nothing to do with him. Not many people would do that.

But trusting him with the facts? It isn't something I can give so easily. He doesn't know the ramifications of what my trust could do to him. Yet, I find myself wanting to trust him. To trust anyone. Because I'm tired of running, tired of being scared.

"Hold up," he growls, his hand grasping my wrist. "You can talk to me, Caitlyn, anytime, about anything. If you don't want to that's fine, but I promise I'm not letting this go. If you and Pea are in danger, I want to help."

My brows pinch together. "You can't help me. Anyone who tries to help me or knows anything about this, find themselves dead, Cage. I'm not putting any more lives at risk. I've said enough already, okay. Just leave it, please," I plead.

"No, I won't, but I can see that now isn't the time to talk about it. You have a little girl a few yards away who can listen in," he states, and his burning stare becomes too much. "What you're going to do is talk to me when we're alone."

"No, Cage."

"I'll meet you after work, and we can talk in private. Okay?" he tells me, ignoring me all together.

I need him gone and Carrie inside. "Okay," I concede, lying.

"Don't say okay and not mean it. I'm a man of my word, Kitten, so I suggest you get used to me, because I don't plan on going anywhere," he declares.

I'm taken aback. "Why? You don't even know me. I'm just some girl who cut your plug and you kissed. That's it. You don't owe me anything and I don't owe you anything."

"That's where you're wrong, Kitten. The minute you came strutting your sweet arse over to cut my plug, you drew my attention. Not many women can do that."

I snort. "That's attraction, not exactly a reason to die for someone," I tell him, groaning at my running mouth.

Why do I keep telling him stuff?

He shakes his head, his lips twitching. "I'm not going to lie to you, Kitten; I want you, but this isn't about that," he tells me, stepping closer and getting in my space. "You can't tell me you don't feel it."

"Feel what?" I ask, tipping my head back to meet his gaze.

He points to me, then his chest. "This. Us. There's a connection."

"That's ridiculous, Cage, and you know it," I snap. I don't like being lied to or made a fool of. If he thinks sweet words are going to make me open up, he's wrong.

He grips my chin, forcing me to look at him. "You can't stand there and tell me that when I kissed you, your world didn't stop for a split second. That your panties weren't soaked from the mere thought of having me inside your tight pussy," he growls, and I feel the words to my core. I shiver, trying not to react. "I knew when I first laid eyes on you that I wanted you, but now, after spending the day with you, I don't just want you. I want it all. I want to get to know you. I want you to be mine."

He can't possibly think that. We just met, for Christ's sake. I can't deny the attraction— there's no point; my body's reaction answers for me. But something more? I don't— won't believe that.

This is too much, too fast.

"You can't possibly be serious. We don't even know each other and you're declaring you are... you are—"

"That I want you?" he finishes, smirking. "I'm not declaring love, Kitten."

I flush, ducking my head. "I didn't say that, but this is still freaking insane."

He grins, and it's not a cheeky grin, it's a dirty grin, and it's doing things to my libido. "I'm not afraid to go after what I want. I'm not some teenager or guy who doesn't know what he wants."

"I'm not safe to be around. Everyone dies when they get involved, Cage. You're not the first person to try and help me," I whisper, glancing away as tears gather in my eyes.

I dreamt of this— of a knight in shining armour. But now that the dream is coming true, I'm not sure I can do it. It isn't just about him trying to help us that scares me; it's him. I have never done this before, and right now, I wish I had my sister to call for advice.

"No, Kitten, I'm probably not. But I'll be the last, I promise," he whispers, pulling me into a hug.

I hug him back, seeking the comfort, if only for a moment. When I let him go, his expression is blank.

"Carrie, come on, let's go inside."

She runs up to me, taking my hand, and I feel his stare burning into me as we head inside.

Chapter Six

CAITLYN

I FIDGET NERVOUSLY AT THE side of the stage as I finish my glass of water. It's just my luck that the bar is packed tonight. I'm not used to singing in front of this many people. Normally, there are no more than ten people in here. Now it's filled with Cage's workmen and the new guests who arrived this afternoon.

I pick up my guitar resting against one of the speakers, pulling the strap over my head. I only need it for one song— one of my favourite songs. And since meeting Cage, Taylor Swift's, 'I Knew You Were Trouble' seems fitting. It's also the one I know down to a 'T' on my guitar. For the rest of my set, I'll sing from the karaoke versions Roy has set up ready for me.

I keep my head down as I walk onto the stage and take a seat on the stool in the middle. I rest my guitar on my knees and take in a lungful of air. I begin to strum the keys to the song before lifting my mouth to the microphone. It's not until the first line flows out of my mouth that I begin to relax.

Once upon a time, a few mistakes ago
I was in your sights, you got me alone
You found me, you found me ...

The rest of the set goes the same. I keep my eyes closed, my head a little tilted to the floor, and I fly through the songs, each one tugging at my heart.

When I sing to Carrie, it's different. I sing to comfort her. It isn't out of pressure; it's just me and her, and I enjoy it. Sitting here, starting my last song for the night, I feel judged, all eyes on me.

This last song was one of my sister's favourites. When the melody of Snow Patrol's 'Chasing Cars' begins to play, I feel like I'm back in my bedroom, singing it to her. I lift my head when a tingle shoots down my spine.

I scan the crowd, something I've avoided until now. When my eyes land on Cage, my cheeks heat. The intensity almost smothers me, and tingles run all over my body.

The pitch gets higher, yet I lower my voice, keeping it low, seductive, and even through the crowd I can see his pupils darken. He shifts in his seat, leaning forward over the table as he grips his glass in his hand.

What surprises me is that I'm no longer nervous. In fact, I feel like a boost of energy has shot through me. I can't take my gaze away from his.

As I finish the last line, I stand, ready to make a run for it. I take a step away from the chair, when the deafening sound of applause stops me in my tracks. I've never had an audience congratulate me like this. I gape, my heart racing at the cat-calls and whistles. I scan the audience, and my knees begin to shake at the standing ovation.

I give them a small smile and a wave before making a hasty exit. I thank people as I move through the crowd, my face flaming with each praise.

"Hey, Kate, what do you need me to do?" I ask, coming around the bar.

"There are some glasses outside that need collecting. You were great up there; Tillie's good, but when you're on stage… it's like you mean every word you sing. It's beautiful."

"Thank you," I answer, ducking my head.

I double back from behind the bar and head towards the exit. I'm reaching for the door, when Cage blocks me, his expression unreadable.

I still can't believe I told him what I did earlier. My mouth is going to be the death of me.

"Hi," I murmur.

"Fuck, you can sing," he rasps, and my breathing escalates at the heat in his gaze. He shakes his head, running fingers through his hair. "As soon as I walked in, your voice captured me. It was like I was frozen. You were magnificent."

His words meant a lot to me. It wasn't a pick-up line; he was genuine in his praise.

I tuck my hair behind my ear, unable to meet his gaze for a moment.

"Thank you. I'm glad you enjoyed it," I declare, picking at the hem of my top. "I don't normally sing. A girl named Tillie is usually up there, but she phoned in sick, so I covered for her."

I inwardly groan when I realise I'm rambling. He doesn't want to know about Tillie. He doesn't care.

He grins, his eyes flashing with amusement. "Cute."

Clearing my throat, I gesture to the bar. "You getting another drink?"

He shakes his head and blanks his expression. "I've got to go see Roy, but I'll meet you after and walk you home," he states.

I wave him off. "It's fine. I can walk by myself," I assure him, then point to Roy's office. "Roy is in there."

I step past him and press the palms of my hands to the door. He pulls me back to his chest, leaning down to brush his lips across my ear.

"Do I need to remind you of what you agreed to earlier, Kitten? I'm walking you back when you've finished. Then we're going to talk. You aren't getting out of this, Kitten," he warns me, keeping his voice low. He presses his lips below my ear, and I shiver, my heart racing. "See you in a few."

His body heat leaves, and I fold into myself, groaning. Why does he continue to get to me? Huffing, I push through the door, stomping to the seating area to collect the glasses.

"He's so goddamn bossy," I hiss to myself.

"Hey there, pretty girl."

I whip around, a startled yelp slipping through my lips. My heart races at the older man, a shiver racing down my spine. His clothes are torn, dirty, like they have seen better days, but it isn't his attire that has my skin prickling.

It's the darkness lurking in his gaze as he rakes his prying eyes up and down my body. My skin crawls, and I wish I could cover myself up. In only a mini skirt that ends above the knee and a black work shirt, I feel exposed.

"Hi," I reply, not wanting to be rude and ignore him.

Dismissing him, I head over to the next table, but I can still feel his presence behind me, and I begin to shake.

Something about him is off, and my head is screaming at me to run.

Which is what I do. I place the glasses down on the table and turn quickly, ready to head inside, but he side-steps me, blocking my way.

"Sorry," I choke out, trying to step around him, but he blocks me again.

"Not so fast, pretty girl," he warns, taking a step closer.

I take one back and try again to move past him. "Look, I have to get back to work."

Suddenly, with movements quicker than I thought he was capable of, he grips my chin, shoving me backwards until my back slams into the wall behind me.

I yelp, the breath leaving my lungs in a painful rush. I tilt my head, ready to scream, but the sharp backhand across my jaw has me paralyzed.

He hit me.

"W-wha—"

"Shut up," he demands, lowering his head until we're inches apart. "I have a message for you."

Robin.

"I—"

"Give him what he wants, or next time I'll be doing a lot worse," he threatens, then leans back to glance down at my chest, his pupils dilating. "Although, if he had told me how pretty you are, I would have come sooner. Just so you know, I love brunettes, so maybe before I kill you, I'll have a little play."

Tears leak down my cheeks as my entire body shakes. "I don't have what he wants. Leave me alone."

"Oh, sweet girl, you do have it, and I'll be around until you give it back."

Noise near the exit has me flicking my gaze in that direction. The couple laugh and my eyes widen as I go to scream. His hand clamps down on my mouth, muffling the sound of my plea.

I notice the couple turn in our direction and a frustrated sob tears from my throat when they keep moving on. From their perspective, we probably looked like a couple making out against a wall.

We aren't, and it terrifies me that no one is coming to my rescue.

"Leave al—" A choked noise slips through my lips when he slides his hand up my side, up to my breast. I whimper as his hand squeezes them, his touch bruising.

I struggle in his arms, trying to push him back as another sob threatens to escape. It's no use. He's much stronger than I am.

He leans down, sniffing my neck. "I'm hoping you don't deliver what he wants, because I can't wait to have a play," he whispers.

Suddenly, he lets go and I slump to the floor on my knees, crying out. I glance up in time to see a fist coming towards me. I clench my eyes shut, crying out when his fist lands across my cheek. I collapse to my hands, gasping for breath when the panic cripples me.

A choked sob escapes when he lifts his booted foot back, kicking me right in the ribs.

"Help!" I cry out, just as his boot connects with my stomach once again, knocking me into the wall behind me.

I curl into a ball, sobbing so hard my chest aches. I can hear a howl of pain, a noise so feral, so primal, it takes me a minute to realise it's coming from me.

I whimper, pushing into the wall when I glance up to see him bending down. Images of him raping me flitter through my mind and the breath gets stuck in my throat.

He grasps my chin in a punishing grip, his jaw clenched. "You've been warned. See you soon, sweet girl."

His knees creak as he gets up, and I watch through tear-filled eyes as he leaves, disappearing into the darkness of the trees.

I lift my hand but cry out as the burning pain in my ribs has me kissing the ground. Sobs rake through my body.

I'm tired, so tired of all of this.

Cage

ROY IS LOOKING over some papers when I enter the office. I glance behind him to the monitors showing various angles of the bar, hallways, and outside. I watch as Caitlyn speaks to herself, and I grin at the frustrated look on her face.

I turn back to Roy, who places the papers down, sitting back in his chair.

"Care for a drink?" he asks, pulling out a bottle of whiskey.

I take a seat on the chair opposite. "Yeah."

Roy and my dad have been close friends since their teens. They met when they were at school. From the stories I was told growing up, they were both known for getting into trouble. They stayed close after leaving school, even started a club business down in my hometown together. My father bought him out of the business after Roy and Hayley got married.

When Roy's father died, he left Roy the cabins. Back then, the resort was just a few cabins that people stayed in when they were passing through. When Roy took over, he made a lot of changes. With Hayley's help they started a fresh new business that is now well known throughout the country. It took off straight away after they built some more cabins, a children's play area, and a café, which has now been transformed into a restaurant next door. The whole place looks great, and I'm happy he called me in to be a part of it.

But I want something more than this. For some time now I've wanted a new start. I need to get away from all the shit going on back home with Lou. Coming here, for me, is a life-changing situation. I took one look around the place and I finally felt like I was home for the first time in years. I was also closer to my friends and family.

"What did you need to talk about?" Roy asks, handing me my drink.

"Well, I sort of have a proposition for you. Me and the boys have decided to venture out and were wondering if you would rent us the land at the back, by the creek, to build on.

"We want to open up a new garage around that area. I'm thinking of buying that old, run-down house on Barrett's Lane and doing it up, and it would be good if I had a business nearby to run. I scouted the area to see what the town has to offer. Currently you have no garages within a thirty-mile radius. If I open this garage, it will benefit you and people in town. The land doesn't get used down by the creek, which means you'll be making a profit with us renting it," I explain, giving a moment's pause. "What do you say?"

His eyes widen slightly. "I say that's a great idea, Cage, but I'm not taking the money off you for the land. You said yourself, it doesn't get used. The creek only gets seen by hikers and that rarely happens anymore on that side of the track. Just make sure you get permission to build on there. Some of the land may be unsafe."

"I know; we had someone come in to check it out before I asked. Hope you don't mind," I tell him sheepishly. "I just didn't want to come to you with the proposal and not have all the facts. It's in a great area by the road so it will be seen. The creek is five minutes out from where we want to build, so we are in the safe zone area to build on. I'll get back to you on everything else once we finish our plans, if that's okay with you?"

I don't want to get my hopes up, but now it's been put out there, I'm getting excited.

"No, it's fine, son. You do what you've got to do, and just let me know the plans. You have permission to do as you please, as long as you keep it over by the creek and not in the way of hiker trails."

"It won't be."

He watches me closely. "Was there something else?"

I clear my throat. "Yeah. It's about Caitlyn."

His back straightens, and he slowly places his drink down on the coaster. "What about her?" he asks curiously.

"Well, she had a threatening note on her door this afternoon, and by the look on her face, she is scared shitless," I admit. I don't want to break her trust, but it wasn't like she said I couldn't tell anyone. And I'm doing this to help her. I just need to know more. "What do you know about her?"

His chair creaks as he gets up, moving to come and take a seat in the chair next to me. "She's quiet, private, but there's only so much you can keep hidden," he starts.

"What do you mean?"

He swallows the rest of his drink. "If she's had a note, she's not safe— that much I do know. When she arrived, she was in a bad state. I'm surprised she even knew what day it was. She was shaken, not with it. But Carrie can talk."

I grin, knowing that to be true. "So, Carrie told you?"

"Not all of it. She told us they moved around a lot, that there was a bad man, and when we questioned Caitlyn, she told us they had been on the road a lot. They had just lost someone, and although she didn't go into detail, I knew enough to know she wasn't safe, and neither was that little girl. She's lost everything. She has no one but Carrie."

My heart clenches at that. She doesn't deserve to be alone. I blank my expression, not wanting to give anything away. "What is going on then?"

"I had an old friend looking into her for me and it turned out— Holy fuck!" he exclaims, shooting up from his chair.

I turn to look at the screens and my feet are on the floor as he hits the door. Caitlyn is on the floor and some guy is booting the fuck out of her.

I knock into people as I push through the crowd. I hear glass breaking and curses in my wake, but I don't care. I only care about getting to Caitlyn and kicking the shit out of the dickhead harming her.

Pushing through the exit, I turn to find a broken Caitlyn on the floor, sobbing uncontrollably. Roy reaches her first, and I'm close behind. When I reach her, anger boils within me. I don't want to scare her, so simmering down my anger, I turn to Roy, keeping my voice even. "Go check where he went," I order, before turning my attention to Caitlyn.

"Hey, Kitten, come here," I soothe, but she flinches away as I place my hand on her shoulder.

My body jolts in fury at her reaction towards me. I'm not mad at her though. I'm mad at the bastard who did this to her. I reach out slowly, letting her know I'm not going to hurt her. As I lift her into my arms, she hisses out in pain, then starts sobbing harder into my chest.

"Where does it hurt, Kitten?" I ask, knowing her ribs must be fucking killing her. I watched the force of that kick on the screen.

"Everywhere," she chokes out, before whimpering, curling into me.

"Can you tell me who that man was?" I ask.

"He said—oh God—he said I need to hand over what I have, otherwise next time it's going to be worse. He said he's going to enjoy having his way with me before he kills me. What do I do, Cage?" she sobs out. "What am I going to do?"

Hearing her break down while cradled in my arms has me feeling like I've been stabbed in the heart. I want nothing more than to soothe her, to ease all her pain and agony.

"Come on, Kitten, let's get you back so we can talk. Can you walk?"

She shakes her head, hissing at the movement, while clinging to me tighter, as if I'll let her go. Carrying her bridal style, I head towards

Roy, who is running towards us with a concerned expression that doesn't hide the anger evident on his face, especially as he watches a sobbing Caitlyn in my arms.

"I looked around and he's nowhere to be seen. I'm going in to look at the security footage. You okay, Caitlyn?" Roy asks softly.

When she doesn't answer, I give him a nod of reassurance.

"I'm going to take her back to mine. I'll see you in the morning," I tell him.

"No! I need to go get Carrie. We're not safe," she yells, trying to jerk out of my arms. "We need to go."

Watching her wince in pain as she struggles sets something off inside me. Taking a firm grip of her body, I stop her from hurting herself. Something raw inside me just wants to protect her.

Roy steps closer, eager to reassure Caitlyn and calm her down.

"She's safe. If it makes you feel better, I can go home now and check on her. I'll text Cage when I get back," he promises. "Let me go look at the security footage, then I'll get back home and check on her. Okay?"

"Yes, that's fine," I tell Roy. Caitlyn goes to refuse, but I glance down at her. "No, Kitten, I'm taking you home. Pea is safe, so you don't need to worry about her, okay? And seeing you like this would only upset her."

She pauses, biting her lip before she finally gives in, nodding. "Okay," she whispers.

"See you in the morning," I tell him, then head towards my cabin, keeping her firmly in my arms, where she fits perfectly.

Chapter Seven

CAITLYN

Opening my eyes, I take in my surroundings and tense. We aren't in my cabin, but in Cage's. I don't remember much about getting here. I'd laid my head on his shoulder and just spaced out. Whether I'm still in shock is undecided.

My entire body shakes, and I snuggle further into his arms, seeking his safety. Inhaling his scent has soothed me somewhat.

I shouldn't be here though. I should be getting Carrie and running as far as we possibly can from here. Sometimes I wonder what the point is when in the four years I've being trying to hide, he has found me every time.

Cage passes the living area and heads straight to the bedroom. Feeling defeated and beaten, I don't argue with him. Instead, when

Cage gently places me down on his cool bed, I snuggle into the sheets, inhaling his scent on the pillows.

I just want to go to sleep and forget what happened tonight; pretend for one more night my world isn't falling apart again.

Earlier, I fantasised about the future, about what it would be like to have a man in my life, to have a boyfriend and someone to love.

It was wishful thinking.

"I'm going to get some warm water and a cloth to get you cleaned up. Do you need me to get you anything else?" he asks gently.

"Just some painkillers if you have any, please," I whisper.

As Cage walks back out of the bedroom, I can't help but admire his firm backside. I snigger inside at the thought that only I could check out his backside after I've had the crap beaten out of me.

Moments later, he walks back into the bedroom holding a glass of water and two painkillers. I hiss in pain as I try to sit up. He rushes over, placing the glass and tablets on the bedside table to help me. I lean against the pillows, breathing through the pain before taking the water and tablets from him.

My eyes water from his tenderness.

"Be back," he whispers, and quietly leaves through the other door, heading into the bathroom. I swallow down the fear of him deserting me.

I didn't realise until then that I don't want to be alone. I want to be here with him.

Hearing the tap run, I relax and take small sips of the water, soothing my dry throat.

Everything hurts. The side of my face is pulsing, and I don't need to see the bruise or swelling to know it's there. It's pounding, just like the burning pain in my ribs. Each breath I take feels like I'm inhaling fire.

His expression is still blank when he walks back into the room, taking a seat next to me on the edge of the bed.

"I'm going to clean your face first. You have a bit of blood on your lip," he explains and waits for me to nod before continuing. His jaw clenches as he runs his gaze over my face.

I still, watching him intently as he wipes away the blood and dirt from my face. The look of concentration and tenderness as he gently wipes the dried blood from me, warms me, and I melt at the touch.

Even as gentle as he's being, each time he catches the bruise wrong, I hiss, my body jerking. Pain fills his gaze, and my heart flutters and butterflies swirl in my stomach.

"I need to check your body out. Can you take your top off?" he asks, his gaze going to my chest.

I flush, my entire body heating. "I bet you do," I grumble. "Is that how you get all the girls into bed?"

"You're already in my bed, Kitten," he states, grinning.

I blush furiously as he looks at me with one eyebrow raised, challenging me to argue with him. Damn, this man is seriously hot. *How does he do this to me?* I've gone from a quivering mess to a hot mess in the space of five minutes. The man works wonders when he's around me.

"No getting any ideas," I warn him, sitting forward.

His lips twitch. "I promise."

Slowly, so I don't strain my ribs, I lift the hem of my top up, then painfully pull it over my head. I grimace at the sharpness that shoots through the left side of my ribcage. I hear Cage inhale a sharp breath. When I look up, I see his gaze firmly on my ribcage. His eyes are narrowed into hard slits, and he grits his teeth.

He closes his eyes, as if willing himself to remain calm, and I look down to where his eyes were cast and notice my side is covered in an angry purple and red bruise. The area of the bruise is raised and swollen.

"Shit," I mutter under my breath.

"Fuck!" Cage snaps.

I jerk, glancing up at him. "What did I do?"

He shakes his head, squeezing the cloth in his hand. "You did nothing, Kitten. I did. There I am, making you promises that I will keep you safe, and they get to you anyway."

I reach out for his hand, lightly running my thumb over his. "Cage, this isn't your fault. I told you they would get to me whether you helped me or not. I tried telling you earlier, but you didn't listen. You don't know what you've gotten yourself into."

"I don't care about what you think I've gotten myself into, Kitten. I'm helping you now more than ever. No one should have to go through this," he tells me fiercely. "I refuse to let you push me away when I now know what they're capable of." He pauses, glancing down at the cloth. "I don't have any ice packs, so I'm going to run this under the cold tap for a bit."

He leaves once again, and I'm struck by his words. Only two other people offered to help, but it was help that extended only so far. They never offered to help with Robin himself. I couldn't blame them. He's a scary guy.

Starting to feel self-conscious again just laying here in just my work skirt and bra, I try to cover myself as best as I can, doing a terrible job of it. Thank goodness it's a decent bra, otherwise I'd have been mortified. I'm just glad it isn't my plain white cotton one. I'm blessed in the breast department, so finding sexy lingerie that is comfortable *and* pretty is hard. Thankfully, today I decided to wear my black lacy one with black lacy boy shorts.

"Okay, this is cold so be warned," Cage declares as he steps into the room.

He gently presses the cold flannel against my ribcage. I hold my breath as pain radiates through me. I bite my lip to suppress a hiss as he applies a little more pressure.

"Sorry," he whispers, his face closer to me than it was a few seconds ago.

As soon as our gazes lock, all the pain drifts from my mind, and all I see and feel is him. The room feels smaller as the temperature rises, making my skin warm the cold flannel quickly.

"It's okay," I whisper back.

I move, closing the distance between us. Being this close to him, I can appreciate how full his lips are. Remembering the way they felt on mine, I edge even closer to him.

Running the palm of my hand over his face, I relish the feel of his stubble against my skin.

Our gazes lock, and he brings his face down, leaving a little gap between us. My heart races as his breath brushes along my lips.

It's only a moment, but it feels like a lifetime before he breaks the space between us, his lips connecting with mine in a tender, fiery kiss.

The air stops in my lungs for a moment, and once the shock disappears, I find myself kissing him back. I kiss him back with everything in me, putting all my exhaustion and fear from earlier aside. At this moment in time, I am where I want to be, with whom I want to be with. I have never felt like this with any other man. The desire builds within me as I slip my hands around his neck, pulling at the hair on the nape of his neck.

I want this. I want to feel anything but the fear, the paranoia.

I want something for myself.

Without breaking our kiss, Cage positions himself between my legs, pulling me down until I'm flat on my back.

Wetness pools between my legs, and I know I should be feeling some kind of embarrassment or anxiety. I don't. All it does is drive a need inside me to have him closer. It's like my body is seeking, searching for something more.

My fingers clench around his neck; a part of me scared he will pull away.

He thrusts against me, his erection rubbing against my sex. A hiss mixed with a moan slips through my lips.

I barely register the burning pain in my ribs or the slight sting on my face. He's a drug, one that helps me forget about my injuries.

He breaks from the kiss, only to start trailing his lips down my neck, nibbling as he goes. I arch my neck, giving him better access.

If this is what desire feels like, what being turned-on feels like, I want more.

"Oh God," I breathe out, as he places kisses on the swell of my breasts. I go light-headed at the sensation.

"No, Kitten, it's just me: Cage," he whispers, bringing his mouth back to mine.

Every fibre of my being is aflame, and I grind into him, seeking more. He growls into my mouth when I bite down on his bottom lip, and I shiver at the sound.

"Jesus, Kitten, you're so god damn sexy. What you do to me…" he breathes into my neck.

My eyes close as I relish in the feel of his hands running down my sides, his touch gentle, soothing.

I tense a little when his fingers reach for the zip on the side of my skirt. I know I should stop him. I'm not ready for this, or at least, I don't think I am.

I do want him to touch me in places I've never been touched. I do want his mouth over my body. I do want him.

But it's all too much.

A part of me wants to beg him for more or to put things on hold. It's a battle inside my head.

But like my body has a mind of its own, I touch him, and for a moment, I forget what I wanted to say. The tips of my fingers slide under his T-shirt, and my lips part at the feel of the sharp edges of his muscles straining.

A low, primal sound slips through his lips as I run my fingers around, scraping them down his back and into the back of his trousers, gripping his arse firmly. I bring him flush against me and I moan at the feel of him pressing against me.

He leans up and I lose my touch. He unzips my skirt, his gaze burning into mine as he slides it slowly, torturously so, down my thighs.

Throwing the skirt onto the floor, he then looms over me, his gaze running up and down my body, his pupils dilating.

I'm completely bare to him, vulnerable in only my lace black bra and matching boy shorts.

He bends down and I close my eyes, assuming he's going to kiss me again, but my lips part, a gasp escaping, when his lips press against my belly button. When his tongue sweeps across the skin just below my navel, I moan, my back arching off the bed.

"Oh," I rasp, as I roll my hips.

Gently, he places his hands on my stomach, stopping me from hurting my ribs more than I already have by keeping me grounded to the bed. I feel myself growing hotter as he slowly moves down, licking and sucking. I glance down at the same time he looks up, his gaze burning into me as he reaches for my sex. He kisses me through the lace boy shorts, and I buck up with pleasure.

I barely recognise my own voice when an embarrassing moan escapes. His hot breath on my sex through the lace is the most erotic thing I have ever encountered—not that I've encountered much.

My ex-boyfriend went down on me, but it never felt like this. Like my entire body was ready to implode.

His fingers hook underneath the sides of my boy shorts, and I lift my bum, making it easier for him to guide them down my legs. Kneeling before me, Cage discards the shorts to the side and devours me with his lust-filled eyes.

My legs begin to shake from anticipation, but mostly excitement.

He places his hands under my bum, lifting me slightly off the bed, as his mouth latches on to my slit. He slides his tongue around my clit then down into my sex, making sure to taste every part of me as he devours my juices. I cry out in ecstasy, moaning his name when he circles my clit again. I was right; he can make my body feel things that I could never possibly dream of feeling.

As my body reaches the crest of its climax, I thrash my head wildly, crying out his name.

"I'm going to come. Oh God, yes!" I scream as my climax hits me with full force, leaving me dizzy and spent.

Cage lifts his mouth from my sex, giving me one of his sexy know-it-all grins. I blush at his knowing expression but try to cover it. Aware that I'm redder than red at this moment in time is hard, as he stays hovering above me. I cannot believe I just let him do that, but damn did it feel so good. He leans down, giving me a quick kiss on my mouth, letting me taste my arousal on his tongue.

When he lies down next to me, I'm confused as to what he is doing. *Doesn't he want to…? Has he changed his mind? Did I do something wrong?* He pulls me against him, and I wince as my ribs protest against the sudden movement.

Now that the aftereffects of my climax have settled and I don't have Cage distracting me, the pain is back in full force.

I tense, a whimper passing through my lips.

"Shit, I'm so sorry. I totally forgot about your ribs," Cage says, moving me a little but keeping me firmly tucked to his side.

"It's okay," I whisper, hiding my face in his chest.

"Hey, what's wrong, Kitten? Did I hurt you?" he asks.

"No," I lie. Technically he didn't hurt me—my ribs hurt before— but my feelings, however, are another story. Why doesn't he want to take it further? Do *I* want to take it further?

Why is this bothering me so much?

"Don't lie to me. Tell me what's wrong, Kitten," he demands, rolling to his side to face me.

I roll to my side so I can see him, gritting my teeth through the pain. Starting to feel self-conscious, I try lifting the blanket from the end of the bed with my feet. When Cage sees what I'm trying to achieve, he chuckles whilst sitting up. Tucking the blanket over us, he lays back into the position he was in before.

"Tell me," he urges.

"It's just that... you didn't... you know... you stopped. Did you not want to?" I ask him shyly, keeping my gaze focused on his chin.

"Kitten, I want nothing more than to shove my dick inside your tight pussy, but I think you've had enough action for one night."

"What about you? Can I, um... can I, you know, return the favour?" I ask nervously. I never liked going down on my ex-boyfriend. I only did it a handful of times before we broke up. I found it revolting; I mean, he peed out of it, for Christ's sake. But the thought of tasting Cage in my mouth is turning me on.

"I didn't eat your pussy for you to return the favour, Kitten."

"No, but I want to," I whisper, lifting myself over him.

Nerves hit me when I feel his hands grip my hips tightly, keeping me firmly in place. Feeling ashamed, I sit back. I can feel his erection through his jeans, rubbing against my sex.

"I want to do this. Please, let me," I beg ashamedly.

I don't give him time to answer as I bend down and kiss his neck, moving my hands down to the bottom of his T-shirt while ignoring the pain in my left side. When I unsuccessfully try to remove his T-shirt, he lifts himself up, helping me.

My mouth waters as I take in his glorious chest and chiselled stomach. He is seriously ripped in the muscle department. He must work out a lot. His eight-pack is so defined. I start to trace the ridges between the muscles with my finger. I'm told men have sensitive nipples just like us women do, so testing that theory, I take his nipple into my mouth. When he moans, I know I'm doing it right. As I kiss down his muscled stomach, I unbutton his jeans. I place my hands into the front of his jeans like I'm gripping onto handlebars, and I pull them down. I struggle to get them over his tight arse, but Cage helps me by pulling them down and kicking them off skilfully as I still straddle him.

He isn't wearing any boxers, so his huge cock is on full display. It's long and thick, with a vein pulsing down the centre. I can feel myself growing wet, wishing I could take all of him inside me. I know I can't; it will lead to questions I don't want to answer just this second. I know I will need to sooner rather than later, but at this moment in time, I just selfishly want to enjoy my time with him.

Taking in Cage's glorious physique, I make my way down the bed, getting ready to take his hardness into my mouth. When my mouth is a breath away from his erection, I look up at him through my dark eyelashes. His face is filled with desire, lust, and need, and I feel powerful and sexy knowing I'm making him feel those things.

I lick the head of his cock, and it twitches. I'm startled at first at the fact the damn thing moved on its own, but I don't think about it too long as I close my mouth around his hardness, tasting the salty pre-cum that has leaked from the tip. Sliding my tongue up the inner side of his cock, I finally take him fully into my mouth. My head bobs up and down on his hardness, sucking enough to make him squirm. I smile around him before taking him deeper, feeling him at the back of my throat. I pull back before I gag and choke on the length of him.

Cage's moans fill the room, egging me on as I speed up my rhythm. They fuel me to drive him wild, just like he did me.

"Oh fuck, Kitten, I'm going to come. I need you to stop if you don't want me to come in your mouth," he groans, his fingers digging into the side of my head.

I don't even hesitate before I tighten my mouth around his hardness, making sure my teeth don't catch on him.

It isn't long before I feel his cock pulse and hot spurts of cum enter my mouth. I swallow it down quickly, still not liking the salty taste, but there is something about the taste of Cage that makes me want to do it again.

When I've swallowed every last drop, I look up at him and grin.

His breathing is slowing down; his face is relaxed and content. I squeal, through pleasure and pain, as he sits up, gently pulling me up by my armpits and placing me over his hard chest.

"That was unbelievable, Kitten. I've never come so hard in my life," he rasps, his fingers running down my back.

I'm glad he can't see me because my face is in flames right now. I want to tell him I enjoyed it more than he did, but I'm too shy. I snuggle deeper into him, forgetting the sharp pains in my side. I feel safe wrapped around him, so I close my eyes, enjoying that feeling.

"Go to sleep, Kitten, but we will be talking in the morning," he warns.

"Okay," I mumble into his chest.

I knew we would talk eventually. I'm just glad I get tonight before he kicks me to the kerb.

"Goodnight, Kitten," he whispers as he wraps the blanket around us for the second time tonight.

"Goodnight," I whisper back.

With the feel of his arms securely wrapped around me, and our naked bodies pressed together, I close my eyes and find sleep easily for the first time in a long time.

Chapter Eight

CAITLYN

WHEN I WAKE UP, I'M CAUGHT off-guard for a moment as I take in the strange surroundings. It isn't until I feel the pain in my left side that my memory of last night comes flooding back. Then I blush furiously as I remember what happened after the incident, between me and Cage, and the fact that I enjoyed it.

"Good morning, Kitten," Cage greets, walking in the bedroom wearing clean clothes. He's freshly showered by the look of his wet hair.

Suddenly feeling shy and self-conscious from my lack of clothing, I pull the sheet tighter towards my neck. My panties are still somewhere on the floor from last night, leaving me in just my bra.

"Have you got some boxers I can borrow, please?" I ask, not

wanting to put last night's underwear back on. It's gross on so many levels.

He grins. "Sure."

He heads over to the drawers and pulls out a pair of black boxers before moving over to the wardrobe, where he pulls out a white T-shirt. He brings them over to me and I quickly pull the T-shirt over my head, thankful for his quick thinking. I was so busy thinking about my lady parts being on full display that I didn't even think about my chest.

I grab the boxers, sliding them on underneath the covers, grimacing as another wave of sharpness digs into my side.

"You're not going shy on me now, are you?" he asks from where he's standing at the end of the bed.

I refuse to meet his gaze and pretend to look at the clock next to the bed, but my eyes widen when the time registers.

Carrie.

Thankfully, I don't pick her up till twelve, so I have plenty of time to do what I need to.

But glancing back at Cage, I also know I need to have this conversation with him.

"No," I lie on a whisper, because the truth is, I *am* feeling shy.

I don't know what to do now. I feel embarrassed for my actions, knowing I only met him just over twenty-four hours ago. I'm an utter slut. Yet, a part of me doesn't care. I want him regardless of it being right or wrong.

I've never felt anything close to how I feel when I'm in his presence. Is it lust? I don't know. What I feel deep inside goes beyond that, but it most certainly isn't love. That is a ridiculous notion; one that can't be true.

Yet, the voice inside of me is screaming: *why not?* I deserve this happiness, this feeling, even if it only lasts for a minute.

He watches me for a moment longer before replying, "I'm cooking breakfast. Are eggs okay?"

"Perfect," I reply, forcing a smile.

"Come on then, let's go feed you."

He helps me out of the bed, and I stagger on my feet, breathing heavily as I wait for the stiffness to subside.

"Okay?"

I nod. "Yeah."

"Come on," he murmurs, and I reluctantly follow him out of the room, but not before I take one last look at the bed. I just want to get back in, soak in his scent a little more. There is just something about it that is comforting.

WE EAT OUR breakfast while making small talk. We mostly chat about the area, along with his plans to build a new garage up by the creek. I actually thought I'd gotten away with not telling him about my past, but then he drops his fork on his plate and looks up at me with a serious expression.

"Now talk," he demands, his voice firm, even.

"Do you have to be so bossy?" I ask him seriously.

"Do you have to answer a question with a question?" he smarts back. "Start talking, Caitlyn. Now."

Jesus, does he always have to be so demanding? Why not politely ask me? Like, 'Caitlyn, darling, could you please spill your most inner, darkest secrets?' But no, instead he goes all Macho Man on me.

"Now, Kitten," he orders with a gentler tone.

"Okay," I grumble, before taking a deep breath. "Right, you asked for this, remember. Don't come crying to me when you're six feet under. Okay?"

"Caitlyn, after you've told me about all this shit, you and I are going to have a little talk about your faith in me. Okay?"

I nod, not wanting to argue. I just want to get this over with so I can go home to shower.

"Okay, here it goes. When I was sixteen, my sister, Courtney, went away with a group of friends. They went over to America, where she met a man named Robin Quinton. Basically, they fell head over heels in love and ended up getting married. Well, she loved *him,* anyway.

"My mum and dad didn't approve, and made it known—strongly—to both Courtney and Robin that they would never get their blessing. It's when she told them she was pregnant, not three weeks after returning, that things changed. Our parents were livid. They thought if they gave Courtney time, they could get them a quick divorce, but then she told them the news and their plan went tits up. After that, my parents disowned her. They told her that out of all the idiotic things she had done, this one was unforgivable. They didn't like Robin and neither did I; there was something about him that gave off a bad vibe."

I continue with my story as quickly as possible because I still find it hard to talk about. "I don't really think my parents actually disowned her. I think they just wanted to make a point that she was on her own if she stayed with him. After that, my sister became distant, but I still went to see her from time to time. My parents encouraged me to go because, secretly, they were worried about her. When people would comment on Courtney's appearance or her personality change to my parents, they got more worried. Worried what Robin was doing to her."

I take a deep breath before I carry on. "Courtney stopped socializing. She stopped working—everything. She was pretty much a housewife. Towards the end of the pregnancy, my father started looking into Robin, but because he wasn't from around here, they had to hire a private investigator. My mum and dad drove down to meet the P.I when he told them he had some information. My mum and dad didn't return that weekend because they were killed in a motorway collision. Even to this day, I still believe Robin had something to do with it. How could he not have? He always seemed to know what was going on in our lives before we did. It was weird, the hold he had on my sister," I explain, tears forming in my eyes as I think about the devastating loss of my parents.

I try not to think of my parents' death. Even to this day I feel dejected from it all. I didn't want to believe back then that they were really gone. Now I'm older, I still feel like that black cloud is hanging over my head. Every day I wish they were here. Having them taken away from me so suddenly, devastated me. I felt like my whole world was crumbling around me, and there was nothing I could do but sit back and watch. I remember the pain in my chest as the policeman told me about the accident, how I collapsed to my knees and sobbed when he told me they didn't make it. Everything after was a blur. The only thing I can remember clearly was the pain in my chest, in my heart, my soul. I had lost the two-dearest people to me.

Cage makes no sudden movements to come to me while I try to compose myself, which I am thankful for. If he held me while I was this vulnerable, I think I'd break, and I don't have the luxury, not when I need to figure out what my next move is.

"I had to move in with my grandma after my parents died as there were no other living relatives to look after me, apart from my sister. But Robin refused to have a teenager around the house, so living with my grandma it was. She died not a month after I moved in." I pause, shaking my head. "I was just starting to feel something again after both my parents died, but God had other plans by taking my grandma, too.

"The day she died is such a foggy mess to me. My sister had come to the hospital, heavily pregnant, with Robin in tow. Which was a shock since he rarely let her out. I didn't even acknowledge them really. I just felt lifeless and numb, like death was coming for me but kept missing, and instead was taking my family in my place.

"It wasn't until I heard Courtney and Robin arguing that I realised what my grandma dying meant for me: I was alone. Really alone. And I was so swallowed by this grief that I couldn't feel anything. I should have paid more attention."

"It's okay," he whispers as I wipe at my cheeks.

I shake my head because he has no idea.

"They argued about letting me stay with them, and in the end, Robin agreed, but under a few conditions. First, I was never to leave my room—unless for dinner—and I was not to wander around the premises or talk to his staff. I agreed, not caring. I didn't even care that I was unwelcome. I felt so detached from everything around me that I would have agreed to anything, just to be left alone. Which they did. Yeah, I could go see friends, but I was happy to lock myself away.

"It was stupid. Maybe if I had taken everything in, I could have done something more."

"What do you mean?" he asks.

"When we arrived at his house in London, the grounds were covered in guards. It was like he was important, and as far as I knew, he was meant to be a regular guy. But I was blind and ignorant to it. Courtney tried to bring me out of my funk, but she went into labour three weeks later." A wistful smile tugs at my lips. "As soon as my gaze landed on my niece, it was like a revelation. Everything I had been feeling disappeared the minute I met Carrie. I loved her instantly, but deep down I was afraid of losing her, too, so I kept my distance—at first."

Cage's lips open and close. He looks like a deer caught in the headlights. I guess that was a shock to pile on.

"Do you want me to continue?" I ask, my entire body trembling. He knows now that Carrie isn't biologically mine.

"Yeah," he croaks out. Clearing his throat, he asks softly, "So, Carrie... she isn't yours?"

"Biologically? No. Emotionally and physically? Yes, she is. She's all I have."

Cage just nods like he understands. Keeping his big brown eyes locked on mine, he gives me the strength to continue.

"A few weeks after Carrie was born, I caved. I was so deeply in love with my niece that I hated being apart from her. I made sure I was with her every waking moment. Robin wasn't around much at that time, and when he was, he would torment me. Make me feel like I didn't belong. He would let me know I was a nuisance, that my sister was getting rid of me the moment I turned eighteen. Well, a few months before Carrie's first birthday, Robin started acting stranger than usual. My sister already thought he was having an affair, so one night she followed him. She came back shaking, her face swollen from crying. I was scared for her, for me, and for Carrie. When we went up to my room, she told me we needed to leave, that it wasn't safe anymore. I asked her why so many times and all she would say was, 'Robin isn't the man I thought he was', and that it wasn't safe to be around him. We couldn't just up and leave, so we planned to prepare a place we could go to, but we never got the chance. I had never been so scared in my whole life, but I trusted her when she said she had it all under control," I sob out. I take in a few breaths, struggling to say the next part.

Cage reaches out and takes my hand in his, squeezing it firmly, making me want to cry out all over again.

"It wasn't until I found a recording she made of Robin, that everything began to click into place. When she followed him, she thought having a recording of him cheating would help with their divorce. What she didn't expect was to film him killing two men. I don't know who they were; I had to stop the tape before I ran to throw up. I also found files my parents' P.I sent when they didn't show up to his meeting. My grandma had left it all in piles in her house, and it's where Carrie and I waited for my sister to come get us.

"We had spent a few weeks planning to get away. Courtney even had all parental rights put into my name after she got Robin to sign the forms, making him think it was the form he had to sign for my grandma's assets to be signed over to Carrie-Ann. She said she didn't want to risk it if anything were to happen to her. She wanted me to have sole custody of Carrie, not that monster.

"The night we were leaving, we forgot Carrie's bear when we packed up, so Courtney went back to get it while I waited at my grandma's house. It was then that I found the files, along with some pictures of Robin's personal activities. From what I read, he's a known criminal in the United States; he ran drugs, women, and guns. We didn't know any of this, and I will never know if my sister knew more than she let on. We had a friend helping us, who had taken Courtney back to the house to get the bear. When Jeremy texted me to run, telling me she was gone, I panicked. I was so frantic, not knowing what to do. She had everything planned, not me.

"Not long after, I was sent confirmation from Robin. He sent me a picture of my sister hanging lifeless from the beams of an old warehouse. There was blood everywhere; her face, her clothes—everything was smeared with blood. When I read the text telling me to come back, I chucked my phone, smashing it against wall so he couldn't trace me, then grabbed Carrie and ran."

I heave out a breath, and when I close my eyes, it's like I can see that picture all over again. It's so vivid in my mind that it gives me nightmares every time I close my eyes. Her clothes were torn, bloodied and dirty. She'd looked like a dog had mauled her, ripping her skin to shreds.

Even with all the bruises, swelling, and blood, I could still make out her pretty face. Her dark, curly brown hair hung limp in front of her eyes, looking matted and tangled.

I shiver thinking about the horrific picture. The rope gripped her neck in a vice, turning her pale complexion blue.

I took one look at the picture and threw up, tears clouding my vision. I grabbed Carrie and got in my car and left. I was grateful then that Courtney made me do a crash course to pass my test. I didn't stick around to see what he would do to me. I just hated she had thought of everything but keeping herself alive.

I compose myself, wiping the tears away. I can't break, not yet. I want to get it all out so he can see I'm not good to be around. That I'm not safe.

"Robin found us—well, his solicitor did—demanding I take Carrie back home where she belonged. When I produced the papers stating my rights, there was nothing they could do. I had custody rights to Carrie-Ann," I explain, taking a deep breath. "He got my new number and would call me, threatening me. I told him if he didn't leave me alone, I would send copies of the video and the files I had of his criminal activities to the authorities. I told him I wanted to live in peace and that I would leave him alone if he did the same with me. I thought he would listen. He hasn't."

I duck my head, focussing on the breakfast bar. Silence fills the air and a lump forms in my throat.

He sits forward, running a hand over his jaw. "Shit, Kitten, when you said it was a long story, I didn't think it was going to be full of blood and murder. I just thought Carrie's dad was an arsehole, not wanting to let you go. I'm feeling like a bit of a prick forcing you to share this with me," he tells me, before taking a breath. "I know it must have been hard losing your whole family like that. I promise you, though—and I don't break my promises—that I'll protect you with everything I've got. Robin Quinton won't hurt you again, I promise. He may have killed people, Kitten, but I know people, too. I can protect you and Carrie from him ever hurting you again."

"You weren't to know how bad it was, Cage. In fact, it feels good to finally talk about it. Our friend, Jeremy, who was helping us, mysteriously died a few months after we left our hometown on the outskirts of London. I was so scared, Cage, really scared. Not just for my safety, but for Carrie's. I don't want her growing up with him if he kills me, too." I pause, trying to find the right words. "After I threatened Robin, we moved to a little town by Lancaster, where I met with a man who knew my dad. He knew what was going on somehow and offered to help keep me hidden from Robin. He got me to make copies and send them to his lawyer. She said she would keep hold of them and if something were to ever happen to me, she would send them to the right people. They both died not a month later." I glance away, unable to hide the guilt. It was my fault they died.

"The papers and copied video were gone, too, which is why he's still after me. He must know they were copies and not the real version. It's why I don't want you involved, Cage; I can't lose someone else because of this mess. I won't allow it."

I can't have another person die in my life, no matter how badly I need to keep Carrie safe. It took me a whole year to really come to terms with my sister's death. I couldn't even go to her funeral as it wasn't safe for me or Carrie. I was powerless to do anything, like the inevitable was going to happen no matter what I did. I was going to die by the hands of Robin Quinton. I got angry after. I was so fed up of everything around me being out of my control, so I took some power back. I made a promise to myself, and to Carrie, that I would make a life for us both. The same day of this realisation, she called me Mummy. I broke down in sobs, wishing my sister were there to hear her daughter say the word 'Mummy'. I knew I'd do anything to keep that promise, to give her the life she deserved to have. It was a life I knew my sister would have given her had she been here.

"Well, guess what, Kitten? I don't care."

"You don't even know me," I argue. "I'm nothing to you."

"I'm human. Even if I didn't have the hots for you, I'd still help. No one like you should live a life like this. You shouldn't have to be scared. I want to do this."

"He'll hurt you," I whisper hoarsely.

"And I'll be prepared for him when he comes. He's not the only person who knows people, Kitten; you don't need to worry about this anymore. Okay? I'll deal with it," he declares, then he stutters for a moment, like he's debating on whether to say what he wants to. I see the minute the decision has been made. His shoulders drop, yet his fists clench. "Have you ever thought of going to the police? Getting him locked up for good?" he asks.

"Cage, that is the dumbest question you could have asked me. Courtney and I tried going to the police, until we got there and saw a policeman walking out, talking with Robin himself. I remember him being at the house, but I never knew he was a policeman," I explain, my voice heating with each word. "I never wanted to risk going to them again after that. What if he had more than one on his payroll, Cage? What will happen to me then— if he has the information? He is going to kill me with it or without it, so it doesn't matter if I take it to the police or not. He'll find a way to get to me."

Chapter Nine

CAGE

MY JAW HITS THE TABLE AT Caitlyn's outburst. Throughout her story, she has tried to remain calm, but seeing her worked up like this turns my stomach. It's like I'm seeing the tiredness in her eyes and in her voice for the first time. I feel useless sitting here, knowing that no matter what I do, she will still have the weight of all that loss on her shoulders. I can't even imagine what she is going through; losing her parents, then her grandma, and then the only living family she had left, apart from Carrie. That would be rough on any person.

My heart tears for her. All through her entire story, I was on edge, forcing myself not to go to her. But I knew she needed me to give her space. I don't think she'd have been able to finish had I held her like I wanted to.

From the minute I laid eyes upon the little firecracker, there was something that drew me to her. It wasn't just her balls at cutting that plug, it wasn't her attitude or sexy as fuck looks. It was her. There was a pull between us and no matter how many times I told myself it was crazy, that we didn't know each other, I couldn't deny that connection was there.

For the first time in a long time, I have something to fight for. I had lost that fight for so long. Everything had become predictable, chicks were predictable. Life was. But she isn't. She's anything but.

But even without all of that between us, there is no way I can let an innocent live a life in terror, too scared to get close to anyone because they're worried they'll die. My will to keep her safe runs deeper than the physical attraction I have for her.

Her strength is admirable. She has done this alone, and I wish she'd let me be there for her.

"First of all, he isn't going to get to you. I will not let him. Last night was a mistake, one I won't be making twice, Caitlyn. I'm going to move my shit in with you while this is going on. Then I'm going to ring my best mate, Nate, to come up as well. He runs my security business and is good at what he does. He can protect you when I'm working. Now that we've got that sorted and agreed on—"

"Hold the fuck up! I haven't agreed to anything. You most certainly are not moving in with me, Cage, and you're not ringing your friend to babysit me. I'm twenty-one, not twelve, for fuck's sake," she snaps.

Even furious she is without a doubt the sexiest woman alive. Even my dick twitches in my jeans listening to her sass at me.

"Listen, Kitten, I'm not taking no for an answer. Plus, Roy could use my cabin for other guests when I move into yours," I tell her. Technically, it's not a lie, because he could use it for paying guests.

"There are other cabins, Cage, and you can see my cabin from here."

"Say what you must, but I'm not budging. I'm coming to live with you at your cabin, whether you like it or not. In fact, it's a great idea. Nate can stay here, and I'll stay with you," I declare, before pushing back on my stool and getting to my feet. "Now, moving on to the issue of you not having faith in me."

Her eyes widen as I walk around the breakfast bar. As I get closer, a smirk pulls at my lips because I'm affecting her. Her breathing picks up, but once I bend down, bringing my lips millimetres from hers, it's like she stops all together.

"Breathe," I demand, and her chest inflates as she takes a deep breath. I blink up at her through my lashes. "Listen now and listen carefully because I'm only going to say this once. I'm twenty-six years old and have seen some shit in my life. I'm not one to brag about my achievements, but I'm very successful at what I do and what I did previously, which was MMA fighting. I can take care of myself, Kitten, and I can take care of you and Carrie. But most of all, I hate it when people question my abilities. I want you, Kitten, more than just protecting you and getting in your pants. If last night was anything to go by, you're just as hot for me as I am for you. Don't question me again. Are we clear?"

I try to keep my voice as calm as possible, but it still comes out more of a demand than a request.

Her pupils darken and her chest rises and falls heavily. I can see a lecture brewing, one I know will piss me off, so before she can open that pretty mouth of hers, I slam my lips down on hers, capturing her in a fiery kiss.

She tenses for a moment, but like me, she can't deny the sparks, and soon, she's kissing me back with as much enthusiasm.

An impulsive need to consume the woman in front of me has me groaning in the back of my throat.

Her lips part, and I massage my tongue against hers, whilst my hands run down the side of her ribs, down to her hips. I grip them tightly and lift her up onto the breakfast bar, stepping between her legs.

I break apart from the kiss, grinning as she sways towards me.

"Are we clear?" I demand breathlessly.

Her swollen lips part, but no words come out. Instead, she nods her head. I need her to say it though. I need to know she understands I'm serious.

"I need you to say it," I whisper, my gaze flicking to her chest with each rise and fall. She looks good in my T-shirt. Really fucking good.

"Yes," she whispers back.

I lean back, making sure she actually spoke the words and I didn't dream it. When her hooded eyes meet mine, I can't hold back anymore. I take her mouth again. What this girl does to me with just a kiss both arouses and scares me. I've never been like this with a girl; I'm usually a wham-bam-thank-you-ma'am kind of bloke. With Caitlyn, though, it's different. I could be content for the rest of my life just holding her in my arms and kissing her.

The kiss becomes more heated as the passion builds between us. Lifting her off the breakfast bar, she automatically wraps her legs around my waist. I smile against her lips, loving how attuned our bodies are with each other.

I head down the hall, to my bedroom, kicking open the door. I lay her gently down on my unmade bed, keeping my mouth securely on hers.

My dick is hard as I move above her, resting myself between her legs. I grip the hem of the T-shirt and lift it above her head.

Her eyes widen as a puff of air escapes her lips.

Fuck, she's hot.

In only her bra and my boxers, she's a man's wet dream.

I lift her up a tiny bit, undoing her bra clasp before placing her back down. Sliding the bra fully off, I chuck it to the side.

I groan as I reach down, sucking her nipple into my mouth. My cock is rock hard, pressing against the rough material of my jeans. I want to rip them off and sink inside of her, but I know she deserves more. She deserves more than a wham-bam-thank-you-ma'am.

Her body writhes beneath me, her back arching off the bed as I reach for her other nipple, flicking my tongue across the tip.

I'm not even inside of her and I want to come. It's the way she submits to me, the way she melts, and the little mewling sounds coming from her mouth.

And although I'm dying to come, I also want to prolong her pleasure.

I pull up, locking my gaze with hers as I slide my T-shirt over my head. She licks her lips, her gaze following my hands as I reach down, unbuttoning my jeans. I keep my movements slow, steady, giving her enough to time to change her mind if this isn't what she wants. It would kill me, but I'd respect her wishes.

Free of my clothing, I lay down next to her, watching as her chest rises and falls with each breath she takes.

She's nervous.

I glide my fingers down her chest, over her smooth, toned stomach, mindful of her injuries. I lean over, kissing her deeply as my hand moves under the waistband of her boxers.

I groan as my fingers slide through her wetness, feeling her arousal. Her hips arch off the bed as I swirl my fingers around her clit, the mewling sounds getting louder each time I press down harder.

"Cage," she whispers, silently begging for more.

My dick pulses as I slide my fingers inside her, feeling her clench around them. I add another finger, thrusting them in and out, and she moans and writhes beside me.

I press my thumb to her clit, rubbing gently, and within seconds, I feel her sex start to clamp around my fingers harder, right before her body tightens and she screams out my name.

"Cage. Oh fuck! Cage."

Hearing my name on those sweet lips nearly undoes me, and I

reach over to the bedside table for a condom before I embarrass myself. I slowly guide it over my girth, along my cock, before pumping it in my fist, groaning with pleasure.

Caitlyn is lying blissfully unaware of my movements as she comes down from her orgasm, her eyes clenched shut. But the minute I position myself between her legs, sliding my cock up and down her tight, wet pussy, she opens them, blinking up at me with so much vulnerability. She shivers, her hands shaking as she reaches up to grip my biceps.

"I want you," I rasp.

"I want you, too," she replies breathlessly.

I guide the tip of my dick to her opening. The minute the tip enters her sex, I feel her body tense up, going rigid beneath me. I bend down, pressing my lips to hers.

She's tight, really tight, so I keep still for a moment, letting her get used to my size. As soon as her body melts against me, I slide further inside, careful not to ram inside of her. I don't want to hurt her or cause her more pain with her injuries.

Her breathing speeds up, and to relax her, I lean down, capturing her nipple between my lips. She moans, her hips arching towards me, causing me to slide further inside. She clamps down and I groan, clenching my eyes shut. I can't trust myself not to slam inside of her.

I push slowly— and come to a barrier, stopping me from penetrating any further. My entire body tenses at the realisation. This beautiful, sexy woman is a virgin.

A rumble makes its way up my throat. Even knowing the fact, I want her more. I like that I'm her first, that she chose me.

"Kitten," I rasp, locking my gaze with hers.

Her forehead creases, and for a moment, her vulnerability shines, replacing the lust and need in her gaze.

"Are you sure you want to do this?" I ask her again. I feel like a pussy, talking while I have the tip of my dick shoved inside her sex.

"What do you mean?" she asks, placing her hands around my neck, pulling me down to her.

"I mean the fact you're a virgin, Kitten. Are you sure you want to do this? We can stop, baby. I don't want to hurt you," I tell her, kissing the tip of her nose.

She blinks, avoiding my gaze. "I… I'm sorry. I didn't know how to tell you. I knew you wouldn't want me if I told you, and I want you— this— so much."

"Hey, I still want you, Kitten. I just wish you would have warned me. We've only known each other a few days. Are you sure this is something you want? I really don't like the thought of hurting you, and the first time always hurts."

"I want this, Cage. I want *you*. I've never gone this far before. I have never felt any desire to. But this is mine to give. This is real. I've been running for so long I forgot what it truly means to be alive, what it means to feel wanted. I want this. Please, make love to me."

I watch as she cringes at her words. And if any other woman had said those words to me, I would have run for the hills.

This is different. I can feel her need to be present, to be wanted.

And deep down, I want to be the man who makes love to her. After everything she has been through, she deserves that much.

There are no more words to exchange. We both want this, want each other, and there is no going back. I lean down, capturing her lips in a heated kiss as I push further inside of her.

I want to own every inch of her body. My heart expands, knowing the importance of what she is giving me.

I inch in a bit more, feeling her sex tighten around my dick. I clench my teeth together, trying to hold back, trying not to shoot my load before it's already begun.

She clamps around me and I groan. "You need to relax, Kitten."

"I can't, it hurts. Can't you just break the barrier and get the hard part over with? I mean, I read in a book that it gets easier once the barrier is broken," she tells me, and before I can open my lips, she's reaching around to my arse, pulling me against her, grazing her nails down my back. She grabs onto my firm backside, pushing me into her.

She cries out as I slam inside of her, tearing the barrier of her virginity. I still, catching my own breath. After a moment, I reach down, placing kisses along her jaw, to her lips.

I have never been with a virgin, so this is a first for me too. I hadn't expected it to be this tight. It feels good, and a reminder of what she has just given me.

"Are you okay?" I croak out, watching as a tear slips down her cheek. I capture it between my lips, smirking at her inhale of breath. "Do you want me to carry on?"

I know my size doesn't help. I'm bigger than average, and it must have hurt her.

"Yes, I'm fine. It just stings," she assures me, her lashes fluttering. "Just, please, go slow."

She's driving me crazy. Each thrust is driving me to the point of insanity. It's torturous having to go slow, but when her lips part, I begin to pick up my pace, thrusting harder with each roll of my hips.

She tightens around me, and her fingers dig into my biceps. She rolls her hips and I groan, the sensation running down my spine.

I'm not going to last much longer. I lean down and our lips clash together.

"Cage," she pants out, and I lean up a little, slamming inside of her, her back pushing up the bed.

I nip and bite at her skin—anywhere I can get to her—as she drags her nails down my back. I feel ready to explode when her body starts to move in sync with mine, and I moan into her neck. I lift up, locking gazes with her, and something inside of me stills. It isn't just fucking her. This feels like more.

Her pupils dilate and I lean down, our kiss softer but no less heated.

"I'm so close, Kitten. You're so god damn tight I don't think I can last much longer," I rasp.

"Please," she pleads. "Harder."

The control I was barely holding onto, snaps with that plea. I pull out until only the tip is left inside of her, then slam inside of her.

She cries out, tightening around me, bringing me closer to my release. I slam inside of her with urgency, our bodies slapping together as sweat mingles in the air.

She's close.

Lifting myself off her, I place one hand on her hip and the other to her clit. She screams out my name as I bring her to the crest of her climax. At the first feel of her orgasm, I shoot my load inside of her, moaning through my pleasure.

Holy shit!

I've never had an orgasm that strong before; it seems to go on forever while we each ride out the waves of our climax.

I collapse beside her, trying to get myself under control as my breath rises and falls.

I turn my head to the side, glancing over at Caitlyn, who lays there, her eyes closed and breathing heavily.

Fuck, she's sexy. Sated, satisfied, and fucked, she's a fucking wet dream.

And although this is the part where I usually leave, I don't want to. And it's all because of her.

I don't know what will become of us, and I don't care. I just know I can't ignore this storm brewing inside of me.

Chapter Ten

CAITLYN

THAT WAS… I'M NOT SURE WHAT words to use, but it was everything. Do I feel any different? Yes, in a way I do. It isn't life altering, but it is something. Something I will treasure and remember for the rest of my life.

Cage, he was… he wasn't who I pictured ever being with like this, and I think that was a good thing, because my expectations would never have been met, not if I knew it would have been like that. And it had been everything.

I'm sore, really sore in fact, but I dismiss the pain because it had been worth it. All of it had been worth it. And although there is an inkling of shame, I ignore it because I don't regret the act itself or it being with Cage.

He made it a moment to remember.

I feel alive. My blood is humming through my veins as the events of what happened play through my head.

He makes me hope for a better future. He makes me want this again and again, and not just for the sex, but the connection, the rush of emotions that flittered through me each time he touched me, each time he thrust inside of me.

It had all been worth it.

My body is spent, and although I feel self-conscious about being fully naked in front of him, I don't pull the covers up to hide. I'm done with hiding.

He's still breathing heavily beside me, and I turn to scan over his sculptured body. That same feeling I got inside of me when he entered me, returns. I want him again. I want to roll over and cuddle up to him. But I'm not sure if that's what he wants.

For all I know, this was a one-time thing, and it probably is. I'm not under any promise or notion that this was anything more than it was. Although I desperately wished it could be.

I know he has been with other women. I'm not stupid. But my sister's warning so long ago echoes through my head. She said men only want one thing and to make sure I never gave them it, not unless they worked for it and he was the one.

My brows pucker in a frown as I wonder what she would think of me now. I had lost my virginity with a practical stranger.

Will he kick me out now he's got what he wanted? The thought hurts, but then again, I don't really know much about the man beside me. He could be a serial killer for all I know.

I turn to get more comfortable, and a hiss passes through my lips at the discomfort.

"Are you okay?" he asks, rolling on his side to face me, his hand running over my stomach. "Did I hurt you?"

"No, you didn't hurt me," I whisper. "At first it hurt, but then it faded a little bit. I'm just stinging down there at the moment."

I inwardly cringe at my running mouth. I should have just said yes and left it there.

I shuffle on the bed, uncomfortable. I don't know what I should do. Do I leave? Do I say thank you? Should I get dressed and leave the rest to him to decide? Do I make small talk? Cuddle?

I shake my head as an inward groan vibrates through my chest. I'm clueless. So fucking clueless when it comes to stuff like this.

Just as I decide to leave, he speaks up. "Come on, let's get you showered, Kitten," he tells me. "You must be sore."

I grimace as I sit up. "I, um, I need to get going actually. I'll take a shower at home."

It's then I notice the bloodied bedsheets, along with splotches of dried blood between my legs. My face flames as I chance a look at Cage to see if he's noticed. He has.

God, someone kill me.

"Um, I think I'll take that shower," I tell him sheepishly. "I'm sorry about your sheets. I'll change them before I go. Hayley will be doing the rounds this afternoon after I get Carrie, so you'll have some fresh sheets before tonight."

"I don't care about my sheets, Kitten," he tells me, leaning over to press a kiss on my lips.

"But there's blood——"

"I don't care," he assures me, smirking. "Let's get you in the shower."

I nod, sliding my legs off the bed. I watch his firm backside head over to the bathroom and a sigh escapes me.

I should feel disappointed nothing else was said between us, but I can't muster up that kind of negative energy. Not after what happened.

What will be, will be.

I have to believe that. It's the same mantra I've told myself since I started to run with Carrie.

I hear the sound of the shower turning on and seconds later, Cage peeks around the corner, his brows bunching together when he spots me still on the bed.

"Everything okay?" I ask.

He heads towards me, and a squeak passes through my lips when he gently lifts me off the bed. I wrap my arms around him, groaning at the sensation of being pressed against him.

"I'm not showering alone," he warns me.

"W-what?"

I don't need an answer. Not when he steps into the shower, pushing me under the spray, still in his arms. I moan when he leans down, kissing the side of my neck.

I guess we're showering together.

I TRY TO IGNORE the ache between my legs. It isn't a pain, just a dull ache, reminding me of what we did earlier.

Each time I glance at Cage, who insisted on walking me home to get changed, he catches me, his lips pulling into a smirk.

I'm not sure why he wanted to come with me, but I'm not complaining. If this is a one-time thing, I want to drag it out as long as possible. It hurts to think this will be the end, or could be. It's bizarre, but I really don't want it to.

And the more he talks about himself, about his family, the more I like him. But that could be the great sex talking.

I sigh, not knowing what it is, and I hate that it's the only thing running through my mind when I have more pressing matters.

"You okay?" Cage asks as we reach Hayley and Roy's.

I nod. "Yeah, just worried I'll scare Carrie," I partially lie. It might not have been what I was thinking before, but I had thought it. And I'm worried. She has been through too much to see me like this.

He opens his mouth to say something, but our attention is pulled to the front door when I hear it click open.

A pale-faced Hayley comes running out, and the minute I take in her terror-filled expression, I panic.

My knees knock together, and without thinking, I reach for Cage, gripping his arm as she races towards me. My stomach ties up in knots when she reaches me, surprising me when she pulls me in for a hug.

"Caitlyn," she cries out, clutching me tightly. "Oh, sweet girl."

A hiss slips through my lips at the pressure around my ribs. They're throbbing more since I overexerted myself this morning. I pull back, my stomach bottoming out. "What's wrong? Where's Carrie?" I ask.

She grips my cheeks, her eyes watering. "Oh, sweet girl, look at your beautiful face. Roy told me what happened last night. Are you okay?"

I immediately relax, knowing Carrie is okay. If she weren't, she would have said that first. I can't believe I keep forgetting about last night. I glance at Cage, silently blaming him since he has a way of scrambling my head.

"I'm fine," I assure her softly. "Where's Carrie?"

Before Hayley has a chance to reply, my little bundle of joy comes running down the porch steps, heading straight to... Cage. Instead of running to me, she goes straight to him, and my heart skips a beat as he kneels down to catch her.

He picks her up, swinging her around while she gushes about what she has done this morning.

"I helped Hayley plant some seeds in her little garden," she informs him, before getting more in his face. "And guess what she let me help make? Some cakes! Isn't that so cool?"

A chuckle slips free, and before it can turn into laughter, it really hits me. She went to Cage first. A part of me is glad that Carrie trusts him, but the other half of me is hurt. It's only ever been the two of us. I'm not used to anyone else getting her attention but me.

"That's great, Pea. What seeds did you plant?" he asks her.

"I don't know, but it was so cool. When they grow to be big flowers, I'll show you," Carrie replies, still in his arms.

She looks over to me, and I hear her intake of air as she takes in my face.

"Mummy," she cries, struggling to get down from Cage.

He lets her go and she comes running to me with tears sliding down her face.

"You got a booboo on your face. Did you fall over? Did it hurt, Mummy?" she cries, as she hits her head on my bruised side, causing me to wince.

"It's okay, baby girl. Mummy fell over. It doesn't hurt, I promise."

"It looks sore," she states, her tear-filled eyes boring into me.

"I know, baby. I took a nasty fall, but it's all better now," I assure her, kissing the top of her head.

"Did Cage make it all better?" she asks, and my eyes widen.

"What? Huh. I... He... Um, yes, he helped me put some cold water on it," I stutter out, my cheeks flushed.

I glance up at Hayley when she clears her throat, but I realise she's smothering her laughter. I glare when she grins at me, her eyes twinkling when she then glances at Cage with a knowing look.

"Why do you look funny?" Carrie comments, and Cage does nothing to smother the deep chuckle.

"You ready to go home?" I ask, changing the subject.

"Can Cage come?" she asks, taking my hand. "Oh, and Hayley and Roy said we could have a dog, as long as it's friendly. So, can we go get one today?"

Shit!

I bite my bottom lip, wondering for the millionth time how I'm going to let her down. It's not that I don't want a dog. I do. I just don't have the time for one, nor can I afford to feed another mouth. Not that we struggle for money. I just like saving as much as I can in case we ever need to leave again, and if it came to it, move out of the country. It's drastic, an option I hope I never have to take, but one I will to get away from Robin.

"I don't think that's a good idea, sweetie. What if we need to move again?" I ask her, aware of my audience.

"Mummy, you said we were staying here. I like it here with you and Hayley and Roy. I don't want to move again. Please, Mummy, I don't want to leave," she pleads, her lip trembling as she fights back tears.

My heart stops for a moment. It's times like this that kill me inside. She doesn't deserve to be moved from place to place. She needs stability. And I'm failing to give it to her.

"We aren't leaving, baby, but what if we need to? How can I take a dog with us if we need to leave? It's not fair on the dog," I remind her, hating that her face crumbles.

"I want a dog, Mummy," she whines. "Did you know they can protect you? We wouldn't need to keep running," she tells me, sounding far too grown up for her own good.

"Yes, I know they do, sweetie," I tell her slowly, as her words sink in. "What do you mean run? We don't run. We just move around a lot."

"You get scared in your sleep," she whispers, running the toe of her shoe along the gravel. She stops, her doe eyes staring up at me. "Please can we get a dog? It can protect us both. I promise."

Tears form in my eyes, and I try to hold them back. The lump in my throat is the size of a golf ball when I try to swallow.

I hadn't realised just how much she was picking up on. I thought I was protecting her from our past. It just seems like I'm messing up her future. She shouldn't have to worry about these things.

"Okay, baby, I'll think about it," I tell her, squeezing my eyes shut for a moment.

I have to make this right for her.

"Yes!" she squeals.

"Go get your bag," I order gently.

I stand, and the look Cage gives me causes a shiver to race down my spine. I'm not sure what it means, and I'm glad Hayley is here so he doesn't say anything.

Carrie comes rushing back out, her backpack over her shoulders. She reaches me and takes my hand.

"Are you coming?" she asks, staring up at Cage.

His lips pull up into a smile. "I have to see Roy."

"Don't touch his cookies. He only lets me eat them," she tells him, and his lips twitch.

"I'll remember that," he tells her.

I stand awkwardly for a moment, not knowing what to do or say to him. "Thank you for having her again."

"You are more than welcome," she tells me, her face lighting up.

I smile and turn to Cage, as I run my free hand down my side. "Um, I guess I'll, um…" I grimace, closing my eyes. "I'll be going. Thank you for, um… everything."

"Yeah," he murmurs, his gaze boring into me.

I shiver and give them a lame wave before heading off. Carrie begins to tell me every detail of her stay, and when we reach the bend, I take one last look at Cage, finding him jogging up the stairs to the house.

"Can I name him?"

"Name who?" I ask, jerking my attention to her.

"The dog, silly."

"Yeah," I murmur, biting my bottom lip.

I guess I have that to worry about now too. Hopefully, there will be a book on my Kindle that explains how to look after dogs.

Chapter Eleven

CAGE

"**Y**OU NEED A MINUTE?" Hayley asks, and I realise I'm breathing hard, my hands in fists at my side.

I can't help it. That arsehole is putting their lives through hell. Hell, she won't even get a pet because she's worried sick she'll have to leave it behind.

And Carrie. Listening to her daughter say all that stuff puts the situation in perspective. Carrie needs stability, a routine, and she isn't getting it when Caitlyn is running every so often out of fear because of that prick.

And this isn't because I had my dick inside her only a few hours ago. My need to protect her happened before then. Only, it has intensified now that I know what it's like to be inside her. There's a primal need inside of me that wants to follow her, to make sure she's okay.

I still can't wrap my head around what I'm feeling. It isn't about fucking her— I did it and still feel the same. And it isn't about protecting her because I would have done it for anyone in her situation. She isn't manipulating me, and she isn't playing games. She's genuinely naïve to her beauty and charisma. It draws me to her. And it makes me want her more.

"Sorry," I tell her, wiping a hand down my face. "Where is Roy?"

"Roy is in his office," she answers. "He's been wanting to speak to you too."

"I'm not surprised," I reply.

"She's going to be fine. You know that, right? Roy won't let anything happen to her. Those two girls mean more to us than they realise," she tells me.

"I'm seeing that," I murmur.

"Please don't hurt her, Cage. She's not like your other girls. She's special. What she's been through is tough, and she has stayed strong throughout all of it, even if she doesn't know it. So please, don't hurt her. I don't think she's ready to handle that kind of heartbreak," she declares, her tone a plea.

I stop at the bottom of the stairs and turn to her. I'm not one to talk about my feelings, but Hayley and Roy mean a lot to me, and they deserve the truth.

"I don't plan on hurting her, Hayley," I declare. "She's different from anyone I've ever met. There is something about her that makes me want to wrap her up in cotton wool and lock her away, just to keep her safe. I'm not declaring anything. We've just met, even if it does feel like we've known each other longer. But I'm not going to lie and say I don't feel anything, because I do, and it scares me. I'm in way over my head when it comes to her because in two days, she's managed to screw my head up in the best way." I pause, letting her digest the words. "Does that answer your question?"

Her lips part, then close, before parting again. She takes a deep breath, before saying, "Yeah, yeah, it does," she tells me. "Go talk to Roy before he wonders where you are."

"Will do," I tell her, taking the stairs two at a time.

Heading through the house, I make my way down the hall to Roy's home office. I don't bother knocking as I let myself in, finding him sitting behind his desk, frowning down at his phone.

"What's wrong?" I ask, sitting myself down in the chair in front of the desk.

Roy looks up with a frown still planted on his face, causing me to sit up straighter.

This isn't going to be good.

"Cage, boy, this isn't good. From what I got off the CCTV footage last night, we are dealing with some seriously twisted people," he begins, and I tense, ready for what else he has to say. "If my sources are correct, the bloke who attacked Caitlyn last night is Kane Fernando. He's a known hitman for a corporation run by a Robin Quinton. If this is correct, then Caitlyn is going to need a lot of help. This shit is bad if he came on behalf of Quinton." He sits back, running his hand through his hair. "I don't even know what to suggest, Cage. This is all out of my league."

I had a feeling it was going to be bad. I sit forward, hoping Caitlyn forgives me for telling him what I'm about to.

"Caitlyn told me everything last night. Robin Quinton is the guy who killed her sister, maybe her parents, and anyone who has ever helped her. She has some evidence that could potentially put him inside for a long time. She tried to go to the police once, but when she got there, Robin was walking out, talking with a cop. She said she had seen the copper in Robin's house a few times, so she got too scared to even trust them after that."

"Hold on. Is this Carrie's father we're talking about? What the fuck was Caitlyn doing with a man like him; he's like, what, thirty-five? Maybe older?"

I grimace, rubbing the back of my neck. "Uh, no. Actually, there's more. I assumed you knew," I begin. "I'm not sure if it's okay to tell you, but fuck it, you need to know. Carrie isn't Caitlyn's; she was her sister's child. Long story short, they tried to get away when Robin found out her sister recorded some shit on her phone, but he killed her before they could leave. Luckily, before her passing, they got him to sign Carrie's parental rights over to Caitlyn. They made him believe he was signing something to do with their grandma, who recently passed before."

"How did Caitlyn get away?" he chokes out, his face paling.

"She was at the house waiting for her sister so they could leave. But she never came back. He sent Caitlyn a picture of her sister's hanging body and from there, she ran. She has taken care of Carrie ever since, as her own."

"Well, fuck me," he breathes out, eyes wide. "This is big. Too big for a dainty thing like her to handle. He will chew her up and spit her out." He takes another breath and I watch him struggle to come to terms with it all. "We can't let him hurt her."

"I know," I tell him, feeling just as strongly about this.

"I only knew she lost her family, nothing else. When Hayley first laid eyes upon them both, she took a liking to them. After losing Jesse, she had been out of sorts. When Caitlyn turned up with Carrie, she had finally started to heal and move on. There is nothing I wouldn't do for my woman. Losing those girls will destroy her."

Jesse was their adopted son; they couldn't have any kids of their own, so they adopted Jesse when he was twelve. He died in Afghanistan last year. Losing him has been tough on both of them, but especially on Hayley.

"I'm going to ring Nate, ask him to come down, and see what he suggests we do. I can imagine we'll need to find someone we can trust on the inside first. That information is pointless until we do. We can't let it get into the wrong hands and be destroyed."

"What do you think it is?"

I shrug. "It must be worth a lot to him, especially for him to keep coming after her like this. Why not leave her alone like she asked, knowing she would keep quiet? She thinks she's going to die, whether she hands the information over or not, and I think she's right," I admit. "I'm going to stay with her and Carrie at their cabin while Nate stays at mine. I'll have cameras put up around Caitlyn's cabin and the surrounding area, if that's okay. Also, I'll have some alarms put in. I know it will seem like too much, but at least we will know she is safe. I'm going to have Nate shadow her while she works so she will be safe then, too."

He nods, taking a swig of his drink. "Sounds like a plan. Be prepared for this shit to get ugly. I've heard of this Robin Quinton before, and whoever tries to go against him, ends up dead. I don't want anything to happen to either of you."

"It won't. I'll protect her with my life," I tell him honestly.

"Yeah, I can see that," he states, watching me like he can read my thoughts.

Getting to the door, Roy calls my name. Turning my attention to him, his face is set in a hard expression.

"Don't hurt her, because I'd hate to hurt you," he warns.

"I won't," I tell him, a grin pulling at my lips.

I've been waiting for him to say something, just like his wife had outside. It seems I'm not the only one Caitlyn has gotten to in a short space of time.

* * *

HEADING BACK TO my cabin, I pull my phone out and dial Nate. We've been best friends since we were kids. His mum died when he was a teenager and he got into some seriously bad shit. As his dad wasn't around, he didn't have anywhere to go, so my mum and dad took him in. It took him a while, but he got his head screwed back on not long after moving in with us.

"Yeah," he greets after the fourth ring.

"Hey, Nate, I need a favour. We have a situation."

"Dante hasn't been arrested again, has he? Because I'm not a lawyer, Cage."

I chuckle. "No. There's a girl here at the resort who is in some serious shit. It's all too complicated to explain over the phone. I need you to come down and bring some men with you. I'm going to need you to put in some surveillance cameras and fit some alarms. I will also need you to find as much shit as you can on Robin Quinton. Is that okay?" I ask, not really caring if it's not okay. The fucker is going to do it.

He inhales sharply. "What the fuck, dude? Robin Quinton is into some serious fucking shit. You remember Frank Roberto?"

"Yes," I growl, remembering that sick fucker. He was bad news, and from what Caitlyn said about Robin, Frank was into the same dealings. Frank was well-known in our area and was feared by the cops. Luckily, he was killed three years ago. By whom, no one knew. The reports said it was the result of a gang war.

"It's been heard that Quinton had some beef with him, took him and his men out three years ago. He literally slaughtered the whole lot of them. You sure some chick is worth this, man? You might not get out alive," he tells me, his voice full of concern.

I don't know how to explain it to my best friend without sounding like a pussy, but he needs to know how much this means to me. How much she means to me. "You'll need to meet her to understand. She's been through hell, but she's innocent. I-I think I care for her. No, I know I do. She's special."

"Fuck!" he hisses.

"She has a little girl, man. They've been through too much and don't deserve this crap. I'll never forgive myself if I look the other way just because I might die. She deserves someone to take a stand for her." I take in a breath, coming to a stop outside my cabin. "She has evidence to put him away but doesn't trust anyone on the inside. Do you know anyone who has been working Quinton's case? Maybe we can give them the information? She knows he has cops in his pocket."

He lets out a sigh. "I'll look into it. You need to remember he isn't one to be messed with. He isn't some guy you can fight in a ring, Cage. He's the kind of guy who will rip everyone you know and love apart," he admits. "He moved away to the states with his parents fifteen years ago and came back when he turned twenty. He left again for the states not long after setting up business here. As far as I can tell, the bloke is a whack job. Apparently, he killed his own wife not so long ago, in front of his men."

My blood runs cold knowing he is talking about Courtney.

"Yeah, mate, I know. That was Caitlyn's sister he killed. I told you it's fucked up. Caitlyn has custody of his and her sister's little girl. Her sister didn't know what she had gotten herself into before it was too late. Now Caitlyn is in the middle of it all, without anyone to help her. She thinks he killed her parents too because it happened when they were on their way to meet the person they had investigating him."

"Let me get a team together, brother, then I'll be down. If she is as special as you say she is, then you need to be prepared. This guy is relentless. It's about time someone put him the fuck down."

My brows pucker together. "Why do you sound excited?"

"I've not had this much excitement or a challenge since the Steven case with the missing girl."

I roll my eyes. "I'm going to go; I need to pack up my stuff. I'm going to stay with her for a while, so you can stay at my place," I tell him. "Oh, and before you go, Roy gave me the go ahead on the garage. Rent free, too. I've bought the land up Barrett's Lane, so can you round up the rest of the guys when they've finished their last job? I didn't take any more work on until we've finished here, but with the house and then building the garage, I'm going to need them up here sooner. Is that okay with you?"

"No problem. I should be down there by tonight and I'll start work tomorrow. I need to get as much information as possible before I head down there."

"Okay, see you later," I say, then end the call.

I know I can count on him. Even with the whole messy situation and Robin in the equation, he didn't hesitate to have my back, even if it meant something could happen to him.

I INWARDLY GROAN, wondering for the millionth time since I ended the call with Nate, what the fuck is up with me.

Instead of taking my time packing my stuff up, I raced through it, a need inside me screaming to get to Caitlyn. I wanted to be near her.

It's official, I dropped my man card somewhere.

As I walk across the grassy path to Caitlyn's, I hear a high-pitched scream, followed by some banging and grunts. I start running across the grassy path, my heart racing when I realise it's coming from the direction of Caitlyn's cabin.

As I draw closer, I scan my surroundings for any threats, seeing no one out of place.

A loud clanging sound echoes through the air, and as I push through the trees, I watch in shock as Caitlyn beats the living shit out of a porch swing. Well, what's left of it anyway.

"What did that swing ever do to you?" I tease, walking up the steps.

She must not have noticed me as she startles, spinning around to face me. I steady her when she goes to fall back and laugh at her expression as she pulls away.

"You scared the living shit out of me, Cage. That isn't funny." She scowls, and the laughter pours out of me.

Her nose scrunches up in the most adorable way. I want to reach forward and press a kiss to the tip.

I sigh. There I go again, and just to be sure, I glance down at my dick, making sure it's still there. I can feel it, so that's a good sign.

I swear, around her I have completely lost my mind.

"Sorry, didn't mean to startle you," I admit, my lips twitching. "I was just concerned for the safety of the porch swing. I needed to come before you got arrested for more than attempted battery."

"Seriously, Cage, I wasn't that bad."

I arch an eyebrow, and she rolls her eyes in return. "What has it done to you?"

"The damn stupid instructions are wrong," she grumbles, looking flushed.

"Want me to take a look?"

"What?" she rushes out, a pink flush rising up her neck and over her cheeks. I grin, watching as her gaze jerks down to my dick.

Ah, the little minx was having dirty thoughts.

"I'm good with my hands. I can do it," I tell her, winking at her.

"I bet you can," she mumbles, clearly thinking I can't hear her.

"Yeah, you'd be surprised what I can do with my hands, Kitten," I state, grabbing the instructions off the floor.

I go through the checklist of the items and set it all out in front of me, then start to dismantle the part Caitlyn sort of put together before I came. Once I'm satisfied I have all the metal poles, screws, and Allen keys, I get to work.

After staring at me open-mouthed for five minutes, Caitlyn heads inside, letting me know she's checking on Carrie.

I chuckle as I watch her arse sway inside. Damn, she has a nice arse.

Another five minutes later, I give the canopy swing one more check to make sure it's safe, before standing up, calling for Carrie.

"Pea, come here," I shout inside the front door of the cabin.

Tiny footsteps pad along the wooden floor, and seconds later, Carrie comes running out, her eyes widening when she sees the canopy.

Her eyes light up as she begins to jump up and down, squealing. I want to cover my ears, but there is something about seeing her happy that makes me want to watch and enjoy it. As lame as it sounds, it's true. Here she is, ecstatic and overjoyed over some little swing, and I feel like it's contagious; feeling content and delighted with her.

"This is so awesome. Mum!" she yells, as she takes a seat on her swing. She swings back and forth slowly and smiles up at me. "Thank you so much."

Caitlyn steps out of the cabin door. When she looks to the left and sees the fitted swing, with Carrie sitting on it, her jaw goes slack. She looks to me then back to the swing, as if she's unsure what to say.

"Wow! That was fast," she states.

"Yeah, that's what she said," I tease.

She blinks a few times before getting what I meant. When her cheeks turn pink, she ducks her head.

"Thank you," she whispers, unable to meet my gaze. The urge to lean over and kiss her is strong. The only thing stopping me is the fact I don't want to push her. Not yet.

"That's okay. Where do you want me to put my stuff?"

"Stuff?" she asks, her nose scrunching up.

"Uh, yeah, Kitten, my stuff. Where can I put it before it all gets wrinkled? You're not going to want to iron all my shit now, are you?"

"What? Why would I need to iron your clothes?" she asks, still looking adorably confused.

I sigh, picking my bag up off the floor. "Okay, Kitten, stay with me. Where can I put my clothes away? I'm taking it you have a built-in closet like the rest of the cabins, but what about drawers? Do you need to move some of your shit?" I ask.

"Language, Cage." She scowls at me, looking slightly pissed.

I glance over at Carrie, who is luckily too engrossed in placing her baby dolls in the swinging chair with her rather than to listening to me. The kid really is cute.

"Look, I'm confused as to what is going on. Just because we… you know, and it was… you know, my, um… first time, it doesn't mean you get to move in, Cage. I know it was only a one-time thing and I'm okay with that. It's not like I was waiting for marriage or anything," she rambles on. I smirk, listening to her ramble because I have to admit, I wanted to see where she was going. She's so cute when she's flustered. "I mean, you didn't seem like you wanted marriage. I'm not sure how things like this work but—"

"Kitten, I'm moving in remember, until we deal with your situation," I remind her, and push past her, chuckling when her lips part. I'll find the damn bedroom myself. "Plus, it's not going to be a one-time thing, Kitten. I plan to get reacquainted with your body very soon."

Chapter Twelve

CAITLYN

HE'S... HE'S MOVING IN?

This morning when he mentioned it, I didn't think he was serious. I thought for sure that once we slept together, he would change his mind.

But as I watch him moving towards my room, I can't help but wonder how we got to this point.

One minute I'm staring him down before cutting a plug, the next, I'm in his bed and wishing for it to happen again. And in the next breath, I feel cheap and dirty having slept with someone I barely know. People were right in what they said about not declaring anything during sex. It's the sexual tension talking, not the mind.

Or at least, I thought it was.

I'm not sure what came over me this morning, but I have been through enough to know I can't let it happen again. Good things don't happen to me. And I'm not sure I can handle losing another person in my life.

Then there's Cage. I wasn't blind this morning to the fact I knew he wasn't a one-woman man. He's too good looking, too experienced. His party proved that the first night I met him. He's used to that.

I'm not.

I'm used to reading bed-time stories and getting excited if I get to bed before ten PM.

However, there's no denying my attraction to him, or the warm, fuzzy feeling I got when he called me his. Then there was yesterday. After my parents died, there was only one day I truly enjoyed. It was the day I woke up from my depression and saw Carrie. Really saw her. And although I've spent each and every moment with her since, nothing beat the day I spent with her and Cage.

It was like I was seeing a life play out that we could have. What she could have. I want her to have the world.

And I want to share that with her.

And yes, that dreamer side of me wants it with him too. Because it feels good to be a part of something, to connect with someone.

It's all just a pipe dream, one I have no chance of coming true. Too much is happening for me to even be stressing about this. And yet, my insecurities fester, and all I can wonder is: when will he leave? Will he die by the hands of the monster trying to protect us, or will he leave, realising I'm not worth it?

I sigh, closing my eyes as I lean against the doorframe.

My insecurities are going to be the death of me. I hate feeling like it, but they are there. And each time I look at Carrie, I'm reminded of what I lost and what I've gained. My sister lives on in her, and I'll be forever grateful to her for bringing Carrie into my life, but every day I'm scared, wondering when she will be taken away, too.

"Mummy, is Cage going to be sleeping with you?" Carrie asks, bringing me out of my daze. I must have been staring into space for a while because Cage appears from the hallway, watching me intently.

"I, um..." I stutter, but I don't get to finish as Cage interrupts.

"Yeah, Pea, I am."

I stare, dumbfounded by his response. My daughter squeals, coming off the swing to jump up into Cage's arms, where he happily takes her. He sweeps her up into his big, bulging arms, leaning her across his hip. Both of them stare at me as if they're waiting for me to say something. Carrie has the biggest smile her face can muster, while Cage wears his god damn sexy grin. I already know I'm in deep shit when it comes to these two.

And Carrie is smitten enough to side with him over anything.

Traitor!

"Yes! Does this mean you and Mummy are going to kiss?" she asks him, batting her lashes.

I open my mouth, ready to respond, but Cage smirks and answers before I can. "Yes, Pea, we will be doing a lot of kissing." He places her down on the floor, and whilst her back is to him, he gives me a wink.

"That means you love each other, doesn't it?" she asks. Before one of us can reply, she keeps going, making my heart beat faster. "Does this mean you're my daddy now? I really want a daddy, and you're nice. My mum smiles when she's around you. I like it when she smiles."

I stagger back, the blood rushing from my face at her words. This is my worst fear coming to life.

I always knew a day would come when she mentioned a father, but I thought she'd ask who he was or where he was. I didn't think it would be this.

I grip onto the doorframe, a million thoughts rushing through my mind. How can I talk to her about this? Explain?

I chance a glance at Cage, still feeling like I'm in a bubble underwater when I watch his mouth open and close. His expression is closed off, and yet, he stands like stone, his solid bulk of muscles tense.

And Carrie… she's back to playing with her doll but doesn't hide her attention going back to Cage, her brows puckered as she waits for an answer.

Answers I can't give her without explaining everything that happened.

I inhale sharply, taking a step back.

I'm failing her.

Each time we hit a milestone I wonder what my sister would do. I question everything, even with how I dress her, wondering if Courtney would approve.

It's the same when it comes to Robin. I don't know what my sister would have said or done had she been here right now. Would she tell her who he was, or would she lie and make up some story?

Because this isn't about her asking Cage to be her dad. This is about her needing that gap filled. A gap in her heart I can't fill.

I take another step back, feeling the walls around me close.

"Caitlyn?" Cage calls.

I turn to him, my vision blurred with tears. I open my mouth, but no words escape, and the tightness in my chest gets worse.

I inhale again, the air getting stuck in my lungs. My eyes widen and I turn, racing through the cabin until I reach the bathroom. I can't let Carrie see me get upset, or worse, let Cage see me vulnerable again.

I slam the door shut, flipping the lock across before sliding down to the floor. I bring my knees up to my chest and bury my face into them as a sob tears from my throat.

Her words play over and over in my head. I thought she was okay, that a father figure missing from her life hadn't affected her. But it's another thing I can't control, another thing I can't make up for when it comes to her.

It was the same when she pleaded to go to her nan and grandad's, both of whom she doesn't have. Telling her they were in heaven had been hard.

Then she asked for a brother and sister. I couldn't give her those either. Not when we were running to save our lives.

She asked if she had aunts or uncles like her friends, and again, I said no, the words like acid on my lips because I had to tell her about Courtney, and how she was the best sister in the world.

But she had never asked about a father.

The realisation I'm not enough, hits me, and it kills me inside. Because with all we have been through, her happiness comes first.

The door jars behind me as someone raps their knuckles over the wood.

"Hey, it's me. Open the door, Kitten," Cage calls out softly.

"I just need a minute," I tell him, my voice shaky. My mouth is dry, and snot is running down my nose. So, this would *not* be the right time to open the door.

I get to my feet and head over to the sink, gripping the bowl as I avoid staring into the mirror. I don't need to see the misery staring back at me, not when I'm living it.

I twist the cold tap and lean down, welcoming the cool water as it splashes across my face. Turning the tap off, I grab the hand towel and dry my face. I wince as soon as I see my reflection in the mirror. My eyes are puffy and red, my face pale. The angry bruise across my cheek doesn't help me feel any better, as it's just another reminder of my failings.

"Come on, Kitten, open up before I kick the door down. One…" he orders.

Shit! Is he really going to use the countdown on me? Does he really think I don't know what comes after three? That's right, fuck all.

I head over to the door as he gets to two and pull it open. I force a smile, but it comes out more like a grimace.

"Hey," he greets, keeping his voice low.

"Hi."

"Are you okay?" he asks.

Seriously, do I look okay? I look like a complete head-case, and my daughter just told me she wants a dad… Something else I can't give her. Tears threaten to start up again, but I refuse to let them spill over in front of Cage.

"Shit, I didn't mean to make you cry. Look, it just came as a shock is all. I didn't expect that to come out of her mouth. I really didn't. If you would prefer I go, then I will, for an hour or so anyway. We need to talk about what she said, though. I want to see where we go before we get too far ahead of ourselves. I don't want Carrie getting hurt."

"What are you talking about, Cage?"

"Carrie wanting me to be her dad is what I'm talking about. I'm trying to apologise for not answering her. I can see I've upset you for not saying anything back, and I don't know if it's because I didn't agree with her or not. It's just that we've only known each other a few days. Calling me dad seems a bit rushed, especially if we don't work out. Sex is one thing, but for me to be a dad is another. Help me out here, Kitten, because I'm out of my element. I don't want to break her heart."

I tip my head back, laughter pouring out, and I don't even recognise it as my own. It sounds fake and forced as I pull my attention to Cage, who watches on with a twist of his lips, and a creased forehead.

He rubs the back of his neck. "Um—"

I put my hand up, stopping him. "Look, I'm not upset because you didn't answer her, Cage. In fact, none of that even crossed my fucking mind when my daughter just openly admitted she has always wanted a dad. I'm upset over the fact it's one more thing I can't give her. Like grandparents, a brother, sister, a house with a garden, a dog, friends, stability, structure, and safety. The list goes on, Cage, but nowhere on that list, was you on it," I tell him, my voice rising slightly.

"Ahh fuck, Kitten," he groans, stepping closer. I step back, out of his reach, knowing that if he tries to console me right now, I'll break.

He sighs and moves quicker this time, snagging me around the waist. He pulls me against his chest, resting his chin on the top of my head. As soon as I breathe in his woodsy scent, I do the very thing I swore I didn't want to do: I break down. I sob uncontrollably into his chest as my fingers grip his T-shirt.

And it isn't normal sobbing. It's the ugly kind. The one where weird noises rumble at the back of my throat. Snot runs down my nose. And my chest heaves with each passing moment.

Absently, I wipe my nose on his T-shirt, sniffling. He tenses beneath me for a moment before his chest begins to vibrate and a deep chuckle escapes through his lips.

What the fuck?

I pull back, wiping at my cheeks to find him… laughing. The jerk is laughing while I cry my eyes out.

Insensitive prick!

"Why are you laughing?" I ask, scowling at him.

I want to punch him so he shuts up, but he just keeps laughing. I slap his chest to get his attention.

"Kitten, you just wiped your fucking snot all over my T-shirt. Seriously, how can I not laugh? Who does that and doesn't even care?" he asks, his lips twitching before he bursts out laughing once again.

I glance at his T-shirt and the snot stain smeared into the cotton, and gape, mortified. Until he pointed it out, I hadn't realised I'd done it. My cheeks heat and I reluctantly meet his gaze.

"Sorry. I guess I didn't want snot down my face?"

He chuckles, shaking his head at me. "Well, you're lucky you're cute, otherwise this conversation would have been going somewhere totally different."

"Where the hell *is* this conversation going?" I ask curiously.

"Oh, well now that you've wiped your snot on me, we can forget worrying about getting to know each other more," he states, chuckling.

"I'm sorry for overreacting."

He loses his smile, his expression sobering. "I get it. I guess I overreacted too. I keep forgetting she's a kid and doesn't know the meaning behind those words."

I tuck a strand of hair behind my ear. "Yeah, I think everything that has happened made it more overwhelming for me. I just want this mess to be done with."

"It will be. A lot has happened, but you have me now. You have people here who care for you. Just let us help you. The rest of it will fall into place."

"Nothing is that easy," I tell him, pouting.

He grins. "Nah, but where's the fun in easy," he tells me. "I'm sorry for upsetting you. For what she said."

I wave him off, wiping my tears away. "It's fine."

"Are we going?" Carrie calls out, and I turn to Cage, my brows pulling together.

"Wait a sec, Pea, I'm talking to your mum," he yells back.

"Okay," she sings.

"What is going on?" I ask.

"I was wondering if you and Carrie would like to go out to the pizza place in town. My treat. I thought you could both do with a change of scenery. Plus, they have this whacky play area across the road that Carrie would love. What do you say?"

I'm speechless. Is he asking me out on a date? Or is he trying to apologise? I'm confused as to why he would want to take me out. He got what he wanted this morning. I swear, men say that *women* are confusing; they need to look in the mirror.

"Why?" I blurt out before I can stop myself.

"Why what?"

"Why do you want to take us out? I mean, it's not like you haven't already gotten lucky this morning, so why take me out now?"

I really should learn to keep my mouth shut.

"Because, Kitten, this morning wasn't a one-off thing for me. I told you that already, and I hate repeating myself. With you it's different. You're different."

"Yeah, I am now I'm minus a hymen," I mutter sarcastically. "We aren't going there again, Cage. I don't want to complicate my life any more than it already is."

"Yeah, I know, I took it." He smirks, wiggling his eyebrows at me before letting out a sigh. "You're only fighting the inevitable. This thing between you and me, it's going to happen."

"No, it's not, Cage. I don't want to risk being hurt. You'll get bored with me in a few days. Plus, I'm pretty sure I snore. Why would you want this thing to happen now?"

I'm rambling again.

Shit.

"You're cute when you panic, Kitten. I think most of the population snores, so I think I'll live. Now go get freshened up so we can go feed Pea. I'm fucking starving," he admits, before turning down the hall.

"Language," I hiss out, growing more frustrated by the minute.

He is so damn bossy, so demanding, and yet it's his smug smirk and the way he lights my body up that's getting to me.

He smirks, shrugging. "Kitten, she isn't even here."

I huff out a breath, and when he arches his eyebrow, jerking his head toward the bedroom, I groan and stomp over.

To get changed for this non-date or whatever it is.

Chapter Thirteen

CAGE

WE ENTER THE RESTAURANT, and after a moment of Caitlyn chatting to the waitress we are taken over to our table, which surprises me since normally I've wasted away before they even seat me. It's like they somehow know I'm hungry and just want to torture me more… like starving isn't enough.

Carrie jumps in the seat next to me as Caitlyn takes the seat opposite her. "Why don't you come sit next to me?" she asks.

"No, I want to sit next to Cage," she tells her, immediately reaching for the colouring page and crayons.

Caitlyn's expression is a mixture of shock and jealously. I try to keep my lips from pulling into a smirk, but when her scowl aims at me, a full-on grin appears.

She huffs out a breath, glancing down at the menu.

I lift mine up, but instead of glancing at the words, I can't get over what Carrie said before we came.

Dad.

I froze, a turmoil swirling around inside of me because I didn't realise just how much I wanted to be that person, to be a dad. And Lou made that dream and ripped it away in the same breath.

Then Carrie asked me, and although a part of me wanted to run for the hills, the other part wanted to reach for it.

But it wasn't real. She isn't old enough to understand the ramifications of her words. However, they still hit me the same.

I wish I had known Caitlyn longer, the way I feel I do inside, because I can picture that life with her. With the both of them.

It's like a tornado has come into my life and blown everything to shit. I came here for an escape, but instead, I found something more.

Lou had been my longest relationship, and that only went on for a few months before I became bored and finished it. That's when she came up with that bullshit lie about being pregnant. However, it woke me up to what I was missing, what I wanted.

The moment I laid eyes upon Caitlyn, I just knew I needed to have her, but it was more than that. It was more than sex that drew me to her. I wanted more. Then I went and spent the day with them both and they stole a piece of my heart.

"What do you want for dinner then, Carrie?" Caitlyn asks over her menu, snapping me out of my thoughts.

"What are you having, Cage?" Carrie asks me.

"I think I might have a meat feast, garlic bread, salad, and corn on the cob," I tell her. Her eyes go wide, making me chuckle.

"I'll have what Cage is having, Mummy."

Caitlyn sighs, slumping down a little in her seat.

"Carrie, sweetie, you won't like what is going to be on there. Why don't you have cheese pizza with garlic bread, salad, and corn on the cob?"

"Because I want to eat what Cage is eating," she declares, her adorable face scrunched up.

Caitlyn goes to argue with her, but I interrupt, not wanting Carrie to lose her shit by having a tantrum in the middle of a restaurant. Not that I think she would. You just never know when it comes to kids. They can go off at any second for no reason at all.

"Okay, Pea, listen, why don't you have the cheese pizza like your mum told you to, and if you want to try some of my meal, I'll swap you some for a slice of yours. Yeah?"

"Okay," she agrees, her expression softening.

I turn my attention to Caitlyn to see if it's okay, but she's staring at me, her mouth agape, yet her eyes narrowed accusingly.

I hold my hands up in surrender. "What?"

"Nothing. Nothing at all," she mutters, before her lips set in a fine line.

A YOUNG WAITRESS arrives with our food shortly after ordering. When I see her checking me over, I squirm in my seat. I already know from a quick glimpse that this girl isn't going to care that I'm sitting with a woman and a child. I've met her type a million times before.

She bends down, giving me a front row seat to her cleavage. I avert my gaze, not wanting to be caught, but I see Caitlyn smirking, so I know she has already seen the waitress's attempts to try to get my attention. I shrug, passing it off as no big deal.

Usually, if something like this happened on a date, the woman would go bat-shit crazy at me. Then again, Caitlyn always seems to surprise me. I mean, I never pegged her to be a virgin. The girl is drop-dead gorgeous. Her hair is thick, long, and wavy, ending just above her bum. She has high cheekbones, plump lips and a great arse. But it's the fact she doesn't realise how beautiful she is that draws me to her. It's her zero fucks given about walking across the green in barely a pair of pyjamas and cutting the plug. It's her strength. Her loyalty and love she shows her daughter.

It's her.

"Is there anything else I can get for you?" the waitress asks, looking directly at me. I shake my head.

"Excuse me, Miss," Carrie calls out sweetly.

The waitress stops, slowly turning around to find the source of the voice, but ends up glancing around at the tables behind us, her forehead creasing.

Carrie sighs and leans up, waving her hand around to get her attention. The waitress jerks and turns her attention to Carrie, staring at her like she has two heads.

"Yes?" she replies flatly.

"You didn't ask me or Mummy," Carrie states, pointing to her mum.

My lips twitch as I turn to Caitlyn, who finds her daughter just as amusing.

The waitress clears her throat. "I'm sorry?"

"It's okay," Carrie replies sweetly. "Can I have some tomato ketchup, please?"

"Sure thing," the waitress mutters, stomping off.

Carrie—who is none-the-wiser—carries on like what she said wasn't funny as fuck. She takes a large bite of her pizza and sighs happily. Seconds later, Caitlyn and I share a look before bursting into laughter.

"Why are you two laughing?" Carrie questions us, her nose twitching.

"Nothing, Pea, just eat your food," I tell her through my laughter.

Carrie resumes her eating while waiting for the waitress to bring her ketchup.

The waitress comes back a few seconds later. I feel her eyes on me as she approaches. Instead of walking around to Carrie's chair, the bitch leans over me, pushing her tits in my face, staying there for longer than necessary.

"Give my daughter the god damn ketchup, then get your tits out of my man's face, or I swear to God, I will remove you myself," Caitlyn barks from across the table.

I sag in relief when the waitress does in fact move her tits out of my face. I give Caitlyn a look that tells her I'm thankful, but she's too busy shooting daggers at the young waitress. I would laugh at the scene, but secretly, I like the fact that Caitlyn called me her man.

"Excuse me?" the waitress snaps.

Caitlyn stands up from her seat, making it scrape along the floor.

"You heard me. You're here to work. Not to try and pick up people's dates," she snaps. "Who do you think you are? We have a little girl seated with us, and you're all over him like a bad rash. Either knock it off or get us another server, because you are two minutes away from me calling your manager over."

She's grabbed the attention of a few customers at nearby tables. They're all staring at us to see what the commotion is about. I inwardly groan when the waitress takes a step towards Caitlyn. I stand, ready to intervene.

"I'm not picking anyone up," she snaps, crossing her arms over her chest. "I don't need to. Your man got a hard-on having my tits in his face; I didn't see him pulling away. He was checking me out the minute you arrived, so have a word with him, not me. I'm free game, so if your man wants a piece, I'll gladly give him one."

Caitlyn's face goes beet red as she steps closer to the waitress.

I rush to her side, pushing her back down in her chair.

"Let's eat and then go," I order softly, before turning to the waitress, letting her see the anger. "You need to get some fucking manners. My dick didn't even so much as twitch when you rudely put your tits in my face. I'm sitting here, trying to enjoy a meal with my woman and her girl before you ruined the whole thing with your foul attitude and your foul mouth," I state, my tone getting harder with each word. "Now I suggest you find another occupation. If you let anyone have a piece, you may as well get paid for it. I hate explaining myself, but for you, I will, because clearly you need it to be dumbed down. I didn't respond to your advances; I just didn't want to make a scene in front of a room full of people and my little girl, but then you had to go and rub it in my woman's face, making her feel belittled. Go into the nearest bathroom and take a long look at yourself, because you'd never compare to a woman like her. You'll never even have a man look twice at you when he has a woman like Caitlyn on his arm. So, get gone and get out of our faces."

A round of applause hits the room with a few cheers from the women. I look over to Caitlyn, who slumps back in her seat, stunned.

Taking a seat, I ignore the waitress yet feel her march away. When I glance out of the corner of my eye, I watch a man stalk towards her with a murderous expression. It doesn't take a wild guess to know he's probably the manager.

Good. He can fire her arse for all I care.

"Mummy? Cage said a bad word," Carrie announces, her eyes wide.

Caitlyn and I both burst into laughter. I ruffle Carrie's hair, leaning down to kiss the top of her head.

"I'm sorry, Pea. Mummy can punish me later," I tease, turning to wink at Caitlyn. She turns beet red, and I chuckle, reaching for a slice of pizza.

CARRIE PLACES THE spoon in the now empty bowl that was minutes ago filled to the rim with ice cream. She sits back, patting her stomach. "That was so yummy."

Caitlyn chuckles and leans over, wiping off the mess around her daughter's mouth.

"Messy eater," she mumbles.

Despite the rough start, the rest of the meal was good, and we had no more sightings of the waitress. I glance over Caitlyn's shoulder, noticing the guy from earlier heading towards us, like I somehow summoned him. His grey hair is thinning on the top and his arms have burn scars. He presses a hand down his black buttoned up shirt that has the restaurant's logo on.

He clears his throat, and Caitlyn sits back, her face paling a little.

"Hi, I'm Chris. I'm the manager here," he greets, clasping his hands together. "First, I would like to apologise for the incident earlier. Lorene has been fired and won't be working here effective immediately. The meal is on the house today, and you can have a ten percent discount if you choose to dine with us again in the future." He pauses, taking a breath as he hands over a coupon. "Once again, I am sorry for the intrusion of your evening."

"Thank you for dealing with the situation so quickly," I tell him, not knowing what else to say.

"That's quite all right, sir," he tells me, before addressing the table. "Enjoy the rest of your evening." With that, he tips his head before heading off.

"That was nice of him," Caitlyn murmurs, grabbing her jacket. "I thought for sure he was going to yell or something."

I chuckle. "You did look a little pale," I tease. "If I knew the pizza was going to be free, I probably would have enjoyed it more."

Carrie slides out of her chair and immediately reaches for my hand before taking Caitlyn's in her other.

A pang hits my chest. To the people around us, we look like a family. I never thought I would want this, not after everything. But I do.

And as I watch the smile light up Carrie's face, I can't help but wonder if she has been waiting for this too.

Chapter Fourteen

CAITLYN

IFINISH DRYING CARRIE AS MY thoughts run all over the place. When we got back, Cage got a phone call and once it ended, he told us he had to go out for a moment. That was a few hours ago.

And now I can't help but worry about the possibility I scared him away. I inwardly groan at the reminder. I basically called him my man in front of everyone at that restaurant, and it probably freaked him out.

In my defence, that woman didn't know that we weren't. You see a guy, a woman, and a little girl, and you automatically think family. Not that woman. She had the nerve to flirt with him like we weren't sat there. No morals whatsoever.

But if he was mad, or scared off, why did he stand up for us?

He said we were his and it was hot as hell. He was ruthless. But he probably didn't even realise he said those things —that he called Carrie 'his girl'.

Because he's a nice guy who stands up to people.

"Mummy, are you angry?" Carrie asks, pulling me from my thoughts.

I jerk and realise I was frowning. "Sorry, sweetheart. I just spaced out."

She yawns and falls into me as I finish getting her dressed.

I lift her into my arms and carry her out of the bedroom. A key being pushed into the lock has my heart racing, and I turn to see it being pushed open before Cage steps through. A scowl is painted over his face, but when he looks up and catches sight of us, he smiles, and his entire posture relaxes.

I lift Carrie up higher on my hip. "Hey," I greet.

"Hello, girls."

Carrie begins to squirm on my hip, no longer yawning and falling asleep. I smile as I place her down, watching as she runs over to Cage as soon as her little feet hit the floor. He doesn't even hesitate before he picks her up, giving her a kiss on the side of her head.

"You're back! I thought you left us," she declares, her eyes filled with light. "Can you read me a story in bed?"

He smiles at her enthusiasm. "I'm not going anywhere. I just needed to talk to a few of my guys about work," he assures her, tapping the tip of her nose. "And I would love to read you a book, Pea."

"Yes," she cheers before a yawn takes over.

Cage laughs and tickles her belly. "Let's get you to bed." He turns to me, his smile softer. "I'll be out in a bit."

Once they are gone, I don't know what to do with myself, so I head to the kitchen and grab a wine glass off the top shelf before heading for the fridge and pulling out a bottle of rose. I finish pouring a glass and put away the bottle before heading into the living area.

I really need this, I think, as I take my first sip.

I'm not a big drinker. I have half a glass now and again, mostly on the nights I don't have Carrie.

I glance around my tiny cabin, noticing everything is in its place. There's nothing for me to do. My routine is screwed now Cage is in there reading her a book. Normally it's me who reads to her, and then I leave her to sleep as I come in here and read one of my own books before heading to bed. Those are my free nights. And since I love to stress clean, the place is sparkling.

I'm not sure how long I stare off into space, but footsteps slapping across the floor gains my attention.

Cage strolls into the room, a smirk on his face. "She snores like a pig," he tells me, chuckling. "She'd better not take after her mummy."

"Hey, I already warned you I snore," I tease.

"How would you know you snore?"

"Trust me, I do. A girl knows these things."

He drops down on the sofa next to me, pulling me against his chest. He cups my cheek, groaning when his lips touch mine softly. "I'd love to stay here, but I need to grab some bags out of my truck."

"You have more stuff?" I ask, pulling back, my lips buzzing.

"I went to the shop before I came back," he tells me, not explaining a thing. He stares at my lips, and moments later, he groans, pressing his lips to mine.

I don't refuse, loving the feel of his lips on mine because although there's plenty he can do, his kisses are like magic.

He pushes forward, and I drop back. He follows, looming over me on the sofa. I moan into his mouth, gripping the hair at the nape of his neck.

Any doubts or thoughts flee from my mind as I press into him, needing and wanting more with each touch and caress. The taste of peppermint lingers on his tongue, and I savour every moment.

Desire and power pours through the kiss. The heat intensifies and lust lingers in the air.

Will it always be like this when we kiss?

When we both pull away, we are breathing hard. He rests his head against mine, keeping our gazes locked. My lashes flutter against my cheeks as I blink up at him, still in a daze after that kiss.

His grip on me tightens. "Fuck, I want you so badly," he growls, pressing his erection against me.

I bite my lip, keeping the moan at bay.

"Cage," I whisper, feeling vulnerable and lost. This is all new to me, and I'm scared.

Seeing that, his expression softens, and he pulls back, bringing me with him. I straighten my shirt and gather myself.

"I'll get the bags. Then we are going to have a 'get to know each other' session while Pea is asleep. Okay?"

I open my mouth, but the words don't come, so I nod, which is enough for him. He grins, pressing a kiss to the side of my mouth before leaving.

I wait for him to return and mess around in the kitchen, swigging the wine as I do.

When he walks back in, the wine bottle in one hand and a beer in the other, I tuck my legs under me, getting comfy as he takes the other side of the sofa, facing me.

"So," I murmur, feeling awkward as fuck.

His eyes crinkle at the corners as he laughs. I love watching him laugh, and when he smiles, his dimples show up far more.

God, he is so handsome.

"Okay, I guess I'm starting this off. I pretty much know the situation you're in, so we don't need to talk about that. So… what's your favourite colour?" he asks, taking me off guard.

"Really?" I ask, wondering if that's what he really wanted to ask. "Favourite colour? So original."

He rolls his eyes and after taking a swig of his beer, asks, "Okay, Kitten, why is it you're still a virgin?"

Okay, not the question I was expecting.

"My favourite colour is purple, and I'm not a virgin anymore," I remind him, and his lips pull up into a grin. "Yours?" I prompt, hoping to move on from the question.

"Well, I'll have to be original again," he mutters dryly, with a twinkle in his eye. "But I'd have to say black. It goes with everything." He pauses for a moment to take another swig of his drink, before pointing at me. "Okay, you go next. Ask me anything."

"Um, where are you from?"

"I'm actually from around here. I used to live half an hour away, but I've just bought an old house that needs doing up on Barrett's Lane. I needed a change of scenery, and with us building a new business here, it just makes sense that I move closer," he explains, and I can't help but be interested in that. I want to know more. "Now, I know where you're from, so I'll go next. Why were you still a virgin before I had the privilege of owning it? You're beautiful."

I blush furiously, fiddling with the little thread poking out of my leggings. Fingers grasp my chin, and Cage tilts my head up until we lock gazes.

"Don't be embarrassed, Kitten," he says softly, letting go of my chin.

I let out a sigh. "I don't know. I had a boyfriend before and we did other stuff, but it never went any further. I never felt like I was ready; I never desired it. I wanted it to be with someone I felt that spark with, who could make me feel alive at the slightest touch. Bring me to my knees with just a kiss," I ramble, pulling further into my daydream.

It was a teenager's dream, a stranger's, because I'm no longer that girl. Too much has happened.

"And I did that for you?" he rasps, snapping me out of my daydream.

I blush furiously, realising what I just implied. Even though everything I just told him is exactly how he made me feel—how he continues to make me feel—I still have a pang of embarrassment.

"Yes," I admit, not wanting to pussy-foot around him.

He looks at me with such deep emotions that it sets butterflies off in my belly.

"Where are your parents? Do you have any siblings?" I ask, hoping they are still alive and that he has a good relationship with them.

"My mother died when I was a teenager," he explains, pain washing over his expression. "My father runs a business back where I lived. I have two sisters, one four years older and the other three years younger."

"I'm so sorry about your mum, Cage. I shouldn't have asked," I rush out, feeling terrible for bringing up such bad memories.

"Hey, it's okay. It's a 'get to know you' session anyway, so ask away," he tells me, before rubbing his hand across his stubble.

"It's your turn," I remind him.

He sits up straight, conflict running over his face. "Please don't be offended, but why does Carrie call you mum? I mean, I know you're her mum in that you take care of her, but why not correct her?"

I shrug. "At first it was a shock. I mean, Courtney heard her first word, but it was dada. She never got around to saying mamma before Courtney passed. When she called me mamma a few weeks after her first birthday, it made everything come crashing down. I remember wishing Courtney were here to hear her say it, but she wasn't. I couldn't sleep that night with it all going around my head. It was then that I decided I wasn't going to take away another thing from Carrie," I tell him. "I mean, I know she has a father, but he's dead to us. She doesn't have grandparents, aunties, or uncles— well, I suppose technically she does have an auntie." I laugh without humour, feeling angry once again at what has been taken from her. "I want Carrie to know she is loved and that she will always be loved. I will tell her when she is old enough to understand what it is I'm telling her." Tears well up in my eyes when I think about that day. Because it will come, and a part of me doesn't want to tell her. It's selfish of me. But I love her, and I don't want to tear her world apart. However, she deserves to know who her mum was, and how much she was loved. Courtney would want that. I want that.

"Hey, I didn't mean to upset you," he whispers, reaching for my hand. "I think it's pretty courageous of you to give your life up for her like that. Noble even. She's a great kid, and you've done a fantastic job with her. You should be proud of that."

"I am. I'd give my life up for her every single day if I could," I admit. "Don't get me wrong, at the beginning I was broken. Add Carrie, who was missing her mum, into the mix, and I just existed. I didn't feel like a mum, or a person at all. It was like my body was on autopilot, getting by each day without knowing what was happening around me. It took me a while until I felt like I was in a good place emotionally and physically. Until that note came, and then that man's visit I was still in that place. I'm trying hard not to go back there. So hard. I don't want anything to happen to her, Cage. If I'm honest, I don't want to die, either, but in order to protect her, I will die without hesitation." I wipe at my cheeks, feeling my chest constrict.

I feel Cage shift before he plucks me up effortlessly and places me in his lap. I snuggle into him and let out a sigh, as he begins to strum his fingers through my hair. Tears continue to fall but I remain silent, keeping my sobs at bay. I've broken too many times in front of this man.

"No one is going to die, Kitten; I won't let anything happen to you or Carrie. My mate, Nate, who works my security business, is coming down tonight. Tomorrow, he is going to be installing some CCTV cameras outside the cabin, and then he is going to set an alarm system in the house. It's just a precaution, but it will make it easier if you don't argue the next bit." He pauses, scanning my face, whilst inhaling. It's like he knows I'm not going to like what he is about to say.

"What?" I whisper, dread pitting in my stomach.

"He will be shadowing you until this blows over."

"What?" I screech, sitting up in his lap.

"Calm down, Kitten, it's just to keep you safe. You just said yourself that you don't want to die. If anything happened to you, where would that leave Pea, Caitlyn?" he points out, giving me a stern look. "You said it yourself: she has no one else."

I move back into my chair, relaxing into the cushions. I'm not sure how I feel about someone following me around, but I can't deny it will be good to feel safe again.

"Are you sure your friend can do this? I mean, I have money stashed away. I know these things cost money and stuff—"

"You're not paying for it, and neither will I. We want to help. Plus, he has the time with the new extensions going on and stuff. He can put other men on jobs that come in, and he can run the business from this end. You have nothing to worry about."

"Okay," I agree, praying to God he's right.

"Let's put an end to the twenty questions and watch a movie."

"Okay," I agree, and move to pour myself another glass of wine.

WHEN HE SAID movie, I assumed it would be a comedy, or at best, an action. But nope.

Cage wanted to watch a horror.

After finishing the latest *Paranormal Activity*, I'm a nervous wreck.

My hands shake as he picks up the next movie he wants to watch: *Mama*.

"No way," I argue, and reach for the other two movies. *The Last Stand*, and *White House Down*. I hate horrors with a passion. If I had to choose, it would be *White House Down* because nothing beats going to sleep with the memories of Channing Tatum half-dressed and running around being a bad-arse. Even his wounds make him look hotter.

"Oh c'mon," he teases, ignoring my attempts to change his mind.

"I'm going to have nightmares," I mumble, already knowing it's going to happen anyway. I have nightmares most nights. Some are about my sister, and some are about Robin catching up to me and taking Carrie away.

He waggles his eyebrows. "You can cuddle up to me if you get scared."

I cringe as he puts the movie in. This is going to end badly. When he sits back down, I jump in his lap, not caring if I look a fool. He chuckles as he sprawls himself down on the sofa, tucking me in so my back is to his front. He wraps his arms around me then entwines his legs with mine.

Halfway through the movie, he pulls the blanket over us. Mostly, I'm using it to cover my face, because shitting hell, this movie is making me jumpy.

Why they put freaky kids in movies, I'll never know.

It's coming to another scary part of the movie. My heart is racing to the beat of the ominous music playing, and I know it's coming, know something bad is going to happen or jump out. I can feel it.

I scream at the top of my lungs when there's a knock at the door. I roll, falling off the sofa, and groan in pain as it jars my sore ribs.

Cage looks over the edge and stares down at me, chuckling. "Comfy?"

"Piss off," I groan out.

After helping me up, he leaves me standing there whilst he opens the door.

Hearing another male voice, I head over, finding a young guy at the door. He's good-looking, his mousy brown hair shiny, and his chocolate-brown eyes are enough to melt the hearts of many. He could be Theo James's doppelganger, they look so alike. He's gorgeous, without a doubt. Yet, he has nothing on Cage.

"Hey, Kitten, come meet Nate. Nate, this is Caitlyn. Caitlyn, this is Nate," he announces, and they both step farther into the room.

My cheeks heat under his inspection. I can feel his gaze as he continues to scan me from head to toe, then back again, like he's memorising every detail.

Cage slaps the back of his head when his gaze lingers on my breasts. I try to laugh it off, but it's forced. It's like the room is getting smaller with them both in here. I've gone from having no one to having a village with Hayley and Roy, and now Cage and his friends.

"Kitten?" Nate questions, glancing at Cage with a smirk.

"Yeah, it's a stupid nickname he keeps calling me. In fact, I don't even know why he calls me that," I admit, pulling my gaze away from Nate.

"She was wearing these ridiculous, cute-arse kitten slippers," Cage explains, and they both chuckle at my expense. It's light-hearted and doesn't bother me. I'm struck on the fact he remembered what I was wearing.

"I just heard how you two met from Dante," Nate admits. "He said she likes to cut wires."

"Ha, ha, very funny," I grumble. "They pissed me off; it was, like, three in the morning. You can't blame a girl for wanting her sleep."

"No, you can't," he murmurs, letting out a chuckle. He turns to Cage, a silent conversation passing between them. "It's getting late so I should get going. I saw the light was on, so I thought I'd come and say hi. It's been a pleasure meeting you, Caitlyn. See you tomorrow."

Bending, he gives me a kiss on the cheek, surprising me, and when he pulls back, he gives me a sly wink. My cheeks heat, and I duck my head, but lift it at the sound of another slap echoing in the room.

"Arsehole," Nate grumbles before leaving, shutting the door behind him.

"He's nice," I tell him to fill the silence. "How long have you two known each other?"

"Most of my life. We grew up together. Always had each other's back," he explains. "He's more like a brother. He's been through some tough shit, but he pulled through in the end."

"I like him," I tell him.

"Let's hope not too much," he growls, pouncing on me.

He lifts me up fireman style, and I squeal out, pleading for him to put me down. Ignoring my pleas, he just slaps my arse, chuckling to himself.

"Shut up before you wake Pea up," he warns, and I immediately pipe down. I forgot about Carrie. Though she can sleep through most things, so I'm not too worried.

"Put me down," I beg again, as he moves around, locking everything up.

"Nope," he replies in a stern voice.

We enter the bedroom, where he throws me onto the bed. I laugh as he towers over me, but soon shut up when he presses his erection into my sex, making me wince. I'm still sore from this morning's activities— nothing major, but still, the soreness is annoyingly painful. Especially now I'm all hot and bothered.

"You sore?" he asks.

I nod, and he smirks down at me.

"Well, I'll have to kiss it and make it better, won't I," he states, pressing kisses along my neck.

My body responds to him like a magnet to a fridge. I can't help the moan that slips from my mouth as he reaches for my shirt and pulls it over my head. He continues to place kisses down my stomach and across the mounds of my breasts. I moan louder this time, and he looks up at me with a satisfactory grin.

"We shouldn't be doing this," I pant out.

"Yes, we should, Kitten. Now lay back, relax, and purr for me," he demands, his voice hoarse with arousal.

Sliding his hands into the waistband of my denim shorts, he pulls them slowly down my legs, leaving me in just my knickers. His eyes glaze over with lust, and he licks his bottom lip as he takes in my hot pink underwear. Heat rushes through me, the anticipation killing me. I know what he can do with that tongue.

Bending down, he captures my hard nipple through the thin material of my bra, biting lightly before using more pressure. Moaning, my back arches off the bed, pressing my sex into his groin. The growl that erupts from his chest makes my entire body shiver.

A moan slips free as his fingers pull the cups of my bra down. He leans over, sucking my nipple into his mouth before paying attention to the other with his thumb and forefinger.

"Oh God," I pant out.

I'm so wet, filled with desire, as he begins to trail kisses down my stomach, reaching the edge of my knickers. He kisses me through the fabric and my back bows off the bed, loving the sensation rolling over me.

"Please," I plead.

I feel him grin against my stomach, and before I can plead once more, he grips the elastic of my knickers, drags them down my thighs, and guides them off my legs before throwing them across the room. I squirm, spreading my legs a little more, my body flushing when he looks up at me with lust-filled eyes.

"Fuck, you are sexy," he rasps, prying my sex open with his thumbs.

I hiss out at the touch, but it soon turns into pleasure when I feel the hard swipe of his tongue over my clit.

I moan, arching off the bed as I grip the covers.

He's torturing me with his tongue, and the more he sucks my clit into his mouth, the closer I get to my release.

I know it's coming. It's building and building, and each time he applies pressure with his tongue, or circles my sensitive opening, it brings me closer to the precipice.

"Cage," I cry out, and his hand glides over my stomach, reaching for my breast.

He tugs on my nipple, and a wave of pleasure shoots through me. I cry out, my climax tearing through me like a tornado.

I sag back against the bed, feeling sated, exhausted, and wanted. Lying down next to me, Cage curls his arm under me, and I roll into him, resting my head on his shoulder.

"Goodnight, Kitten," he murmurs, pressing a kiss to the top of my head.

I close my eyes, too tired to do much else. My body still tingles in all the right places and a smile tugs at my lips. "Goodnight, Cage," I whisper.

"Night, baby."

Chapter Fifteen

CAITLYN

THE SOUND OF CARRIE'S GIGGLING stirs me from my sleep. My lashes flutter open to find the other half of the bed empty. I'm a little disappointed, but when I hear my daughter's laughter again, I can't be mad at him for not waking me up.

With a smile, I sit up in bed, stretching the kink out of my back. I reach for Cage's T-shirt on the floor and pull it over my head. When I stand, I'm grateful it hits mid-thigh, but just in case, I head over to my dresser and grab a clean pair of knickers.

After pulling my hair into a messy bun on the top of my head, I walk out of the room, heading towards the sound of laughter and conversation.

Entering the kitchen, Carrie immediately snags my attention, and all I see is her as I slowly move over to the greet her. I bend over, snagging Carrie around the head and planting a kiss on her cheek.

"Morning, baby," I greet. "Did you sleep well?"

"The best," she replies, and I smile, standing up.

I need a cup of tea. When I turn back to the room, I jerk, finding not only Cage filling up my kitchen, but Nate and some other guy, all wearing the same smug expressions.

"Morning to you, too, sweetheart," the one I don't know drawls, his gaze running over my body and bare legs.

My cheeks heat and I step back, pulling down the T-shirt to try to cover more of my legs.

Holy hotness.

"Cage made us breakfast," Carrie declares, her voice filled with excitement. "We got pancakes with bacon and sausages. We never have those."

"Um… that's, um— that great," I reply.

Cage, taking pity on me, wraps his arms around my waist and pulls me against his chest.

"Morning, Kitten," he murmurs, leaving a trail of goosebumps over the nape of my neck.

My eyes close when he presses his lips to the crook of my neck.

"Morning," I rasp, my voice still filled with sleep.

"Okay, you two, get a room, preferably one where I don't have to see this son of a… monkey fool around with his woman," the one I don't know says through a smile, making me laugh.

"Kitten, this is Dante, another one of my men. Dante, this is Caitlyn," Cage introduces.

"Hi, nice to meet you," I tell him, giving him a lame wave.

"This isn't the first time we've met, sweetheart. Last time, you had scissors, which destroyed my stereo," he reminds me, losing that charming smile of his.

Oh shit.

I wince at the reminder. I never really thought of whose stereo it was. I just thought about cutting that goddamn sound off.

"Yeah, sorry about that," I lie.

He surprises me when he bursts into a fit of laughter. I smile, feeling awkward, but only because he shouldn't find it funny.

"Funniest damn thing I ever saw in my life. I thought you were a hot psycho," he announces once his laughter dies off.

"Nope, just a regular crazy woman needing her sleep," I reply sweetly.

"Nate and Dante stopped by for breakfast and a catch up," Cage explains. "Do you want a cup of tea or coffee?"

He steps away to flick the kettle on.

"Cup of tea would be great. No to the breakfast, though. I need to get ready for work before I drop madam off with Hayley."

"You can't leave without having any breakfast; it's the most important meal of the day. Isn't that right, Pea?" Cage comments, his attention turning to Carrie for support.

Oh, he is good.

"Yes, Mummy. You tell me to eat all mine up, so you should do as you're told, too," Carrie scolds softly.

The hot bunch chuckle and I find myself scowling at Cage.

"Okay fine. I'll have some toast."

I hate eating in the mornings; I always have. I can't eat until I'm fully awake, which is usually by midday. I sit myself down next to Carrie, looking over the men.

Dante is taller than the rest, though not by much. Nate has to be the prettiest. He has these incredible pretty-boy looks. Whereas Cage is also a pretty-boy, but he has this rugged look about him. All the men are packing some serious muscle, although Cage, without a doubt, is the fittest. I find myself checking Nate and Dante over, not even realising it until Cage slaps the plate of toast down on the breakfast bar in front of me.

"Stop checking out my men, Kitten," he growls in my ear.

Both men laugh while I try to ignore the heat rising in my cheeks. I turn, aiming my scowl at Cage.

"I was not checking them out," I snap. "I was just observing their beauty and wondering what the hell is in the water back where you live. You're all seriously hot," I tell him honestly, forgetting about everyone in the room.

"Don't say my men are hot in front of me, babe. It seriously pisses me off," he warns me.

"Language in front of my daughter, Cage," I snap.

"It's okay, Mummy. Cage said not to say naughty words if I hear them. He said one this morning," Carrie slips out, before jumping out of her chair. "Oh, I forgot, I have something for you."

I silently question her quick departure with Cage, raising my eyebrow at him, but he looks as confused as me. He shrugs, and we both turn our attention to the hallway when we hear Carrie running back, a blue envelope in her hand.

I frown as she hands it to me. On the front, my name is scripted in black letters that are definitely not hers.

I tense, pulling the card from the envelope, my breath catching in my throat.

No, no, no.

I stand quickly, accidentally knocking the cup of tea over, which smashes when it hits the wooden floor.

No, no, no.

Princess, he isn't going to protect you. I'm coming for you, and next time, I'm ready to play. Give him what he wants, or the brat will be next to meet my fist. This is a reminder of how easily I can get to you. K x

I drop the letter to the table, swaying silently. I'm going to pass out, or be sick, maybe both.

He threatened my daughter.

"Oh God," I pant out, stepping out of reach when Cage goes to grab me.

"Pea, where did you get this?" Cage asks.

"It was by my bed when I woke up. Did Santa bring it?" she asks.

Her words cause me to snap out of my daze, and I stagger backwards, hitting the draining board over the sink. The pots and pans and a few plates fall to the floor in the process.

"Oh God," I cry out.

We can't stay here. We can't. She isn't safe.

"Caitlyn," Nate barks, and Cage turns from reading the letter, his gaze locking with mine.

He knows they're trying to protect me.

I take a step forward, and the ceramic and glass slice through my skin, but I don't feel it, not really.

He was in my daughter's room.

He can get to her any time he wants. I didn't even hear him, and he was in the same room as my daughter.

My breath hitches once again, and the room begins to spin. The blood pumps hard in my veins, my chest rising and falling heavily as my vision blurs.

Every thought, every action runs through my head. I have to get her away from this danger, away from him.

I have to—

My heart races but I can't catch my breath. I can feel it trapped in my lungs, just like I feel trapped in this life. Trapped and bound.

I can't keep her from the danger.

"Fuck," I hear, but the sound is foggy.

I reach out unsteadily, and just as my hand hits something hard, I collapse, the darkness swallowing me whole.

STIRRING AWAKE, THE pounding in my head intensifies and I become aware of the dryness at the back of my throat.

Oh God.

I feel like I've spent the night drinking, which isn't right because I never make it past two glasses.

My lashes flutter open, and like they were a switch, memories of earlier this morning hit me. I jerk up in bed, the room spinning around me.

I groan, cupping my head as I wait for it to stop. Two strong hands reach for me, gripping my biceps.

"Kitten, calm down. We need to talk, and we can't do that unless you're awake," Cage's soothing voice tells me.

"He was in her room?" I choke out. "How did he get in there?"

He runs a hand over my hair before cupping my cheek.

"I don't know, Kitten. I locked up last night, and double checked everything after Nate left," he tells me. "I need you to think for me; have you lost your keys lately? Or do you have a spare hidden outside somewhere?"

I shake my head, tears filling my eyes. "No, I haven't got a spare and I haven't lost or misplaced it. Roy has a spare key in his office and that's it."

"Okay, Nate is going to get on with alarming the house today, so I'm going to be staying with you and Carrie for the day," he announces.

Carrie.

"Shit! Where is she?" I ask, my voice rising. "Is she okay?"

"She's fine. She has Dante playing babies in her room. She was pretty scared when you passed out. You've cut your foot, but luckily not too deep."

I sigh, my shoulders slumping. "We can't stay here. He got to her," I choke out. "What if he had done something?"

"Kitten, it's going to be fine. I promise," he declares, his voice fierce. "You need to get on with your life and let me worry about this crap. You aren't alone anymore."

My lashes flutter as I stare up at him. "I'm always alone. You can't fix this."

"I can," he assures me.

"No, you can't," I snap. "You can't promise us anything."

"He's not going to touch either of you," he bites out.

I push his hand away. "You said that the last time and he was in my daughter's fucking room." I immediately regret the words as soon as I've said them. "I'm sorry," I whisper, getting up off the bed.

"Where are you going?"

"I need to get to work. I need more money to get out of here."

I don't need to see a clock to know I'm late. I doubt Hayley will mind, but I do. I don't want to let her down, not after everything she has done. If I move now, I can whiz through everything and be done on time.

"I called Roy after you passed out to let him know what was happening and that you wouldn't be going in. He let Hayley know, and she has you covered."

"You had no right to do that," I argue, my voice weak.

"I'm trying here, but you need to let me help you."

I sigh, sitting back down on the bed.

"I'm sorry. I'm being unfair. You're only trying to help me," I whisper.

He moves, taking the seat next to me, wrapping his arm around my shoulders. "You're scared. I understand, Caitlyn. I can take whatever you throw at me."

My shoulders shake as a sob tears through my throat. "He was in her fucking room. He could have killed her while she slept, or taken her, and we wouldn't have known about it. What kind of mother does that make me, Cage?"

He presses his lips against my forehead. "I promise you, Kitten, I will die before I let anything happen to any of you. I'm sorry I didn't hear him. He must've had a key because I've checked all the windows and the doors, and none of them have been tampered with," he explains, sounding frustrated. "Nate is going to change the locks and put alarms on the windows. There will be cameras placed around the cabin. We'll be able to see anyone who comes near this place from now on. I'm making these promises to you with every intention of keeping them. If he gets you, I will find you, but I won't let it get that far." He pauses, his gaze boring into mine. "Do you trust me?"

It only takes me a moment to answer. "Yes, I trust you, Cage, more than I let myself admit, but it scares me. It scares me to know you could die trying to save us, and I don't want you to get hurt. We've only known each other a few days. It's one heck of a promise to keep," I choke out.

"I'm not going to get hurt," he declares, pressing his lips against mine. He pulls back before it gets too heated. "It's sweet you care so much about me, Kitten, but you need to realise that I'm not going anywhere."

"Okay," I whisper.

"Go and see Pea. Let her know you're okay," he orders softly, kissing my forehead before leaving me to get dressed.

Once done, I take in a deep breath, composing myself before I face Carrie. She doesn't need to worry any more than she probably is.

Heading out the door, I walk across the hall to Carrie's room, finding the door open.

I bite my lip to smother the laughter threatening to bubble up when I see the sight in front of me. Dante, in all his muscular glory, is sat on the floor whilst Carrie kneels on the bed above, combing a brush through his hair.

But that isn't what's making me laugh. It's the tattooed god holding one of her babies, swaying it side to side.

Clearing my throat, Dante jerks, dropping the doll in his lap. He scowls. "Don't you dare mention this to anyone. *Ever*," he warns.

"Wouldn't dream of it," I mutter, smothering my laughter.

Carrie stops mid-brush at the sound of my voice, her eyes filling with tears. She drops the brush onto the bed and races over to me, sending me back a step when she slams into my legs. I run my hand over her curly locks.

"Hey, it's okay, sweetie. Look, I'm fine," I assure her, pushing her back gently so she can see.

"I was so scared, Mummy. You fell, but Cage caught you before you hit your head," she chokes out. "And your foot was bleeding, Mummy. You wouldn't wake up."

"Hey," I whisper, kneeling in front of her. "I'm okay, I promise. Nothing hurts, I swear."

From my peripheral vision, I watch as Dante rises from the floor, leaving the room so he doesn't disturb us. My lips twitch when the glitter butterfly bobble in his hair sparkles. I'll let him find out for himself that it's there.

"Pinkie promise?" Carrie asks, holding out her pinkie finger.

"Pinkie promise," I swear, wrapping my little finger around hers.

I pull her into a hug, breathing her in. She's safe. I repeat it to myself like a mantra, over and over, so I don't pack up our stuff and leave.

Because as much as I want to run, I also won't survive much longer without help. He got into her room. Had Cage not been here, he might not have left after dropping the letter off. He could have done anything, and I wouldn't have had the power to stop him.

He could have touched her. The thought has bile rising in my throat.

My chest squeezes and I clench my eyes shut, forcing the negative thoughts aside. I can't go there. Not now.

I'm angry with myself for letting it get this far. I'm stuck in a hard place, not knowing what the next step is.

If I relent and give him what he wants, I'm as good as dead anyway. But if I don't, he could do a lot more to me— things that will rip me to shreds.

Trust Cage.

I close my eyes once again, pulling Carrie closer.

I do trust him, and if I want Carrie to make it out of this alive, listening to him is my only option. My attempts to keep her safe have failed, so now I'm putting my trust in someone else.

I just pray there are no more casualties in the meantime.

Chapter Sixteen

CAGE

LEAVING CAITLYN IS HARD. I want to stay with her, but I know she needs a moment to gather herself.

Her words hurt like a knife through the chest, and although I knew they were coming from a place of fear, it didn't make them any less powerful.

I had promised her, and I had failed. And last night, or this morning, could have ended up differently with regards to Carrie.

"She okay?" Nate asks, only stopping for a moment to check on me.

He finishes screwing in the new lock as I reply, "Yeah, she's freaked out more than anything, but she's strong. She'll be okay."

"It's really fucked up," he comments, and I nod in agreement, still musing over what was said in that letter.

Hearing footsteps behind me, I turn, hoping to find Caitlyn, but instead, it's Dante.

I burst out laughing when I see him, pulling Nate's attention away from the lock. He looks up, scrunching his brows together, until he focuses on Dante. Laughter pours out of him.

Dante runs a hand over his face, then his chest, making us laugh harder. He looks behind him, his brows bunched together. "What? Do I have something on me?"

"Oh my God," I burst out, laughing harder.

"What?" he barks, his voice rising, close to hysteria.

Nate sobers, a twinkle in his eye. "You look really pretty," Nate purrs sweetly.

Dante growls and stomps over to the mirror hanging above the fireplace. He inhales sharply— then rips the butterfly bobble out of his hair.

"Next time *you* get kid duty," he growls, and Nate and I double over with laughter.

"Seriously, dude, the sparkles bring out the colour in your eyes," I tease.

"I'm going to make you see sparkles if you don't shut the fuck up," he warns, throwing the bobble onto the mantlepiece.

"Don't be like that. It suited you," Nate mocks.

"Fuck off!" Dante mutters.

"Nah, seriously, mate, you had that look going for you. You might get laid once in a while if you keep it in," I tease, knowing he doesn't need any help in that department. The guy could get a nun to drop her pants.

"I swear to God, Cage, one more word out of you and I'll be ringing Lou to tell her you love her," he warns.

A growl sounds from the back of my throat as I narrow my gaze on him.

"How is the psycho?" Nate asks me, grinning wide.

Dante tilts his head back, laughter pouring out of him before he turns his attention to Nate. "Bro, you missed it. She went bat-shit crazy on him the other day."

"She was here?" Nate asks, his eyes wide.

"Are you seriously that surprised? She turned up at my door, demanding we take another shot at a relationship. She wasn't even listening to a word I was saying as she spat all this shit about us being good together. I swear, if she weren't a woman, I would have laid one on her."

"Seriously, dude, you've got your hands full with that one," Nate comments, his lips twisting together. "You need to be careful. I heard from a mate a few days ago. She said Lou was telling her you guys had sorted it out and were thinking of getting hitched. I don't think she is in her right mind at the minute. With all this going on here, you need to be careful she doesn't try anything stupid."

I grimace at the thought of being tied to that woman for the rest of my life. I'd rather hang myself than endure that for the rest of my life.

"Shit! She is fucking crazy. I still have bite marks from dragging her scrawny arse to the car," Dante declares, holding his arm out.

"I'll keep an eye out, but hopefully she got the message loud and clear yesterday," I announce, letting out a weary sigh. It's Lou. Anything is possible.

"Yeah, you hope. All Caitlyn needs right now is a crazy ex-girlfriend added into her life," Nate warns.

"Yeah, you're right," I murmur, rubbing a hand down my face before turning to Nate. "Did you bag up the card for fingerprints?"

"I've already sent it off with Dez. He came by earlier with the equipment, then took it with him. Shouldn't take us long to run it through the system, but something tells me we won't find anything."

"So, what are we going to do about the evidence?"

"Has she told you where she has it stashed?" Dante speaks up, helping himself to the box of chocolates on the counter.

"No, and I don't want her to just in case someone is listening in. I think it's best to wait until we have someone who can use it and not let it disappear."

"I spoke to Darius, a friend of mine who lives near the Isle of Wight. He works for Dean Salvatore, who is also a PI of sorts. I've asked him to find out what he can about Robin and if he knows anyone trustworthy who will take a copy of the evidence and get it shown before it disappears. He seems to think the more we send out, the harder it will be for Robin's contacts to make it disappear. The more people on the inside who see the evidence, the harder it will be for people to just ignore if it does disappear."

I muse over his comment. He's right about one thing: it would be hard to ignore if every official received a copy. Not everyone is corrupt or bought. "Can you trust him?"

Nate nods. "Yeah, bro, I can. Darius and his boss used to be undercover cops, until Darius got screwed over on a job where his girl got raped and killed. Darius got payback and the evidence he needed to send the gang to prison. He risked his life to get it, but the evidence magically disappeared. He took off when half the charges didn't stick due to lack of evidence and began to work for Dean once he got set up. They don't work outside the law or within the law; they have their own law. They know some respectful cops, so hopefully he can help us."

"Let me know when they get back to you. We need to move fast before all this blows to shit. I don't want Caitlyn or Carrie getting hurt because of this sick fuck."

"Between us, he won't have a chance to hurt them," Nate declares.

I believe him too. After our chat this morning, I know he'll protect her with his life.

When he came by early this morning to talk, I wasn't surprised the conversation was about Caitlyn. He was worried she was another Lou, which is why he really dropped by last night. But he saw it was real, saw she was different and left it alone.

Now he's worried I'm getting too attached.

But how could I not. She's like no one I have met before. She's special.

And every minute I spend with her, each moment we share, my feelings for her grow. I'm so out of my element, it isn't funny.

I'll do anything to keep hold of that feeling, our connection. I'll do anything for her. And it doesn't matter that we've only known each other for a short time. Time can't be measured. But emotions? Emotions are very much part of the present and something I can rely on. It wouldn't matter if I met her five minutes ago; those feelings would be the same.

SWINGING MY LEG off my bike, I glance up at the estate agent standing in front of the house I just purchased.

I didn't like leaving Caitlyn or Carrie, but I knew Nate and Dante would protect them and this couldn't wait.

The house is basically in the middle of nowhere, with the nearest neighbour five miles out. Trees are the only thing separating the houses unless you count the country roads. When I took a drive down here, I knew I wouldn't have any problems with them, not like I did with previous neighbours. Both sides own a cattle market or some sort of farm company. For me to step on their toes, I'll need to be in that business, and I wasn't.

And it's perfect. I wanted something run down, something I could build up and make new. I like restoring things, which is why I love owning the garages.

The house is old, but not too old. It needs a lot of work as the last owners didn't keep it up together.

But it was what I was looking for in a home, and what drew me to this place apart from the peace and privacy, was the architecture of the building. It's beautiful, and after doing some research, I learnt it was built by an American who moved over here when he married his wife. He built the home with the American style in mind yet used British material to get the look. So, it's a brick house, but instead of just stairs or a small garden leading up the door, there's decking that wraps around the entire house.

I head through the small garden, taking in more of the house as I go. The front door is old and will only need one kick to break through so it will be the first thing to be changed once I get a start on it. It's the same for the backdoor, that leads off to a little fenced off garden. That's another thing I like about the house, although they had fenced off a garden area, there was also a gate at the back that led to a trail. I haven't walked to see where it leads, but I can't wait to check it out.

I jog up the stairs, smiling at the woman who greets me.

"Hi, Mr Carter, I'm Judith. We spoke on the phone," she greets. "I'm sorry Tom couldn't be here. He had a family emergency. Here are the keys and the paperwork. Everything is all in there, but I must dash. I have an appointment in twenty minutes that I can't miss out on. Tom said it was only a matter of handing the keys over, but is there anything I can do before I run?"

I happily take the keys off her. "No, thank you, Judith. I'm fine."

She heads down the short set of stairs before stopping and turning back to me. "Congratulations on your new home. Tom's number is in the paperwork. I've written mine down on there in case Tom is still out of the office."

"I'll be fine. You get off," I tell her, excited to look around my new home.

I give her my back, and head to the door. After prying the door open, I enter my new home. It's mostly open-spaced on the bottom floor. The only door down here is the one to my right which will potentially lead to a living room once it's done.

I pull out my phone, making a list of jobs that will need doing, and take measurements as I head into each room. As much as I want to stay, I know I need to get back.

And as thoughts of Caitlyn enter my mind, I can't help but wonder what she will think of the place.

Will she like it?

Now that I'm staring at the large rooms, I have to wonder if I bought this with a family in mind. Because the house is huge. Four bedrooms for one person seems like too much. So, I can assume I did this wanting to fill it with a family.

Shaking my head, I head back downstairs, tucking the phone back in my pocket. But once I hit the bottom of the stairs, the garden calls to me. I know the weeds are overgrown, but I have to know where the path leads.

Heading out, I push through the gate and follow the path. It needs some TLC, but the place is beautiful. The birds chirp, the trees whistle as a light breeze picks up, and the sun shines down, blocking out the chill from the shade.

Ten minutes later, the path widens, and I come to a clearing. There, in front of me, is a reservoir with the bluest water I have ever seen. I stand in awe, staring out into the water, wishing like hell Caitlyn were standing next to me seeing this magnificent sight.

This is a place where I know memories can be made. And although I'll need to check the safety of it first, I can't wait to be here to enjoy the scenery and tranquillity.

This place might have been a little over my budget, but it's everything I could have asked for.

After taking one last glance at the reservoir, I turn back, following the path back the way I came.

As much I want to stay out here, I need to get back. Dante needs to be briefed if he's going to help be in charge whilst I'm not there, and then there's Caitlyn and Carrie. I want to get back to them, see what they're up to.

It's mid-afternoon now, so she is probably getting lunch ready for Carrie. At the mention of food, my belly grumbles, and I pray that I'll be back in time.

***

I SHUT OFF MY bike and swing my leg over, greeting Nate, who is up a ladder installing the cameras.

"Everything okay?"

He jerks his attention away from the task, glancing down at me. "Hey, everything is okay."

He's good at his job. I know that. People from all over hire him to install their security.

He slides down the ladder, coming to a stop next to me. "Did everything go okay with the house?" he asks.

"Yeah, I took another look around while I was there. It needs more work than I originally planned, but I'm not worried," I admit. "The barn or garage—or whatever the hell it is—doesn't have a key, and the padlock on it is pretty solid. You can see where the previous owner tried to get into it. The estate said it hasn't been opened in years, so I'm free to do what I please with it and whatever is inside. Although it makes me wonder why they never just took the doors off."

"Now I'm intrigued. Let's hope there isn't a barn or garage full of dead people. Just your luck, you'll enter it, and it will be a scene from *The Walking Dead*," he replies, letting out a chuckle.

I roll my eyes. "You watch too much shit on television."

"Just remember to go for the head is all I'm going to say," he warns, climbing back up the ladder.

"I'll be back out after to help," I tell him, and get a nod in response.

I climb the stairs of the cabin as Caitlyn emerges from the door. She's changed into a pair of cut-off denim shorts, paired with a blank tank top, and I eye her legs, my dick twitching.

"Do you want a sandwich— Oh hey, you're back," she greets, her entire face lighting up when she sees me.

I run my gaze up her body, over the flush in her cheeks. A smirk tugs at my lips as I swagger forward, watching her breath hitch.

"Hey yourself," I murmur, pulling her into me.

She wraps her arms around my back, melting into me. Leaning down, I press my lips to hers. It was meant to be a light, quick kiss, but as soon as my mouth touches hers, the fire burns within me, and I want more. She moans as I slide my tongue against hers, bunching my T-shirt into her fist as she grips it, pulling me closer.

"Ewww," a little voice cries out.

I chuckle against Caitlyn's mouth, before giving her one last quick peck on the lips.

Pulling back, I turn to Carrie, laughing when I find her hands over her face, her fingers spread so she can peek through the gap.

"Hey, Pea," I greet.

She closes the space between us, holding her hands up. Knowing what she wants, I lift her into my arms, tucking her into my side.

In the few days I've known her, I can see why Caitlyn fell in love after all the loss she had received in her life. Carrie draws you in, and I know without a doubt I'm going to have a hard time saying no to the girl.

"Hey," she sings, giving me a kiss on the cheek. "I'm not kissing your mouth. That's just gross. Mummy, will you catch germs?"

I chuckle, and then hear Nate, who is still up the ladder, laughing down at her.

"No, sweetie," Caitlyn replies, and when Carrie looks away, she narrows her gaze on me before turning her attention to Nate. "I'm making sandwiches. Do you want one, Nate?"

"Please, I'm starved," he replies, winking down at her. "No preferences on what to put on it though. I like anything."

I narrow my gaze on him, silently imagining payback when he smirks like the cocky bastard he is. We may be mates, but that won't stop me from kicking his arse.

"What about me?" I ask, feigning hurt.

She rolls her eyes. "I knew you'd say yes," she admits, her cheeks turning pink once again. "I put a joint of pork in the oven after you left this morning, so, I hope you two don't mind having pork with stuffing baguettes."

"Oh, good heavens, if he screws up, let me know because I think me and you would make a great couple," Nate pleads, gripping the ladder.

I watch her lashes flutter, and a small smile I've only seen her reserve for me lift at her lips. The fucker has gotten to her.

Lucky for him, I'm still holding Carrie in my arms, otherwise he'd be off that ladder in a second.

Like he can read my thoughts, his grin spreads. "What?"

"You're so lucky I've got Pea in my arms, Nate, otherwise your face would be meeting my fist. Don't proposition my woman," I warn him.

"Scared she'll take me up on it?" he taunts.

"No, just worried for your safety," I growl at him, which only causes him to laugh harder.

"Okay, you two, pack it in," Caitlyn scolds lightly. "Come on, Cage, I'll make you a coffee."

"Thanks, babe, I'll have two sugars in mine," Nate calls down.

"She wasn't talking to you, arsehole," I growl, forgetting Carrie on my hip until she smacks her hand over my shoulder, her face scrunched up in a pout.

She points her finger in my face. "Naughty word. You have to put money in the jar. Ten thousand pounds every time someone says a naughty word. Mummy made it when you were gone. She said it would teach you all not to use naughty words when I'm around," Carrie scolds.

"Did she now?" I mutter as I enjoy watching Caitlyn squirm.

Carrie nods, her chest puffing out. Placing her down on the ground, I then reach into my back pocket, pulling out my wallet. I hand her a ten-pound note. "Okay, Pea. You go and put that in the jar, and I'll try my best not to say any more naughty words."

She glances at her mum then gestures for me to lean down.

"I wouldn't say them either," she whispers. "I heard Mummy telling Dante off before he left. She said that if he said one more word, she was going to cut his tongue off. Then he said Mum liked her scissors, but she gave him The Look." Her eyes widen, silently telling me what look it was. I chuckle as she shakes her head, like the reminder of mum's scolding scared her. "It's okay. He promised not to say them again."

I ruffle her hair, grinning. "Come on, Pea, let's get you fed."

Chapter Seventeen

CAGE

Tonight, I have a surprise for Caitlyn. It's Friday and after persuading Roy and Hayley to give her the night off and getting Dante to baby sit, I'm finally getting her alone.

We've gotten to know each other over the past few days but I want her to myself tonight. I want to give her a night where she doesn't need to worry about Robin or any of that mess.

Since the letter, things had been strained. She hasn't been sleeping and when she does, she's restless, waking up screaming from a nightmare. Hearing her call for me, or for Carrie, tears me apart. It's just more proof that she needs us.

"Are you ready yet?" I call out.

When I announced our plans, she said she wanted to get changed, even after I told her what she was wearing was perfect. But she's taking her sweet-arse time.

"Ready," she calls back and moments later, she steps out the bedroom.

Raking my eyes down her body, my dick stirs. The tight brown blouse clings to her chest, giving me a great view of her tits. Her skinny jeans look like they're glued to her, and when she grabs her bag off the sofa, I can't help but admire her arse in them.

Fuck, she's killing me. If we don't leave, I'm going to fuck her, and I want to give her more time before we're intimate again. When she spoke about her virginity, it made me realise how quickly it happened and that it wasn't what she expected. So, I want to give her more, show her this is more than sex.

"Is this okay?" she asks, reaching for her leather jacket. Although it's still warm outside, it won't be on my bike. She just doesn't know we're taking it instead of my truck.

"You look fuckable," I rasp, and her lips part as I scan over her once more.

Because my woman looks good in those jeans.

"Okay, come on, before we never leave," I groan out, grabbing my keys off the side.

"Where's Carrie?" she asks, searching outside.

I lock up behind us as I answer. "Dante took her to get some ice cream."

"Oh, okay, will they be alright?" she asks, biting her lip. I know she's worried about leaving Carrie in his care, but she has nothing to worry about. Dante might be a dick when it comes to women in his life, but he's a good person. He'll take care of Carrie. "She hasn't had dinner yet either."

"They're fine," I assure her. "If it makes you feel any better, I told him to go to a McDonalds so they can go through the drive-through."

When Caitlyn heads straight for the passenger side of the car, I snag her hand, pulling her away. Her brows pull together. "What are you doing?"

"We're taking the bike, not the truck, Kitten."

Her expression morphs into horror and her hands shake as she steps back, and chancing a glance at the truck, her gaze is almost pleading. "Can we just take the truck?"

"No," I rush out, chuckling. "Now, come on before it gets dark. I want to take you somewhere."

She hesitates for a moment before following me to my bike. I get on and hold my hand out to her, which she takes.

"Just put your leg over the side, then hold on to my waist," I instruct her.

"Is it safe?" she asks, doing as I said.

"Kitten, I've been riding since my feet could touch the ground. I promise you're safe. Here, put this on," I order, handing her the helmet over my shoulder.

I glance over my shoulder, checking she's done it right, and when I'm happy she has, I pull her arms around me. She grips me tight, holding on for dear life when the engine roars to life. As I push off, she squeals, her arms squeezing my stomach.

I keep the bike at a steady speed as we leave the resort, but once my front tyre hits the paved road, I gun the throttle, racing to our destination.

After five minutes, I feel her relax against me, and she begins to laugh. My lips pull into a smirk because this is what I wanted her to experience the freedom of the ride.

I GLANCE UP AT the sky when we pull into our destination. The sun will be setting soon but before that, I want to show Caitlyn the house. If we left it much longer, we wouldn't have been able to look around, not since the electric still needed to be sorted.

"Whose place is this?" she asks, mesmerised as she climbs off the bike.

"This is the house I was telling you about."

"The one you bought?" she asks, turning back to the house, her eyes lighting up with excitement.

"Yeah, she doesn't look like much now, but once you picture the finishing piece, it will be worth it."

"You're going to fix her up, aren't you?"

"I am," I answer, grinning at her enthusiasm.

"When will you start doing the work?"

"I need to make sure the cabins are sorted first. But after that, I'll get started. I have a few people coming up to help and with the garages."

"Can we take a look inside?"

"Yes, come on."

She races up to the door, and I follow, unlocking it. She pushes through the door, and with energy I thought only her daughter possessed, she bounces from room to room, talking animatedly about each room.

I relax, not realising until this moment how much I want her to like the house.

"Oh my God, Cage, this is beautiful," she gushes, as she moves on to the upstairs.

Each room we enter, I find myself making notes of all her ideas, liking every one of them.

By the time we are downstairs, her cheeks are flushed. "Cage, this place is beautiful."

"So are you," I tell her, pressing my lips to hers.

"It's going to be incredible when it's finished," she gushes.

"This isn't the surprise I wanted to show you," I tell her, pulling her towards the backdoor.

"It's not?" she asks, and the surprise in her tone makes me laugh.

When I lead her through the garden to the back gate, she tugs on my arm. "Is this where you kill me, then bury my body?" she asks.

I snort at her overreaction. "Come on, you dork."

"Hey, I'm not a dork," she protests.

It's not long until we reach the clearing and I stop, letting Caitlyn go ahead. Her lips part as she comes to a stop, taking in the beautiful scenery.

She takes another step, heading towards the blanket I laid down earlier, where I've got a picnic waiting for us.

"You did all of this?" she breathes, taking in all her surroundings.

I chuckle, reaching for her hand. "Yes, now come sit," I command lightly.

She obliges, taking a seat on the blanket. I pull the cushions out from the rucksack I brought over earlier and set one behind her.

She stares longingly over at the water before turning back to me, her eyes glistening. "I don't know what to say. No one has ever done anything like this for me before."

Leaning over, I steal a kiss, groaning at the taste of her. She parts her lips, and I deepen the kiss, my heart racing as that same sensation I get each time I'm with her, intensifies. I pull back, and stare into her eyes, mesmerised by her beauty. Needing to break the tension, I pull back a little and clear my throat.

"Just tell me you're hungry," I tease.

"Starved," she states, her lips twitching.

"There's baguettes from that sandwich place in town, some cheese and crackers, and a chocolate fudge cake. That all okay with you?"

"It's perfect," she whispers, and watches me as I begin to pull everything out, including the bottle of wine and the two glasses.

I pour her a glass and she takes it, taking a swig. Her eyes close and again, I'm paralysed by her beauty, that she's here with me.

"This is amazing. You're amazing," she states in awe.

"I know, people tell me that often," I tease.

She smacks me playfully on the arm before grabbing her turkey sandwich. She unwraps the foil before leaning down, her luscious lips wrapping around the baguette, taking a bite. She moans, her eyes closing.

I shift, pressing down on my dick when it begins to harden. I want her lips wrapped around my dick and watching her with that baguette only makes me want it more.

"Ahhh, Kitten, you need to stop making noises like that," I warn, my voice hoarse.

"Like what?" she mumbles, licking a crumb off her lip.

Fuck!

"Like that," I groan and lean over, pressing my lips to hers.

Her eyes droop and she sways a little. "What was that for?"

"For being you," I tell her truthfully.

We sit back, finishing off our meals and after staring up at the night sky for a long while, I sit up, grabbing the lantern I remembered to pick up. I switch it on and use the light to find the chocolate cake.

"You got a full cake?" she asks, laughing as I pass her a fork.

"I did," I tell her, chuckling because it was overboard now that we're here. "Let me just cut you a slice."

"Don't bother," she tells me and shocks me when she stabs her fork right in the middle of the cake.

Fucking hell. She's perfect.

I follow suit, taking a large chunk out the middle, but the fork pauses near my mouth as I watch her lips close over the fork, sensually sliding down the metal.

I gulp, wishing like fuck she would do that over my cock.

When another moan slips free, my cock is painfully hard again.

"Kitten," I warn hoarsely.

She pulls back, her eyes round, full of vulnerability as she flutters her lashes at me. And it's that look, that feeling inside of my chest, that snaps the control I have been holding onto.

I capture her soft lips, deepening the kiss as I push forward, causing her to drop onto her back.

I'm not sure what I have done to deserve this, to deserve her, but I'm not arguing. Heat curls in my stomach, to my chest, my breathing laboured.

Her lips part once more, a moan slipping free, and I come to, becoming aware of my hand under her top, cupping her breast.

Tonight isn't meant to be about this. It's about her. I want to give her a tiny piece of what she gives me when I'm around her. It's like a sense of peace washing over me.

I'm not a romantic guy. I'm not normally this in-touch with my feelings, but she brings them out of me.

"Please," she pleads, her fingers scraping along the side of my ribs. I pull back, letting her lift my T-shirt over my head. I drop it down on the ground next to me, before staring down at her.

"Your turn," I rasp, and instead of going for her blouse, I go for her jeans, but first, I pull off her boots, throwing them behind me. She watches me, her eyes hooded as I pull her jeans down her legs, groaning at the sight of the thong barely covering her pussy.

Fuck, she's killing me.

"Cage," she rasps.

Grinning, I slide them down her legs, enjoying her intake of breath. I run my hands up her smooth skin, kissing the inside of her thigh. Her hips arch into me, and I grin, pulling back. Her eyes fly open, watching me in confusion.

I grip her hips and in one fast movement, I sit back, pulling her into my lap. Feeling the pillows against my lower back, I lean back a bit.

"Your turn," I tell her huskily.

"But I—"

I lean forward, pressing my lips against her neck as I unbutton her blouse. She inhales sharply and I grin up at her.

Her pupils dilate and she leans forward, kissing me. I slide the blouse off her arms, palming her back and pulling her against me. Her bra is thin, and I can feel her nipples rubbing against my chest.

I growl, unclasping the clip. She leans back, discarding the bra to the ground beside us.

Her hair falls in waves, blanketing us from the outside world. Her lips brush against mine, soft, sweet, and the taste of chocolate still lingers.

She pulls back, running her fingers through my hair. "Your turn," she rasps, unbuttoning my jeans.

I lift up, causing her to squeal as she balances above me. I grin, pushing my jeans down my thighs, grateful for not putting on any boxers. I toe off my boots before kicking my jeans the rest of the way off.

She's featherlight when I lift her, sitting her down on my lap, my cock rubbing against her folds.

I groan, my dick tightening. "Fuck!"

"Condom," she pants out.

"Shit," I mumble, and take her by surprise when I lift up and lean forward, taking her with me as I reach for my jeans. I grab a condom and sit back, but not before stealing a kiss, earning a long moan in return.

God, she tastes so good.

Pushing her further down, I then work the condom down my length, my balls tightening from the touch.

I want inside her so goddamn bad.

She inhales sharply when I roughly pull her back up, her chest flush against mine.

"God, you're so beautiful," I rasp, before sealing the compliment with a kiss.

Her kisses have all thoughts escaping from my mind, and when she tugs the hair at the nape of my neck, I lose all self-control.

Positioning myself at her entrance, I silently ask her if this is okay. The words don't need to be said. I can see it in her eyes. Just like most of her emotions. I can read her well.

"Cage," she moans, sliding down my hard length.

"Fuck," I growl, gripping her hips. She's tighter than I remember, so fucking tight.

And it's enough to snap all my control. I cup the back of her head, bringing her forward. Our mouths clash together in a fiery kiss, her moans driving me wild.

I press one hand on her hip, guiding her to move. The minute her luscious hips roll, I nearly come undone there and then.

"Oh God," she pants against my mouth.

She's killing me.

I reach between us, cupping her tit and pushing it up. Pulling away from the kiss, I lean down, sucking her nipple into my mouth.

She writhes and moans, digging her fingers into my shoulders until I feel them tattooed into my skin.

"Fuck," she breathes out.

Kissing my way up her chest, I reach her lips, pouring everything into the kiss. I grip her hips, guiding her movements and with each thrust, then yank her towards me harder.

The sound of our skin slapping together mingles with our heavy breathing.

She's close, so fucking close. I yank her hips closer, pushing them back before impaling her onto my cock. She cries out, thrusting her chest out, and I lean down, grazing my teeth across her nipple before sucking it into my mouth.

With a tug, she cries out, her orgasm tearing through her.

My balls tighten and I follow, our movements jerky as I empty my load inside of her.

"Fuck!" I growl, smashing my lips against hers.

Pulling away, she melts against me, panting heavily. "That was... That was—"

"Incredible," I finish for her, lying down with my cock still inside of her.

I hope it will always be like this between us, like a match to a flame, setting us alight. Because it has never been this good.

Chapter Eighteen

CAGE

THE STARS TWINKLE IN THE night sky, the warm breeze now cooling. Luckily, I packed a spare throw blanket, just in case, to cover us.

We're still naked, content to just hold one another, enjoying the peace and serenity. I know we'll have to start making a move soon, but I honestly can't muster up the energy to leave. I want to stay right here with her.

Caitlyn leans up, resting her chin on my chest. "Tell me something about yourself."

A smirk tugs at my lips. "I like being here with you."

She rolls her eyes. "Not what I meant."

"Ah, so we're doing the twenty questions thing again?"

"No, more like a get to know you thing. I feel like I already know you inside of my heart, but I don't actually know much about you."

"True," I murmur.

"Who was your first girlfriend? And what was your favourite and worst subject at school?" she asks as I settle in.

I run my fingers through her hair. "Well, first girlfriend that I can remember was a girl named Emily. My favourite subject had to be art, along with sports. I loved them both. The worst subject I would have to say was science. No matter how hard I tried to understand it, I could never wrap my head around it." I chuckle at the reminder. The amount of detentions I had for that lesson alone wasn't fun. It made me hate it more. "What about you?"

"Well, my first boyfriend was Jake. We were five," she admits, and it's cute she remembers. "Favourite subject had to be English, because it was easy to understand, plus I got to do papers on my favourite books. Worse subject had to be maths. I hated everything to do with it, and even the pervy teacher I had. I hated him; every girl in the school did. He kind of looked like Hagrid out of Harry Potter, only he was a creep."

"There's always one," I tell her, chuckling.

"What is it that you actually do? You have all these businesses, but what is it *you* do?" she asks, taking me off guard.

No other girl I've been with has actually cared about what I do. Yeah, they've cared about my bank balance and how big my dick is, but nothing else.

"I like working on bikes but it's not a passion. It was just good business sense to start up. It's the construction side I love to do, mostly designing a lay out," I admit. "I'm good at it."

"Roy said you were making changes."

"I am. He sent over the prints for the design he got from the previous builder, but it wasn't going the way he had hoped. It wasn't the vision he saw. I looked them over, drew up some new ones and brought them over to him. But after taking a look around at the space he has, I pictured more, which is why we are building a spa treatment block."

"He wants families to enjoy being here and have something for each of them to do."

I nod in agreement. "The park he had put in after his parents left him the estate helped. But even that is becoming outdated. There isn't much to do around the resort unless you go into town."

"Yeah, but it's peaceful out there. No one to disturb you—well, until you and your goons came anyway," she mutters, feigning annoyance.

"Hey, me and my goons can be peaceful," I tease, pressing my lips against hers.

"No, you and your goons ruined my peaceful bliss. Well, them and their bikes."

"Don't talk bad of the bikes," I warn, my lips twitching in amusement.

"You said you had sisters. What are your sisters like?"

"Well, Laura is opinionated, stubborn, funny, bossy, and motherly. Danni is quiet, shy, and the kindest person you could ever meet. I had to look out for her when we were kids; she would always get picked on for being the quiet one, not having many friends. The friends she did have loved her unconditionally. She had a few that would take advantage of her kindness and it pissed me off. Then she got to the age where boys started sniffing around, which drove me mad. I don't like to say this, but she's naïve; she always sees the good in people. I didn't want boys taking advantage of that."

"I bet she loved you for it, though," Caitlyn whispers.

"Yes, we get along really well. Laura is another story; we always end up in a fight if we see each other. After mum died, she took on the mother role of the house, and she took it seriously. She did a lot for us as kids, but she always seemed to have a problem with me when we were younger. When Nate moved in though, I settled down a little; I got a job, grew up, and so did he. We all get on fine now though, but Laura and I still argue from time to time," I admit. "What about Courtney? Tell me something about the two of you."

"Courtney was always the rebel in the family. I suppose I was kind of a tomboy as a child; always climbing trees or playing video games. When I started high school, everything changed. I got into doing my hair, hanging with friends, wearing girly shit, but I still loved video games, books, movies, and would prefer to do that than be social. Courtney would tease me constantly. She was the total opposite of me. She loved pissing our mum and dad off, saying it was to keep them on their toes. She would come back drunk, stoned; sometimes she wouldn't even come home. She was always getting into trouble." Her smile dims a little at that. "She changed when she turned eighteen. She started to act more mature. She worked a lot too, which I think helped her grow up. However, when she went to America, she came back a different person. My parents were so disappointed in her. They thought she had grown out of her rebel ways, but then she came back married and pregnant."

"What about your parents? What was their relationship like?"

"Oh God," she groans, pressing her face into my chest. "They acted like love-sick teenagers all the time. They couldn't keep their hands off each other." She lets out a wistful sigh. "They had been together since they were fifteen and loved to remind us constantly of how they got together. Mum was a geek at school and Dad was a bad boy. She was helping him with some homework when they fell in love. They never got bored with each other like most couples their age do.

"Mum got pregnant with Courtney when she was seventeen. Shortly after their eighteenth birthday, they got married. They never broke up once the whole time they were together. They argued, but they never stayed mad at each other long. They always brought the best out of each other," she tells me, her voice breaking a little. "I miss them so much. Some days I forget they're gone, and I find myself going to ring them. If I knew that day that they wouldn't be coming home, I would have changed the last thing I said to them.

I told them to get lost—they were in a heavy make-out session in the kitchen—and was so embarrassed seeing them making-out. I remember covering my eyes and screaming at them to get a room. They laughed. They always laughed when we reacted that way. But it was the last thing I said to them, instead of telling them I love them, like I usually did when they left the house. I've dreamt of that moment so many times and I always say I love you. But it's just a dream and it hurts when I wake up and realise that."

"Caitlyn," I murmur, hating the turmoil in her voice. She forces a smile, her gaze dropping to my chin. Knowing I need to change the subject, I start to tell her about my parents. "My parents loved each other, but they argued nonstop. They would fight like two blokes in a wrestling ring. I remember one day my dad came home drunk from work. Mum had left his dinner in the oven to keep it warm. When he took it out, he started screaming up the stairs at her. She went downstairs after putting us to bed and I could hear her shouting at him outside. I looked out of my bedroom window to see my dad in the middle of the garden, digging a hole. When she asked him what he was doing, he told her he was burying the food. When she asked him why, he told her to make it fucking grow, that there wasn't enough to feed an infant on his plate. She was so mad at him that she started smacking the baking dish across his head. Three nights he slept on the sofa, and Mum refused to make him dinner. Laura and I watched the whole scene, but we knew, no matter what, that they loved us and each other."

Caitlyn's lips go from gaping open to a big smile, laughter pouring out of her.

"That sounds like something I would do. If you ever bury my cooking, Mr Carter, you'll have more than a baking tray across your head."

"Your cooking is amazing, so no worries there," I tell her, as a shiver races over her. I pull her against me, letting out a sigh. "We should be heading back."

"Yeah, I want to make sure Carrie's okay."

"She will be," I promise her.

"I wish all this would be over so we can get on with our lives. I hadn't realised until recently how much we've been missing out on."

I help her sit up and reach for her bra, passing it to her. As we dress, I reply to her comment.

"I promise I'll sort it out," I assure her. "You won't need to worry anymore."

"Cage?" she calls as she finishes pulling on her jeans.

"Yeah," I answer, glancing up from my boots.

"You know when it's sorted… do you think you'll still want me?" she asks, unsure.

I stand, pulling her into my arms. "Of course, I will," I declare, wondering where that came from. "What has made you think I wouldn't want you?"

I'm crazy about her, and I thought I was coming on too strong already.

Maybe I need to up my game.

She tucks a strand of hair behind her ear. "I don't know. I thought… maybe the only reason you stuck around was because of the situation with Robin. You have a protective personality—from what I've seen anyway. I just thought you'd be bored after everything settles down, so to speak."

I cup her cheek, tilting her head back until her gaze locks with mine. "Look at me, Kitten," I demand softly.

Her lashes flutter open and my breath stalls in chest when I see her eyes moist with tears.

Today isn't about tears. It's about making her laugh, smile, and I feel like a prick for bringing up bad memories and making her doubt me. She has nothing to worry about when it comes to me. I'm not going anywhere.

"If you haven't gotten it already, baby, then I'll explain it to you. I'm not going anywhere. I'm this for the long haul."

"But—"

I press my lips against hers, shutting her up.

"I'm not sure where you are, but I'm in this. I'm not going anywhere, not even when this crap is over." I take in a breath as I open myself up to her. "One of the reasons for me moving in was so I could protect you. But the other reason is because I wanted to get to know you. I was scared you'd retreat or make excuses. This seemed like the best way for you to get to know me, to get to know you. I want you to take a chance on me too."

"Why?" she whispers. "I'm plain and boring."

A deep chuckle erupts from my chest. "You are anything but boring. You are perfect. From the minute I laid eyes on you, I wanted you. It's crazy, I know, but I want more with you. I guess sometimes you just know. And right now, I know you are what I want."

"I want that too, but I'm scared."

"Of me?"

"No, of it all going to shit. Everyone around me dies. I'm scared if I let myself get any closer, I'll lose you."

"You aren't going to lose me. I'm not going anywhere until you tell me to, and even then, I'll fight for you. Okay?"

She nods, before closing the distance between. She wraps her arms around me. "This is all so much."

"I know, but for once, I'm not going to question it. You were brought into my life for a reason, and, Kitten, I want you there."

"Okay, but I need to process this."

"Let's get you home," I murmur.

Chapter Nineteen

CAITLYN

WHEN WE PULL UP TO THE cabin, Carrie, Dante, and Nate are all sitting on the porch playing a game. Watching my daughter interact with others, and having fun, makes my heart skip a beat. I'm overjoyed she finally has this kind of joy in her life: being surrounded by people who care for her, people who will protect her and love her. And by the way she seems to be clinging to Nate, I can tell she loves them, too.

It's late, and although Carrie should already be in bed, I'm glad she isn't. It gives me a chance to tuck her in and find out how she's doing with everything. Since the note the other morning, I haven't been sleeping well. I'm constantly feeling on edge. I know both Carrie and Cage have picked up on it, though they haven't mentioned it. If anything, they've been trying to help ease my mind as much as possible.

My mind won't still, and after Cage's declaration, I know tonight is going to be another long night. Tomorrow night I begin work again and after what happened the last time, I'm wary about going. But I can't put it off any longer. Roy has hired a new waitress and since I'm assistant manager, it's my job to train her.

It's all becoming too much, and although I told Cage it was okay, it isn't. I'm scared. Scared of what's happening, how quickly it's happening, and I know there won't be much more I can cope with.

Work is something that normally takes my mind off things and now that's tainted. Even with the new schedule and rules, it's going to be hard to grasp normalcy. They don't want me to work routine shifts. They think it will give Robin's men chance to form a plan. The only one they can't change is the cabins. I clean each of them like clockwork every morning and there is no way I can lose the money by not doing it.

Having the entire day off has been refreshing. I never get the chance to just relax. And when Cage said he was taking me out, I assumed it would be to a restaurant. What he gave me was so much more. It meant more to me than he'll ever realise.

And although I played it off, his words tonight scared me. I wanted what he was offering so badly. I wanted Carrie to have it.

But as we passed the house as we were leaving, I couldn't help but feel like I've failed. We would never have that. We were never going to settle with Robin at our back.

The further we drove away, the more reality hit me, and the night just feels like a dream. Good things don't happen to me. And I have a horrible, gut-churning sensation that things are going to end badly. For all of us.

Seeing Carrie laugh at something Dante whispers to her, my heart aches. I'm a fool. Such a fucking fool to think this could be our life now.

Carrie spots us heading towards them and jumps off Nate's lap. She runs over to me, and I meet her on the steps, catching her in my arms.

"Hey, beautiful, are you having a good time?" I ask her.

"Oh my God, Mum, Uncle Dante let me play dress up with him. I didn't have any clothes to fit him, so I just did his hair and make-up. He washed it off after Uncle Nate came though. He brought us Buckaroo. It's so cool, Mum, come see," she says, dragging me across the porch to where they are, in fact, playing Buckaroo.

I don't miss the fact she called both Nate and Dante, Uncle, and neither did they or Cage, because they were all looking at Carrie with big grins on their faces. My daughter seriously knows how to make friends.

"One more game and then it's bedtime. It's getting late," I tell her.

"Pleeease can I stay up, please?" she begs.

"No, it's late, and you'll only be tired in the morning, and grumpy all day, so no."

"That's so not fair. You get to stay up, so why can't I?"

"Because I'm the adult and you're the child. You'll do as you're told, young lady," I scold her.

She gives me her best 'I hate you' look, then struts back over to sit on Nate's lap. He glances over at me, silently asking me what to do.

I open my mouth but it's Cage who answers. "Pea, baby, you can't talk to your mother like that. She said you can play one more game, then you have to go to bed, okay?"

"Okay," she mumbles.

Cage ruffles her hair, taking the seat between Dante and Nate. Looking around for a chair, I notice there aren't any left. Before I have a chance to go inside to grab one, Cage is pulling me into his lap.

"So, have you all had fun?" I ask, glancing from Nate to Dante.

They haven't said anything since we got here, but I can see that they've wanted to—well, at least Nate has wanted to. Dante looks like he's in a sulk.

"We sure did," Nate states, as he relaxes back into his chair, grinning.

"What have you been doing?" Cage asks, his tone curious.

"Oh, for fu… monkey's sake. Carrie here," Dante growls at her, which causes her to giggle, "made me have my make-up done, along with my hair, and if you think that wasn't bad enough, jackass here walked in when I was having my eyeshadow done and took a picture. He didn't just stop there though. He posted it on Facebook." He gives Nate the side-eye.

We all burst into a fit of giggles, but Carrie jumps off Nate's lap to go and park herself into Dante's lap. Dante immediately makes room for her, hugging her close.

"Don't laugh at him," Carrie grumbles, her lips tipped down. "He looked really pretty. The eyeshadow matched his eyes."

I can't hold it in; I double over, leaning my forearms on the table in front of me as I burst out laughing. I laugh so hard my sides hurt, my cheeks hurt, and I feel like I can't breathe. It only gets worse when Nate shows us the picture.

"Here she… I mean *he* is," he teases, holding up the phone.

I nearly fall off the chair when I see it. Tears stream down my face—thankfully, for once, they are happy tears.

In the picture, Dante is leaning against Carrie's bed, his legs stretched out and crossed at the ankles. Carrie is sitting by the side of him with a makeup brush to his eye. He's got bright red lipstick on that looks like it's more smudged into his face than actually on his lips. He has bright pink blusher staining his cheeks, with bright blue eyeshadow. She must have nabbed my mascara because he has black under and above his eyes.

"Right, I'm off. I'll see you tomorrow, Carrie." He turns, glaring at the rest of us. "As for the rest of you, don't ask me to babysit the beautician. It's your turn next, boys. You try saying no to her when she goes all puppy-dog-eyed on you," he states, giving them all a warning look. "Oh, and before you say anything, I did say no. I said no a thousand times, trying to get her to play something else, but no, she wanted to play dress up. After trying to get me into a Rapunzel dress, she gave up, saying she would do my make-up instead. I point-blank refused, telling her men don't wear sh … sugar like that. Then she went all out by putting the water works on. Seriously, dudes, you're all done for. Good luck saying no."

"You didn't want to play with me?" Carrie asks, her bottom lip trembling when he sets her on her feet.

Dante's eyes widen as he bends down. "You can do my hair any time you want, sweetheart."

Her eyes light up. "Really?"

"Yeah, just don't tell the rest of them. They'll get jealous."

"I won't," she whispers.

He ruffles her hair before jumping down the stairs, sticking his middle finger up at the guys when they begin to laugh.

Hearing Carrie yawn and seeing her rub at her eyes, I know it won't be long till she's asleep. If she pushes through it and goes past tired, she's a nightmare to deal with the next day.

"Let's get you to bed," I tell her softly, getting up off Cage's lap.

"I want you and Cage to take me, Mummy," she mumbles, and Cage lifts her up in his arms.

Since he had been staying with us, Carrie has demanded Cage or both of us put her to bed each night. It was a little weird at first, but now I can't picture him not being here when she goes to bed. It's like a new routine.

And as I glance at them together, I can't help but let that fear consume me. Is this really everything he said it would be?

Is he playing me? Although, as soon as the thought crosses my mind, I banish it.

I know it had nothing to do with that. And yet, I'm scared. So damn scared. It has only ever been us for so long.

"Okay, Pea, let's get you to bed," Cage orders softly.

Nate stands, leaning over to give Carrie a kiss on the cheek.

"Bye, Uncle Nate," she whispers.

"Night, baby," he whispers back, right before Cage heads inside.

My eyes clog with unleashed tears as I watch this play out in front of me. I know both guys can see but I don't care. This moment means everything to me. It might not be real, but for the moment, it's real for her, and this is all I ever wanted for her.

To have a family.

I rub at my chest, fighting back the panic threatening to consume me.

"Thank you for coming to look after Carrie with Dante. It means a lot," I tell Nate.

"They were no trouble," he declares, and surprises me when he pulls me in for a brief hug. "I can see you're scared, but don't be."

"W-what?" I stutter.

"She's precious, Caitlyn. You're an amazing mother, and I promise I'll do anything to keep you both safe. Not just for me, but for Cage; you make him happy. But don't be afraid to be happy. We will protect you both."

He leaves without waiting for my reply. When he's gone, I whisper to the night sky, "Thank you."

Because it was like he had read my mind. He couldn't have known what I was thinking, but he answered my fears like he could. I just wish I knew how to let go of the fear and believe that what was happening was real.

Needing to get Carrie into bed, I quickly pack up the game before heading inside behind them.

As I step into the bedroom, Cage is tucking her teddy, Missy, into bed with her as she tiredly tells him how much fun she had today.

I walk over, waiting for Cage to step back before sitting on the edge of the bed. I lean down, placing a kiss on her cheek. "Night, baby."

"Night, Mummy," she returns, and I get up, smiling down at her. "Night, Pea."

We both head for the door when she stops us. "Will Cage be staying?" she asks, a slight tremble in her voice.

"Of course, Pea, I'm not going anywhere," he promises.

She fiddles with Missy, pulling at her ears. "It's just, Mummy smiles more now that you're here. I like her to be happy all the time," she whispers. "I want us to be a family, a real family. I want you to be my daddy. I want us to be together forever."

The tears slipping down her cheeks have me moving before I know it. I kneel next to the bed, taking her hand in mind.

"Hey," I begin, feeling Cage take a seat on the bed. "I'm happiest with you."

Cage clears his throat, placing a hand on her arm. "Pea, you do know I'm not your real daddy, don't you?" he asks, and I whip my head up, narrowing my eyes on him.

How dare he say that to my daughter. Can't he see this is a sore subject for her? He doesn't pay attention to me, his focus solely on Carrie, but it doesn't matter. I know he can feel me glaring at him.

Her chest begins to shake as a sob tears from her throat. I reach for her, but Cage gets there first and has her up and his arms.

"Cage," I warn.

He ignores me and brushes Carrie's hair out of her face. "Carrie, do you understand what I'm saying?"

She shrugs, sniffling into his chest. "I-I think so."

"Cage," I warn, my voice firmer.

This isn't his conversation to have. It's mine, something I should have done when she first brought it up. The crap around me kept distracting me.

"Firstly, I want you to know I'm not going anywhere, baby. But I'm not your father. You mean a lot to me, so for a little while, why don't we just enjoy getting to know one another."

I gape at him in shock, appalled he'd even say that to her. This isn't his place.

"Do you not want to be my daddy?" she asks, swiping the tears away on her cheek.

"It isn't that, baby. It's just that me and Mummy just found each other. It's still new. And although I'd love nothing more than to be your daddy, right now, I'm just Cage. You can be Carrie, and Mummy can be Mummy. Then we can talk about this at a later date, okay? I promise I'm not going anywhere."

A lump forms in the back of my throat and I close my eyes as a wave of pain hits me in the chest.

It means a lot that he'd do this for her. He's being honest, giving her no false hope. Yet, it's killing me inside because this is something she wants. How I missed it all, missed the ramifications of having him move in, I don't know. It had been me giving her false hope.

"You promise you won't leave us?" she asks, snuggling into him. "We don't want to be alone anymore."

I choke on a sob as I duck my head, stifling it.

Failure.

Terrible mum.

"I promise," he assures her. "Are you okay now, Pea?"

"Yes, I just want us to be a real family. I can wait," she declares.

"Okay, well go give your mum a hug, then let's get you back to bed."

"Okay."

She crawls on her knees over to me, wrapping her tiny arms around my neck. I hold on tight to her as tears threaten to fall.

"I love you, Carrie," I declare, my voice filled with so much emotion.

"I love you more, Mummy," she replies.

"Always."

"And forever," she finishes, making my heart stop. God, I really do love this child.

She lets go of her tight grip, flopping back down on the bed. Cage tucks her back in, pulling the blanket up to her neck. She moves to her side, snuggling up to Missy. I lean over, kissing her forehead one last time.

"Goodnight, baby girl," I tell her.

"Goodnight, Mummy. Sweet dreams."

"You too, honey."

"Night, Pea," Cage murmurs, pressing a kiss to her forehead.

"Night, Cage, I love you, too," she tells him, once again making my heart beat rapidly.

"I love you, too, Pea," he tells her.

I leave, knowing I won't be able to keep it together much longer, and head for the kitchen. I hear Cage following behind me as I reach for a glass, then the wine out of the fridge.

After that, I need one. A large one.

I hear him rummage through the fridge a moment later, grabbing a beer. I take a large gulp of wine, trying to compartmentalise my thoughts.

"So…" he murmurs, breaking the silence.

"So…"

"What happened in there… I know you're mad, but she had to know. I didn't want to give her false hope, not when this is all new."

I snort. "It wasn't your place to tell her," I argue.

"Maybe not, but I wanted her to hear it from me. She deserved that much from me."

"You are no one to her," I yell, feeling my chest tighten.

The walls close in around me. This is all too much.

"Yeah? You go ask her what I mean to her," he barks. "See how she thanks you then."

I slam my glass down on the side. "It wasn't your place to say anything to her. I had it under control. I was going to talk to her. Now she thinks it will happen eventually."

He throws his hands up. "Did you not listen to anything I said earlier to you?"

"Yes, I did, but it's too soon."

"It's not happening too soon, Kitten, and you know it. You feel for me like I feel for you. I can sense it. You're just being scared and pushing me away, which I expected to happen."

"I am not doing that at all. I'm—"

"Scared. I know. I'm in the same boat," he tells me. "I've had my life mapped out for as long as I can remember. I like structure. After what happened with my ex, I knew what I was searching for and what I wasn't. Or I thought I did. Until you walked into my life. Now I want it all and I want it with you and Carrie."

I shake my head, taking a step back until my back hits the counter. I know I'm running, running from him, the commitment, the fear of losing him, the fear this is just a dream, one I'll wake up from soon. But it doesn't stop the words coming out of my mouth.

"You have your life mapped out. You said so yourself. I don't. I don't know what tomorrow will bring."

He gives me a side-eye and I can see he is growing frustrated with me. He forces out a laugh.

"When I was showing you around the house earlier, I took in everything you said. I watched how your eyes lit up when you described something. I wanted that for you. I want to *be* the person who gives that to you. That's how much I'm in this. And I know you want that too."

My eyes widen as my vision dims a little. This can't be happening.

I'd love to be your father.

I'm this for the long haul.

You were brought into my life for a reason.

I want to be the person who gives that to you.

The looming threat of Robin suffocates me.

"We are temporarily living together and now you want me to move into your house?" I ask. "You keep forgetting that my life here is temporary. The only reason I'm staying is because I'm giving this a chance. I'll do anything to keep her safe, even if that means packing up and leaving. I can't give you promises. I can't have you give them to Carrie either."

He drops his can on the side.

"You two aren't going anywhere," he grits out. "You feel this too. Why run from it? Why give him more power to control your life?"

"Yes, I do feel it, Cage, and that's what scares me. I told you that earlier. But it doesn't change the fact that if we need to run, my daughter's heart is going to be broken. I got too close."

This isn't too soon.

"Listen to yourself," he spits out. "Are you really willing to put your daughter in danger because you are that scared of being happy?"

My back straightens and I push off the counter.

"Are you kidding me? What the fuck, Cage? Everything I've done is to protect her. Don't you dare tell me I'm putting her in danger."

"No? Then why the fuck would you take her away from people who can protect the pair of you? You have people here who care about you. Roy, Hayley, Nate, Dante and me. Instead, you're willing to flee the country, where you will know no one at all? You're insane."

"Fuck you, Cage," I scream. "I haven't even said I'm going. I'm just telling you how it is. And don't you dare tell me how to look after my own goddamn daughter. I've been doing just fine without you. I don't need you."

"Yeah? You've been doing so well on your own that your goddamn daughter is scared that she's going to have to leave again. You're willing to put her happiness aside? Fucking think for a second," he snaps. "Goddamn it, Caitlyn."

"How fucking dare you," I grit out, feeling every muscle in my body tense.

"How dare I? How dare you! Hayley and Roy idolise that girl in there," he declares, pointing to the direction of Carrie's room. "The boys love her. They are willing to put their lives in danger in order to protect you both. I'm willing to do that. Does that mean nothing?"

Anger consumes me and the pulsing in my ears rings.

"I never fucking asked them or you to protect us. I never asked for any of this," I choke out.

"Caitlyn," he murmurs, taking a step forward.

I hold up my hand, warning him off. "Get out!"

"No, we need to—"

"Get out," I scream. "Just get the fuck out, Cage. I mean it. I don't need you sitting there telling me how to raise my daughter or how to keep her fucking safe. If I have to leave in order to protect her, I will. Don't ever tell me how to raise her again."

"You know what? Fuck this," he snaps, throwing his beer across the kitchen. I flinch, my heart racing as he grabs his jacket and keys off the side.

I startle as the front door slams shut behind him, my breathing escalating.

I slide down the side of the cabinet, tucking my knees to my chest as a sob breaks free.

He's gone.

My words run through my mind, and I flinch at each and every one of them. I was cruel, unkind, and now I've lost him.

I stare at the door, hoping he'll return, but the door remains shut, the silence of the cabin deafening.

Out of all the things I've lost in my life, none have been because of my own stupidity.

I lied to Cage, though; I lied to him when I said I didn't need him. I do need him. I've never needed or wanted anyone as much as I do him. And those feelings he talked about? I had them. I had them so damn bad I was consumed by them. But I was also scared of them. Whenever I opened my heart up to hope, to love, it was taken from me.

He was right; when you know, you know. A life can't be measured, it's only added up in moments, in actions and love. And although society says it's too soon, what I felt wasn't. It had been weeks now since I met him. Weeks of skipping steps in a normal relationship. The tension and drama pushing us closer together in a way a normal couple wouldn't.

But I know him. I know his heart.

And I just ripped it out by my cruel words, letting my fear win.

It all comes barrelling down on me, knowing I just lost the best thing that has ever happened to me since Carrie.

"What have I done?" I whisper to an empty room.

I'm not sure how much time passes, but when I finally pull myself up off the floor, my eyes feel swollen and my body aches.

I head to my room, a fresh wave of tears hitting me when I stare at the empty bed.

It's going to be weird not having him here. I'm going to miss his cuddles, his sweet words and kisses.

Getting undressed, I go to reach for my PJs but notice Cage's T-shirt lying on the floor. I reach for it, bring it up to my face, a sob breaking free when his woodsy scent fills the air.

I pull it on before dragging myself over to the bed, curling up into a ball under the covers. I cuddle the pillow to my chest, sobbing until my throat is raw and my tears dry up.

Only then do I let the darkness pull me under.

Chapter Twenty

CAGE

MY THOUGHTS ARE SCATTERED IN my head, and anger pumps through my veins as I pour myself my fifth or sixth glass of Jack Daniels.

I can't believe that just happened. One minute we were fucking next to the reservoir, me putting myself out there, only to get back and start fighting.

And at this point, I'm not even sure what it was about. I know she was pissed about me talking to Carrie. I could feel her anger burning in the side of my head.

But it feels like more that.

And I have to wonder if it was worth it.

A dry chuckle escapes me. I should have known it was too good to be true, that I could find someone as perfect as her.

Did nothing about today mean anything to her? Do I mean anything to her?

I've never met such a stubborn woman in all my life. I respect her need to protect Carrie, I truly do, but she isn't alone now.

"Are you going to finish or are you going to keep staring into your drink?" Nate asks.

I tell him everything that happened, stopping to yell about how unfair she was being.

I was surprised to find a full-on party going on when I got here. It hadn't been that long since they left Caitlyn's, but if anyone could manage to throw a party and find a group of women staying for a hen party, it was Dante. It's like he can sniff pussy out.

The bride is already passed out on the sofa.

Nate and I moved to the kitchen where I poured myself a hefty glass of Jack. He did try to introduce me to everyone, but I wasn't in the fucking mood. I'm still not.

After a beat, he replies, "Mate, I wasn't there, but I don't think being here is where you need to be right now."

"What do you mean?"

"I think you need to go back and talk to her. She's not a stupid girl. I saw her earlier when Carrie called us uncle and she was scared. And I think it's because she desperately wants family in her life, whether that be blood or not."

"It's just me she doesn't want."

He rolls his eyes at me. "She didn't say that."

"She didn't need to," I argue. "I've been ignoring the signs from the beginning. This is just *temporary* for her."

"You don't believe that," he declares.

I rub a hand over my jaw, sighing. "No, I don't, but I don't know what to do either."

"I'm telling you, dude, you need to go back and sort it out. Being here drinking yourself stupid isn't going to get you anywhere."

"You weren't fucking there," I snap, wishing he'd stop pushing me to leave. "She told me to go."

He throws his hands up. "I never pictured you to be a pussy. Even I can tell you are really into her. You want to fuck that up, go ahead."

"Fuck you," I growl. "Fuck her. I'm done."

"Whatever, it's your funeral," he snaps.

"Yeah, what the fuck would you know? The longest relationship you've had is with the cheese sandwich you have in your gym bag."

"Fuck you, Cage. Caitlyn is a good woman. She isn't like any of your other fucking mutts that you usually date. She actually has feelings for you. Take this situation from her point of view. She has lost everyone she has ever cared about—all tragically, and may I add, all close to each other. The only person she has left, she is going to protect. She needs reassuring that she's safe here, that nothing can harm her. And instead of proving it, you pushed her too soon. And now you being here, acting like a dick, is going to make it worse."

"She told me to go," I remind him.

"Yeah, and you've been here for over an hour drinking your fucking sorrows. She's probably regretting everything she said, likely waiting for you to return. Either that or she's sat crying her fucking eyes out."

"I'm not going back. I'll talk to her in the morning before Pea wakes up. I'll let the air clear out before I step back in there."

"I'm telling you, mate, you're making a bad decision."

"You're not my dad," I snap.

"No, I'm your fucking friend. Caitlyn has been through a lot. I don't want to see her get hurt. She doesn't need that, but worst of all, Carrie doesn't need that. This isn't going to get you anywhere."

"You have known her five minutes. How the hell do you know what she's been through? You don't even know her!"

"Neither do you," he fires back.

"I fucking know her," I growl.

"Whatever. She doesn't deserve this. She's scared. I can see why you fell for her so quick. She's fucking special. If she were free, I would have taken a shot."

"Don't," I warn, earning a smirk.

"This is what I'm talking about. Just go to her," he tells me.

I scrub a hand over my face. "No, I'll go in the morning. I've fucked up enough tonight."

"At least you admit it."

Grabbing the bottle, I pour myself another glass. "Are you going to have a fucking drink with me or are we going to keep talking in circles?"

He doesn't say anything for a moment, but then snatches the bottle away from me, a frown creasing his forehead. "Yeah."

Dante comes in, his shirt ripped off. "Let's get this party fucking started."

"Fuck!" Nate groans.

Dante turns to me, his grin spreading across his face. "You gonna get out your mood?"

"No," I snap.

He nods, like that's okay. "Well, Mr Frowny Face, let's get you fucked up."

"I don't think that's going to help," Nate warns.

Dante scoffs. "It always helps."

I STUMBLE INTO the living room, collapsing down onto the couch. I'm not sure what time it is, or what day.

My eyes immediately shut when I reach the couch, my head spinning out of control.

Fucking Dante.

When he got the tequila out, I knew I should have said no, but the argument with Caitlyn hit me and I grabbed the bottle, taking a hefty swig.

Now, everything is a blur. The room spins, and as my head lolls to the side, I glance at the half naked bodies on the floor.

"Caitlyn," I grumble, regretting our argument.

I want to go to her, but I know in this state, I won't make it out the door. I need to tell her I think I'm in love with her, that I miss what we shared.

"I can be Caitlyn."

A warm hand presses against my bare chest and I stop fighting to keep my eyes open and enjoy the sensation. "Caitlyn," I whisper.

"That's right," I hear whispered, but the voice doesn't belong to Caitlyn.

At least, I think it doesn't.

"You told me to go," I slur.

"I don't want you to go anywhere," she tells me, kissing the corner of my mouth.

Her scent is all wrong. Even in my drunken slumber, I know this doesn't feel right.

"Stop," I growl, reaching for the person sitting on my lap. Feeling bare skin, I open my eyes, finding double of everything. "Fuck!"

"Yes," she hisses, rubbing herself against me. And even drunk, my body responds.

"No," I snap, pushing her away.

"Hey now, baby. I wanna make you feel good," she tells me, her voice loud against my ear, causing me to wince. She lifts her hand, pressing it against her bare breast. "Yes!"

"Fuck!" I growl, pushing her away.

She squeals, grabbing onto my hands before she falls to the floor. It causes her to rub against me, and I groan, wishing I could control my body's reaction. She leans forward, rubbing her tits in my face. "You want me."

"Not interested," I mumble, trying to get off the sofa, but I'm pushed back and with little energy, I fall, my eyelids drooping as I fight to stay awake.

A hand reaches between us, and I feel something at the button of my jeans.

"Come on, let me suck this big cock of yours and make it all better," she rasps.

No, this isn't right.

Why isn't this right?

Caitlyn.

"No," I growl, fighting to stay conscious. "Caitlyn!"

She brings my hand up to her boob again and I use it to push her away, but it only causes her to thrust down on me and a moan slips free.

"That's it," she whispers, and in my foggy brain, I wonder if she's slurring too.

"I said fucking no," I snap, but she ignores me, rubbing herself against me.

"Fuck off," I growl, twisting my hips, but she moans, rubbing herself harder against me.

I wiggle, trying to buck her off, but instead, her pussy straddles my thigh and I feel her rubbing herself against me.

Her moans grow louder, and I slump back against the sofa, the alcohol pulling me under.

Her scream jerks me awake, and just as I think I'm imagining it, I feel lips press against my chest, working their way down my stomach.

"I'm going to make you feel good. It can be our secret."

"Fuck off!" I growl, my hand connecting with her face as I push her away. I hear her stumble to the floor, and I grimace, hoping I didn't hurt her.

I need Caitlyn.

I need to make this right.

"W-what?"

"Caitlyn," I whisper, right before the darkness pulls me under.

Chapter Twenty-One

CAITLYN

AFTER A NIGHT SPENT TOSSING AND turning after waking up from a nightmare, I'm exhausted. Beyond exhausted. It's like I can't rest my mind for a single moment.

And I know why.

I regret everything last night and now I'm scared I can't fix it. I had hoped I would have heard from him by now, but it has been radio silent. And if it wasn't for Nate not turning up, I would have thought there was a chance, but it seems likely they are done with me, with us.

Nate normally accompanies me to work, following me around each cabin, but he wasn't there when I woke up. And I don't blame him. He was only there because of Cage. I can't expect him to stick around after what I did last night. It hurts because I didn't just come to care for Cage. I care for them all.

I caved once Carrie woke and was upset Cage wasn't there. So, I sent him a message, explaining how sorry I was, but I stared at the phone until I had to leave, and I got no reply.

If I could just speak to him, I could get him to understand why I said what I said.

"She okay?" Hayley asks, watching Carrie storm into the house, sulking.

"Yeah, Cage, um, he wasn't there this morning, but she'll be okay. I promised to take her to the cinema after work tomorrow since I won't have time between shifts," I admit, tucking a strand of hair behind my ear. It was the only way I could get her to calm down, but she went from crying, to sulking.

"You look tired, honey," she states. "Do you need me to get someone to cover your shift?"

I wave her off and force a smile. "It's okay. I'll speak to you later."

She nods, biting her bottom lip as she watches me rush off. When I round the corner, I take in a deep breath, composing myself.

I head towards Nate's, hoping if I start the clean-up in that cabin, I will get a chance to bump into Cage—unless he's gone to work.

My steps are brisk as I race to get there, glad it's still early. If he isn't there, I'm going to leave a message with Nate.

As I come to a stand outside Nate's cabin, my nerves begin to flutter inside of me. What if he doesn't want to see me again? Am I making a fool out of myself?

Knocking on the door, I take a step back, but when I get no answer, I step forward, unlocking it using my master key.

As soon as I step into the room, my stomach revolts. The smell of stale alcohol lingers in the air, along with some serious bad odour. Striding over to the front room, I take in the half naked women and a couple of men, my heart stuttering in my chest.

Movement from the couch catches my attention. I slap my hand over my mouth at what I see, covering the cry ready to slip free.

Cage.

Cage is slumped over to the side, his chest bare whilst his hand is pushed inside a woman's knickers, gripping her arse.

"No," I whisper, my heart tearing apart.

The blond bimbo moans as she snuggles closer to him. My knees lock together, and I freeze, unable to look away from the scene in front of me. I reach out, grabbing the doorframe beside me when my legs threaten to give out. It feels like I have been stabbed in the gut. It wasn't even twelve hours ago that he was buried deep inside me, before he moved on to another woman.

And I did this. I pushed him to this.

In my peripheral vision, I catch movement, and I jerk to find Nate stepping into the room. He jerks to a stop, his eyes taking in the room before they land on Cage. He grimaces before turning to me, his expression pained.

"It's not what it looks like," he swears, stepping closer.

"It's not what it looks like?" I ask, my eyes widening as I take another look at them on the couch.

The one good thing to happen to me since Carrie and I ruined it. I pushed him into the arms of another woman.

And it isn't what it looks like?

He doesn't want me.

"It's not," he promises.

Is he not seeing what I'm seeing?

"I think I'm going to be sick," I tell him.

He takes a step towards me, but movement from the couch has us both freezing. Cage groans, but it turns into a moan as he presses the woman closer to him. "Caitlyn?"

Caitlyn?

"I'm Jemma, dickhead," the woman groans.

His eyelids fly open, and he stares in horror at the woman in front of him. He shoots up, pushing her to the floor with a thud.

A whimper escapes my lips when I see she doesn't have a top or bra on.

"Hey!" she snaps, covering up her breasts.

"What the fuck!" he yells, wincing from the noise.

I should rejoice in his pain, but I can't. All I can see is him and her.

"Jesus, keep it down," she snaps.

"Yeah, some of us are trying to sleep," another person in the room grumbles.

"Who the fuck are you?" Cage growls. "Why were you next to me?"

She opens her mouth to answer, but I take a step back, knocking over a vase while trying to make my escape. Another whimper slips free.

Cage's gaze shoots to mine, and horror washes over him. "Kitten?"

He turns his attention back to the woman, then to me, and he jerks like he's been slapped.

I open my mouth to tell him where to go, but I can't. I can't find the words to say to him.

I came here to apologise.

Not for this.

Last night, I was fooling myself in thinking I could protect my heart by keeping an emotional distance.

I was already invested.

Too invested.

And for the first time in my life, I'm experiencing true heart break.

"It's not what it looks like," he tells me, using the same words Nate threw at me earlier.

He trips over a bottle on the floor trying to get to me and I use that to race out of the cabin.

"Caitlyn," Nate roars.

I stop, turning to face him, seeing him through the tears blurring my vision.

"Don't. And don't come after me," I warn him, a sob tearing through me.

He listens, taking another step inside, and I hear him yelling at Cage, but I don't stick around. I want to go back to my cabin, to get into bed and forget about the last few weeks, but I can't. He will know where to look for me.

Instead, I grab my work supplies off my cart and race towards a cabin, hoping my job will help me forget.

MY FEET DRAG as I enter the last cabin of the day. It has been just over an hour of sobbing into toilets, rubbish bins and the dust cloth. All I want to do is get Carrie and call it a day. I don't even have the energy to go to work tonight.

I can't keep my mind off what I walked in on.

Pushing open the door, I sigh with relief that the place is already empty. All it needs is a once over for the guests arriving later today.

I make quick work of going over the kitchen and living area. It isn't until I reach the main bathroom that the hairs on the nape of my neck stand on end, like a feeling someone is watching me.

Playing it off due to the stress of the morning, I give everything a wipe down, loading the toilet roll and placing out new towels.

The feeling doesn't go and when I enter the bedroom, my day turns from bad to weird. Rose petals are scattered over the bed.

My eyebrows pull together as I check my chart, making sure I have the right cabin. I don't want to be walking into a romantic surprise and ruining it. Normally, Hayley would inform me if a request like this was made and usually, it was more who organised it.

Looking over the chart, it clearly states that the guests arrive later on this evening. I bite my bottom lip, wondering if someone else had been in here, but then spot a vase of roses next to the bed, a card resting against it.

Stepping closer to get a better look, I freeze when I see my name. *No, no, no.*

My hands shake as I reach for the card similar to the one we found in Carrie's room.

Caitlyn, I'm coming for you, princess. Be ready. You were warned. I'm a man of my word, and Robin wants to meet with you.

See you soon, K x

The letter once again isn't signed, only marked with the letter K. I feel my skin prickle as I re-read the note. This was the man who attacked me, the one who was in my daughter's room.

My entire body trembles with fear, the fight leaving me.

Why couldn't he leave us alone? Why go to this much trouble when he knows I won't speak out if he does?

We were never going to be safe.

Not then. Not now.

A sobs rattles through my chest and I collapse to the bed as my legs give out. Twice today my world has shattered. Twice today the rug has been pulled out from under me.

It isn't a reminder that Robin can get to me, that he can touch me whenever he likes; he's doing this to taunt me, to torture me until I break.

And it's working.

I'm tired of fighting him, tired of running.

I have little fight left inside of me. With everything that's happened, I have little energy to pull myself up.

I'm dispensable to everyone. Hayley can get a new cleaner. Roy can get a new barmaid.

And as much as it pains me, Carrie can get another parent to love her. Maybe not as much as me, but she can. And they could probably open up a new world for her, one I haven't been able to give her.

And after last night's revelation, it isn't because I'm keeping her safe. It's because I'm scared.

So damn fucking scared.

There is no one else who cares about me, not really, and the people that could have, or might have, I pushed into another woman's arms. He went to the next woman so easily. He didn't try to work it out; he didn't compromise or give me a chance.

Because I'm not worth it.

I close my eyes, tears slipping free as the shame of my thoughts hit me.

You have people here who love you.

Cage's words are like a hammer to the heart. It crushes it, and I cry out, the pain unbearable.

The burden I carry only grows much heavier. If I pull them in close, I'm putting them in danger. Robin will use them as my weakness, and it will work. It's the same with Cage, the one person I fell for, and he's willing to protect me.

I couldn't bear it if one of them were to get hurt because of me.

I clutch the pillow in my arms, sobbing uncontrollably.

"Courtney, please, please tell me what to do," I cry out.

My sobs fill the air and I clutch the pillow tighter.

I have never felt so alone in my life.

I fucked everything up, done it all wrong.

And now I'm paying the price.

"Courtney, I wish you were here," I choke out, crying until the tears dry and the tiredness pulls me under, my heart praying that when I wake up, the last twenty-four hours is nothing but a dream.

Chapter Twenty-Two

CAGE

"Look, you need to calm down. Caitlyn will listen to you if you tell her what happened."

"Calm down? I was lying half naked with another fucking girl in my arms. Even if I do explain that shit to her, she isn't going to forgive me. I saw the look on her face, arsehole. She looked like her whole world just got torn from her. She looked devastated beyond belief. Who the fuck is that chick?"

The woman in question walks in, fully dressed this time. "I'm so sorry. I'm Jemma. I had too much to drink last night and I get horny when I'm drunk. I swear, I thought you were my fiancé. We like to role play."

I choke on air. "Did we?"

She holds her hands up, shaking her head. "No, I, um… I got off. I think."

"What?" I roar, turning to Nate. "Who the fuck is she?"

"She's the bride-to-be, man. You were passed out on the kitchen counter when I went to bed. She was on the sofa. Clothed."

"I sleep naked," Jemma replies.

"Not now," Nate mutters before turning back to me. "I couldn't put you in my room. I had a couple of chicks in there."

I take a step forward, ready to punch him, but Jemma's next words stop me. "Nothing happened. Not like that. I kind of rubbed myself against you. Unless I was dreaming. I got off, and I remember trying to go down on you, but you pushed me off. I can't remember getting on the sofa again. But I swear, nothing happened."

"You were in no state to get your jeans back on, so she's probably right."

"I know I am," she bites out. "Once he pushed me off, I came to my senses, realised he wasn't my fiancé or all that into it and fell asleep on the floor. I'm not sure how I got back on the sofa."

"Can you guarantee that because that was my woman who walked in on us and I'm not going to lie to her."

"You were pissed. You probably couldn't even muster a hard on," Nate mutters.

"Oh, he did, but it wasn't fully hard," Jemma announces.

I grit my teeth and glare at her. "Get the fuck out of my face. I don't think trying to fuck someone incoherent and inebriated is something to be proud of."

"I wasn't… we didn't—"

I close my eyes, remembering pushing her off. "Because I pushed you off."

She beams. "You remember?"

"That I do."

She nods. "Yeah, so you know nothing went beyond my embarrassing attempt to seduce you. Well, my fiancé."

Nate sighs, running a hand down his face. "This is so fucked up."

A redhead stumbles through the front door, looking a little green. She grips Jemma's arm. "We need to get back."

"Why are you walking funny? And where have you been?"

"You know the large guy with the tattoos?"

"Dante?" Nate asks, stepping forward.

The redhead nods, her face paling. "He has a monster cock, and just when I thought it was over, he was back inside of me. If it wasn't for the fact he gave me a lecture about not using Viagra, I would have thought he had taken a packet."

Nate chuckles. "Yeah, he doesn't need that."

"Really?" Jemma asks, her lips parting.

The redhead whimpers. "My vagina is so fucking sore."

Jemma grins, holding her hand up. The redhead high fives her as a growl erupts from my lips, my lethal gaze boring into them.

"Fucking leave."

Redhead whimpers, jumping back. Jemma blushes and takes her friend's hand.

"Come on, let's go." They head for the door, but Jemma stops at the door. "I really am sorry, and if you would like me to explain everything to her, I don't mind."

"I think you've done enough," I bite out and wait until she leaves before turning to Nate. "What the fuck am I going to do?"

"Mate, tell her the truth."

"It's not just about this morning. I said some uncalled-for shit to her last night. I meant it, but not the way it came out. She's the best fucking person and mother I know, Nate. I don't want her to think she's not taking care of her girl, when she is doing a great job. I just wanted her to understand that all I want is to protect her and Carrie. If anything happened to them it would kill me. I don't even know when my feelings got so invested in them both. It's all messed up." I take a deep breath, clutching my head. "What sort of man gets infatuated with a woman the minute they meet? The whole situation is foreign to me. I've never had an argument like that with a chick, apart from with Lou. Even then, it was to tell her to stop being such a bitch and a psycho."

"Lou's different because you didn't give a fuck about her. With Caitlyn, you do, mate. Go get changed, you can borrow some of my clothes so you can take a shower here, and please go now, because you fucking stink."

"Nice," I say sarcastically. "I need to go and find her, explain what happened."

He places a hand on my chest, stopping me. She left twenty minutes ago now, and it's killing me. I just needed answers from the blonde bitch first, but she had locked herself in the bathroom before I got a chance.

"Mate, there is nothing you can do or say right now to make this better. Let her calm down for a bit."

"I can't do that," I tell him.

"I'm not going to let you work her up even more, man. She was fucking broken out there. I saw it. What you need to do is take a fucking shower, let her finish her shift and then go speak to her."

"Last night you were forcing me to go see her."

He lips twist. "That was before she saw you wake up with a blonde in your arms and your hands in her knickers."

I pull at my hair, growling. "Fuck!"

"Just give her time."

"Till the end of her shift," I warn him.

"Now can you please go shower."

I stomp off down the hall, praying like hell she listens to me and forgives me. I can't make excuses for last night. I put myself in that position by getting in that state. It could have been a lot worse. As images flicker through my head, I remember touching her, feeling her rub herself against me. And I feel ashamed to admit that had this happened before Caitlyn, I wouldn't have hesitated to fuck her.

But I have Caitlyn. I know what it feels like to have her, and I wouldn't fuck that up.

Still, I hate that she had to witness it, but I swear once I go to her, I'm going to tell her everything, let her know I fucked up and I'm sorry. For all of it. For spewing all that crap at her and for the woman I woke up with.

I might be a dickhead at times, but there's one thing I've never done. Cheated on a woman.

I'm not going to start now.

I PACE THE length of the kitchen floor, my phone in hand. It has been two hours since Caitlyn finished work and I've heard nothing from her. I've sent over a dozen messages and called, much to Nate's dismay. He still thinks she needs more time.

I can't give her time though. I need to sort this out now, especially when I finally charged my phone and saw a message from her early this morning.

I'm sorry. Please, please forgive me. I didn't mean it.

I was so fucking stupid. I should have listened to Nate last night and gone back because now this may be truly done. And the longer she believes something happened with that woman, the worse it's going to get.

"Have you seen her?" I ask Nate, who I forced to check over her security cameras while he had the live feed on the other screen.

"Dude, I'm telling you, she needs time to calm down. You go in there, guns blazing, she isn't going to listen. Trust me, I watched it happen with my mum and dad."

He's right, but then he isn't. We aren't his parents. We don't have years of marriage to tie us together. We only have weeks, and with the way she doesn't easily attach to people, I probably don't stand another chance.

My ringtone blares through the kitchen and I answer without looking at the screen.

"Caitlyn," I greet.

"No, it's Roy," he mutters, drawing his words out. "It's actually Caitlyn I'm calling about. Hayley just called me, and she hasn't been back to pick Carrie up. She normally picks her up after her shift then brings her back later on tonight. She should have finished work two and a half hours ago. She only had to do the right side of the lot today as the left is empty for a few days."

I grip the counter and Nate looks up, watching me warily. "What?"

"I said—"

"I know what you said, Roy. What I mean is, why the fuck didn't you ring me sooner?"

"Well, I thought she would be with you or Nate," he states.

I run a hand down my face. "No. We had an argument last night over something stupid. I stormed out, then this morning…" I stop myself before I can finish the sentence. I don't want him to know I fucked up. I like my dick where it is.

"What the fuck did you do?" he growls.

Shit.

"Look, it was a misunderstanding. Caitlyn walked in on some chick half naked asleep on me."

"She what, boy?" he roars.

Fuck!

"Calm down before you give yourself a heart attack, old man," I demand calmly. "Nothing happened. It was a misunderstanding on the woman's part. She thought I was someone else, into something else, but before she could actually do anything, I pushed her off. I was fucking out of it, but I know I didn't willingly do anything."

"And you expect me to believe that?" he grits out.

"I don't care what you believe. It's the truth." I shift the phone to the other side. "Can I have my head back now or do you need to chew me out some more?" I mutter dryly.

"So, she could be anywhere?"

"Yeah," I admit, my shoulders sagging.

"It's not like her to forget Carrie, Cage. Remember, after the attack she still got up and collected Carrie. This isn't like her. I don't like it," he murmurs, and I can hear the worry pouring down the line.

"Fuck," I growl, stomping over to where Nate was working. Roy is right, nothing would stop Caitlyn from getting her daughter, not even a broken heart. "Have you still got Caitlyn's camera feeds on there?"

"Yes, it's been on the screen in the corner while I've been working through this morning's feeds. Apart from when she left this morning with Carrie, she hasn't been back. And the only person who's been there was Roy not long ago."

"Did you hear that?" I ask Roy.

"Yeah. I was looking for her. Which is why I called you. I've just reached the cabin she should have cleaned first. I'm going to follow her routine, see if I can find her at one of them. I'm hoping she may have been held up by something," he admits before letting out a weary sigh. "I swear to God, Cage, if something has happened to her, I will cut your fucking dick off then feed it to you. Meet me at the east side cabins. She usually starts there."

I don't even get a chance to say anything before he hangs up.

Nate stands, grabbing his phone. "What's going on? Has something happened?"

"Caitlyn hasn't been back to Hayley's to collect Carrie. She was meant to finish earlier than usual today, so they're both worried. It's not like her."

"Come on then, let's go. Oh, and Cage, if anything has happened to her…"

"Yeah, yeah, you'll cut my dick off. Got it," I growl, slamming the cabin door shut behind us.

Chapter Twenty-Three

CAGE

WE'VE BEEN WALKING FROM CABIN to cabin for the last hour, asking the occupants if they've had their cabins cleaned this morning. Most have said yes, but then there are some on the list that are vacant, which we needed a key for. Now we're on the last one, where the guests didn't turn up, even though they paid for the room in advance. Roy pushes open the front door, gesturing for us to enter the dark cabin.

All the curtains have been drawn, blocking out the sun shining outside. It's eerily quiet and the hairs on the nape of my neck stand on end.

Turning the corner, I see her cleaning supplies near the bathroom door. I run over, with Roy and Nate following, and I push the through the door.

"She's not here," I mutter, walking back out.

Turning towards the master bedroom, I notice a dark figure on the bed. Nate notices too and turns to Roy.

"Flick the hallway light on," he whispers.

My body jerks like I've been hit when I see it's her lying on the bed. She's curled up in a protective ball, her cheeks bright red and under her eyes puffy.

And she's fast asleep.

What worries and concerns me are the rose petals beneath and surrounding her.

There is a bouquet on the bedside table, but that seems to be a whole bunch, so whoever scattered the rose petals brought extra.

"Maybe she was tired," Nate comments.

I hum under my breath and take a step closer, spotting a piece of paper tucked securely in her hand. I gently pull it from her grip, careful not to wake her.

My jaw clenches when I realise what it is. It's another threat, and I have to wonder what he's waiting for. He had the opportunity to take her, just like he had with Carrie, but he's biding his time. I would have thought if it were for the information, they would have used Carrie to get it. There's nothing she wouldn't exchange for her daughter and Robin must know that.

Guilt shames me. I left her unguarded all day. If I hadn't walked out, or if I had just gone back like Nate had told me to, then she would have been with Nate today. Instead, he was with me, trying to sort my shit out.

I hand the note over to Nate, who makes a noise in the back of his throat when he reads it. I know what he's thinking without him saying it, and I don't blame him. This is completely my fault; I should have handled last night better. I place my hand gently on Caitlyn's arm, giving her a light shake. She stirs, mumbling something under her breath. I try again, but this time she shoots up, knocking her forehead against my jaw. I hiss out a breath when my teeth clamp down on my tongue.

"What the ..." she grumbles before flinching and opening her mouth to scream.

"Shhh, Kitten, it's me. I'm with Nate and Roy. We came looking for you," I tell her, pulling her into my arms.

She clings to me so tight I feel like my oxygen is being cut off. I don't say this though; I just let her hold me while I hold her back in return.

"I'm sorry," she chokes out. "I didn't mean it; I do need you, but not just to keep us safe. I want you, all of you. I love being here. I don't want to leave you, Roy or Hayley, or anyone else. I'm so sorry for the things I said."

"No, Caitlyn, I'm sorry. I understand where you were coming from. I just wanted you to understand how much I want you to stay to fight this. What I said was wrong and uncalled for. You're everything to Carrie. She needs you, but she needs other people too."

"I know. I'm sorry. I know you didn't mean any harm with what you were trying to tell me. You were just being there for us. I was being stubborn and stupid; saying things that I didn't mean."

"It's fine, baby," I murmur softly.

She tenses for a minute, pulling back. She avoids meeting my gaze.

"No, it's not. You moved on and I understand why. I come with too much baggage, so I don't blame you for wanting to," she whispers.

Although I would have preferred to have this conversation without Roy and Nate in the room, it needs to be said.

"Kitten, what you saw this morning wasn't what you thought. Well, maybe it was, but you got the wrong idea. Nothing happened," I admit.

"I saw—"

"I know what you saw," I tell her, my voice low. "When I got to

Nate's last night, he was having a party. The bride-to-be was already passed out on the couch when I arrived. Me and Nate went into the kitchen and had a drink. Which led to more drinks." When her breath hitches and tears begin to roll down her cheeks, I pause, wiping them away. "Nate left me in the kitchen, where I had passed out over the counter, but at some point during the night, I must have got up to find somewhere else to sleep."

"With that girl?" she asks, her lip trembling.

I force a smile. "It's all a blur but I swear I was looking for you. It doesn't change anything. I ended up on the sofa and the woman thought I was her fiancé. They, um, like to role play and she was fucked up. Nothing sexual happened on my end. I didn't touch her, but not for lack of her trying. I pushed her off and she got the hint. She said she fell back asleep on the floor but somehow ended up in my arms again. I don't remember much, but I know I didn't touch her like that."

"You didn't?"

"No, kitten. I would never do that to you, or anyone. I was fucked and was pretty out of it, but even in that state I knew she wasn't you. She even offered to speak to you before she left. She felt bad," I tell her. "I was being a dickhead last night. I let my stubbornness keep me from coming back to you."

"You left though."

"Because you asked me to and because we were getting loud. I didn't want to wake Carrie up and scare her."

"And nothing happened?" she whispers.

"No, I swear to you. If something did, I wouldn't be here," I begin, my lips twisting when I glance at Nate and Roy. "I would be at the hospital getting my dick sewn back on."

She chuckles lightly, wiping under her eyes.

"I'm sorry for the things I said," she tells me.

"It's okay. Believe it or not, I understand now where it was coming from," I admit.

Nate steps over to the window, pulling back the curtains to let some light in.

Which reminds me. "Why were you cleaning in complete darkness?" I ask, helping her sit up straighter.

"I wasn't. I mean…." Her brows pull together. "They were open when I came in and started cleaning. Then I came in to do this room and I saw the roses and the note… oh God, the note," she cries out, her eyes wide.

"We got it, girl," Nate declares.

"He isn't going to give up," she states, her breathing deep and heavy. "He's not going to stop."

"Calm down. We are going to sort this," I promise her. "I shouldn't have left you to come into work by yourself. I'm sorry, Caitlyn. I just wanted to give you time, you didn't need me getting in your space, it won't happen again."

She closes her eyes for a moment, catching her breath. "It's not your fault. I would have gotten the note either way. It wouldn't have mattered who was with me."

"What do you mean?" I ask, sharing a look with Nate who shrugs in return.

"The note was already here. It was like the room had been set up for me to receive that note. The roses, the petals on the bed and the note resting against the vase," she states, but then pauses, her lips puckering and her brows pulling together. "None of the curtains were drawn though."

I share another look with Nate, who reads me easily when he pulls his phone out. The guy was here while she was asleep.

"Oh my God, he was here, wasn't he?" she declares, looking from Nate to me. "He was here whilst I was sleeping."

I rub the back of my neck. "Most likely. If you didn't draw the curtains, then he must have. The curtains are drawn throughout the cabin, not just in here."

"I never did that. They were all open. Oh my God. He could have touched me. He might have… oh my God," she cries, wiping furiously down her body like it will remove his touch. That's when I see something white sticking out from the front pocket of her jeans. I lean over to pull it out. Caitlyn freezes and glances down, her eyes widening at the piece of paper I have between my fingers.

I lean back and unfold the note, frowning at the words. 'Look under the pillow," I read it out loud.

We both go for the pillow to find another white envelope. With shaky hands, Caitlyn reaches it and passes it to me. "I-I can't. Not again," she whispers and takes a step back into Roy, letting him hold her.

I pull out the card, but something flutters down to the floor. Caitlyn bends down before I can and her breath hitches. "What is it?" I ask.

"It's a picture of me," she whispers, her voice trembling. "I think I'm going to be sick."

"Hang in there," Roy orders, holding her close.

I take the picture from her before she shoves her face into his neck, sobbing uncontrollably. I glance down, anger pumping through my views. It's of Caitlyn lying on the bed in the same position we found her in. Only this time, a knife is held to her throat. She's completely unaware.

I'm going to fucking kill him when I find him.

Nate hisses out a breath when I pass the picture to him. "Fuck!"

I glance down at the other note, this time not reading it out loud.

Next time, I'm tying you to the bed and fucking the confession of where the information is out of you. Then that knife is going to slice through your neck. Last warning. K x

Caitlyn lifts her head from Roy's shoulder, her tears still streaming down her cheeks. "What? What does it say?"

Nate steps out of the room, taking both the note and the picture with him.

"Trust me, you don't want to know, Kitten," I warn her.

"I need to know," she tells me, a plea to her tone. "What does it say?"

"Pretty much what the other said," I lie.

"You're lying to me," she accuses.

"Yeah, but for your own good. I promise I would tell you, but given your current night terrors, and with that picture now burnt into your brain, I'm not giving you something else to worry about. I'll take care of this, okay?"

"Okay," she agrees.

"Come on, let's go get Carrie, then head back home," I order, pulling her into my arms.

She rests her cheek against my chest. "Okay," she murmurs.

"You can have the night off, girl," Roy declares, nudging her under the chin.

"No, I need to keep my mind off things. I need to be there. I promise I'll be fine. If I'm not, I'll let you know. Okay?"

"Okay," Roy agrees reluctantly.

We step outside just as Nate puts the phone down to someone. He turns, his cold gaze meeting mine, and I know this isn't good.

"Need a word," he murmurs, gripping the picture in his hand.

I nod and turn to Roy. "Take Caitlyn with you. I'll meet you back at yours when I've finished speaking to Nate."

He gently pulls Caitlyn to him, gritting his teeth as his gaze flickers from the picture. "See you in a bit, boys."

Whoever this Kane guy is, he's messed with the wrong person this time. If he thinks he can get to her, he's got another thing coming. He will have to get through all of this.

"We're going?" Caitlyn asks, and turns to me, startled. I don't think she realised I handed her off to Roy.

"Yeah. I need you to go with Roy while I speak to Nate. I'll be there in a bit, okay?" She still looks lost, and it's killing me. I walk over, pressing my lips to hers. "I promise I won't be long."

"Okay," she whispers and let's Roy steer her away.

I turn back to Nate, giving him my full attention once they are out of sight.

"What's going on?"

"That was Darius on the phone. He spoke to his boss, Dean, and they've found someone we can trust."

"Who?" I ask, hope filling my chest.

"A detective called Rome. Apparently, he's already been working on building a case against Robin."

"How are we just hearing about this?"

Nate runs a hand over his jaw. "Because it's been kept on the down-low. He noticed whenever Robin's name came up, evidence disappeared, or his bosses or colleagues avoided filing an investigation. It doesn't take a rocket scientist to realise that's because whoever goes against this guy ends up dead.

"This guy, Rome, has an informant who works for Robin. Together they've been working on building a case."

"Then why do you look like this isn't good news?" I ask, feeling like the rug was about to be pulled out from under me.

"Because his informant hasn't checked in. He hasn't shown up in over a week and he's worried. He has a list of who he thinks or knows is under Robin's payroll."

"So, Robin could already know about him?"

He shrugs. "I don't know. He's been careful. Dean told Darius that Rome has connections with people who are willing to take the case to court as soon as they have the evidence to do so," he explains. "What do you want to do?"

"I think we need to check out this Rome guy first to see if what Darius says is true. It's better to be safe than sorry. If everything you find pans out, get in touch with him and set up a meet," I order. "I'll talk to Kitten tonight about the evidence, see if she's ready to give it up. I think we are going to need to take some huge precautions from now on with this guy lurking around. If he catches on to what we're doing and the evidence doesn't make it to the right people, we're screwed."

"I'll get straight on it," he promises. "Get back to Caitlyn. I'll be back around seven to take her to work. Are you looking after Carrie tonight or is she staying over with Roy and Hayley?"

"I think I'm going to spend the night with her. She was pretty upset before bed last night."

"What do you mean?"

I rub the back of my neck. "She wants a dad and I think having me around made her think I was. Then she thought I didn't want to be her dad. It was pretty messed up."

When I filled him on everything last night, I skipped out the part where Carrie asked if I could be her dad. I didn't need another lecture from him.

He looks stunned for a moment. "What did you say to her?"

"Just that, for the time being, I was Cage, she was Carrie, and Mummy was Mummy. That, at a later date, we could talk about it again. I don't want to make her promises in case I can't keep them. As strongly as I feel towards Caitlyn at the moment, none of us know our future. And it's too soon for anything like that. I still feel shit though."

"She's a great kid, Cage. If this were any other situation, I would tell you not to let her call you dad when you aren't biologically her dad. Hell, you've not even known them that long to be that figure in her life," he explains. "But something like that can get messy. Like you said, she's a kid. Either way, it's gonna hurt and confuse her."

"I know. It's a struggle because she has a way of making you want to give her everything."

He chuckles. "You are good with her. With both of them. I'm not gonna lie, when I see you with them, you're different. It's like she's pulled out the best parts of you. They both do. But just be careful. She's young, so fucking young, and it could impact her for life."

"I know. I don't want to hurt her."

"I know. I can see you've got feelings for them both. I see the way you are with Carrie," he states, before slapping me down on the shoulder. "Either way it doesn't affect me. I'll always be Uncle Nate and I love it."

"Fucking prick," I grumble, yet can't help the smile that tugs at my lips.

"Right, I'll get back and find out what I can in the few hours I have before I come to get Caitlyn. I can take the laptop while she works; it just means finding a spot away from Caitlyn in the back, where no one can see the screen," he warns me.

"Whatever you need to do, brother," I tell him, trusting him to take care of her. "If it helps, I can ask Roy for permission to set up the camera feeds to your laptop. That way you can see who is coming and going without worrying where to sit." I pause, something else occurring to me. "And you won't need to worry about Caitlyn leaving the bar. She's only allowed to move away from the bar to go into the office or out on the floor to collect glasses. She has no reason to go anywhere else."

"All right, I'll catch you later," he murmurs, already scanning his phone as he leaves.

"See ya," I call out and he lifts his hand in a salute.

As I make my way to Roy's, I have to believe we can end this. And soon. Because I want to build a future with Caitlyn, with Carrie.

I finally have something truly good in my life, and I'm not about to let it get taken away from me.

I spent years with women using me or me using them. None of them were right. And although there was a time—a short time—when I thought Lou was the one, she wasn't. Even at the beginning I had doubts.

With Caitlyn, I have none. She is all I can see.

All I want.

Chapter Twenty-Four

CAITLYN

THE DAY HAS DRAGGED, AND AS I finish putting my hair up, I can't help but look longingly at the bed. I'm exhausted, even after sleeping the day away, and I think it's because of everything that happened with Cage, then the new notes.

Pulling myself up, I head to the dresser, grabbing my work clothes, memories of the day fluttering through my mind.

I had to paste on a happy face for Carrie but inside, I felt like I was dying. *Will I ever be strong enough to protect her?*

She must have picked up on the tension because she glued herself to my side or Cage's the entire day.

I hadn't realised just how attached she had grown to him until he returned from his conversation with Nate. She raced over to him, rattling off a bunch of questions as to where he had been and if he was coming back with us.

He did. And together, they both pulled my mind off my nightmare of a life. We had lunch, then spent the day in front of the television watching movies, one being *Frozen*.

Even with the distraction, I could see Cage wasn't as okay as he seemed. Every now and then I would find him watching me, like he was waiting for me to break down again.

I didn't.

I knew the woman from this morning was also playing on his mind, because he kept asking if I was okay with us, like he needed it confirmed.

And it was.

I hadn't realised it, but I naively forgave him before I even knew the truth. I wasn't sure why, but I did. Whether that was because deep down I knew I misunderstood what I saw, I don't know. I just did.

But I couldn't deny the relief I felt when I found out nothing happened. Not because of him anyway. When he brought it up when Carrie fell asleep, he told me how she rubbed herself against him, that he was pissed at himself for getting in a state that he put himself in that position. I believed him though. I believed him down to my core that he wouldn't intentionally hurt me or cheat on me.

The bedroom door opening brings me out of my thoughts, and I glance up to Cage stomping inside, flopping down on the bed.

He pouts up at me. "Are you sure you're okay to go to work?"

I finish getting dressed. "Yes, I'm fine. Can you please stop worrying? Nate is going to be there, and so is Roy. It will be okay."

"That's not the only reason I don't want you to go. You've had a bad day, and I had a major part to play in that."

"I said I believed you and it wasn't just you," I tell him, giving him a pointed look.

"I want you here. I want to make it up to you."

I sigh, sitting down on the bed next to him. "You can't keep doing this to yourself. You can't protect me from everything that happens."

"But I want to," he declares. "You've been through so much stress today. I don't want something happening in work that makes it all come rushing forward. It's not good for you."

"I'll be fine," I assure him. "I know you think I'm not dealing with this, that I'm ignoring it, but it's not like that. I've been dealing with this for so long, Cage. I had my breakdown earlier and now I'm going to push through this. I've always been like this."

He cups my jaw, his pupils dilating. "You might think that's how you deal, but it isn't. You might not think about it during the day, but it comes to you in your nightmares."

"I have to be okay for Carrie," I whisper, unable to meet his gaze. "I'm all she has. I can't afford to break. I need to keep some kind of normalcy for her."

He sighs and for a moment, I think he's going to argue. "Alright, Kitten, normalcy it is," he declares. "Get your sexy arse outside because Nate is here."

I lean over, pressing my lips to his before pulling back and smiling. "I'll be fine."

His gaze heats. "Yeah, you will be."

IT'S AN HOUR into work when the new worker, Kelly, turns up for her first shift. My first impression of her is a good one.

Thank God!

The chick I tried to train a few days ago didn't make it to a second shift. She wasn't a social person and was rude and incompetent taking a standard order.

Kelly, however, was already proving to be a good fit. She arrived ten minutes early, giving me enough time to get her outfitted in our uniform.

Her blonde hair is pulled to the side in a fishtail braid, her makeup light since she doesn't look like she needs it.

She's gorgeous, and I have to wonder what she's doing working in a place like this. It isn't a dive, but it also isn't a posh establishment, somewhere I think Kelly would fit in better.

"Are you sure that's her?" I ask Derek, the barman.

"Sure is," he states, before moving off to serve a customer.

Heading around the bar, I meet her on the other side, smiling as I greet her. "Hi, I'm Caitlyn, the assistant manager."

"Kelly," she introduces, shaking my hand. "It's lovely to meet you."

Polite and formal. I like.

"Let me show you around the bar, then I'll go through everything you need to know," I tell her. "Then we can put you to work. Sound good?"

"Perfect. I've worked at a bar before, so drinks won't be a problem."

"That's fantastic," I reply, before pointing into the mini kitchen we have. "That is the kitchen. We don't have much in there since the restaurant is next door and handles all that. It's mostly storage and has all the glass washers. The main storage room is through the door at the end of the bar."

She nods, taking it all in as I point to the next room that she doesn't really need to go in. "That is the office. Roy mostly uses it so if you need anything, you can go there or come to me if I'm on."

"Okay," she agrees and follows me behind the bar.

"You'll find pint glasses down here on the bottom shelves, wine glasses above you. There are three tills. You'll be designated your own, unless it's packed, which means we have more staff working.

Then you'll share," I explain and pull out the piece of paper with her log in. "Here is your login code. You can set up your password now."

She types in the code, then I glance away, waiting for her to set up a password. "Done."

"The rest is self-explanatory. Beer is under beer, soft drinks under soft drinks etc. There are a few new added items on, but you'll find it under 'other' until we have it changed and put under the correct category. I'll give you some time after to get a feel for it." I take a deep breath before continuing. "We serve at the bar; we don't do table service in here. And we take turns glass collecting. Do you have any questions? You said you've bartended before, so I assume you know how to pull a pint and make drinks?"

"I do," she assures me. "When I spoke to the manager, he said I'll be focused on closing. Does that mean I have to count tills?"

"Not right away. Derek, who you met earlier, will be doing that, or Roy. I normally do it, but I'll be finishing earlier after tonight. When the time comes, I can go through everything with you. And someone is always here to answer questions. You will be expected to do clean-up. If kept on top throughout the night, it doesn't take that long," I admit. "Is there anything I've missed?" I ask because my head still feels foggy.

"No, just point me to where you want me," she tells me.

She hasn't even done a full shift but from first impressions, I know she is going to be a hard worker. Just the thought has relief pouring through me. I will no longer have to run myself ragged to get things done. Except for Derek, I can't stand any of the other staff. They're lazy and do more talking and taking fag breaks than they do serving people.

THE CLOCK BEHIND the till keeps pulling my attention away from work. I'm close to finishing and I'm counting down the minutes until it all ends and I can go home to bed. Roy has been gracious in letting me finish early, even though I was meant to be training Kelly. He said he couldn't bear to watch me struggle another minute on his cameras and knew I wouldn't leave right then if he asked. So, I agreed to finish an hour early.

My only saving grace was Kelly. She's everything I hoped she would be and worked her arse off all night. She picked everything up in no time and anything she didn't know, she asked about.

She was also observant and noticed Nate straight away, asking if we were together when she noticed him watching me. I had to tell her he was a friend and was walking me back after my shift. I couldn't risk her being in danger because she knew the truth. The little she knew, the better.

However, after I revealed he was just a friend, I noticed her watching him more than once, like she was either trying to figure him out or get his attention. He was good looking, so I couldn't blame her.

"So, how long have you worked here?" Kelly asks me when the bar quietens down, and we're left doing nothing.

"Not long, it's only been open for a few months. They did an extension on the restaurant that's next door. I mostly clean the cabins, but when they opened this place a month after moving here, they offered me a job and I took it," I explain, turning to her. "Where did you work before?"

"Just a small bar back home," she answers vaguely.

In the short time I've known her, I've come to realise she's not very forthcoming about herself. Every time I have tried to ask her about her life, she has given me vague answers. Which I don't mind because it's something I still do. It's just strange how she can be so talkative yet stay quiet at the same time.

"So, where do you live?" she asks as she wipes down the bar.

"Oh, I'm staying in one of the cabins with my daughter," I tell her.

Something flashes across her face, but it's gone before I can figure it out. "You have a daughter? How old is she?"

I chuckle. "She's four going on fifty."

She chuckles. "What's her name?"

"Carrie-Ann, but we just call her Carrie."

"That is a beautiful name. Hopefully, I'll get to meet her. I'm new in town and staying at my brother's friend's house back in town. I'm hoping to save up to get my own place soon, though," she explains, taking me off guard. That's the first time she has given me anything remotely personal.

Knowing what it's like to be new in town, I decide to invite her over.

"She'd love that. She's a people person. You should come by for dinner one day to meet her and we can hang out," I offer. "How are you liking it here so far?"

She turns back to wiping down the bar, not meeting my gaze.

"I would love that. I don't really have anyone here or any girl friends to hang out with. When you're up for it, let me know and we can arrange something," she replies before turning to me. "It's okay here. I don't know anyone so it can be lonely at times. The weather has been great, too, but with England, it doesn't last long."

"That's true," I reply, laughing somewhat. "Well, how about Wednesday, say about three-thirty? I'm off that day and night, so we could do a BBQ if the weather holds up. It's meant to stay nice, but with my luck it would rain the day I decide to do a BBQ."

She smiles warmly at me. "I would love to. If it rains, we will figure it out. I need some girl time, and of course need to meet little Miss Carrie."

Nate heads over just as a customer heads to the bar, waving Kelly down.

"You ready?" Nate asks.

I wipe my hands on the dish towel and nod. "Yeah, just let me go grab my coat."

He sits on the stool at the bar while I run off into the back, heading into the staff room. I grab my stuff and make my way back out, finding Nate where I left him.

Kelly finishes with her customer and heads over to me. "You finished?"

"Yeah, Roy has let me go early. He said you're doing amazing and can handle the rest on your own. Derek will be here if you have any questions."

She winks. "You get off. I got it handled. I had a great teacher."

"She must be awesome," I tease. "See you tomorrow, chick, and it's been lovely meeting you."

Her lips tip down for a moment before she masks it, pasting on a smile, and it makes me realise how lonely in must be for her in a new place.

It wasn't just her without any girl friends around. I hadn't made any friends, except for Roy and Hayley, and the people I work with. Even then, I still keep them at arm's length.

And lately, I have desperately needed another woman's advice. The day I lost my virginity had been one of them and it killed me I couldn't pick up the phone and call my sister.

I had no one.

But from now on, I'm going to listen to Cage; to Carrie and I'm going to live my life.

"Goodnight," she tells me with a soft smile. "It's been lovely working with you."

"You too, honey."

Nate jumps off the stool and once again, her attention pulls to him. I bite my lip, kicking myself for not introducing them to each other. "Nate, this is Kelly. Kelly, this is Nate, my boyfriend's best friend."

It feels weird calling Cage my boyfriend, but I'm not sure what else to call him. We're everything a couple are. And I'm so not introducing him as someone I sleep with and desperately want more than anything.

"Hey," Nate murmurs, his gaze flicking from her back to his phone.

"Hey," she greets back, watching him curiously.

She's a knockout, and I could kick Nate for not giving her a second look.

I roll my eyes as I turn to her. "See you later."

CAGE IS ON THE front deck waiting for us when we arrive back home.

"Hey, Kitten, you have a good day at work?" he asks, getting up from his chair.

"Yep, the new girl is amazing," I tell him, walking into his arms. I press a kiss to the corner of his mouth, then smile up at him. "How has Carrie been?"

He grimaces. "She's still a little upset over my absence this morning. Took me a while to get her to go to sleep because she thought I would leave again," he explains and when I go to reply, he continues. "Don't worry, I told her I'm not going anywhere."

"She'll be fine," I assure him, but it's more to convince myself than him. I'm worried about her.

"Hope so, Kitten. I hate seeing my girl sad and scared."

That is so sweet, like really sweet.

"How did it go?" Cage asks Nate, who is leaning against the post.

"Good. No problems at all," he declares. "I linked up the feed when I got there. I kept an eye on the feeds all night and didn't notice anything out of the ordinary. I also had Pug outside, patrolling the area. He got nothing, either. So, either this guy knew how to stay hidden or he wasn't around tonight. My guess? He sent the message he wanted this morning then went away to set up for his next play." He runs a hand through his hair, staring directly at Cage. "We need to figure this shit out. I'll be back in the morning with that information we talked about. I got most of it, but there are still some leads to follow. I'm going to get back, so I'll see you later."

"Keep me posted," Cage orders, sounding distracted.

Nate nods, then walks over to me, kissing me on the cheek. "Night, girl. Don't get into any more trouble while I'm gone."

"Pffft, your life would be boring without me," I tease, trying to lighten the tension.

He smirks. "It sure would." He gives us a wave before heading off, breaking into a run with his laptop shoved under his arm.

"He's a good guy," I tell Cage, who wraps his arms around my midriff.

He rests his chin on my shoulder after pressing a kiss to my neck. "He sure is, but you better not be hung up on him," he warns me.

I turn in his arms, smiling as I wrap my arms around his neck. "Why would I when I have a macho badarse as my boyfriend, who I gave myself to, willingly?"

"Willingly, huh?"

"Yep."

"Well, how about me and you get into bed, so I can see just how willingly you come?"

"Oh, it will be *very* willingly, and if you're lucky, I'll willingly return the same gesture," I purr seductively.

I go to take a step, but he surprises me by swinging me up in his arms and over his shoulder. I let out a high-pitched squeal when he slaps his hand over my arse.

He locks up behind him before strolling down to our bedroom, where he kicks the door shut behind me him.

He throws me down and I land on the bed with a bounce.

"Now, let me show you how willing I am," he rasps before he pounces.

A giggle escapes as he lands on me, but it turns into a moan when he reaches under my top and my bra, cupping my breasts.

"Oh God," I moan out.

"No, Kitten, it's all me."

He pulls his hands out and grips the edge of my T-shirt, pulling it up until it reveals my green lace bra. I lift my arms, helping him take it off. I lie back down, my body heating as he stares down at me, lust filling his gaze.

I spread my thighs a little, giving him a little tease.

He shifts, sliding off the bed to remove his own clothing, and when I see he isn't wearing any boxers again, I arch my eyebrow at him.

"Did you think you were getting lucky tonight?" I ask, glancing up from his erection when he grabs it, pumping it once, twice, in his hand.

"Kitten, I was lucky at just the thought of you going to sleep in my arms. This… This is just a bonus," he tells me, a wicked gleam in his eyes. "A seriously fucking good bonus."

I bat my lashes at him. "Then don't keep us both waiting."

Chapter Twenty-Five

CAGE

I WIPE THE SWEAT OFF MY forehead after throwing the last of the kitchen into a pile to the side.

Since things have been quiet over the past few weeks, I have been able to concentrate on the house. But I knew I couldn't do it on my own, and with the cabins, the spa at the resort, then the new garages, I couldn't pull any of my men off their job to help. But thanks to my dad, who told me about a company who were going out of business due to lack of work, I managed to hire a new team at a reasonable rate. I think they were just grateful for the work.

They're hard working, and after the house is done, I'm going to speak to the guy who runs the company to see if he'd like to work for ours or at least let us contract them when we have too much work on.

And since we started work, a few teenagers have come up asking for work. Since I can't hire untrained guys, I put them on garden duty. After that, they can help me clean the garage out. I'm hoping with all the new additional help, it will be finished in no time.

It feels good to take a break though. For years, work has been my life. I had nothing outside of it to go back to.

Now I have Caitlyn and Carrie and life with them has been blissful. It's a nice change to want to go home and then have someone there waiting for me, someone I want to spend time with.

And since Caitlyn decided to take more time off, life is good. A change has come over her and it's for the better. She laughs more, smiles, and she lights up like she's experiencing life for the first time.

Even with the threat looming over her, she carries on like a rock, pushing forward like the trooper she is.

It doesn't mean things are perfect. They aren't, but none of it has been like the night I fucked up and ended up on Nate's sofa with a half-naked chick.

It's small things. Things that don't really matter. But the one that does is rent. I took over paying, and she found out and didn't like it.

My lips twist at the reminder. She had been so mad at me for it, but I didn't care. I was staying there, and it was my way of contributing.

For a few days she tried everything to get me to cancel it, even going as far as to use sexual blackmail on me. It always ended with me teasing her to the point she gave in and screamed my name. It was fun watching her think she could get her way though. I think the only reason she gave in was because I told her how strongly I felt about it.

Her happiness isn't because of just me though. She's finally embracing life and she couldn't look any more beautiful for it. She's let everyone in, showing them the kind, funny person she is.

She organised a barbeque for her colleague who had become a good friend a few weeks back and it ended up as a party. I invited close friends from work, and we spent the day laughing and enjoy each other's company.

Everyone got to meet each other, and it went well. For most of us. Dante had tried to hit on the new girl, but she wasn't interested. It was hilarious to see him shot down, because I have never seen him fail with any other chick.

Caitlyn's new friend is okay, but over time, I noticed she wasn't talkative unless it was Caitlyn or Hayley. And she was jumpy around men, except Dante, who she loved giving the cold shoulder to.

Kelly was actually the other argument Caitlyn and I had. I told her she was a little weird. She observed people to the point you would consider it a staring problem. I watched her, and a few times, she got caught and would flush, glancing away.

I wasn't sure whether she thought I was hitting on her, or what. I just knew she was a little weird. And to be careful, I had Nate do a background check on her. Things had been easier since then as it came back clear. Caitlyn didn't like it, but she didn't need to. I was just taking care of her.

I wipe my hands down my trousers as the front door is pushed open. "Cage?"

"In here," I call out, looking at the mess I made. I had stayed later than the other guys, but I know in the morning, they will clear up the mess I made.

"You got a minute?" Nate asks, stopping at the kitchen door. He takes a look around, his eyes widening. "Shit, you really ripped it all out."

I snort and step over a pile of doors. "What brings you here?" I ask, then glance behind him, my brows pulling together. "Where's Caitlyn?"

"She's in the car waiting. I wanted to speak to you first."

"Did something happen?"

"Yes and no. I got all the information we needed. Everything I can find on Rome has come back clean and you know I've done a thorough search."

"Is he going to meet us?" I ask, hopeful.

"I've set up a meet with him. He's going to drive down tonight and be here tomorrow. He wants to book into a bed and breakfast first to get a few hours' sleep, then he'll ring us to set up a meet," he tells me, shrugging. "If you get a good vibe when you talk to him, then I guess you'll need to tell Caitlyn what we've been doing and see if she's willing to hand it over. I would advise you talk her into letting us have it sooner, so we can make copies. We need to make sure we don't get screwed over. Even Rome agrees and is emailing me a list of people who we can send the information to. The more people that see the information, the harder it will be to erase."

"I can talk to Caitlyn when I get back. This is what we needed."

"You'll have time to yourselves too because Carrie is sleeping over at Hayley's tonight. Something about making decorations for a party they're planning on having in a few weeks."

"Let me just lock up," I tell him, grabbing my tools. "Hopefully after today I can be home more. I've just been busier this week trying to organise everything and give everyone a job."

"Did you want me to carry on back with Caitlyn or have you got it covered? I wasn't sure if you brought your bike instead."

"I've got it covered. I've got my truck with me, even if my girl does prefer my bike," I tell him, a grin tugging at my lips.

He grins, shaking his head. "I bet she does," he murmurs. "I'll follow you back."

I finish grabbing my tools together before I head to the door. I lock up behind me and when I turn to leave down the stairs, I come to a stop, my gaze burning into Caitlyn as she leans back against my truck, looking hot as fuck.

"Hello, gorgeous," I greet, strolling towards her.

She pushes off the truck. "Hey, handsome. Do you want to go get something to eat to take back home?"

"How about we go back to change, then go to that Chinese restaurant in town?"

"Sounds like a plan," she agrees.

Leaning down, I give her a kiss on the mouth, something I've been yearning to do since I saw her sexy arse leaning against my truck.

Damn, my girl smells good.

"Hop in." I wink at her.

I pull open the door and she gets in. I nod to Nate as I jump in, starting the car up and pulling off the drive.

Travelling back to the cabin, we talk easily about everything. Since I've been with Caitlyn, we never struggle for conversation. We always feel comfortable talking about everything and anything. As we talk about her day, she starts telling me about Carrie's activities. I love this part of my day. If I've come home to Carrie already in bed, Caitlyn will sit and fill me in on what she's been doing.

"So, they are making cakes for a pretend party that is now going to be a real party?" I ask, trying to make sense of what is going on.

"Basically," she answers. "Carrie wanted to spend some time with you because she misses you, but I felt like being selfish. I wanted to spend the night with you alone, so I was trying to bribe her into staying with Hayley for the night, but she wasn't having any of it. Hayley, thinking quickly, made up a story about a party that they could practice making cakes for. Carrie bought it. Only downfall is that we are having another barbeque in a couple of weeks."

I grin. "I enjoyed the last barbeque, so I'm looking forward to the next one."

We are heading down Birmingham Lane, which is a straight road heading towards the cabins. Making sure the road is clear, I lean over, giving Caitlyn a quick kiss on the lips.

Straightening in my seat, my chest is filled with happiness. It consumes me. Tethers me.

But in a blink, that all comes crashing down around me.

All in one painful moment, as my mind registers what is about to happen. Even if I was paying attention before, I know there was no avoiding it, no way to evade the inevitable.

The colossal impact jerks me to the side, and the sound of metal banging together, along with the horn and Caitlyn's screams, echo in my ears.

I grip the steering wheel, trying to maneuverer the car, but it's no use. The car is pushed over the side of the road and then begins to tip. My face smacks off the steering wheel, glass shatters, shards cutting into my skin as we roll, maybe one, twice, before landing on its side, a hissing sound echoing around us. It happens so quick, and in that moment, all I can think about is Caitlyn.

A deafening silence, all but the ringing in my ears hits me. Disorientated, I try to gather myself and focus on the other sounds around me. Tyres squeal against the tarmac close by, followed by one coming to a screeching halt. At least, I think it does.

Warmth flows down my cheek as I slowly lift my hand, peeling a piece of glass off me. "Caitlyn," I choke out, blinking through the haze.

"Cage? Caitlyn? Can you hear me?" I hear Nate shouting. "Hello, there has been an accident down on Birmingham Lane. A car just hit another car and it's gone over the bank. Yes, they're friends of mine. Okay. Hurry."

It wasn't a dream. A car really had hit us.

I struggle to move, hissing out a breath as I turn to Caitlyn. A choked roar tears from my throat as I see her slumped against the window at a weird angle, a large gash on the top of her head, pouring with blood. She's unmoving, and I struggle to get free of my confines.

"Caitlyn," I choke out again, tears forming in my eyes as I tug at the belt, frustration welling inside of me. "Caitlyn."

I don't take my eyes off her, staring at her chest for any signs she's breathing.

The crushed metal creaks and the car shakes as Nate climbs up, staring into the broken window at me.

"Fuck, are you okay?" he asks, then looks down at Caitlyn, his eyes widening. "Shit!"

A wave of dizziness hits me. "Get to Caitlyn," I croak out. "She hasn't woken up. I don't know if she's… if she's…"

He jumps onto the bonnet, sliding down until his feet hit the trunk of the tree. He rips off his jacket and begins to pull the glass free.

"Caitlyn, can you hear me?" he calls out, moving enough glass to get his arm through without cutting himself. He leans in, checking her pulse. "She's breathing."

I struggle to get free, a growl of frustration escaping me. I needed to get out of here, get her out of here.

"Keep still," Nate scolds, turning to look at me. "The ambulance is on its way. She's got a pulse, brother, she's just unconscious. She is going to be fine," he says, trying to reassure me.

It doesn't work. The fear of losing her, when I've just met her, is enough to send me into a despair.

I can't lose her.

In the distance, I hear the sirens coming closer. Nate climbs back up the car, leaning in to help with the belt confining me inside.

"Stay with her," I choke out.

"Let me help," he demands.

I turn to her, praying so hard that she wakes up. I've never believed in God, but right now, I'm hoping someone hears my pleas, because I don't want to be without her.

I love her.

I fucking love her. I don't care that it hasn't been long. I don't care that we're still fairly new.

She is mine.

And I am hers.

She makes me laugh even on a bad day. She turns me on like no other ever has. She's kind to those who don't deserve it. She's the strongest out of the people I have ever met.

To lose her now… I'd lose myself.

"Did you see the car?" I ask Nate, as I hear people yelling close by.

He looks away from where the noise is coming from, his lips twisting.

"Yeah, I got the number plate down. I got to tell you, though, from what I saw, it looked like a woman driving."

Before I have a chance to reply, the firemen are there, moving him out of the way.

"You are free to go," the nurse announces, handing me my discharge papers. I don't wait around for her to change her mind. I need to get to Caitlyn. Nate's updates weren't enough to tamper the worry I have inside of me. I have a few cuts and bruises, nothing compared to Caitlyn, who, from the last I heard, still hasn't woken up. That was four hours ago.

Reaching the ward Nate said she was on, I head to the nurse's station. "Hey, do you know—"

"Cage, she's through here," Nate announces, standing in a doorway. He turns to the nurse and lies. "This is her fiancé."

She nods, going back to work. I head towards Nate, bracing myself when I reach the room. She looked fucking bad in the car, even with the memories foggy in my mind. The image of her lying there, unconscious, is forever burnt into my memory.

"How is she?" I ask, stepping past him into the room.

I nearly buckle at the sight of her lying in the bed unconscious. She's cleaned up now, but the bruises have already formed and there are stitches in the wound on her head. The rest are superficial, which doesn't explain why she is still asleep.

I turn to the machines she's hooked up to, my heart racing. The only thing keeping me together is the steady rhythm of her heart on the machine.

There's an IV in her right hand and her left is now wrapped in a cast since she broke it trying to keep herself upright when we turned. Or at least, that's what Nate guessed when he came to see me.

"She's doing good. They have her on some monitors, as you can see, but it's just procedure. She has a broken arm that will be in a cast for six to eight weeks, the stitches are dissolvable, and she has three bruised ribs. And obviously a few scrapes and bruises."

"When did the doctor say she will wake up?" I ask, sitting in the chair next to her bed. I grab hold of her hand, placing a kiss into her palm, careful not to knock the IV lead.

"He said she will wake up when she is ready. She took a nasty bump to the head when it smashed through the window; it's common with head injuries for the patient to take time to heal and wake up. I gave the police my statement when we first got here, so I'm still waiting to hear back from them. They should be here soon to come get yours."

"I don't remember what happened. All I remember is the lane being empty, me leaning over to give Caitlyn a kiss, a flicker of colour and a car, then the sound of metal breaking. It's all a fucking blur. Even though it felt like it all happened in slow motion, it was over so quickly."

He takes a seat on the opposite side, gripping the bed rails. "Look, the car hit you on purpose, Cage."

"No," I murmur, but I know his words are true.

"I was, what, three, four car lengths behind you? I saw a car come from the left, from one of those dirt paths. It had no intention of stopping. Whoever hit you didn't wait around to see if you were okay. They just took off. In the time it took me to comprehend what the fuck happened, they reversed and drove off. It was definitely a woman, though, that much I could tell."

"You're sure?"

"Yeah, I saw her hair."

I'm about to ask him more when two uniformed police officers walk into the room. When I get a good look at their faces, I sit up straighter in my seat. Whatever they're here to tell me doesn't look good.

"Are you Mr. Cage Carter?" one policeman asks.

"Yes," I answer.

"Hi, I'm Officer Johnson and this is my colleague, Officer Marcus. We're here to ask you a few questions about the incident that happened earlier," he explains, standing at the end of the bed. "Do you know a woman named Louise Cunnings?"

"Yes, she is an ex-girlfriend. Why?" I ask, already knowing what they are going to say. I knew the bitch was crazy, but to try and kill me? I never thought she would do that.

For hours I assumed it was Caitlyn's past that had caused today's event.

But it wasn't. It was mine. And I hate myself for it.

It gives me an insight into how Caitlyn felt when we first met. Because had I known Lou was this fucking crazy, I wouldn't have gotten involved with Caitlyn. I wouldn't have put her in danger, just like Caitlyn had done when we first met.

"The vehicle involved with the collision down on Birmingham Lane was indeed Miss Cunnings'. We had officers go to her house, but she isn't there. The damaged vehicle, however, is. We believe Miss Cunnings may be in hiding," he states, knocking the breath out of me. It really was her. "Is there any reason as to why Miss Cunnings would want to hurt you, Mr. Carter?"

I snort. "Yeah, she's a crazy bitch. We were an item a long time ago. I broke it off with her, and then she told me she was pregnant. When I found out that it was all a lie, I kicked her arse out. She didn't like it and has done nothing but stalk me, begging me to take her back, ever since. She came to Cabin Lakes, where I am staying, a few weeks back. She kept going on about shit, saying that we were good for each other, that we were getting back together, even after I point blank told her I wasn't interested, and she needed to get gone. In the end, I had a buddy of mine remove her from the premises."

He looks up from his pad. "We have a statement from Mr Mathews here. Can you give us anything new?"

I shake my head. "No. We were driving down Birmingham Lane when it happened. The roads were clear," I tell him, missing out the part where I leaned over to kiss Caitlyn. "It all happened so fast. One minute we were talking, the next we had been hit and were rolling."

"Thank you, Mr Carter. We will be in touch if we have any further questions, or if we have any more news on Miss Cunnings whereabouts. If you can think of any more information that can help us find her, please call me or my colleague here," he orders, handing me his card.

"I will, thank you."

"Goodbye, Mr Carter."

"Yeah, bye," I murmur, my mind racing. Once they are gone, I turn to Nate. "Fuck!"

"Yeah, did not see that coming."

Chapter Twenty-Six

CAITLYN

Internally groaning, I slowly come to, my lashes fluttering as I peel my eyelids open. They feel heavy and my head is pounding like someone has put a hammer to it after a long night of partying. God, everything hurts; my head, my hand, my body, it all hurts.

What the hell happened?

"Kitten," Cage calls, bringing a small smile to my face, but even that hurts.

Frowning, I turn to the sound of his voice, finding him watching me, his expression filled with pain.

"What happened?" I croak out, sounding like I have a frog shoved in my throat.

"We got hit by a car," he states vaguely, glancing down at my hand he's holding.

He's hiding something.

I close my eyes, pushing the pain away so I can concentrate on remembering. We were driving. We were happy then everything around us exploded. I remember the blinding pain as my head smashed against the window, the breath being ripped from me as I was jerked back into my seat. Everything after is a blur, although, the smell of burning rubber and burning metal still stings my nostrils.

"What are you not telling me, Cage?"

He sighs, gripping my hand a little tighter. "It was Lou, my ex, driving the car," he admits, glancing away.

I knew about her. She was the girl I met the day I walked in on Cage showering. She was acting crazy then, but this?

Why would she do this?

I can understand her being gutted over losing Cage— he's everything you could want— but to go to this extreme? It doesn't feel right.

Glancing up at Cage, I watch as the guilt pours out of him, and I know he has spent the time sitting next to me riddled with it, blaming himself.

"Crazy bitch. She could have killed us," I announce, taking him off guard.

Cage stares for a moment before shaking his head, chuckling. He lets out a weary sigh before bending over, pressing his lips to mine.

"You continue to surprise me," he murmurs, before pulling back, and I inwardly groan, wanting his warmth back. "But you're right, she could have. The police are going to want to ask you a few questions, but they have everything they need for the moment."

"How long have I been here?" I ask, my brows pinching together.

"It's six in the morning, so I'd say thirteen hours, give or take."

I try to sit up in bed, hissing out in pain. "Carrie— oh my God, Carrie. Does she know?"

He gently pushes me back down.

"Relax. I spoke with Roy last night and he said he has everything taken care of. The doctors and nurses have been coming and going all night. The doctor said as soon as you wake up, they will check you over and, hopefully, you can be home by tonight."

"She's okay?" I ask, needing to know. I don't want her to feel abandoned again and that's how she felt when I was late picking her up after the visit Kane paid at the cabin and when Cage stayed at Nate's.

"She's fine. I've even spoken to her," he assures me.

"Have they got Louise in custody?"

"No, they found her car parked outside her house, but no sign of Lou anywhere. They have police searching for her, but my guess is she has taken off."

"Great, so not only are we dealing with my sister's crazy ex, but life decided to throw in yours, too. This is just bloody fantastic," I mutter, wishing this would all end. Things have been so good the past few weeks. I want it to be like that forever. I had Cage and with him, I felt like we were a real family for once. We were also surrounded by great friends. Life is good. I shouldn't be surprised something had to ruin it.

He smooths my hair away from my face. "Hey, they will find her. She took us by surprise, Kitten. I didn't know she would stoop this low to get my attention."

I groan. "It isn't your fault. I'm just pissed that nothing seems to be going easy for us. I could have died in that crash, and where would that have left Carrie, or you? What if you had died? Where would that have left me or Carrie."

The heartbeat monitor begins to beep rapidly. "Let's not think about that. I can't think about losing you. Yesterday nearly killed me. You wouldn't wake up and I was scared shitless. I don't want to lose you, *ever*." I begin to calm when he leans over, pressing his forehead against mine. The desperation in his voice is nearly my undoing. "Never," he swears.

"Okay," I whisper.

He pulls back and stands to his full height. "Let me go get the nurse. They said to call them if you woke up."

"Don't be long."

"I won't," he promises and leans over, pressing another kiss to my mouth.

Even banged up, bruised and in pain, that burning need to have him soared inside of me. He pulls away far too soon with a knowing grin on his face. Giving me a wink, he leaves the room to find a nurse.

* * *

BY THE TIME the doctor came around to do his rounds, it was seven in the morning. He wanted me to stay longer for observation but said I could leave tonight. Only, to be discharged, we needed another doctor to give the okay. By the time she came, it was eight o'clock at night. Then we had to wait around for the nurse to discharge me, and then again for them to get me a prescription of pain meds to take home. Waiting around isn't one of my strong suits, so I spent the day agitated and grumpy.

It's gone ten now, and we are only just pulling up to the cabins. I'm grateful to be back home, even after it took me a while to get into his replacement car. It's only temporary until he gets his fixed or his insurance pays out. Still, flashes of the crash hit me, and I was scared about getting into it.

I glance at Cage and can see the frown lines on his forehead and the top of his lip. I sigh, wondering if he's going to let it go.

Before we left the hospital, we had an argument. Not a big one, but still, it happened.

My arm was sore and causing me discomfort, but it was my head that had me wanting to curl in a ball and cry. It was throbbing and Cage noticed I was hurting and told me to take the painkillers before we left.

I said no. They were making me drowsy, and I didn't want to fall asleep. I missed him, and each time they had given me some today, they had put me out of it or sent me to sleep. Something also occurred to me at the hospital, and I wanted to address it with him in the privacy of our own home and not when we had nurses and other patients listening in.

He called me stupid and said we weren't leaving until I did.

Obviously, Cage won the argument, which is the reason why I've been forcing my eyes open for most of the drive back. Every time I closed my eyes, I had flashbacks of the crash, and I would shoot up in my seat, gasping for air. The pain in my ribs is excruciating, but it's manageable.

He's not long finished talking to Nate, who let him know work and the house had been taken care of.

It was what hit me at the hospital and why I wanted to talk to him. He has more than one business to run, along with so much work going on right now, and I'm holding him back. He has taken so much time off to deal with my shit and now this crash. He thinks I need him to stay home and look after me, but I don't want him missing out on more work.

In fact, looking at him, he has never looked so worn out. And I'm the reason.

"Hey, we're here," Cage murmurs softly. I was so deep in thought that I didn't even realise we had pulled up outside our cabin. "Come on, let's get you inside."

Cage leaves the car, walking around to my side. He opens the door, and before I can even move, he has my seat belt undone and is picking me up bridal style out of the car. He carries me up the steps, and then efficiently opens the door with the key.

Locking the door behind us, he carries me down the hall to our bedroom. I'm so worn out, I don't even argue as he starts to strip me out of my clothes. Usually, being treated like an imbecile would piss me the hell off, but with Cage doing it, I know he is doing it because he cares.

"Thank you," I mumble through my hazy state.

"It's okay, Kitten," he whispers, pressing a kiss to my head.

When we are finally in bed, both of us lying on our sides, facing each other, I finally work up the energy to bring up the work issue.

"Cage, we need to talk about your work," I tell him.

"It's all sorted. You haven't got to worry about any of that, Kitten. Between me and Dante, we have it covered."

"That's not what I meant. I want you to go to work tomorrow. You can't keep having all this time off because of me. I'm betting my *Pretty Little Liars* boxset that you are falling behind. So please, can you just go into work?" I plead.

"Look, I don't want to have another argument. We're both tired and worn out, and we need to get some sleep. We were both in that car crash. Yes, I came out with only a few scratches, but I think I'm entitled to some time off from work, given the circumstances. I'll meet you in the middle, though; I'll have tomorrow off, then go into work on Thursday. How does that sound?"

"Perfect," I tell him sleepily.

"Night, babe," he whispers.

He gently gives me a kiss on the lips, only to pull away and tuck me into him. My plastered arm goes around him, resting on his torso, with my head on his chest. It's only seconds after closing my eyes that I fall into a deep sleep.

My phone has been blowing up all morning. I was overwhelmed by people's well-wishes. I never had people to care before, but the proof was there from the minute Cage presented me a new phone. Nate had purchased them this morning since ours got broken in the crash. He replaced the sim cards with ours and in no time, we had them charged and messages and missed calls poured through.

I'm expecting Kelly to be here soon. Her messages were sent last night after Roy informed her why I wasn't at work.

I cherish our friendship. I know she has secrets, but I never push her. Her demons are hers to share, and I know when the time is right, she will come to me. After all, that is what friends do.

There's a knock at the door, bringing me out of my thoughts. I go to push myself out of the chair, but Cage places a hand on my shoulder, pushing me back down. "I'll get it," he tells me, heading for the door. He pulls it open. "Hey, Kelly, come in."

Kelly comes in, wearing a short denim skirt, paired with a tight white tank top, covered by a short-sleeved blazer.

I sigh, envious of how good she looks. In fact, I have yet to see her dishevelled. She always has her hair done, light make-up on, and is dressed well. Me? I'm in my Minnie pyjamas, my hair a mess on the top of my head, and my face has cuts and bruises. I can't put anything else on. It feels too constricted and painful against my injuries.

"Hey," I greet when she spots me.

Her eyes widen at the sight of me. "God, you look like you've gone ten rounds with Mike Tyson," she declares, sitting down on the sofa. "Please tell me they've caught the person who's done it? Dante mentioned to me last night at the bar that they knew who it was."

"No, the police rang earlier. They're still out searching for her."

"It was a woman?" she asks, her lips parting.

"Yes, it was one of Cage's ex-girlfriends, to be precise."

She grimaces. "Well, shit."

"I know," I reply, lightly chuckling.

"How are you feeling?"

"Really fucking sore. I have had my painkillers, but they aren't really helping me much. In fact, they are making me feel worse. I feel sick and really tired when I take them. How has work been?" I ask, hoping to change the topic. I'm sick of talking about the accident. I feel like I've repeated myself twenty times to fill people in today.

"Busy. Roy helped out last night as one of the other fill-ins called in sick."

"I bet Roy wasn't too happy about that," I state, chuckling. "He really hates working in the bar."

"He may have mentioned his feelings about it once or twice," she wearily answers.

Roy prefers to work in the restaurant, and I'm confident, as the bar's assistant manager, that I will soon have everything back under control, so he can go back to the restaurant to do what he loves best.

"That I can believe," I state, glancing up when Cage walks in, his phone in his hand. "Everything okay?"

"Yeah, it was Hayley on the phone. She wanted to let us know she was coming back with Pea soon."

"I'm dying to see her," I tell him. And I am. As sore and as tired as I am, my need to see the little nugget overrides that.

"I'll go so you can have some time together."

"You don't need to," I rush out, enjoying her company.

She waves me off. "It's fine. I can understand you wanting to be with her," she explains, reaching for her jacket. "When do you think you'll be well enough to come back into work?"

"In a week or so, I'm hoping. It will kill me not having anything to do. Obviously, there isn't much I can do at the bar, so I'm hoping Roy gives me some invoices or something to do. There isn't a lot I can do with one hand."

Thinking about it, I don't know what I'm going to do about

work. The doctor said my arm will be in the cast for six to eight weeks, depending on scans. So, that leaves me with little options. How am I supposed to manage to pour pints, carry drinks, and wash glasses with one hand? Not even going to go there about cleaning the cabins. It will be okay once I'm able to use it but right now, it hurts even if I knock it.

"I suppose not," she murmurs absently, then her eyes widen. "Hey, did you hear the singer girl quit?"

"She did?"

"Yeah, and from what I heard you have an amazing voice. Maybe you could fill her spot until you're well enough to go back," she suggests.

I smile, and hope blossoms in my chest. "That's a great idea. I can't play my guitar, though I'm sure I'll cope."

"Think about it. I'm sure Roy won't mind," she tells me, getting up.

"You really don't need to go."

"It's fine. I have a shift in a few hours, and I'd like to get home and change first."

"Alright," I reply, getting to my feet. "I'll try to pop in the bar during the week sometime."

"Definitely. We can have a catch up," she suggests.

We get to the door, and she pulls it open. "Oh, I forgot to mention that we are having another barbeque in a few weeks if you want to come. It's a long story but I bribed Carrie into staying at Hayley's so Cage and I could have one night to ourselves, and it ended up with her thinking we are having another party. So, a party is what she'll get, even if our night alone was spent in a hospital room," I muse.

"I'll be here," she agrees, beaming at me. "See you soon, and I hope you feel better."

When she suddenly pulls me in for a hug, careful of my injuries, I'm struck with surprise. She has never been affectionate towards me before, and I've watched her tense when Hayley has given her a hug during her goodbyes.

"See you," I whisper, still frozen as she pulls back.

She waves and jogs down the steps before getting in her car. I watch as she reverses out of the designated parking space out the front. Two arms wrap around me from behind and I smile, leaning back into Cage's embrace.

"Do you want me to take Carrie out for a bit so you can lie down and rest?"

"No, I've missed her. Plus, we need to get this over with. As soon as she sees my arm, let's face it, she's going to freak."

"Yeah, you're right, she will. Maybe I should sweeten the pot first, go get her a McDonalds or something?"

Laughing softly so I don't hurt my ribs, I turn around and face him, placing my arms around his neck. I press my body against his as I lean in, giving him a kiss on the lips.

"Are you saying you're going to bribe my daughter into not having a hissy fit?" I ask sweetly.

His eyebrows rise. "Do you think it will work?"

I chuckle and shake my head. "Probably, or probably not," I admit, watching his hopefulness drop into a frown.

Leaning up on my toes, I press my lips to his, moaning when he opens his mouth, massaging his tongue against mine. I shiver in response, desperately wanting more. Every time he touches me, he has this effect.

We both pull away when we hear Carrie laughing in the near distance. We smile at each other, then I move away to straighten up my rumpled pyjama top. Once I'm somewhat presentable, I turn to the stairs, waiting for her to come into view.

"We will continue this later, Kitten," he whispers in my ear, sending shivers down my neck.

"Is that a promise?" I purr seductively.

"It sure fucking is," he declares, giving me a hard slap on my arse.

I immediately squeal as I turn around, glaring at him. He winks before heading off into the house. I'm about to go after him, wanting to get him back, but feet hitting the bottom of the stairs has me turning around.

I barely turn before Carrie is pummelling into my legs, knocking me back a step. A hiss slips free when her head bangs into my side, I try to cover it up by muffling the sound with a cough. The noise must have sounded like a wounded animal because Cage comes barrelling back outside, searching for a threat.

"Are you okay? What's wrong?" he asks, before glancing down at Carrie, realisation dawning on him.

"It's fine," I assure him, running my hand over her head.

"Does it hurt?" she asks, staring at my cast with fascination.

I hold my hand up. "No, baby," I lie, not wanting to upset her. "You can even write on it if you like and draw me a pretty picture."

"Cool," she breathes out, her eyes lighting up. "I'll go get my pens."

"She took that well, didn't she?" I mutter to Cage, who smiles in response.

We follow her inside, and moments later, Hayley steps through the door, out of breath. "She's fast," she pants out, but jerks to a stop at the sight of me. "Oh, my girl, you look terrible. How are you feeling?" she asks, rushing over and pulling me in for a hug, mindful of my injuries.

We pull apart and I give her a reassuring smile. "I'm fine. I wish everyone would stop worrying about me," I tell her. "I actually wanted to talk to you; Kelly came over today for a chat, and she mentioned work. It got me thinking about what I'm going to be able to do one-handed, which isn't going to be a lot. With everything going on, I never really thought anything through. I can't get my cast wet, I can't lift anything, and I can't even make a bed one-handed. I know you said I'm covered, but I need the money." She opens her mouth and I hold my hand up. "Before you say anything, hear me out. Kelly said Tillie quit, and that you'll need to replace her. How would you feel if I take her place? Just until my hand gets better."

A smile lights up her face. "Actually, Roy and I were talking about this last night. We were both going to ask you the same thing, until the accident happened. You have a beautiful voice," she tells me. "So, it's settled, you'll continue to do Tillie's sets?"

"Yes," I answer, smiling.

Although I'm nervous at the thought of singing every other night in front of an audience, I'm secretly a little giddy. I've never really done full gigs before. I only usually fill in when Tillie can't make it into work.

"Okay, well you go rest now, dear. I will come by to check on you tomorrow. I was also going to come and take Carrie out for a while. She wants to go down to the lake, and as you can't get your cast wet, I kind of already told her I would take her. I hope you don't mind?"

"Of course not. She will love it."

She clasps her hands together. "Great."

"Thank you for taking care of Carrie for me. It means so much to me. You do a lot and I love you for it. We love you. I'm not sure I tell you enough, but I don't know what we'd do without you in our life," I state, grateful to have her in my life.

Her eyes take on a wet sheen. "It's always a pleasure. You know that, darling."

"Goodbye, Hayley."

She leans in, pressing her lips to my cheek and giving me a one-armed hug. "See you tomorrow."

When she leaves, I close the door behind her, before turning around and bumping into a hard chest.

"Hey," I greet, tilting my head to look up at him.

He tucks a strand of hair behind my ear. "I wish I had you to myself," he growls, pressing a kiss to my lips. I moan, clutching his biceps. "But we need to go get Pea her pens."

"They're in her room," I tell him, my brows pulling together.

He rubs the back of his neck. "No, they're not."

"They're not?" I ask, feeling even more confused.

"No," he declares, grimacing. "I hid those fuckers when I caught her drawing on her wall. The pictures weren't small either."

"And when, exactly, did you do this?" I ask him, trying to hold my laugh in.

"Last week. I went into her room to get her ready. When I walked in, I caught her in the act and scared the shit out of her. She knew what she was doing was wrong. I had a word with her about it, and she promised she wouldn't draw on the wall again, but she had that mischievous look about her. One that said, 'I may do it again on a different wall'. I knew then and there that she might not draw on *her* wall, but she will on someone else's, so I took them before things got out of control."

Standing there looking at his serious expression, I can't help it: I burst into a fit of giggles, trying not to hurt my side as I continue to laugh at him. When I finally calm down enough to look back up at Cage, his face is stern, and I have a feeling he is about to lecture me.

Uh-oh.

"I'm being fucking serious, Caitlyn. She was drawing big-arse pictures," he tells me, and my lips twitch in response.

I lean up on my toes, kissing him on the mouth, and then pull back enough so he can see me smile at him.

"Okay, let's go get the pens," I tell him softly.

His eyes go warm again, making my belly twirl. He leans down, kissing me once more as he grips my arse, pressing me flush against him. My good arm shoots out and presses against his chest to steady myself as he deepens the kiss.

It's short-lived when Carrie comes barrelling in the room, shouting about her pens.

"I can't find them anywhere," she cries. "I promise I looked further than the end of my nose. I looked in my drawers, under the bed, in my toy box, and even on my desk. I can't find them." She huffs, folding her arms across her chest.

Cage is smirking down at me when I chance a look at him. I don't need to hear it, but I can tell he's laughing inside.

"Let's go find them," he tells her, sweeping her up into his arms.

I watch them leave, a smile on my face. These are moments I live for.

Chapter Twenty-Seven

CAITLYN

IT HAS BEEN TWO WEEKS SINCE I came out of the hospital and a week since I returned to work.

The first few days of being on stage were terrifying, but in the end, I let the music flow through me, allowing me to forget where I was and what I was doing, and each night it got easier.

It was nice to get back to normal, or as normal as my life could get considering. The first week I got to spend with Carrie whilst Cage worked and then on the evening, we did things together. It was lovely getting that quality time. It might have only been me and Carrie for so long, but it hadn't been until last week that I realised how much I had been missing when it came to her. She was growing before my eyes, and I was missing so much.

That said, it hadn't been all fun and laughter. I missed work. I missed keeping busy. And it sucked at times trying to entertain a tiny human.

We also had an incident at the end of last week when Louise's mother came banging down my door, accusing Cage of being the reason for her daughter being crazy and for why she is missing.

Cage had been ready to phone the police, but as I stared down at the grieving, concerned mother, I did what I was brought up to do. To care. I walked over and I held her as she tore herself wide open in my arms. Once she had calmed down, Cage took her home, which I knew was hard for him since we could have died in that car crash.

Her daughter was missing though. The police had come back to get a full statement and to update us on what was happening with the investigation. That was when we found out none of her family or friends had seen her since the morning of the day of the crash. It was concerning, but since I had only met her once in passing, there wasn't much I could do to help. And Cage hadn't seen or heard from her since then either.

Right now, none of that matters. What matters is being surrounded by the people I love, who have become like family to me.

When Hayley and Carrie wanted to continue with the barbeque, I didn't argue. I thought it would be good for everyone, maybe ease some tension that I knew Cage felt.

I take a seat in the deck chair as Cage places my burger on the table in front of me, along with my glass of wine.

"Enjoy," he orders, pressing a kiss to the top of my head before heading back to the barbeque.

He and Dante are in charge of the cooking this time, so I get to sit down and relax.

My lips twitch as I watch Dante prancing around in Hayley's apron, which is frilly, pink, and far too small for his large frame.

Cage steps up, ready to take some of the food off, but Dante slaps his hand with the spatula. "It's not ready," he snaps, nudging him out of the way.

I know the only reason Cage hasn't given up is because he's worried Dante will set something on fire, or himself.

When he told me that, I laughed, thinking he was joking, but then he went on to tell me about a time Dante lit candles for a girl, and ended up setting his sofa on fire. Then he told me there was a time when they went to a bonfire, which ended up with Dante having burnt hands from trying to cook marshmallows using his fingers.

Although Cage assures me Dante is clever, strong, and dependable, he still has a brain of a ten-year-old that will get him doing some stupid shit. He is such a bulk of a man. If I didn't see some of the shit he does with my own eyes, I wouldn't believe it.

Although, I hope he never loses that. The other day, Carrie had him making a secret den with her. She hadn't even finished telling him what she wanted to do before he was going into detail about a tree house that he and his dad made when he was a kid. Carrie, being Carrie, ate the whole thing up. Together, the two made up loads of impossible ideas on how they could make theirs. As soon as they left the house, I rang Cage to let him know what they were doing because I thought it was seriously cute. Anything Carrie asks, when it comes to Dante, she gets. No matter what. So, when I informed Cage of this latest adventure of theirs, he burst out laughing, warning me to go supervise. He went on to tell me about Dante and his dad's tree house, and how the wood used for it ended up being used for a bonfire the same year because it collapsed a few days after being built.

"Hey, what are you smiling about?" Kelly asks, snapping me from my thoughts.

"Just musing over how domesticated Dante looks in his apron," I admit, chuckling.

She chuckles, looking longingly over at him. "Yeah, he does, doesn't he?"

My gaze flicks to Cage like it always does and he catches me watching him. Smirking, he then gives me a wink. I duck my head, feeling my cheeks heat.

"God, you two are so sickeningly cute together. I swear it's like you're both attuned to each other. Even with Dante yelling at him, he could feel you watching him."

Her words are a compliment, but I hear the sadness in her voice. "Are you okay?"

She fiddles with the burger on her plate. "I guess I'm feeling envious," she admits, before letting out a sigh. "I know I don't share much about my personal life, and I do it because it's not been the best. I've had a lot of shit happen and it's been hard for me to move forward."

"Hey, you have us. You can talk to me about anything."

She forces a smile, and her eyes glisten with unshed tears. "I just want you to know you should hang on to him. Love like that is rare, and when you capture something so beautiful, you should hold on to it. Not all love is like that."

"He is the best," I whisper, going back to watching him. "He's always doing stuff for me."

"Oh, I know. I'm still not over him getting up in the middle of a football match to get you painkillers and a glass of water. He didn't ask if it was hurting, he just knew and did something about it," she reminds me. "No guy gets up from a football match unless it's to get a beer. You seriously lucked out when it comes to a man."

"Yeah, I have. He's the best man I've ever met," I agree, before taking a chance on asking her about her life. Normally she shuts us down. "What about you? Do you have a boyfriend, an ex-boyfriend, or maybe one that got away?"

Her lips tip down, and she begins to pick apart the napkin. "I don't trust men at all. I'm not ready to tell you the full story—I might never be—but let's just say my ex… he made me false promises and then took everything from me. He lied, he beat me, then was the reason I had the one thing in the world that means anything to me, taken away."

"What did he take?" I whisper, not feeling good vibes.

This is the first time Kelly has ever opened up to me; the only time she's spoken about anything personal really. I don't want to ruin the moment and have her close up, but I also don't want her to think she can't talk to me about it.

"My son," she answers, her voice breaking.

I sit up, nearly knocking my glass over with my cast. I reach for it with my good hand and turn to her.

"What? You have a son?" I ask, keeping my voice down. I'm a little hurt she never said anything, but I can also understand not wanting to talk about painful memories. I have plenty of those I haven't told her about. "Oh my God."

"Please, don't say anything. I don't want to talk about it. It's a long, complicated story, one I will share when the time is right."

I want to ask where he is, who he is with, but the torment in her voice threatens to choke me. My first assumption would be social services have him, but gut instinct tells me there is more to it.

"Okay," I promise.

She turns to me, her eyes filled with determination and promise. "I'll get him back if it's the last thing I do. It's the only thing that keeps me going."

"Okay, honey, just know, when you are ready, I will be here. If you need anything at all, you only have to ask. I'll do anything to help you," I swear to her.

She smiles at me, gripping my hand. "I know that," she chokes out, before turning away to pull herself together.

"Good. Now, I think you need another drink. What would you like?"

Her shoulders slump. "I'd love one but I'm driving. Thank you though."

A commotion pulls me away from our conversation and I turn to see Dante, Cage, and Roy fighting around the barbeque.

And the barbeque that was cooking the chicken has high flames and smoke bellowing from it.

Kelly and I both turn to each other, breaking into laughter.

"Holy crap!" she howls, slapping her thigh.

Yeah, life is good, and moments like this make everything worthwhile.

THE NIGHT WAS a success, even with the fire incident. Cage and I finished cleaning up and had put Carrie to bed an hour ago. She was so wiped out from the day's activities that she went out like a light.

Now Cage and I are both lying in bed, snuggled into each other. I have my arms wrapped around his torso while he has his fingers drifting up my naked back. I usually sleep in a nighty, but my man likes to feel my skin on his, so I just go to bed in my knickers now. Sometimes I go in a T-shirt, but with the summer heat, the nights have been stuffy, so the lack of clothing is welcomed.

"Are you ready for tomorrow?" Cage asks.

Tomorrow, Detective Rome is coming down here to get the information I have on Robin. Nate had to cancel the original meet due to the accident. Rome was okay with it and said it gave him more time to put things into plan.

I'm nervous. I'm not going to lie. I don't trust very easily, but I trust Cage, and if he thinks we can trust Rome, then that's what I'm going to do.

I'm also ready for this to come to an end and hopefully tomorrow, that will start to happen.

I still haven't told anyone where the stuff is. Cage didn't want to know, not until he knew it was safe. But tomorrow, we will be getting them copied and sent out, then hopefully get them back in their safe place.

I can't wait for them to be gone. What Cage doesn't know, what I haven't told him, is that they are closer than he thinks. It's one of the reasons for my nightmares, why every time I come to bed each night, a tightness compresses my chest and I feel like I can't breathe.

They're underneath the bed, stored under a loose floorboard that only takes a knife to lift up.

He did ask last night if I will need time to get to them, but I assured him we didn't, that they were at hand. He was worried, I could tell, but after I assured him they weren't in my underwear drawer or somewhere obvious, he began to relax.

"Yeah," I murmur. "I will be glad to get the ball rolling. I should have figured out a way to get this done a long time ago."

"You've got me now," he promises.

"Are you sure we can trust him?"

He doesn't answer for a moment. "You don't need to trust him. Trust me. I don't know him, Kitten, but from what I've learned over the past few weeks, he's a good man. He doesn't even want the originals, so that is saying something. He wants us to keep a hold of them until he can get the rest to the people who can use them. All we have to do is sit back and wait for them to do their work, and then hope Robin doesn't fuck up in the meantime."

"What do you mean by 'fuck up'?" I ask, biting down on my lip.

"I know this isn't what you want to hear, but he's getting desperate and desperate men are unpredictable," he admits. "If he gets wind of what we are planning, there's no telling what will happen. I might not know him, but I can tell there's nothing good or redeemable in him."

My hope for this to be over pummels to the ground. "So, it's not over. Not until he's behind bars?"

"We're getting a step closer," he declares, his tone fierce.

"But we're going to have to watch our backs until this is all over. I don't want anyone getting hurt."

"Kitten, I'm not going to let anything happen to you. I know this isn't what you had hoped for, or planned, but we will get through this," he declares. "As long as you keep working with us to keep you safe, nothing will happen. I've got you. I've got Carrie."

"Okay, honey," I whisper.

"I love it when you call me honey," he whispers huskily, pressing a kiss to my neck, before pressing another one along my jaw, working his way up.

His lips finally reach mine and I smile against his mouth. My toes curl as he takes his time, savouring the kiss.

But it doesn't last long.

It never does.

And moments later, the kiss deepens, and within minutes, he has my knickers off and is deep inside of me.

Bliss!

Pure, utter, mind-blowing bliss.

Chapter Twenty-Eight

CAITLYN

I TAP MY FOOT RESTLESSLY against the floor, my thoughts focusing on everything but what is happening.

Mo, who I met when we arrived at the café over an hour ago, is Dante's mother. She is loud, outspoken, and took my mind off everything instantly, until she had to leave and get back to work.

Listening to her tease Dante about how he was dressed had been fun. Personally, I think he looks good, but it never hurts to take him down a peg. He needs it.

What I loved the most was hearing stories about Cage as a kid and all about the shenanigans they got up to.

The funniest story she told was about Elena, Cage's mum. She had walked in on them once measuring their own dicks to see whose was the biggest. I couldn't stop laughing, especially when Cage went bright red and blamed it on a dare.

I didn't enjoy hearing how his father worried about him getting some girl knocked up as a teenager and coming home with an STD.

Dante got her back to work, but at this point, I'm wishing she would come back.

Rome was meant to have been here nearly an hour ago. Something has happened. I can feel it.

"It's going to be okay," Cage assures me, placing his hand over my leg and stopping my tapping.

"Sorry," I murmur, gripping my mug. "Why isn't he here? Do you think something has happened?"

He grips my hands. "No," he declares. "He said he wasn't sure if he could arrive on time and to hang on, unless he rings to tell us otherwise."

"But how can he ring if something has happened to him?"

"Stop thinking like that," he orders gently. "Talk to me about something. Anything. Because I can't take another foot tap."

"Here, here," Dante teases.

I narrow my gaze before turning to Cage, teasingly asking, "Whose was the biggest?"

His cheeks redden, and I chuckle, ducking my face. He squeezes my hand, glowering at me, which doesn't help fade my amusement.

"Mine, Kitten," he declares.

Dante gasps. "No, it fucking wasn't."

"Are you sure? All men say they have the biggest do-dah."

"I would love to prove it to you, Kitten, but I'm not a fan of you looking at my friends' dicks, or any other man's dick for that matter."

"Me either," I mutter, scrunching up my nose.

"Are you not listening to me?" Dante cries out, banging his fist on the table. "Mine was the biggest."

"You wish," Cage mutters.

I open my mouth to reply, but the bell signalling the door pulls my attention away from them and I turn, spotting a tall, handsome man stepping inside. He's gorgeous—like, seriously gorgeous. He's smartly dressed in black suit trousers and a white crisp shirt that has the top two buttons undone and the sleeves rolled up to his elbows. He pushes his mirrored shades up and places them on his bald head. He scans the room, coming to a stop when his attention lands on our table.

Holy fuck!

I was so busy taking in his appearance that I don't feel the atmosphere change in the room. Cage tenses beside me and when I look up, Dante is already out of his seat, ready to spring into action.

"No breaking my shit, son," Mo yells.

Dante rolls his eyes, groaning.

The hot guy begins his way over to us and stops at our table. "Are you Mr. Cage Carter?" he asks in a gravelly voice.

"Yeah," Cage replies. "Are you Rome?"

The man jerks his head into a nod, before turning to me, running his gaze up and down my body. I shiver from the intensity, feeling it from head to toe. He is seriously hot, and he could easily be mistaken for Dwayne Johnson's doppelganger.

"Are you Caitlyn Michelson?"

"Y-yep," I choke out, feeling flustered all of a sudden.

Cage wraps his arms around my waist, and I jerk, not realising until then that I had stood up.

"Sit down, Kitten," he orders gently.

Taking my seat, I barely register anything else as Rome gets straight down to business, taking the seat in front of me and next to Dante.

"I'm sorry it took me so long to get here. I just wanted to make sure I wasn't being followed," he explains.

"It's fine," I lie, not filling him in on the fact I've been a nervous wreck.

His lips twitch like he can read through my lie. "When word leaks that I'm back working this investigation, things are going to be difficult for me *and* the two of you. I need to know what you have. You haven't got to give me anything yet, but I need to know if this is going to be worth it."

I'm taken aback for a moment, hit with the realisation of why we are here, and although Cage said we could trust him, I can't, not yet.

"Can you show me some identification first?"

"Sure," he agrees without hesitation.

Pulling out his wallet, he shows me his driver's licence, plus his badge. I settle in my seat to begin. Cage has kept silent, scanning the area while still keeping an eye on Rome.

"Okay," I murmur, handing them back. Cage rests his arm along the back of my chair, his fingers twirling a strand of hair. I clear my throat as I begin to relax. "I don't understand some of it. There are pages of accounts, numbers, and addresses with a list of names. Then I have a DVD. I played it once, though I turned it off when I saw a man tied to a chair with Robin standing by the side of him holding what looked like either a bat or a plank of wood."

"Do you know the man who was in the chair?" he asks, sitting straighter.

I shake my head. "No. There's also a recording of him with someone else, and again, I don't know what any of it means, but from what I could make out it was about a deal. There are pictures of him at various places, and then some not so nice pictures of him doing bodily harm to people. There's also one he sent me of my sister's dead body," I whisper.

"I'm sorry about your sister," he whispers.

I wipe under my eyes and glance away. "Thank you."

"That should be enough to get him," he admits. "I need to get a copy of everything you have straight away, if you've got it handy. I need to take off soon to get it back to my superior. We have some things tied up to Quinton, but we were told that in order to get him sentenced, we needed more evidence. This is exactly what we've been looking for." He stops, turning to glance at Cage and Dante. "Does anyone else know about this apart from these two?"

I reach for the napkin on the table. "Just Nate, but none of them know where it is or have seen it," I admit. "Robin knows I have the information, although I don't think he knows exactly what it is."

"You need to keep all this information within a tight net of people you trust."

"Have you ever been this close before?" Cage asks.

Rome's expression falls. "Once. But the guy they had on the inside fell in love with Quinton's wife and it went to shit."

I inhale sharply, my head snapping up.

"Courtney?" I ask, my lip trembling.

His gaze hits mine, taken aback, before he quickly recovers. Whatever that look was for, he sure didn't want me to see it.

"Yes, Mrs. Quinton. How do you know her?"

"She's my sister."

"She was your sister?" he asks, his jaw dropping.

I nod. "Who is the person who fell in love with her? She never said anything to me about this," I tell him. "I don't get it. If you knew all along about his criminal activities, why not just arrest him? Surely if you have someone on the inside, you could have found something out by now."

"That's confidential, Caitlyn."

"Did he die too?"

"No. He is currently still working on the inside, but since the night of her murder, Quinton has kept his affairs private, like he somehow knew he had a leak. He's only letting certain members of his men into the fold."

"I... I don't get it. Who? Why didn't he save her? She's my sister," I demand, feeling hysterical. "I deserve to know."

"Caitlyn," Cage whispers, taking my hand. I grip him back, but keep my gaze on Rome, pleading with him to tell me.

"Your sister was with a serious crime mob," he reveals, and I hate that pitying look. "All I know is that when he met her, he had not long started and was doing odd jobs here and there. Evidently, he caught her snooping through Quinton's office and suspected what she was trying to do. He was worried she was putting herself in danger in the process, so he took it upon himself to watch out for her. We advised him to stay clear, but he didn't listen. They started spending time together, from what I was briefed. Then he tried to help her get out of Quinton's hold. She confided in him a few weeks before her death that she found some stuff out. She told him she needed to get her... her sister and daughter safe. So, he did. The night she was murdered she was meant to meet him somewhere, but she never showed up. He never heard about what Quinton was planning to do to her, otherwise, I promise you, he would have stopped it."

I'm frozen. I don't know what to say. *What can I say?* I've just been told my sister could have been saved. This mess could have been put to an end years ago. I keep my head down as tears threaten to escape, while I let Cage and Rome continue the conversation. All I can think of is the last night my sister was alive. How she said she needed to go back to get Carrie's teddy, something easily replaced. I never got it. But if she was meeting him, why not meet at our grandma's house?

"Let me get this right, you're saying that you've had a man on the inside for what, years? And none of you have had enough evidence to put this fucker behind bars?" Cage bites out.

"Yes. You have to understand, Mr. Carter, we have rules we have to play by. Anything we do outside those rules can jeopardise the investigation."

"Are you sure this man of yours didn't tip Quinton off? That it wasn't him who was feeding Quinton information, and that's the reason he's conveniently not in the fold?"

"I can assure you he is good at his job. He has been on the case for eight years, and believe me, he is no crook. He is risking his life every day to put Quinton behind bars. He has fed us useful information that we have used, but nothing to ever pin Quinton on."

"Right," Cage mutters, jaw hard.

"Can you get the information for tomorrow? We can meet here at the same time," Rome suggests, turning to me now.

"Yes," I whisper.

"I'm going to get out of here. I don't want anyone to see me with you and it getting back to Quinton. I need to make sure this information reaches the right people, before he's tipped off that we are working the investigation," he explains, before handing me a card. "That has all my information on. To be safe, I want you to use a secure email account, along with a safe computer to send me the recording and DVD. Don't use your own computer or email address. If Quinton is watching you, he will have them tapped, along with your phones and workplace." I nod, still reeling over the news about my sister. "It was nice to meet you both."

He stands up to leave, but before he turns for the exit, he looks back at me with a serious expression.

"Stay safe, Miss Michelson," he orders, then nods to Cage before leaving the café.

As soon as I see the back of him disappear into the street, I exhale with relief.

Everything is falling into place, and after having it all spiral out of control for so long, it's a nice change. Now we have Rome, we can finally take a step forward instead of ten steps back.

"What do you think?" I ask, addressing Cage.

"I think we can trust him, but then again, I think it's the only choice we have left to take."

"Will this keep us safe, though? I mean, I know he is planning to put him behind bars, but can't Robin control his men from inside the prison? If he has all this power like you say he does, where does that leave us? Will we always be watching our backs? Carrie's life is at risk too, her entire life is. If she ever finds out her father is a murdering son of a bitch, it will shatter her."

"Calm down, Kitten. We can't keep living by 'what ifs'. What are the alternatives? Either way, he doesn't get to win."

Dante raps his knuckles over the table. "Men like him don't stay in power long. There's always someone who is willing or wanting to take over and to do that, they'll do anything."

I rub a hand down my face, exhaustion seeping through my system. "I'm just scared," I admit, then tilt my head up, facing them both. "I'm so sorry I've got you all into this mess."

"You didn't drag me into anything. I want to be here. With you," he admits. "And as sick and fucked up as this is, it brought you to me and I could never regret that."

My eyes glisten with tears from his words. This strong bulk of a man had been my undoing from our first meet. He's driven me insane, and can be infuriating, but I can't imagine life without him. He has become a part of our world.

"Cage," I whisper.

"I don't regret it either," Dante interrupts, breaking the moment. "I want to be with you too."

His mum, Mo, takes that moment to walk by and rolls her eyes. She slaps him across the head, muttering under her breath.

"How did the meet go?" Nate asks, and I jump. Cage's hand over mine tightens and he turns, glowering at Nate, who has taken a seat in the chair Rome was occupying.

"Good," Cage answers. "We need to head back and get a start on the copies."

Nate's expression turns concrete. "So it begins."

"It begins," Cage repeats, before turning to me. "Kitten, it's time. We need to know where the information is. Mo's place is safe to talk.

As you can see, it's just us, along with those three over there, who are here." He points at the other three customers, and I nod. "I asked Mo when the best time would be to come here, so that we wouldn't be surrounded by people who could easily listen in."

I didn't even think of that. I knew Cage was being cautious on the way over here—always looking behind us in the rear-view mirror for anyone following—but I didn't think anyone would actually know what we were doing. I didn't even know Nate was here.

"How long have you been here?" I ask Nate now the thought has come to mind.

"I've been here since you guys got here. I travelled behind you at a distance to make sure no one was following."

"Why didn't you come in?" I ask, my brows bunching together.

"I wanted to make sure there were no other interruptions and keep an eye on the place in case someone was watching."

"Oh," I murmur.

"Kitten," Cage urges. "The information."

Oh yeah. I forgot.

"It's under the floorboard in my bedroom," I whisper. His mouth opens, then closes, before his expression morphs into a scowl. "What?"

Anyone would think I had just told him they were on the kitchen side.

"You hid it in your floorboard?"

"Yes. Why?" I answer, annoyance building inside of me.

"Kitten, you put yourself in danger right there. You should have taken it somewhere away from you."

"I didn't want to risk losing it. I wanted to know where it was at all times."

He shakes his head before standing, helping me to my feet. "Let's go get it."

"I'll meet you at yours," Nate announces. "Your place isn't wired, but just in case, don't talk about it. If you do, use the term 'bills' and not information."

Cage and I nod before we leave, my heart racing as we do.

This is nearly over.

Chapter Twenty-Nine

CAITLYN

I GLANCE AT THE CLOCK ON THE wall, knowing I need to start making a move if I want to spend time with Carrie before I go to work.

She wanted to stay with Hayley. It warms my heart with how close she is to Roy and Hayley. I'm glad she has them in her life.

Even still, my gut churned when I left her there. It was just a bad feeling I had in the pit of my stomach. I kept running over what Robin will do when he finds out what I've done. Will he kill everyone I love because he has no reason to keep them alive? Will he kill his own flesh and blood? I'm ready to explode, and I can't wait until I start work. Tonight, I'm not singing, I'm going over some books for Roy, which will no doubt keep my mind from everything.

I head into the kitchen to grab a bottle of water, passing Cage and Nate who were still going through the files they ripped up from under the floorboard.

I offered to help but after a few minutes of glancing at papers, I didn't have a clue what I was looking at or what I should be looking for, so I left them to it.

"Hey, Kitten, what are you doing?" Cage asks, snagging me around the waist when I walk past.

I smile down at him. "I'm going to get ready. I promised Carrie I would go see her before I started work. Roy needs me to go over the books."

"Let me know when you're ready and I'll walk you over."

I wave him off. "No, it's fine. You've got more important stuff to do," I remind him, pointing down at the papers.

"You're more important. This stuff is worthless if you're dead or kidnapped by one of Robin's psychos."

"Good point," I mutter. "I'll be ready in ten."

Nate snorts, sifting through papers. "Make that an hour then."

Cage chuckles as he turns to Nate. "No, brother. When she says ten minutes, she means ten minutes."

"No way," Nate denies.

"Honestly," Cage promises, his lips pulling up in amusement.

"Lucky fuck," Nate grumbles, before pulling his laptop in front of him.

Making a mental note not to take more than ten minutes, I walk out of the room and head to the bathroom. Even though it doesn't take me long to get ready, the universe would shit on me by making sure I go over by a few minutes. Then I would never hear the end of it, from Cage or Nate.

I walk out of the bathroom less than ten minutes later to find Cage putting on his boots, still sitting at the table.

"You ready?"

"Yeah, I'm going to come see Pea for a while, walk you to work, then either Nate, Dante, or I will pick you up later when you've finished. We don't want to leave all this lying around unattended."

"Did you get anything useful from them?"

Nate drags his attention away from the computer to explain. "I didn't know what any of it was at first, so I started to look into his background," he begins, letting out a weary sigh. "He's quite the thief. He's doesn't just run the business; he scams other gangs and steals *their* business too. It's not just them he scams but massive corporations, earning millions in profits."

"No," I whisper, eyes widening.

Cage nods. "We've managed to find information on past drug runs, weapon shipments, and a list of storage containers he owns that he thinks he has hidden."

Nate points to the pile. "The police will know what to do with all that though. I'm actually hoping this Rome guy keeps us informed after they catch the sicko. It's intriguing," he tells us, his eyes lighting up. "With the videos, voice recordings, and all of this paperwork, there is enough to send him to prison for a fucking long time."

"Even though it's old?" I ask, biting my lip.

"Yeah. You said he doesn't know what information you have, and my guess is, he knows it's old and probably thinks he has nothing to worry about," Nate answers.

"But he does?"

"Yeah, because it means he didn't cover anything up, probably didn't see the point. And even still, half of this information is still concrete evidence. There's no talking his way out of this or paying off people."

"Thank God," I breathe out. "I really hope this all pans out."

"It will," Cage promises.

I lean down, capturing his lips. "Come on, lover boy, let's go see our girl," I demand.

Cage tenses for a moment before he stands, his gaze distant for a moment before he masks it.

"Are you okay?" I ask, chewing on my thumbnail.

He snaps to attention and beams at me. "Yeah, everything's perfect, Kitten."

I don't believe him. "Cage," I whine. "You froze up for a second."

"I didn't freeze up, not really. You just took me by surprise."

Took him by surprise? My brows shoot up. "Cage," I demand.

He rolls his eyes as he reaches for me. "So demanding," he murmurs. "You just said something I liked the sound of is all."

He reaches for my hand and begins to pull me towards the front door. When we reach it, I dig my feet in, keeping them firmly on the floor. "Tell me what it was."

He stops, turning to me. "You said *our girl*."

"Oh," I reply, scratching the top of my head. I hadn't even realised I said that. I guess it just came out.

"Yeah, *oh*. I liked it, I liked it a lot," he admits, his gaze warm.

Seeing the truth in his words, I can't help but melt against him. I wrap my arms around his neck, leaning up to kiss him.

This man is perfect. He has taken my baggage, my daughter, and made them his own.

Our relationship may have progressed fast, but I regret nothing. I wouldn't change the time we have shared for anything. I have to believe he was brought into our lives for a reason, that I took a chance on him for a reason.

I might not have thought it or voiced it, but I think I trusted him and felt something for him from the first night I met him, yet the trauma of my past would only let me access that trust subconsciously.

It was like someone with amnesia. They don't remember, but somewhere deep down, something will become familiar to them, like they had lived or seen it before. I felt this way with Cage, and as corny as it sounds, it feels like I have known him my whole life yet woke up the night I cut the plug.

I pour my love into the kiss, showing him without words what he means to me. I love how he argues with Dante for no reason. I love how he teases and makes my daughter laugh. I love it when he reads to her, cuddles her, or treats her like the precious treasure she is.

I love the way he's gentle with me yet firm in the bedroom, respecting my limitations. I love the way he anticipates my needs before I know what they are. I love how he's stayed by me this entire time and showed me what it's like to live.

But it won't last.

Stopping my thoughts, I pull back from the kiss, gazing up at him. I watch his pupils dilate, his expression softening as he pulls me closer like we aren't already close.

It won't last.

I push the thoughts away. I know it's my past and fear talking. Just because my crap is coming to an end, it doesn't mean we are.

Because when he promised he was in this for the long run, I believed him. And I still do.

"I love kissing you," he rasps, pressing another to the corner of my mouth. "I love doing other things too. Are you sure you have to work?"

I squeeze my thighs together, my lust, desire, and emotions running wild. As I stare up at him unblinking, I'm assaulted by it all.

By his devotion.

His love.

His loyalty.

His bravery.

And his ability to render me speechless.

"I love you," I blurt out, unable to stop the words from tumbling out of my mouth.

They come out so easily, and although I'm shocked I spoke them out loud, I can't regret them.

Because this is love. There are no ifs or buts, no 'you've not known each other long'. It just is.

However, feeling him tense in my arms has me rethinking my verbal vomit.

I'm so fucking stupid.

"You love me?" he breathes, rocking back a step.

"I… I didn't mean to say it," I whisper, ducking my head.

He takes a step closer, gripping my chin. "Do you love me, Kitten?" he growls.

"I… I… I know you don't feel the same way, but it's how I feel. I'm sorry if it's not what you wanted to hear," I tell him, fighting back tears.

"Kitten," he rasps, and the plea in his voice has me tilting my head back to look at him.

"What?"

"Say it again," he demands, placing his palm on the bottom of my back to push me closer. "Say it."

I run my hand up his chest, feeling his heart race under my palm. My lashes flutter as I look up at him. "I love you."

He slams his lips against mine as he picks me up by my hips, slamming me against the cabin, right next to the door. My breath hitches when he pulls back. "I love you too, Kitten," he declares, before kissing me once more.

He loves me.

I grip the hair at the nape of his neck, pulling at the strands as he thrusts against me.

Fuck!

"I love you," he repeats, his voice stronger, determined. "Fuck, I love you."

"I love you too," I pant out, rolling my hips.

He clenches his eyes shut. "I'm trying to come up with a good reason why we can't kick Nate out because I want you naked and lying across the kitchen table."

I smile against his mouth before he pulls back, kissing along my jaw to my neck. "I think he'd understand," I reply breathlessly.

"Yeah, he would."

He leans down, and his lips brush mine just as his phone begins to ring from his pocket. He groans, resting his forehead against mine. "Fuck, I should get that."

I nod as he drops me to my feet. He takes a step back, pulling his phone out. His brows rise when he glances down at the screen and he takes a step back, cursing.

"What do you want?" he answers. "What? How in the hell did you find out? I'm going to fucking kill him. No. No, you're not. No, Laura. Fuck's sake, okay. We can come tomorrow. Caitlyn has the day off, but we have shit to do in the morning. Yes, I'll fucking bring them. Whatever. Bye."

"Who was that?" I ask, trying not to laugh at his put off expression.

He pockets his phone. "My eldest sister, Laura. She wants us to go around to Dad's tomorrow so they can meet you and Pea. It looks like fucking Dante was bragging about a girl called Carrie. They all thought he found *the one*," he explains, chuckling. "When he explained who she was, they got together and made plans. Now they want to meet you both."

"Oh God," I groan, stepping forward to grip his T-shirt.

"It's okay. We'll go around two tomorrow and get it over with," he assures me, misreading me. "It was either us go there or they come here, and if that happened, we would never get fucking rid of them."

I bite my lip. "What if they don't like me?"

His eyes widen. "They're going to love you."

"Who's going to love you?" Nate asks, stepping outside.

Cage wraps his arm around me. "Laura called. Evidently, Dante opened his big mouth yesterday about Carrie. Things got mixed up and he then explained who she was. You know what Laura is like. She has to stick her nose in. She wants us to go around Dad's tomorrow for a barbeque so they can meet her."

"They?" Nate asks, seeming more interested now.

"Yeah, Laura, Dad, and Danni, but you know what Laura is like; she will invite the aunts and uncles," Cage replies absently.

Nate pauses for a moment before replying, "I'll come if you want."

Nate tenses, bracing himself, and I turn rigid, wondering what's going on.

"Of course you can. It's your funeral, though," Cage tells him, and I come up more confused.

There was a weird vibe coming from Nate and Cage hadn't picked up on it at all. It was weird.

"They can't be that bad," I comment.

"Oh, trust me, they are," Cage utters.

"They aren't. He just hates being ganged up on by a girl," Nates teases.

I chuckle, squeezing the hand on Cage's hip. "I bet."

"It wasn't like they weren't going to meet you. I just wanted to keep you to myself," he explains. "Is that too much to ask for?"

I relax against him. "I believe you."

Nate snorts. "He's trying to get out of it already."

Cage narrows his eyes. "Don't you have shit to be working on?"

Nate laughs. "Yeah," he replies, before turning to me. "And they'll love you."

I force a smile as he heads back inside, turning when Cage pulls me into his arms. "Do you really think so?"

"Yeah, they will. And they'll adore Carrie," he assures me, pressing a kiss to my lips.

"Then I guess we are meeting your family tomorrow," I murmur.

He grins, pulling me close. "We should get to Carrie before you have work but don't think I've forgotten we were interrupted."

"Later," I tease.

"Later," he promises, his eyes darkening.

Chapter Thirty

CAITLYN

I'M STILL WALKING ON CLOUD NINE as I enter the bar an hour later. The man I love told me he loved me back, and I spent the last hour laughing and joking with my girl.

"I'm just saying, if she wants the doll, she can have the doll. I'll go out and get it when I next have time," Cage tells me, talking about the doll Carrie had conned him into buying.

"And I'm just saying; she has you wrapped around her little finger."

He laughs, tugging on my arm and pulling me against his chest. "She has everyone wrapped around her finger."

I sigh, placing my casted arm over his chest. "That she does."

"Hey, Caitlyn, Cage," Kelly greets.

I beam. "Hey, you okay?"

"Yeah, I'm good."

"Roy in his office?"

"He's not going to be back until later, but he said he piled it all on his desk for you."

I give her a chin lift and make my way through the bar to the office. Entering, my eyes widen at the mess.

"Shit," Cage murmurs.

I sigh, knowing this will take a while for me to get through. "You can say that again."

He kicks the door shut behind me and picks me up at the waist. I squeal, gripping him tightly with my good hand. "Hey, what are you doing?"

He places me down on the desk and then bends down until we're eye level. "Remember, no leaving unless it's with me, Dante or Nate, okay?"

I run my hand up his chest. "I know. I heard the first time you told me."

"Smart arse."

I grin. "I know."

His smile turns devilish and my breath stalls in my chest. "Now, on to another matter."

"What matter would that be?" I breathe out.

I close my eyes when I feel his hands run up over my thighs and under my skirt, stopping before he reaches my sex. He spreads my thighs apart before stepping into them.

"Roy isn't here," he comments, pulling me from my daze.

"Huh?"

He runs his hands further up, reaching under my top. When he grips the end, pulling it up and over my head, my eyes widen, and I quickly cover myself the best I can.

He grips my good wrist whilst gently taking the other, pinning them down. "We are going to finish what I started earlier."

"Here?" I squeak.

He leans down, kissing the corner of my mouth. "Yes."

A moan slips free when he tugs my skirt up before pushing his hand into my knickers. "Cage," I cry out, feeling his fingers slide through my sex.

I'm already turned on, and as his thumb presses down on my clit, the desire builds.

His mouth smashes back down to mine in a hungry, ravishing kiss. His tongue collides with mine and I moan. We grab at each other, touching, feeling… everything.

I faintly hear him undoing his zipper as he continues to kiss me hard and fast, making me forget about everything around us and the fact we are in Roy's office and on his desk.

I can't get enough of him. Reaching between us, I pull his T-shirt out of his jeans, working quickly and roughly as I pull it up over his head. He slides his hand around me, unclipping my bra, letting it slide down my arms.

Being vulnerable, naked in what is a potentially public place, only heightens my arousal. I moan when he presses against me.

"Please," I beg, wrapping my legs around him to bring him closer to me.

"What do you want?" he asks, looming over me, his voice filled with sex.

"You."

His lips twitch as he slides a finger inside of me. "You have me, Kitten."

"Don't tease me, Cage. Fuck me," I plead.

Sliding his hand out of my knickers, he then pushes them aside, gripping his cock with the other. He lines it up at my entrance, and as if he anticipated it, he slams inside of me at the same time his lips crash down on mine, swallowing the moan.

He thrusts harder, and in the distance, I hear the sound of the music in the bar, voices moving past. The desk shakes, items knocking to the floor, but it doesn't matter. None of it matters.

Only he matters.

"Harder," I beg, and he complies.

"Fuck, you feel good."

I grip his shoulder, my back arching off the desk as he reaches the spot. I cry out, my stomach tightening.

"Tell me again," he demands, his hands pressing down on my pelvis as he thrusts harder, sweat beading at his forehead.

"Harder," I breathe when he begins to slow down.

"Not until you tell me those three words."

What he's talking about dawns on me, and my stomach tightens.

"I love you," I declare, staring into his eyes as he begins to pick up the pace once again.

"Fuck!" he rasps. "I love you too."

I grip the edge of the desk with my good hand, my stomach tightening. "Cage," I moan, closing my eyes as pleasure rolls through me.

"Are you close?" he rasps, and my lids flutter open, finding him watching where we are joined.

It's hot.

So fucking hot. I know I won't last much longer.

"Yes," I pant, gripping the desk harder when that feeling coils in the pit of my stomach. "I love you."

"Fuck," he grunts, then slams into me harder. "Fuck, I love you, too, Kitten. I love you so goddamn much."

His words send me flying over the edge, and I scream out his name, just as he leans down, pressing his lips to mine.

He pulls back a little, his breathing hard, and moments later, I feel his entire body tense, his fingers digging into my hips as he empties his load inside of me.

Moments later, he drops his weight over me, panting heavily. I run my fingers through his hair, feeling content and blissfully sated.

"God... that was... I don't even know what that was," I murmur.

"Well, I'm good. Did you expect anything less?" he teases, wearing a triumphant grin.

"Cocky much?" I mutter, slapping his arm playfully.

His grin spreads. "Only with you."

I smile back, giving him one last kiss before I push him away so I can straighten out my skirt and put my clothes back on. I grab some of the tissues from the desk to clean myself up, before disposing them in the dustbin. Cage grabs his T-shirt off the floor and starts to get himself dressed, too.

When we are both decent, I glance over at the door, biting my bottom lip.

Anyone could have walked in and caught us. Hell, Roy could have come back and walked in on us. And Kelly? What if she had needed something but heard what we were doing?

As great as it was, I'm still embarrassed. But it was Cage, and he has more control over my body sexually than I ever have.

Cage chuckles when he sees where I'm looking. "Stop worrying, Kitten, no one gives a fuck what we were doing. The music is on out there, so they wouldn't have heard you screaming like a banshee," he teases.

I glare, making him smile wider. "I was not screaming like a fucking banshee," I snap.

He arches an eyebrow. "Yeah, Kitten, you were."

"Whatever," I grumble, walking around the desk to the chair. I need to get some work done before Roy comes back with more. Although, I'm not sure how I can be in this room with him knowing what Cage and I just did.

He chuckles, leaning over to press a kiss to my head. "I'll let you get to work but call me if you need me or you're leaving."

"Yes," I promise, flicking the computer on, my gaze going back to the spot where we just fucked.

"Stop worrying," he says, still grinning, the cocky twat.

"Roy could have walked in on us fucking like school kids on his desk," I tell him, worrying over it. What if someone did but we just hadn't noticed or heard them?

"Did you enjoy it?" he asks, losing his grin.

"You know I fucking did," I snap, feeling my cheeks heat.

"I know. Like a banshee."

I go to slap him, but he jumps back out of reach. "I was not screaming like a fucking banshee," I yell.

"Tell that to the people outside," he chuckles, pulling open the door.

I grab the nearest thing to me, which happens to be a book, and lob it across the room towards Cage. He ducks out of the way and through the door. I growl in frustration, wanting to strangle him for being right. I did love it, and I probably did scream like a banshee. Kind of.

"You're horrible," I call out.

He pops his head around the doorframe. "No need to be pissed, baby. I love it when you scream my name," he tells me, winking.

"Go home before I chuck something more likely to hit you," I warn.

"See you later, Kitten," he tells me, turning to leave.

I admire his arse in his tight jeans as he leaves, and I drop in my chair, exhausted yet happy. My lips pull up into a smile, my gaze going to the spot where we just fucked. Yeah, I can't complain. Not really. Life is about taking chances and I was too scared to make any of those over the years. This is one chance I'm willing to take. Because sex with Cage makes everything worthwhile.

And he loves me.

I STRETCH MY back, trying to get the kink out of it. I have been going over his files for a few hours and am not making much progress. He needs to either keep on top of these or pay someone to do it.

There's a knock on the door and I'm grateful for the distraction. My eyes are beginning to sting from staring at the screen.

"Come in," I call out.

Kelly pushes open the door. "Hey, you busy?"

"No," I groan. "Please, come in and distract me."

"You still going over the books?" she asks, staring down at the desk.

"Yeah," I sigh. "What can I do for you?" I ask her.

"Nothing really, I was just wondering if you fancied going out next weekend into town or something? Dave, the bloke I'm staying with, asked me to go out with him and a few of his mates. As much as it would be great to get out, I don't have any girlfriends here and I'm not keen on going out with a bunch of guys."

I grimace, but then a thought occurs to me. "I thought you were staying with your brother?"

She opens her mouth, pauses, then pales a little. "Yeah, this is, um, his friend's house."

Ah, that explains it. "I'd love to, but I have Carrie, and with work and stuff—" pause, exhaling heavily. "Honestly? I do have Carrie, but if I'm honest, I'm not really a going out person. Going out clubbing doesn't appeal to me."

"It's okay. It was just a thought. It would have been nice to have some girl time."

"Well, why don't we organise a girls' night in? We could watch some movies, order takeout and gossip about whatever you want to," I offer.

Kelly has come so far since I met her and has really come out of her shell. I hate that the first time she has asked to spend time with me, I've rejected the offer. But I wasn't lying when I said it doesn't appeal to me.

I want to make her happy. Lately, that sad, depressed vibe pours from her, and I know without asking that she's internally struggling with something, and I know it has everything to do with her son. I haven't brought him up since the barbeque. I had hoped she would come to me, but maybe it's time to get her to open more.

In some ways, she reminds me of me. She has secrets, she holds demons, and she's fighting for her child. I can relate to that more than anyone.

She sags with relief. "That sounds awesome if I'm honest."

"That's settled then. We can get a bottle or two of wine, but I will tell you, I only need one glass and I'm a goner. I'm a lightweight," I admit, laughing.

"Me too," she admits, shrugging. "Right, I'd better get back to work because we both know Frey is going to be sat out there polishing her nails. It makes me wonder how she has kept this job for so long, especially with the restaurant being so busy all the damn time."

I wince, feeling for her. I only worked with Frey once and she's lazy. She's here temporarily to cover my shifts, whilst Kelly covers the rest, but normally she works in the restaurant, and compared to here, that place is a no rest zone. At least we get to have somewhat of a rest whilst working here.

Frey, however, doesn't know the meaning of work and takes it upon herself to do as she pleases. How Roy keeps these girls on is beyond me.

"I'm sorry. I'm planning on talking to Roy about setting up a staff meeting this week. Things need to change and not just sharing the workload. Some of the customer reviews we receive regarding the same members of staff have the potential to ruin the business' image."

"Thank God," she breathes out. "If I had to work one more

night doing everything on my own, I was going to take matters into my own hands."

I can't blame her. We're busier than normal, and we need staff to be at their best, not slacking around.

I push up out of the chair. "I'm going to come out to get a drink anyway, so I'll tell her to get her skinny arse to work."

"I wish I could record this," she mutters, making me laugh as she follows me out.

Chapter Thirty-One

CAITLYN

CLOSING TIME IS UPON US AND I'm beginning to get a headache. Roy dropped by earlier, but he's due back any moment.

After tonight, he needs to hire some serious help. Not local kids who just want to earn money by doing nothing. He needs to hire people who want the job. This isn't because he's doing a bad job; this is because he's too kind and lets them walk all over him.

The door pushes open, and Roy drags his feet inside, a steaming cup of coffee in his hand. He yawns, dropping down on the chair in front of me, and I take a moment to take in his appearance. He's exhausted, and he's going to run himself into the ground if he doesn't do something about it. The only other assistant manager aside from me is Dominic and he runs the restaurant.

"Hey," I greet softly. "You look exhausted."

He runs a hand down his face, glancing up. "I feel it, girl."

"Have you thought about hiring more staff? Not more Frey's or Kacey's, but more Kelly's."

"More you's?"

I grin. "Well…" I shrug.

He chuckles. "I'll get on it. I've just got a lot going on."

"What's wrong?" I ask, wondering why Hayley never mentioned anything earlier. I'd like to think we're friends, and that she would come to me if something was happening. "Can I do anything to help?"

He sits back, kicking his feet up on the desk. "No, nothing for you to worry about."

"Roy," I warn, dropping my pen down on the stack of paper.

He rolls his eyes before sitting up. "It's fine. I've just been trying to get some work done with the new development, but it's turning out to be harder than I originally planned."

"What do you mean?" I ask, reaching for my own cuppa.

"I want some new CCTV set up around the grounds, but with privacy laws and all that bollocks, it's where to set them where they aren't a waste of money."

"Have you spoken to Nate?"

"Yeah. He's got some stuff going on but he's going to look everything over and come up with a plan," he explains. "I just wish it could be done now. We need it now more than ever."

His words are like a blow to the gut as the blood drains from my face. Guilt eats at me. He wouldn't need to up his security system if it weren't for me. He wouldn't have to waste money on an updated system had it not been for me.

And he's running around stressing about it all, because of me. Because he cares for me.

"I'm so sorry," I whisper, my voice breaking.

He looks up, his brows pinched together. "What for, honey?"

"It's because of me. I'm the reason you need the extra security. If I didn't bring my shit here, you would have been okay. You wouldn't be stressed like you are now."

He sits forward, leaning over the desk to grab my hand. He gives it a squeeze. "Oh, honey, it isn't because of you."

"Don't try to make me feel better," I demand softly. "I'm not worth this."

"Caitlyn, listen to me. You are one of the reasons, I'm not going to lie, but it was worth every penny if it meant keeping you safe."

"Roy," I whisper.

"But it's not just about that. We've been having problems with vandalism over on the east side of the cabins. We reckon it's local kids getting in and doing it, but we aren't too sure," he explains softly. "And as much as I don't need the reminder, I hate that someone got into the cabins without us being aware and planted that stuff. This should be a safe place for our guests and our staff. Please don't worry about any of this. I've got it handled."

I sit up, my eyes widening at the news about the vandalism. "Someone has been vandalising? When did that happen? Have you reported it to the police?"

"Yeah, we have an incident number, but they have nothing to go on other than there have been other vandalism reports from residents in town."

I open my mouth to question him some more but there's another knock on the door. I groan, rolling my eyes at Roy. "I bet it's Frey again asking if she can go home."

"I need to fire her arse," he mutters.

I slump back in my seat. "Come in," I call out.

It's not Frey who walks in. It's Officer Johnson, and his expression has a shiver racing down my spine. I share a look with Roy, who looks just as tense.

"Officer Johnson," I greet, standing.

"Miss Michelson," he replies tersely, his gaze flicking from Roy. "Can I please have a word with you in private?"

I turn to Roy, disliking having to remove him from his own office. He stands, forcing a smile. "It's okay," he assures me.

"Are you sure?"

He nods, but when his gaze flicks to Officer Johnson, he doesn't look too pleased. "Yes. I'll be in the bar," he tells me, and it sounds more like a warning.

Once he leaves, I turn to the officer. "Please, take a seat," I tell him, retaking mine.

I want to cry. All I want to do is get back home and go to bed, but I can see this taking a lot of time.

"I'm sorry to catch you so late in the evening."

"How did you know I was here?" I ask, clasping my hands together on my lap.

"I didn't, but I remembered you telling us you work nights here, so I came here first to check," he explains.

"Okay," I murmur, feeling my heart race for reasons unbeknown to me. "How can I help you? I've already told you everything I know."

"You were fully aware of the warrant out for Miss Cunnings' arrest?"

"I was," I tell him, wondering where he is going with this.

"And that we filed for a warrant to search her premises?"

"I thought you said her mum checked her house?"

"She did, but to do a full sweep, we needed a warrant."

"I'm not sure why you are telling me this," I admit.

"Miss Michelson, we found Miss Cunnings' body at eight this morning in her home."

My hands slap down on the table, my lips parting. "What?"

"I need to know your whereabouts on Monday the thirteenth between four AM and eight PM."

She's dead?

His question hits me and the blood drains from my face. "I…
uh… oh my God!" I pull my hair out of my face, my heart racing. "I
don't know. I can't think."

"I need you to answer me, Miss Michelson."

My eyes widen and I rub at my chest. "I didn't kill her if that's
what you're asking. I don't even know where she lives," I admit, my
voice rising.

Oh my God. I'm going to be arrested.

He thinks I killed her.

"I need you to think about it for me. What were you doing on
that day?"

I struggle to catch my breath. "I don't know," I all but yell. "Give
me a minute. You've just told me someone has been murdered, and
then you expect me to know what the fuck I was doing a week ago.
Can I call my boyfriend? He will know."

"Go ahead, Miss Michelson," he orders, leaning forward. "But
first, I'd like to know how you think she was murdered. I never said
that."

I pause with the phone in my hand, and I look up, a ball forming
in the back of my throat. "W-what?"

"I never said she was murdered," he repeats.

I'm beginning to get angry. He's playing mind games with me.
"You wouldn't be here asking me where I was on a certain date if she
had killed herself. What else was I meant to think?"

"I suppose," he mutters, then jerks his head to the phone in my
hand.

I dial Cage's number just as the office door is pushed open. I jerk
to my feet, nearly collapsing when I see it's Cage walking in.

He rushes over to me, pulling me into his arms. "What's going
on?" he asks as I cling to his shirt. "Why are you here this late?"

"I think you need to sit down, Cage," I warn, my voice low.

"No, not until he tells me why he's here."

I glance up at a shuffle and see Mr Johnson stand from his chair. "Mr Carter, I was going to visit you after Miss Michelson here."

"Well, you've got both of us so start talking," Cage grits out.

Officer Johnson sighs. "We found Miss Cunnings' body during the early hours of this morning. We need to know your girlfriend's whereabouts on Monday the thirteenth between four AM and eight PM," he demands, his voice firm. "This will also include your whereabouts too."

Cage's arm tightens around me, and I close my eyes. I know she tried to kill us, that she did a lot of shitty stuff to Cage, but she was still his ex. "I'm sorry, but I'm failing to see what that has to do with us. She probably killed herself after nearly trying to kill us," he snaps.

"She was murdered," Officer Johnson replies.

Cage jerks. "And you think one of us fucking did it?" he growls. "Caitlyn doesn't even know her."

"I'm just doing my job," Officer Johnson reveals, losing his patience. "Before I can continue, I need to know where you both were. Please think hard. Where were you between those times?"

"Monday? Well, if it was the Monday after the accident then we were both at the cabin. We both had the day off. I can't really remember if I'm honest, but we have surveillance around the cabin that has a time and date stamp. I can't give you a definite answer until I look at the videos, but I'm more than positive we stayed in."

Officer Johnson pauses, lifting his pen away from his pad. "Why do you have surveillance around your cabin?"

Cage's fingers tighten against my waist. I know we can't tell Officer Johnson the reason why we have the surveillance, but I'm worried we might have to, to save ourselves a prison sentence. We're getting so close to finishing the Robin situation, but it looks like it could all come down on us in this single moment.

If he finds out the surveillance is because of Robin, then spreads the news, we are fucked.

"We have a four-year-old little girl, Officer Johnson," Cage partially lies. We do have a four-year-old, but she isn't the reason the surveillance is up. "Now, can you tell me why you were questioning Caitlyn?"

He doesn't look away from Cage for a moment, but when he does, his hardened expression drops. "Whoever killed Miss Cunnings left a note."

My body grows tight at his words. Cage's muscles bulge beneath me and I have to bite my lip to stop the sob from escaping.

Johnson doesn't know. He can't. But if that note is from who we think it's from, I'm the reason she was killed.

Bile rises in my throat, and I clutch Cage tighter, not letting go.

Why can't this just stop?

What did I do in another life to deserve this happening? I didn't even know Lou, but now she's dead because of me. Another life on my hands.

When I get my hands on Death, I am going to wring his fucking neck for taking all these lives, then feed him to the sharks, and if Death happens to be a woman, then God help her, because I pray that her next period is in a shark tank.

This is what I've been afraid of. I didn't want anyone around me being hurt, and now someone has been. But what I don't get is why Lou? I only met her once and it was brief, and we didn't even share words. And why after she tried to kill us?

"What did the note say?" Cage asks, his jaw tight and his focus entirely on Officer Johnson.

"Here," he offers and pulls out a piece of paper.

I pull back from Cage when he leans over to take it. He moves away, blocking me from seeing it. I bite my lip, unable to look away as I watch his expression harden. If his reaction is anything to go by, this is bad. Really bad.

He tries to hand it back, but I snatch it up, seeing they've scanned the card onto this piece of paper.

"Kitten, don't," he warns.

I give him my best I'm-doing-this-with-or-without-your-permission look, but he just glares, shaking his head with disapproval. Before he can take it back, I glance down at the piece of paper. The scripted lettering is just like all the others I received, and my skin prickles as I read over the words.

A present for you, my darling Caitlyn. Let's hope you will be as fun as Lou here. Let this be a warning to you. Lou won't be the one to kill you, I will! See you soon, K.

Holy mother of all that is Jesus. He killed her. *For me.*

I take a step back, the piece of paper slipping through my fingers.

"Caitlyn," Cage calls softly.

He killed her because of me. Because he wants to kill me.

Bile rises in my throat as the words replay in my head.

He's going to kill me.

Cage reaches out for me, but I launch to the side, grabbing the bin next to the desk and throwing up today's consumption of food.

Cage kneels next to me, rubbing my back as I continue to empty my stomach.

"Shhh, it's okay."

"I need to ask some more questions," Officer Johnson announces.

Cage's hand clenches over my shoulder. "Really? Right now? She's fucking throwing up," he snaps.

"I know, but the quicker I get answers, the better." I begin retching again, my stomach throbbing. "I know this is a shock, but we need to get this done now."

How can he not think that this would come as a shock? The woman who tried to kill us—who nearly achieved that—has been found murdered; murdered by someone who wants to kill me.

"Shock is an understatement," Cage bites out. "We will answer your questions but not tonight."

"Mr Carter—"

"Not tonight," he barks. "We have prior arrangements in the morning, but we can be there after. Is that good enough for you or do you enjoy terrorising young women?"

"Make sure you are there," he warns, sounding pissed.

"We will," Cage replies, and I can hear he's barely hanging on.

"Very well. I'll see myself out," he mutters, and I hear him take a few steps before he stops. "Be well, Miss Michelson, and please, do not miss tomorrow's appointment."

I hear the door faintly close, but I take no notice. Cage's cool hands rest on my forehead as he scrapes the hair from my face.

I collapse against him, clutching his T-shirt. "What are we going to do? He killed her, Cage. He killed her. And it's all because of me."

"No, it's not," he bites out. "I'm not sure what is going on, but either way, this is not your fault. It's not."

"He killed her," I whisper.

"It's going to be okay."

Will I always feel the guilt of the people I lost so strongly? Why am I alive and they're all gone?

When will this end? With me dead?

I tilt my head up, struggling to focus on him through tear-filled eyes. What started out as a good night has ended up one of the worst nights ever. I've only ever known about men like this Kane guy from movies or books. Never in a million years did I ever think someone like that would manifest in my life. Then again, I blame all this entirely on Robin fucking Quinton. Who does he think he is? How can he live with himself day in and day out knowing he has taken the lives of so many innocent people?

I pray he burns in hell for his crimes. "What are we going to do? All this with Rome was for nothing if we have to tell him what is really happening."

"Let me figure that out. Nothing is ruined."

"Can you take me home, please?" I whisper, my voice hoarse and sore from retching.

"Sure. Go clean yourself up while I go talk to Roy for a moment. Okay?"

I nod, and he continues to hold me, like he's scared that if he lets go, I'll break down once again. I can't even assure him I won't because I feel the walls tumbling down around me.

"Okay," I agree, pulling my knees to my chest. The minute he leaves, gut-wrenching sobs are ripped from my body.

Chapter Thirty-Two

CAGE

Fuck, I don't know what I'm supposed to do. She's breaking inside. I can feel it, and I don't know how to fix it.

Lou doesn't deserve her grief. Whatever she got herself into is no one's fault but her own. I can't be sure that she was working with Kane and got herself killed that way, but I also wouldn't put it past her to do that. She tried to kill us— nearly succeeded.

And although I thought she should pay for her crime, I didn't want her dead— not that I'm going to lose sleep about it. It might make me a prick, but I don't care. I could have lost Caitlyn.

That said, this is too fucking much. I know there are sick people in the world, but I have never come across someone like this. He's playing games and enjoying it. He enjoys the kill. There's no remorse for his actions whatsoever and I blame Robin for bringing him into her life.

Roy glances up when he hears me approach. "What's going on, son?"

I hold my finger up, letting out a weary sigh. "I need a shot of Jack, please, Kelly."

Leaning my elbows on the bar, I tug at the ends of my hair. This is a fucking mess. Much more and she won't recover. Even the strongest can break. And now she's grieving a woman she didn't really know because she blames herself for her death.

That's the kind of person she is; how big her heart is.

Kelly places a glass of Jack in front of me before moving around the bar, heading to clear the tables. Once she's out of earshot, I turn to Roy.

"They found Lou, my ex, dead in her house," I tell him. He already knows who she was and what she tried to do. His eyes widen. "The officer came in to question Caitlyn about her whereabouts, then he was going to come and question me."

He leans back, letting out a breath. "Fuck, this shit is messed up. Who would want to kill Lou? I know the bitch is an evil spinster, and had enemies, but this?" He shakes his head. "Do you know what happened?"

"We only know a note was found on her body and it was addressed to Caitlyn."

"Fuck, what did it say?" he asks, paling.

"That he did it for her and that he's the only one who gets to kill Caitlyn. I think he saw Lou as a threat and decided to eliminate that threat."

He glances at the office door, concern colouring his face. "Does she know about the note?"

"Yeah. She fucking read it," I tell him, taking a gulp of my drink. "You should have seen her. The colour drained from her face and her eyes became unfocused. She fucking threw up because of it and now she's blaming herself. She thinks she killed her, Roy."

"That's ridiculous," he growls.

"I know," I agree. "I don't want to lose the girl I love over some sick, twisted psycho. I need her to be strong. I don't want her to blame anyone other than the person who did it."

"Is there anything I can do?" he asks.

"Actually, there is. I need you to get me CCTV from the night Caitlyn was attacked. They're going to want to know what the note is about, but more; why it was on Lou's body. We can't risk giving them the truth. Not yet."

"What are you going to do?" he asks.

"Twist the truth," I tell him, shrugging. "We can tell them he attacked her, and that ever since she's been getting death threats. If he asks why we didn't report it, then we can say she was too scared to."

"And the death threats?"

I shrug. "Maybe say we thought it was Lou trying to break us up or something."

"Just be careful, son," he tells me, clapping me on the shoulder. "I'll bring it by first thing in the morning."

"We're meeting Rome in the morning, then heading over to the police station after that to make an official statement. I'll need to pick Carrie up after if that's okay?"

He waves me off. "We can take care of her for the day again, it's no trouble. You just keep your mind and attention on your woman. Make sure she really is going to be okay. I worry about her a lot."

My lips tug into a smile. "You can't. Laura rang me earlier demanding to meet Caitlyn and Carrie. Dante, the dumb twit, was telling them about Carrie. They thought he had found himself an immature girlfriend who loved building playhouses, so when he explained who she was, Laura rang me," I explain. "So, after we get all the shit done in the morning, we will be heading over there. If you want to join us, you're more than welcome. Dad is going to be there, and probably a dozen more people."

I inwardly groan. As much as I'd love to get out of going, I think it might keep her mind off everything.

"Rather you than me, son," he taunts, chuckling. "I'll see what Hayley is going to be doing tomorrow. Hopefully, she will be fine with taking a break from her blooming garden, and we can make it. I'll arrange for some cover in the morning in case you need me for anything. Now, go get your girl home."

His gaze goes over my shoulder, and I turn on my stool, watching Caitlyn dragging her feet as she makes her way over to me.

I slide off my stool, coming to attention when I catch a glimpse of her bloodshot eyes and red cheeks. She glances up, meeting my gaze, and I'm taken aback by how dead she looks inside. It's like a light has gone out within her.

I close the space between us, wrapping my arm around her shoulders. "Are you ready to go home, Kitten?" I ask softly.

"Yeah, I'm so sorry, Cage," she announces, not sounding at all like herself.

"What are you sorry for?" I ask, taken aback.

"I'm sorry for everything that is happening around us. What turned out to be one of the best days of my life just got tainted by death, *again*. I got her killed. I could get you killed. She's dead and it's my fault and I'm so sorry, so god damn sorry," she tells me, tears spilling down her cheeks.

"What did I say, Kitten?" I demand.

"I know, and I'm going to be strong. I can't let them scare me, but damn if I am. I'm so fucking scared. Freddy Krueger would have a field day in my nightmares. It's all my fault. I should never have taken those files and given Robin another reason to come after us."

"Honey, none of this is your fault. You have just been dealt a shitty hand. You have family here who love you more than anything. Please don't give up on yourself or blame yourself for a scum bag like him. What happened to Lou isn't your fault, and if you didn't take those files, then he may or may not have still come after you. It's all a bunch of what ifs, but you're a fighter, Caitlyn. You are one of the strongest people I know and what you're doing…" he pauses, shaking his head. "You are fighting for a future, one where you aren't looking over your shoulder. Don't you want that?" Roy asks, watching her in concern.

When Caitlyn finally makes eye contact with Roy, she sniffs and wipes at her eyes. She steps out of my embrace and pulls him in for a hug. A slight whimper passes through her lips and the sound… God, the sound. It's like a knife being twisted in my gut. I can't keep watching her break and being powerless to do anything to help.

"I love you, and Hayley too. You both mean so much to me. If anything happens to either of you, it would be like losing my parents all over again," she chokes out, and at her words, Roy's eyes mist and he pulls her closer.

Kelly rushes over to join our huddle when she spots Caitlyn in Roy's arms. "Are you okay?" she asks, and her body tenses when she reads our expressions.

"Yeah," I answer, reaching for Caitlyn. "She's not feeling well, so I'm going to take her home."

We can't tell her the truth. The less people who know, the better. We can't risk it being leaked.

It isn't that I don't trust Kelly, I just don't know her. Sometimes I feel like she's hiding something from us, but then I see that haunted look in her eyes and know to leave it alone.

"Oh, sweetie, go home and get some rest. I hope you feel better in the morning," she tells her, leaning over to press a kiss on Caitlyn's cheek.

"Speak to you soon," Caitlyn whispers, not sounding with it. It was almost robotic.

She's emotionally drained but is fighting to keep it together. I can tell. As much as I want to go and find this Kane guy and end him, so she doesn't have to worry anymore, she needs me more right now. Sitting around and doing nothing is something I loathe, but for her, I'll do anything. And right now, she has my full attention.

"See you later," I tell them both.

"Take care," Roy whispers, leaning forward to press a kiss to her forehead. He pulls back, and the heartache has my breath hitching. He really does love her. Caitlyn hasn't been in their lives long, yet they have adopted her as their own.

I pull her closer and begin to lead her out of the bar. Her feet drag, and once we exit the bar, I sweep her up into my arms. She doesn't even protest as I start carrying her home. She just lays her head on my shoulder and snuggles into my neck.

I FINISH TELLING Nate what happened, his face a mask of shock and horror. He had the same reaction I did, only he isn't being questioned for murder.

"That is so fucked up I don't know where to start," he hisses, keeping his voice down since Caitlyn is in bed resting. This is all getting out of hand."

"I know," I admit. "Did you finish everything?"

"I have. I sent out the last email before you got back."

"We're going to have to keep a closer eye on her."

"I'll up security," he promises. "She'll be protected."

I glance towards the bedroom door. "She's barely keeping it together. I'm worried about her."

"How was she when you left her?"

"She seemed more focused, but still…" I shrug, not knowing what else to say.

"Our girl is stronger than that, Cage. You just need to give her some time to process it. All this shit is surreal. It doesn't happen every day. Give her time. Eventually she will realise she isn't to blame for any of this."

"I hope so."

"Let's get this hidden again so you can go be with her," he announces, holding up the stack of information. He points to the other pile. "They are two lots of copies. I've already sent Dante off with another two and we will hide those."

I pause with my fingers gripping the stack. "I'm not sure if I've said this but thank you. For everything. It's not just us at risk, but you are too."

He grins. "It's been nice to use my skills for something more than minor things."

I snort, shaking my head. "Come on. You can help move the bed."

We head down the hall to my room, and as I push through the door, I find Caitlyn laying on the bed, half out of the covers. Her leg is over the blanket, showing off the globes of her arse.

"Well shit," Nate mutters. "Now I really get it."

I turn, finding him gawking at my girl. "Eyes off, dickhead," I warn, before moving over to the bed.

"What are you doing?" Caitlyn asks groggily, sitting up. "Has something else happened?"

"No, nothing's happened. We need to put all of this back, so we need you to jump off the bed for a minute."

"I mean, we can't put it anywhere other than your brilliant hiding space," Nate declares.

Her lips tug into a smile and I relax. "It is a brilliant spot," she declares.

I chuckle, pressing a kiss to her lips. "I know, Kitten, now up."

She huffs before sliding off the bed and moving out the way. Nate heads to the other side and together, we move the bed towards the door, making room for us to get to the loose floorboard.

Nate grabs the pile of stuff and shoves it back in before securing the floorboard. He gets back, and together, we move the bed back.

"I'm off," he announces as Caitlyn drags herself back into bed. "I'll follow you in the morning. You won't see me, but I'll be there."

"See you then, and thank you," I tell him.

He nods and heads over to the bed, and I inwardly groan when he pulls her in for a hug. She's braless under that tank top. I know what it feels like when she's pressed against me wearing it, and if it weren't for the fact that he's my best mate and wouldn't cross the line, I would have ripped him off her by now.

"Don't let this tear you down, babe. You need to stay strong. Get some rest and I'll see you tomorrow."

She pulls back and hugs the blanket to her chest. "Are you, Nate Mathews, going all mushy on me? Are you going to start talking about your feelings?"

He laughs, knocking her on the chin with his knuckles. "Wouldn't dream of it, babe."

"All righty then," she mutters, before a yawn slips free.

He turns to me. "Come on then, pretty boy, walk me out," he orders.

"Back in a minute," I tell her, and walk out with him.

Once we reach outside, he jogs down the stairs before coming to a stop. "Don't worry about tomorrow, brother. I know you're eager to get this shit done but use your head. Caitlyn needs to see that you're dealing with all this shit."

"I am dealing," I snap.

"Yeah, then why do you look like you're about to commit murder?"

"My woman is blaming herself for the murder of Lou, Nate. Don't be a dick. I have it under control."

"All right," he mutters. "See you tomorrow."

Once he's gone, I lock up the cabin, checking all the windows and double checking the door. When I head back to the bedroom, I stop at the door.

She has been through so much, and Roy and Nate were right in saying she's strong. She is. I can't disagree.

But am I?

She's my beginning and end. She's more than a woman who has come into my life. She isn't a friend like she is to Nate or Dante. She isn't an adopted daughter like she is to Roy and Hayley.

She has become my everything. She makes me appreciate life. She gives my life meaning.

I'm not just a brother, a son, a friend, or a business owner. I'm Cage. I'm hers. I'm Carrie's.

She's easy to love, but what's driving me… it isn't just love. It surpasses that.

And I'm scared of losing it. Losing her.

Pulling away from the door, I head back into the living room and pull my phone out of my back pocket.

I dial the number I need and wait, listening to it ring.

"Hello," Rome answers.

"Rome, it's Cage. We have a problem," I announce.

"What sort of problem?" he growls.

I fill him on everything that happened tonight, informing him of my plan. I don't want to go in there and lie to the police if it's only going to make things worse. We can't keep the lie forever— eventually they'll find out the truth— and I need to know he has our back.

"I need to know you aren't going to throw her under the bus."

"Not you?" he asks.

"I don't give a shit. This is about her. I just want this over with," I admit.

"I'm not going to mess with your head. This isn't going to be easy for anyone. Right now, we need to get the information to the right people. Anything else we can deal with later."

"That's what worries me," I mutter.

"If Quinton gets wind of us messing around in his life, it could go one of two ways. He could go underground, become a ghost and let it play out, or he could kill a lot of innocent people trying to recover that information."

"I just want her safe."

"I'm working my hardest to make that happen. I've got someone on the inside but recently, they've been pulled from the inner circle. I'm waiting to hear back. All you can do now is take it one day at a time. Don't act out of character in case it tips off the people watching you."

I groan, running a hand through my hair. "We've emailed out the copies and made a few of our own to send out."

"Good. I'll meet you in the morning as planned. As for the police officer, just keep with the plan you have made. It's the best you've got. And if he asks about anything to do with Robin, act stupid. You don't let on that you know him and make sure your girl knows that too."

"All right."

"Take care," he rumbles, before the line goes dead.

I sigh, beginning to feel less stressed. I needed a moment to lose it, but I also needed to know there was someone who had it together. I trust Nate and Dante with my life, but if something were to happen, I need to know she isn't alone in this, that she has someone on her side, willing to do anything to get that information out there.

My feet drag as I make my way back to the bedroom. Tonight has dragged, and with everything that's happened, I'm spent. I have no energy left. After going through all those papers and memory sticks, I'm done.

Pushing through the bedroom door, I strip down to my boxers and slide in next to Caitlyn.

She stirs and snuggles back into me. "You were gone awhile."

"Just talking to Nate," I whisper, kissing her neck. "How are you feeling?"

She rolls onto her back, then to her side so she's facing me. It crushes me to see the hurt evident in her eyes. The brightness that once plagued them is now masked over with a sharp dullness from reading that goddamn letter. I want to see her eyes shine again, I want to hear the life back in her voice, and I want to see her smile.

"Are *you* okay?"

My eyebrows pinch together. "Yeah. Why are you asking *me* that? It's you who's had a bad day."

"She was your ex," she whispers. "No matter what she did, she was still something to you and now she's gone."

I sigh, wanting desperately to roll my eyes. Only she could be worried about something as trivial as that.

"I don't want to sound like a soulless prick, but she has been dead to me for a long time. She's my past," I admit. "Did I want her dead? No. And I can't change that."

"I was worried you'd hate me," she whispers.

"I could never hate you. I don't blame you for her death and neither should you. It had nothing remotely to do with you. You've never once asked for this."

"But he's here because of me," she chokes out.

I tuck a strand of hair behind her ear. "If that were the case, why aren't you blaming your sister?" I ask, regretting the words.

"Cage," she hisses.

I groan, pinning her against me. "I didn't mean it like that. I just meant; how can you shoulder all of this blame like you are the cause when it isn't you who brought Robin into your life," I explain, hoping she understands. "Do you blame your sister?"

She tenses for a moment, and I think I've lost her. She tilts her head up, her eyes filling with tears. "There was a time when I did. It was once, and I regretted it immediately."

"And why did you regret it?"

"Because it wasn't her fault," she breathes out. "She would never have asked for this kind of life, for that kind of man. She's innocent in all of this too."

"Exactly, and so are you. You can't take the blame for other people's actions, Kitten."

"I need time," she whispers, and her lashes flutter as she looks up at me. "Are you sure you're okay?"

"Yes, you and Carrie are my top priority. I don't care about anyone else, just as long as you two are okay. Lou's death is an inconvenience because all it's done is give you more stress."

She weakly pushes at my chest. "You say the sweetest things," she mutters dryly, and I chuckle, bending down to press my lips to hers.

"Yeah, but you love me," I whisper.

"Yeah, I really do," she whispers back, snuggling into me.

Chapter Thirty-Three

CAITLYN

Y HEART IS A BALL OF NERVES as I grab my bag off the table. I'm still not okay. I don't feel okay, and I don't think I will until the exchange is done.

My nightmare that woke me up early this morning was about the exchange and my future after. It didn't end. None of it did, and Robin was still coming after me. And I have to wonder if there was any truth into it. It scares me to death that this could be my life, and I'm wondering if it's worth it anymore, or if I should get Carrie somewhere safe and just let Robin end it.

But that isn't me. It can't be. I'm a fighter, goddamn it.

"Are you ready?" Cage asks, startling me.

I pull my gaze away from the window. "I just need to grab my coat," I tell him. "Are we coming back here before we get Carrie or are we getting Carrie then heading to the barbeque?"

"Shit. I forgot about the barbeque," he grumbles. "We can come get Carrie after the station then go straight there if you want. Why?"

"I need to grab Carrie's bag then. I packed it this morning while you were in the shower," I tell him, moving to the hallway.

"Why'd you pack a bag for Carrie?" he asks, tilting his head to the side.

"I don't know what she will be like there, or if she will want toys or something. We don't go anywhere, Cage. We haven't been on a family outing before, so this is all new to me. I want to be prepared. I want her to have everything she needs to make her feel comfortable."

"She's good with people," he reminds me.

"I know, but I just want to make sure."

His gaze softens when I reach him, her bag in my hand. "Let's go," he orders. "And, Kitten, she will be fine. Today will be fine, I promise."

I nod, swallowing past the lump in my throat. I can't answer. After yesterday's news, I can't think of it. Cage said he has a plan and I trust him.

And Carrie is going to be fine at his dad's. She has Cage and Cage is her favourite person.

I REST MY head against the window of the car. I can feel Cage's stare on me every time we come to a stop at the lights, but I'm exhausted. The meet with Rome hadn't been what I expected, and it's made me nervous. We literally handed over the information and then he left.

Gone.

He didn't realise the significance of what he held in his hand or what it meant for me to hand it over. Those files are what will decide our future.

I can understand him not wanting to hang out and paint a bull's-eye on his head, but he could have said something, anything, to calm my nerves. It was a big moment for us.

Now we are on our way to the latest hurdle.

The police station.

Cage informed me of the plan on the way to meet Rome, and what he's going to say about Kane.

He pulls into an empty spot and shuts off the car. Turning to me, he grips my hand. "Are you sure you are up to doing this? I can try to talk to him."

"No. I want to get it out of the way," I admit.

"Remember, do not mention Robin Quinton," he warns me. "They can't know about him or the real reason you're receiving those letters."

I squeeze his hand. "I know. It will be okay."

He leans over the parking brake and cups my cheek. He pulls me in, pressing his lips to mine.

"Let's go," he rumbles.

Walking into the police station, I'm surprised to find Officer Johnson is already in the reception area with another guy wearing a suit. I have never seen him before, but the way they are sharing notes... I can't help but wonder if he's going to be interviewing us too.

I share a look with Cage, and he leans down, pressing a kiss to my temple, then whispers into my ear, "It will be fine."

I nod and force a smile when Officer Johnson spots us. He says something to the guy next to him and together they head over.

I'm wary. I know not all policemen are crooked, but with everything still on my mind and fresh, I don't trust the guy coming in.

"Mr Carter, Miss Michelson, this is Detective Marker from out of town," he introduces, side-eyeing the detective. "He's recently transferred to help out with the investigation. If you walk this way, we can get the interview underway." He gestures down the hall, and it hits me that he hasn't made eye contact with me.

This's weird. Too weird.

"Good to meet you," Detective Marker introduces, shaking Cage's hand before stepping away.

We follow Johnson into the interview room and take a seat opposite.

"Do you have the recordings you mentioned?" he asks, glancing up from his pad.

"Yes, we were both indeed in the cabin that day, between those times and longer. It's all here," Cage confirms, handing over one of the discs.

Johnson places it to the side before clasping his hands together. "Now, I understand last night was a bad time for you both, but this is a murder investigation, and we need to ask these questions."

"We know," Cage replies, his brows pulling together.

"Do you know anything about the note that was placed on the deceased's body?"

"Yes *and* no," Cage answers, looking strongly at Detective Marker.

Detective Marker sits up, folding his arms over the table. "Care to elaborate?"

His tone sends a shiver down my spine, but Cage, unaffected, places another disc on the table.

"On this disc is the man I think you're looking for. He attacked Caitlyn a few months ago while she was outside her work collecting glasses. I, along with her boss, Roy Carpenter, was lucky to be in the office at the time of the incident and caught it on the CCTV before it got even more out of hand."

"What does that have to do with the notes?" Johnson asks.

"The next day, she received a threatening note from the person who attacked her. It's the same handwriting on the one I saw last night. Caitlyn's had been on a piece of card."

Johnson looks surprised by this, but Marker, as I predicted, doesn't.

"This person— do you know him?" Johnsons asks, addressing me this time.

"No, I had never seen him before that night," I tell him honestly.

"What about now? Do you know him now?" he asks, shocking me.

I shake my head. "No, I've met him once; the night he beat me. I have no idea why he is coming after me."

"Why wasn't this reported to the police?" Marker asks, using a hard tone I rather don't like.

My hands clench into fists under the table. "Because I felt stupid. I should have known something was wrong with him when he approached me. I was late trying to get away."

"That doesn't answer my question," he demands.

"She was—"

"Let her answer, Mr Carter."

He's a dickhead. "I was scared to, okay? I didn't know the guy. I was worried if I went to the police and they did find him, he would come after me. As far as I was aware, he knew nothing about me. I was safe and it wasn't going to happen again."

"These notes, do you have them with you?" Johnson says.

"No, I didn't even think about keeping hold of them. They didn't really seem like something I'd want to hold on to as a keepsake," I snap.

We couldn't bring them, not with the information that was on them. It would only lead to more questions.

"So, you're saying you got attacked by the man you think left the note on Lou's body, and didn't report it," Marker asks.

"Yes," I grit out.

"Then continued to receive threatening messages but you didn't report them either?"

This isn't going good at all.

"No, I didn't. I didn't feel the need to. I didn't take them seriously.".

Marker sighs and looks like he's holding back an eye roll. "We don't have those notes, Miss Michelson. How are we meant to know they are real or if it is the man on the tape you're accusing? You don't have proof about any of this."

"No, she doesn't," Cage bites out. "She came here voluntarily to answer questions. She didn't come here to do your job, Detective."

Marker's lips twitch before he covers it. "Just a few more questions."

I answer each one the best I can, repeating the same answers over and over until I'm blue in the face.

The time ticks on, the sound echoing around the room with each minute. My head is throbbing.

We're going around in circles.

"Stop," Cage demands, pushing back in his chair.

"Where are you going?" Marker asks, who has taken over the investigation. Johnson looked done an hour ago.

"Unless you have something new to ask, we are done. We've spent hours answering the same questions, which, I might add, is voluntarily. Unless you are arresting us, we are done."

"Mr Carter," Marker warns.

Cage pulls me out of the chair, glaring at the officer. "We have a right to leave, and we are leaving. We have a prior engagement to get to and you've delayed us long enough. If you don't mind ..." Cage murmurs, turning to Johnson for confirmation.

Johnson gathers up the papers, his gaze flicking to the prick beside him. "No, that will be all. If you can think of anything then please don't hesitate to call. No matter how little, it could help our case," he tells him, before his gaze flicks to mine. "If you have another note, please, don't throw it away. These threats are taken very seriously."

"Thank you," I whisper, my voice hoarse from all the talking. I turn to Marker, but don't offer the same.

Cage turns, pulling me with him to the door. He grips the handle, pushing it down when Marker's next words stop us. "We will be watching, Mr Carter," he warns.

A cold chill races down my spine. I turn, finding him looking directly at me. Not at Cage. But at me.

The blood drains from my face as I tighten my grip around Cage's hand. "Bye," I whisper to Johnson.

The entire interview, I felt something was off. Maybe even before it began. I felt like I was being baited into telling the truth or to maybe lose my cool. He did everything to push me.

And when Johnson tried to end the interview, Marker pulled rank and demanded they needed to get everything now.

And what was worse, they hadn't directly accused us of anything. It was weird, and I think halfway through, Johnson realised that too. We had given them everything they needed.

"Fucking dickhead," Cage bites out when we reach outside.

I suck in a lungful of air, feeling like I can breathe for the first time since we arrived. I pull him closer to the car, keeping my voice low so we aren't overheard.

"Cage, I don't trust Detective Marker. There was something off about him. Did you see him at the end when he warned you that he'd be watching you? He was looking right at me," I explain, shivering. "I'm telling you, he gave me the creeps, more than that Chinese kid off *The Grudge*."

He helps me into the car before walking around to the driver's side. Once inside, he turns to me, his expression serious. "Yeah, I fucking saw it. Who the fuck does he think he is asking you questions like you're the suspect? Why would you leave a note addressed to yourself if you had killed Lou? The man's a dick."

"That's not what I mean," I tell him.

His brows pull together. "You think he was there for another reason?"

I shrug. "I don't know. He just gave off bad vibes. And Johnson was picking up the same thing by the first hour," I tell him. "You didn't?"

He grips the steering wheel. "No. But then I was too pissed with the way he was interrogating you."

"I was probably seeing things," I tell him, trying to wave it off.

"We just need to be careful. You've been under a lot of stress."

I arch an eyebrow because he's still gripping the steering wheel. "And you aren't?"

He rolls his eyes. "He's fucking me off. Now, can we go get Carrie so she can cheer me the fuck up?"

"Okay," I say, dragging the word out as I clip my belt into place. "Let's go get her."

He pulls out of the space and drives out of the car park. Hitting the main road, his gaze flicks to me. "*The Grudge*? Really? Out of all the horrors there are, you picked that?" he asks, before chuckling.

I snort, trying not to laugh. "Shut up and drive."

"ARE WE THERE yet?" Carrie asks.

I chuckle under my breath because it isn't the first time she has asked, and we've been driving awhile. She has been a ball of energy since we picked her up from Roy and Hayley's, who were following behind us once they made sure everything back at the resort was sorted.

"No, sweetie. I packed your DS; it's in your Dora bag. Why don't you get that out and play on it?"

"Okayyyy," she whines, like I've just asked her to clean her room.

We travel in silence the rest of the way, with the odd conversation or grunts coming from Carrie. She throws a tantrum whenever she can't complete a level on Super Mario, and it isn't like she has Cage to help her. He's busy driving.

"They keep killing me," she mumbles.

"We're here," Cage announces as we pull into a driveway of a bungalow. I sit in awe as I take in the size of the place, and the mere beauty. I can't picture Cage growing up in a place like this. I can't pinpoint exactly why either.

"It's beautiful," I tell him when I slide out of the car.

"So are you," he declares, meeting me on my side. He bends down, capturing my lips in a kiss before opening the backdoor, helping Carrie out of her car seat.

I reach for Carrie's hand after he helps her put on her backpack. We take two steps towards the front door when it flies open, and two women and a man come rushing out.

"You are real," one woman yells, smiling wide.

She looks a lot like Cage; dark hair, short to her shoulders, with dark brown eyes, but hers seem to shine more, sparkling like they're glistening with tears. She is slim, but with curves in all the right places. She's wearing a fitted summer dress with a floral design on it, paired with a pair of plain pink flip-flops. She's gorgeous.

"Hey," I greet, waving lamely.

She ignores my hand and instead moves in for a hug. I'm taken aback at first as we just met. As her arms snake around my body, I can do nothing but respond, and I hug her back.

I close my eyes as a thought occurs to me. I'll never get to do this for Cage. He'll never get to meet my sister or my parents. They'll never get to meet him, and I think they would have loved him.

I love him. He's a part of us whether I'm scared of it or not. He has become our everything.

She pulls back and beams at me. "It's nice to finally meet you. Dante has told us so much about you. This jackass neglected to mention he met a woman who finally got him to think with his heart and not his—"

"Don't say another word, Laura," Cage warns as he covers Carrie's ears.

"Oh, I forgot. Dad, make sure you watch your language today," she warns, making us all laugh.

Cage points to the guy. "Caitlyn, this is my dad, Jim. Dad, this is Caitlyn, my girlfriend. You've met Laura," he tells me, pointing to the woman who hugged me before. "This squirt here is Danni." He pulls the timid, pretty brunette to his side, "Danni, this is my girlfriend, Caitlyn."

Danni is just as gorgeous as her other two siblings. She has light brown hair nearly as long as mine, and cheekbones people would sell their soul for. But she also looks like she'd rather be anywhere but under the spotlight, and I can relate. I hate being the centre of attention.

"Yeah, they kiss a lot, too," Carrie declares, rolling her eyes.

Cage grins as he ruffles the top of her head. "This here, everyone, is Carrie, Caitlyn's daughter."

"Isn't she adorable," Laura coos, walking over to Carrie.

"Hello," Carrie greets, giving them all a wave.

"Hello, beautiful," Laura greets back. "Would you like to go play in the garden? Jim can go start the barbeque while you play. I bet you're hungry."

Carrie let's go of my hand and take's Laura's as she licks her lips. "Yes pweaze."

"Why don't you say hello to Jim and Danni first, Carrie," Cage orders softly, sounding fatherly.

She waves at the two. "Hello, Danni. Hello, Jim."

"Hi," Danni replies, her lips twitching in amusement.

Jim steps forward. "You can call me grandpa, kid."

"What!" Carrie shrieks happily, placing her hands on her cheeks.

Everyone pauses as she continues to breathe heavily, her squeals of happiness waking up the birds on the street. Tears gather in my eyes as she suddenly charges at him, nearly knocking him over as she wraps her arms around his legs.

"I always wanted a grandpa," she declares, sounding choked up. "I wished for it."

Poor Jim is as frozen as I am. When she pulls back, her eyes are glistening with tears. "Oh, sweetie," I murmur, holding my hands out to her. She immediately runs to me, and I kneel on the floor to catch her in my arms.

My fun, loving daughter is easily pleased. I have to hold back the tears, which is proving to be hard as I hear a sob draw from her throat. When she crashes into me, I hold on to her for dear life.

She really hid all of this from me. It was something she wanted, and as my mum always said, blood doesn't automatically make you family. Love does.

"I have a grandpa," she whispers, but loud enough for everyone to hear.

Cage comes to kneel by our sides. I meet his gaze, and his eyes go warm before he turns my daughter and pulls her out of my arms.

"Yeah, you do, Pea. And you have aunties, too," he tells her softly.

My breath hitches. Before, this scared me. I was scared this wasn't real and that it would hurt when it was taken away from her. But I have learned over our time together that he's serious about this. He doesn't make rash decisions. He's a thought-out man. And although we were together quickly, it didn't make it a rash decision. He's in this all the way. And he has spent months proving that to us.

And how can I not allow her to have this one simple joy in her life.

"Are we all a family now?" she asks when she pulls back, her lower lip trembling.

"Of course we are," he declares fiercely.

"But how? You said you weren't my daddy," she chokes out. "I want us to be a family. We can keep loving each other and get a dog."

He glances up, looking to me for help. I tuck her hair behind her ears. "He can still be a part of our family. But, honey, Cage isn't your daddy. You had one," I choke out, the words like bile on my tongue.

"But Hayley said she had a baby and that she wasn't their real mum, that she was gifted them," she argues, and I think she's talking about the child Roy and Hayley adopted, who is no longer with us. I close my eyes as pain washes over me. "Can't I be a gift too? Please. I want you to be my dad."

"I'm in this for always," Cage declares, directly addressing me. "I'm not going anywhere."

I know what he's saying to me, what he wants to give her. Tears slip free and I nod, then fall back on my knees.

"You can call me whatever you like, Pea, and I'll always be honoured."

"I can call you daddy?" she asks, her lip trembling.

She squeals, wrapping her arms around his neck, squeezing tight. He holds her just as tight, and I watch the two most important people in my life make a pact.

He wouldn't have taken on this roll had he not meant it, and for that, I couldn't love him more.

He stands with her still in his arms, and on shaky legs, I try to follow, but collapse, my chest contracting. Her sobs are breaking me apart.

Two strong hands reach for me, and I glance up at the man who has the same eyes as my boyfriend's. They soften, and gently, he pulls me up off the ground.

"Thank you," I choke out.

He beams. "Welcome to the family," he declares, tears forming in his eyes.

"Where's my loving?" a voice booms from behind me, making me jump.

I turn around to see Dante and Nate getting out of their car.

"Uncle Dante, guess what?" Carrie yells, pulling back from Cage. Her cheeks are still bright red, tears still falling down her cheeks.

He shares a look with Cage, and I know he's silently asking why she's crying, but Cage shakes his head. "What, princess?" Dante replies, playing along.

"I have a grandpa," she tells him, puffing her chest out proudly.

His eyebrows meet his hairline. "That's, um, awesome. Where?"

Carrie giggles and points towards me, where Jim is standing next to me.

"There, silly head," she tells him. "That's not all; Cage wants to be my daddy now. I'm super happy. I have a mummy, daddy, grandpa, and aunties and uncles. That's like a thousand people."

Dante chuckles, walking towards her to take her from Cage. "It sure is, princess, but who's your favourite uncle?"

She wraps her arms around his neck and kisses his cheek. "You, because you're my best friend in the whole world."

"It must be the same age mentality wavelength," Laura replies, chuckling.

"Shut it," Dante warns Laura, but turns to Carrie, smiling.

Nate steps up to the circle and I watch as Danni steps back, her cheeks flushing red as she watches him.

"Come on then, let's get this barbeque on," Jim announces, heading up to the house. "We've got more to celebrate."

Dante's stomach rumbles. "Yeah, I'm starving," he states.

"You're always hungry," Nate, Cage and Laura say simultaneously, making Carrie giggle.

Cage heads over to me, pulling me into his arms as we walk through the house. It's stylish, very modern, and clearly has a woman's touch to it. I remember Cage saying Laura has her own place but comes by every now and then to give the place a clean.

Danni, however, I know is looking for a new place because I caught Cage looking through listings a few weeks ago. He said she's staying here until she can find somewhere.

I don't get to see much of the house because we reach the back and head out into the garden. The garden is huge and goes back quite a bit.

I glance out over the decking, my eyes widening at how big it is. It's beautiful, and I love the pond feature he has in the far corner.

Cage pulls me towards the large glass table, big enough to sit at least five families on it.

They must do barbeques a lot.

"Cage, come help me with the barbeque," Jim calls out from the other side of the deck.

"Just a minute," he calls back before pulling me away from the others. "Are you okay?"

Honestly, I wasn't this morning. I wasn't when we met with Rome or when we left the police station. But now... now life couldn't be any better.

"I really am," I admit.

"Are you sure? What just happened is a big deal and I didn't talk to you first," he begins but I lean up, placing my finger across his lips.

"What happened was beautiful, Cage. I was scared before but I'm not anymore. Not with you anyway. Not with you anyway. I want us to be a family and I love that you did that for her."

"I didn't do it only for Carrie; I did it for me. I want to be that person for her. Fuck, I already feel like I am. I know it's a complicated situation, but please know, I promise to always be there for her. I love her. I love you. And if I had any doubt in my mind, I wouldn't have given her that hope outside. I wouldn't play with her emotions like that, Kitten."

"What will happen if we ever do break up?" I ask softly. "Not that I'm saying we will. But where does that leave her?"

"Nothing will happen because we are never going to break up. You're it for me, and I hope I'm it for you," he declares, his voice firm, a promise. "But if you're worried, then don't be, because I'll never leave her. I'll always be in her life. And one day in the future, I hope we can make it official, because I was being serious before, Kitten. You're mine. She'll always be mine. No matter what happens between us."

Tears gather in my eyes as I lean up, pressing my lips to his. "I love you."

His gaze softens. "I love you too."

When I pull back, I catch both Danni and Laura watching us with tear-filled eyes, yet both beaming at us with love.

I let out a contented sigh. This is my life now.

And I couldn't ask for anything more.

Chapter Thirty-Four

CAITLYN

THE BAD ALWAYS HAS A WAY of balancing itself out. Although it never seems like it when the bad happens, it does, whether it be big or small.

Today, my happiness came from being surrounded by my new adopted family. Roy and Hayley turned up not long after we arrived, and from then, the stories began, and everyone started loosening up.

Laughter echoes around me, and as I sit back, watching the people who have become a huge part of my life, I'm blissfully happy.

And scared shitless, but I think that's going to happen until Robin is out of our lives.

Carrie is in her element. I'm yet to see her alone. If she isn't getting fuss off her new aunts, Cage, or her grandpa, it's one of the others. One mostly being Dante. The two share a connection I missed somewhere along the way. I knew they were close, but they have inside jokes I was unaware of until today. She loves him, and he loves her. If someone had told me he was a kid person, I would have laughed. He looks like he eats kids for breakfast.

Although they've all made me feel welcome, I'm overwhelmed by it. I answered when I was spoken to, I carried on a conversation so as not to be rude, but mostly, I observed them. It made me feel warm inside watching them, yet made me miss my family profoundly. I wish they were here with me now, meeting Cage, along with his family.

I don't dwell on it too much, not wanting to ruin the day. Instead, I turn my attention back to Danni. She's fascinating to me. Her personality is eccentric. She can be shy and quiet, yet loud and funny in the next instant.

And I think she has a crush on Nate. He's either watching her when she isn't looking, or she's watching him. He has caught her a few times and it made him smirk each time.

I sense a story there. It isn't just because of the sneaky glances. It's the way they look for Cage first, making sure he isn't watching.

And the sexual tension whenever they speak to each other... They bicker, yet they're polite, but the sexual tension is palpable, and it seems like no one but me has picked up on it.

Danni finishes telling Hayley about a new book she has read when her phone vibrates across the table, blaring a ringtone.

My brows pinch together when she pales, her hands visibly shaking as she snatches the phone off the table, glancing down at the screen.

She bites her lip, and I watch as she visibly shivers. I can't see the screen with the sun blaring down, but whoever it is, she doesn't want to speak to them because she swipes her finger across the screen.

"Excuse me," she whispers, pushing back in her chair.

"Are you okay?" I whisper as she stands.

"Yes, I, um, I need to use the bathroom," she explains before stumbling away from the table.

I feel more than see Nate tense on the other side of the table, watching as she rushes inside the house. His jaw clenches.

He pushes his chair back, glancing around the garden until his attention lands on Cage, who is swinging Carrie around by her ankles. His shoulders sag, and in the next instant, he is up out of his chair and following her inside.

Well, shit.

I jump when Cage takes the seat Danni vacated. "Hey, Kitten, are you having fun?"

I smile, my gaze flicking over to where he's left Carrie on a blanket with her crayons and paper. "Yeah, your family is amazing. They're so welcoming."

"Why wouldn't they be? You're an incredible person," he tells me, pressing a kiss to my temple.

I laugh. "I am, aren't I."

"Where's Danni and Nate?" he asks, scanning the garden for them.

Shit.

I shrug. "Danni went to the bathroom. I'm not sure about Nate," I lie.

"How is the house coming along, Cage?" Roy asks, taking the seat across from us.

"Quicker than I expected. I thought I would be going through my money more quickly, but I've saved a ton with favours people owe me."

"You getting on with the new team you hired?" he asks.

Cage nods. "They're really hard workers. Even the kids I hired from town have worked hard. Upstairs is nearly complete, and I've got an interior designer coming in to decorate the rooms. Then everything is done."

My breath stalls at the news, my body tensing.

"That's great to hear. When do you think it will be ready for you to move in?" Roy asks, taking a swig of his beer.

"A month, maybe two. I'm not sure. It all depends if we finish on time," he states.

I grip the glass in my hand. I hadn't realised it was nearly finished, even though he came back every night from work and told me what they had done. It never occurred to me until now. He wasn't just working on the house. It was his house and soon, he would want to move in there, leaving me and Carrie.

I glance up at him, trying to catch my breath. I really do love him. It's only a thought right now, but soon, him moving out will become a reality and I don't want it to happen. I like him being there, with us.

"Daddy," Carrie cries happily as she races over the grass towards us, causing Cage and I to tense. "Look what I've drawn."

Although he declared himself her father, she has yet to say the word until now. And it doesn't hurt or make me mourn, it only makes me happy. My sister isn't here to approve or disapprove, but she loved her daughter and died making sure she got away from her biological father. I truly believe she would want this for her. And sometimes, I wonder if this is why she left her in my care.

"Daddy," he whispers, sounding choked up.

Carrie skids to a stop between us and lifts up her picture.

I take a look around, feeling all eyes on us. "This is precious," Hayley whispers.

Cage lifts Carrie up, dropping her down on his thigh before taking the drawing from her hand.

"Look, Daddy, it's me, you, Mummy, Grandpa, and all my uncles and aunties." She points to each figure as she calls out who they are. Looking over at me, she smiles. "I can finally call Roy and Hayley nanny and grandpa, too, now, Mummy. Roy said Cage was his family, so that means I am, too," she tells me in a sing-song voice.

I beam back at her. We went from being an us, to having a large family. And it's all because of the special little girl in front of me.

Hearing a breath hitch, I turn, finding Hayley snuggled into Roy's chest, her eyes shining with pure joy and love as she watches my daughter.

She shouldn't be surprised by this though. She must have known we love her too, that she means everything to us. I couldn't argue with Carrie even if I wanted to. They have been our family since the day we drove onto the site and asked for a job.

"They always have been, sweetie," I declare, my eyes glistening with tears.

A strangled sob tears from Hayley's throat and she pushes back in her chair, making a quick escape.

"Did I do something wrong?" Carrie asks, her lips tipped down as she watches Hayley leave.

"No, my darling. Hayley is just overjoyed, is all."

Her nose scrunches up. "What do you mean?"

"She's just really happy you want her to be your nanny, sweetie," Roy murmurs softly, his voice choked up.

My eyes mist over as loves fills my chest. I spent so long not getting close to anyone, and looking back now, it was a mistake. I'm not alone anymore.

Carrie isn't alone.

It's a monumental moment for us.

And if my family were here for me now, they would want us to have this.

Carrie slides off Cage's lap and runs over to Hayley, who is standing over by the back gate. She kneels down to Carrie's height, listening intently to what she is saying. It must be something that means something to her, because from my vantage point, I watch as Hayley's expression grows softer, more tears falling down her cheeks.

My phone rings in my bag, distracting me from Hayley and Carrie.

I get up from my seat to take the call. "I'll be back," I tell Cage, and he nods, his gaze never leaving Carrie.

"Hello?" I answer as I move into the house, standing inside the kitchen.

"Hello, Caitlyn, it's Rome. I tried to get in touch with both Cage and Nate, but there's no answer."

"I'm with both of them now. Would you like me to go get one of them?" I ask, taking a step towards the back door.

"No, you'll do fine," he tells me, and I stop short.

"Is everything okay?"

"I can't go into detail as I've just pulled over on the motorway, but I need you to tell them that I just heard back from Judge Morrison, whom they sent an email out to last night."

"Okay," I reply, not understanding what that means.

"Caitlyn, he's put a warrant out for Quinton's arrest."

I sag against the counter. "Oh my God," I whisper. "This is great news, right?"

"It is. I'll be in touch as soon as I get back. Let them know I will be ringing them and to turn their fucking phones on."

"I will," I reply, but he doesn't hear me as he's already put the phone down. I glance down at my screen, frowning. "Well, goodbye to you, too, happy."

As I'm already in the house, I decide to tell Nate first. Walking through, I hear voices coming from around the corner. I stop just as I hit the corner to what I think is the living area and hear Nate and Danni arguing.

Shit.

"I said it's none of your business," Danni snaps.

"None of my business? You get a call in the middle of a family fucking barbeque, go pale as a ghost, and then I hear you crying at someone to leave you alone. Tell me, Danni, how the fuck is this not my business?"

"Just because you're Cage's best friend, it doesn't mean you have the right to treat me like you own me. You don't get to be in my business anymore," she hisses.

I take a step back, not wanting to interrupt what is obviously a private moment between the two. I'm not sure what's going on, I just know it's not my place to get involved.

"Danni, don't be fucking ridiculous. You can't hold that against me forever. You need to tell me what the fuck is going on. I know you've moved back in here. What I want to know is why. And why were you crying?" Nate growls at her, sounding impatient.

"I'm not telling you anything, you arsehole," she snaps.

Her voice sounds closer, and I panic, not wanting them to find me eavesdropping on them. Everything happens in slow motion as I take another step back, knocking over a vase that is on a little table next to the door.

Shit.

"What the...?" Nate mutters, rushing around the corner.

"Hey," I cheerfully force out, before turning to Nate. "I need to talk to you and Cage. Can you go get him?"

"How long have you been there?" he asks, watching me closely.

I flutter my lashes. "Been where?"

"Doesn't matter," he grumbles. "I'll go get Cage." He turns to leave but stops at Danni's side and leans down to whisper in her ear. I don't hear what he says, but from the frown and glare Danni sends his way, I can tell it's not good.

"I need to go and see if Dad needs help. I'll send Cage in," Danni announces, flustered as she scurries out of the room.

"You're such a terrible liar," Nate states when Danni disappears.

"Yeah, well, you're the dick taking the blame for this vase," I tell him, chuckling.

His lips twitch as he shakes his head. "I don't think so. You're on your own there."

"What the hell has happened here, guys?" Jim asks, stepping into the room with Cage.

I point to Nate, sighing in disappointment. "Nate. He needs to watch where he's going."

Nate snorts and nudges me in the shoulder. Cage looks between us, then chuckles, clearly reading between the lines as to who really broke it.

"So, you can move around a building and not be heard, be practically invisible doing it and what not, yet you just knocked my vase over? Why don't I believe, with your job skills, that you were the one to knock the vase over?" Jim muses.

"She's a terrible liar, isn't she?" Nate states, chuckling.

I groan and turn to Jim. "I'm so sorry. I didn't mean to. I had a phone call and I needed to tell Cage and Nate about it. I saw Nate walk into the house a while ago, so I thought I'd get him first. It was an accident. I really am sorry. I'll clean it up once you point me to where the dustpan and brush is. And I'll replace it."

He laughs, pulling me in for a side hug. "Don't worry your pretty little head over it. I'm glad you smashed it. It's fucking ugly," he declares.

I bite my lip. "Still, I am sorry."

He waves me off and pulls away. "I'll let you get on with what you wanted to tell these boys. See you guys outside," he tells them before turning to Nate. "Oh, and Nate, you know where the dustpan and brush is. Do not let her clean that up."

Nate grunts. "Yes, boss."

When he leaves, Cage turns to me. "Who were you on the phone to, Kitten?"

"Rome," I tell him.

"Rome? Why the fuck didn't he ring me?" he asks, grabbing his phone from his pocket. "Shit, my battery's dead."

"There's your answer. He tried you, too," I explain, and then glance at Nate. "And yours. He was ringing to tell you Judge Morrison has sent out a warrant for Robin's arrest. He will ring you once he gets back."

"Fuck, now things are going to get heavy," Cage stresses before addressing Nate. "You need to see if you can move up the security camera job at the cabins."

"Already done," Nate states.

"Thanks, bro," he breathes out, pulling me into his arms. "Kitten, Carrie's getting tired. She started singing *Frozen* tunes after you came in and my head can't take it."

I burst out laughing. For the past two mornings, Carrie has woken us up by singing 'Do you want to build a snowman' outside our bedroom door. I think it's cute that she's trying to re-enact the scene from the movie.

"Okay. It is getting late. And Hayley said she woke up early this morning."

Nate lets out a dramatic sigh. "I need to get Dante back, too. It's way past that boy's bedtime."

I laugh and follow them back out into the garden. Carrie is occupying Hayley's lap, reading a story. My girl is clever for her age. I don't know whether it's all the home schooling, but she has picked up so much. She's advanced, very advanced, and sometimes comes across older than what she actually is.

Cage clasps his hands together and announces, "Hey, kids, it's time to go. It's getting late," Cage says.

Dante snorts, glancing up from the picture he's colouring in. "Kids? And you were meant to be the clever one. There is only one here, Cage." Nate chuckles, slapping his hand down on Dante's shoulder. Dante growls. "Hey, you made me colour outside the lines."

"You'll live," Nate mutters. "What Cage was trying to say is: we need to get *you* back."

"What?" he asks, looking adorably confused. "I'm an adult."

"Yeah, but you act like you're five," Laura states, chuckling.

"I'm nearly five," Carrie announces, making everyone laugh.

"Whatever, I'm tired anyway. That chick I was… playing games with had me up all night," Dante grumbles, thankfully skipping what he was going to say.

He does that a lot around Carrie, and it warms my heart that he cares enough to do it. I don't want her picking up bad habits. When Carrie isn't around, all bets are off, and he swears like a sailor and has no issue filling us in on his conquests. You'd think that with the way he acts, he would have a problem getting laid. He doesn't. If anything, I think it helps him get laid.

"Dante," Cage warns.

"What game did you play?" Carrie asks, glancing up from her book.

Everyone glares at Dante, who is unaffected by it, and stares at Carrie like she just asked him to be her husband. Which, by the way, is a horrified look.

"We, um… we… oh God! We played football. I scored every time," he states, proud that he finally came up with something, even if it is absurd.

"Can I play next time?" she asks sweetly.

Roy and Jim choke on their drinks. I know Carrie doesn't understand the meaning of Dante's 'every hole's a goal' comment, but we do. I don't know whether to laugh or smack Dante around the head at this point, so I opt to interrupt the conversation before it gets more out of hand.

"Dante, do you remember the first night we met each other?" I ask, to which he nods, his brows pinching together. "Well, I still have those scissors, so if you say one more word, I'm going to cut your manhood off. Comprende?"

He gulps. "Yep."

His horrified expression has the group bursting into laughter.

Even when he pales and turns to Cage for support, but Cage only arches an eyebrow. "I'll help."

"You're so mean," he hisses, slapping the crayon on the table.

"Come on then, Pea, say goodbye to everyone so we can get going," Cage orders.

Carrie doesn't argue, which surprises me. She slides off Hayley's lap and turns to pull her in for a hug.

"Bye, Nanny."

Hayley leans down, her eyes growing misty again as she kisses Carrie on the head. "Bye, my sweet girl."

She runs over to Roy next, doing the same with him before moving through everyone. My heart is in my throat the entire time because she is loving every minute.

When she reaches Laura, she turns timid. "Can I come again?" she asks politely.

Laura melts in front of us, her gaze softening. "You can come anytime you please, baby girl," she promises and pulls her in for a hug.

"Does that mean I can sleep over, too?" Carrie asks, blinking up at her.

"Yeah, it does. Only, I don't live here. Grandpa and Danni do."

"That's okay. We can take it in turns," Carrie offers, nodding like it's already a set up place.

Everyone laughs as Laura ruffles her hair, grinning. "Okay, kid, it's a deal."

Once Cage and I say goodbye to everyone, we head off back to the cabins.

It has been a home to us for so long, but it wasn't meant for long-term living, only temporary, short stays. It feels weird calling it home after today.

I want more for Carrie. For us. I want a place we can put our own mark on.

IT'S COMING UP to midnight when Cage and I get into bed. His earlier conversation about his house nearly being finished and what it means is still playing on mind. I can't push the dreaded thoughts away. And I need to straighten things out before it eats away at me.

"Cage," I whisper, pulling his attention away from his phone. He drops it on the bedside table and faces me.

"You okay?"

"What happens when you move into your new home?" I blurt out, not holding back.

A look of puzzlement crosses his features. "What do you mean, Kitten?"

"Well, you're living here right now. When you move out, I'm worried how it's going to affect Carrie."

"She will get used to it," he states, yawning as he lies down.

He did not just say that.

"What?" I snap, sitting up and clutching the blanket to my chest. I'm disgusted with how insensitive he is being.

He sits up at my tone, his eyebrows bunching together. "What's wrong?"

"Are you being serious?" I ask. "You really think she'll *get used* to it?"

"Yeah," he replies, lying back down like it's no big deal. I want to grab the pillow and suffocate him.

I opt to nudge him in the chest. "Cage."

He blinks one eye open. "Caitlyn, go to sleep and stop worrying. All kids go through changes and are fine. Carrie will be one of them."

"Stop worrying?" I cry out, hoping I'm reading this wrong. He can't really feel this way.

"What is your problem? What is going on?" he rumbles.

"What's *my* problem? What the fuck is *your* problem, Cage? Today you made a promise to her. Do you really think after living with you for months, that she'll really *get used to it* when you leave?" I ask, my voice rising.

He sits up, his eyes wide. "Woah, woah, woah. Hold on a second there, Kitten. Who said anything about just *me* moving out? All I meant was she would get used to the move."

"What?"

"Did you really think I would move out and not take you with me? I've been here for you, Caitlyn; there is no way I could live without either of you. I thought I made myself clear that you were moving in. How could you even think I would say that about Carrie? I always think of what she will like, how she will feel, all the goddamn time," he grits out, his expression pinched.

My expression crumbles as I reach for him. "Oh God, I'm so sorry, Cage. I thought you were moving out on your own. I panicked and then you said that stuff and I—"

"You thought wrong," he finishes, clenching his jaw.

I close my eyes, feeling like an idiot right now. "I didn't mean to piss you off. It's why I brought it up. I don't want you to live somewhere that isn't with us and vice versa. I'm so sorry I jumped to conclusions."

He sighs, pulling me into his arms. I sag into him, seeking the comfort. "It's fine. I probably need to start telling you things straight instead of deciding in my brain what we will be doing in the future, and then thinking you'll just go along with it."

I chuckle because that's kind of what I just did. Built up all these scenarios in my head and spoke about them as facts.

"We're moving in together?" I whisper.

"Never apart," he promises.

Excitement bubbles through me. "I'm sorry if I hurt your feelings."

"You can make it up to me," he purrs, rolling until I'm above him.

I grin down at him. "Oh yeah? And how would I do that?" I tease.

"Naked apology," he murmurs, rolling over once more, until he's above me. I squeal, and moments later, it turns into a moan.

Yeah, I'm totally down for a naked apology.

Chapter Thirty-Five

CAITLYN

THERE'S A KNOCK ON THE DOOR just as I finish putting my hair up in a bobble. Tonight, Carrie is staying over with her auntie Laura for the first time so I can have a girls' night in with Kelly, and I asked Danni to join us. She's met Kelly a few times now and they get on, just like I knew they would.

They met during the sisters' visit to the bar where they came to watch me sing.

From there, we became close. Not only has Cage brought family into my life, but he's given me friends. Without him, I wouldn't have Laura or Danni. They have become a permanent fixture in our lives, and I couldn't be happier about it.

Cage has headed out to the bar with the boys to give us space, not wanting to get involved in the girly crap—as he put it.

And there will be girly crap, because since the barbeque, I haven't had a chance to talk to Danni about what was up with her and Nate, and tonight I'm hoping to find out.

As I head to the front door, I can't hold in my excitement. I desperately need the distraction as well.

Since Rome's phone call, things have been quiet. Apparently, the warrant has reached out to other towns, and by now, Robin will have heard about it. He just hasn't reacted. Not yet.

But the cabin is surrounded with security, which is why Cage felt it was safe enough to leave us here. I'm grateful because I need some normalcy back in my life after been shadowed for so long.

Reaching the door, I double check the peephole Nate installed for us. Seeing Kelly and Danni both standing there, I open it, letting them in.

"Hey. Are you ready for some fun?" I ask, grinning.

"Hell yeah," they cheer, heading inside.

Danni holds up a bottle as she heads for the kitchen. "I brought some wine. I hope you like it."

Kelly holds up hers too. "Great minds."

"You'll have to open the bottles," I tell them, holding up my casted arm.

My cast comes off in a week or so. *Thank God.* I cannot wait. I've been sticking knives down my cast just to scratch an itch. It's torture not being able to reach it, and sometimes, trying to only makes it itch more.

I grab the glasses down from the cupboard and place them on the table. Kelly pours us each a glass before we head into the front room, sitting down on the blankets I threw down on the floor earlier. It's childish, but it was something I never got to do as a teenager. And there's the fact the seating in this place is limited. It isn't like some of the other bigger cabins.

I take a sip of my wine and sigh. "I needed this."

"I think it touched my soul," Danni whispers.

"It touched mine," Kelly agrees, using the sofa as a back rest.

I chuckle. "I ordered pizza. Is that okay?"

"Love pizza," Danni replies.

Kelly nods. "Where are the guys?"

"They've gone to the bar," I tell her, shrugging.

Her brows pinch together. "It's weird."

I laugh at her puzzled expression. "Why is it weird?"

"Because in all the time I've known you, one of them have been glued to your side."

I duck my head, hoping she doesn't see my cheeks heating. I can't tell her the reasons, not until it's safe to. "I guess he's just protective."

Danni, reading between the lines, snorts. "That's my brother. Always protective."

I force a laugh then change the subject, and Kelly is none-the-wiser as she joins in.

The night goes on smoothly. We eat pizza, pop on a movie, talk about the movie like we didn't watch it together, and as the credits roll on the second one, I begin to feel a little tipsy.

I gulp down the rest of what has to be my fourth glass of wine and begin to laugh when the room starts to spin.

"You're so drunk," Kelly accuses.

"I don't care," I admit, laughing. "And this was my last one. I know when to stop."

"Fuck that, pass me another bottle," Danni orders, reaching out for the bottle in Kelly's hand.

Laughing, Kelly hands it over.

"I wonder if the boys are having a good time."

Danni snorts as she finishes pouring herself a glass. "Dante probably has them contemplating murder."

I hold my empty glass up and she knocks her glass against mine. "True."

"What about you, Danni— you seeing anyone?" Kelly asks.

Danni jerks and her lips twist. "No." I snort, and she turns to me. "What did that mean?"

"You know what."

She rolls her eyes. "I'm not a mind reader."

"You and Nate," I declare, saying no more.

"No," Kelly drawls out, eyes wide. "You and Nate?"

"There is no me and Nate."

I turn to Kelly. "There totally is."

Kelly grins and turns to Danni. "Now you have to tell us."

She shrugs. "There's nothing to tell."

"Liar," I accuse.

She holds her hands up. "There isn't. I swear."

"Then what was that at the barbeque the day we met? I know you know I heard you both arguing."

She ducks her head, a blush rising in her cheeks. "I don't know what you mean."

She is so darn cute.

"Is there something going on between the two of you? You can tell me."

Her eyes widen. "Are you kidding? Have you seen Nate? Why would you think there is something going on between us?" she rushes out, flustered.

"I heard the two of you, remember. It sounded like something was going on. Plus, I have eyes. I saw the way he looked at you."

"You're seeing things," she accuses.

"And the way you looked at him," I finish, daring her to deny it.

"He is hot. Like seriously hot," Kelly slurs, as she gulps down more of her wine.

I laugh. "You're seriously drunk."

She shrugs and turns back to Danni. "I wouldn't blame you if you had a thing going on with him." She pauses, lifting her glass in the air as she mouths, "Hot."

"He really is," I agree, nodding. Kelly clinks her glass against mine, causing wine to slosh all over her hand.

"Nothing is going on," Danni denies, but with us staring her down, she exhales, sagging against the sofa. "All right. I had a huge crush on him when we were kids. I tried it on with him once and he rejected me. It was so embarrassing."

I sit up, sobering a little. "What happened?"

"This is going to be juicy," Kelly murmurs, her gaze unfocused as she squints in Danni's direction.

Danni picks at the thread on the blanket. "I got drunk at a party."

"It always starts at a party," Kelly grumbles.

I press my lips together and think about it. "That might be true. Cage and I technically met at a party."

"We're listening to Nate and Danni's story," Kelly whispers.

"Go on," I demand, chuckling.

"Yeah, so I got drunk and had to call him to pick me up. I was so out of it I forgot to go back with a friend. I don't remember much. I must have passed out in his car, so he had to carry me to bed. I woke up as he was pulling the sheets over me," she explains.

"And?" I push.

"I drunkenly ended up confessing my crush on him and then stupidly tried to kiss him," she admits, groaning. "He shot me down and a part of me died that night. I could never look at him the same after. He had been living with us a few years when this happened, and it was weird after."

"And his reaction at the barbeque?"

She shrugs. "I don't know what the fuck his problem was that day, but he doesn't care about me. He was sticking his nose in because I'm Cage's little sister. They've always been protective of me."

I tusk. "I don't think it's because you are Cage's little sister. How old were you when you kissed him—or tried to, anyway?" I ask her, curious.

"He had not long turned eighteen. He had not long passed his driving test."

"And how old were you?"

She muses over it. "I was fifteen, I think. It doesn't matter. It was a long time ago."

"You don't think it was because of your age that he turned you down and not actually because of you?" Kelly mutters, eyes wide.

Danni points her glass in Kelly's direction. "See, I thought about that for a long time after, but I don't think it was."

"Why?" I ask, seriously curious.

"Because he didn't care who he fucked. He always had girls coming and going. He's never had a relationship, but the girls he slept with were all drop-dead gorgeous. I know I have huge boobs, long legs, and a curvy body, but I wasn't like all the girls he was with back then. I'm not his type at all."

I snort. "Danni, you are drop dead gorgeous. He would be a fool not to see how incredibly beautiful you are. Your mum must have been a knockout if you look anything like her."

"She was beautiful," she murmurs wistfully.

"She's right though," Kelly interrupts. "I don't think it's because you aren't his type. I've not seen you together, but I can't believe it's because of that."

"Oh, they were electric together," I tease.

"He's so far out of my league, it's not even funny," Danni declares. "And even if he wasn't, there's the fact Cage would pitch a fit if he ever found out I had a crush on him, let alone if anything ever did happen between us." She groans, rolling her eyes. "Oh God, I don't even know why we are talking about this when he doesn't even see me in that way."

I shake my head, hoping one day she opens her eyes. "I think you're wrong. I think Nate would be the lucky one for you to notice him."

She ducks her head and I end the conversation, seeing this is getting to her.

There's a knock on the door, interrupting us.

"If that's the boys, I'm going to kick Cage's arse," I declare, giggling when I begin to sway while getting up.

"That or cut his supply off for a week," Kelly yells.

I pause at the door and turn to her. "Supply?"

She laughs, shaking her head. "Sex, sweetie."

"Oh," I mutter, still not getting it, but then my eyes widen as it hits me. "Ohh."

There's another knock on the door and I lean up, checking the peephole. A woman glances around on the other side, a bouquet of flowers in her hand. I pull open the door, my brows pinching together.

"Hi, can I help you?" I greet, startling her.

Looking around the bouquet of lilies, she smiles. "I have a delivery for a Miss Michelson."

"That's me," I state, reaching the flowers when she hands them over.

"Have a nice night," she tells me, before rushing down the steps to her van.

I have no idea who could have sent them. Cage has gotten me flowers before, but he always gets me daisies, knowing they're my favourite. Sending me lilies doesn't make sense, but I'm not going to be ungrateful about it.

Danni and Kelly look up when I walk back in. Danni rolls her eyes. "Who knew my brother could be so freaking romantic."

"Who knew any man could be so romantic," Kelly mutters, then begins to laugh to herself.

"I wonder what he's done to send me these. If he's the one who broke my Kindle, I'm going to have a hissy fit, then smash his bike up," I warn them.

"Someone broke your Kindle?" Danni asks, her expression horrified.

"Yeah. It was either the kids or Cage, but none of them are owning up to it."

"Kids?" Kelly asks, looking from Danni to me.

"Yeah, Carrie and Dante," I murmur, feeling a little dizzy.

Kelly and Danni giggle at my answer. I place the flowers down on the table by the door, then take the card that is poking out of the top.

I stagger back when I pull the card out of the envelope, seeing the same scripted black writing as I had in the others.

No.

No, no, no, no.

Princess, you did a really stupid thing. Time's up. K

I collapse to my knees, my scream frozen inside my throat as I stare down at the card in my hand.

It's happening.

This is it. What we have all been waiting for.

Chapter Thirty-Six

CAGE

I SLAM MY FIST AGAINST THE brick wall outside the bar. I just got off the phone with Rome and there still isn't any news. They haven't found Robin. There's no trace of him, so either someone who we sent the documents to tipped him off, or when the warrant for his arrest was issued, an officer tipped him off. No one disappears that quickly.

He ended the call, warning me to keep an eye on Caitlyn, like that isn't what I have been doing all this time.

Taking a deep breath, I push through the doors of the bar and head back to where we were sitting. The other two spot me walk in and finish their game of pool.

"Hey, handsome," a woman purrs, sliding onto the stool next to me.

"Not interested," I tell her as I take a swig of my beer.

"I'm glad I have my library card with me," Dante dramatically announces, sliding between me and the woman.

"Why?" she replies, and I glance over, finding her smiling up at him seductively.

He smirks, leaning in a bit. "Because I am totally checking you out."

I snort and roll my eyes at Nate, who joins me on my other side. He grins, just as amused as I am.

I glance at the time on my phone, groaning. It has been four hours since Kelly and Danni got there. I checked on the cameras. It has to be over by now. I want to get back to her. It feels weird her not being with us.

"What's your name, beautiful?" Dante flirts.

She giggles. Actually fucking giggles. "Candy," she replies.

"Oh, I like `em sweet," he rasps, and I swear I gag a little.

"Can he be any cheesier?" I whisper to Nate.

"Probably, it is Dante after all."

"So, you like your treats?" she teases.

"I sure do," he admits as I take a swig of my beer. "Hey, I'll be Burger King and you can be McDonalds. I'll have it my way and you'll be lovin' it."

I spray my beer all over the bar, earning a glare from Derek.

Nate chuckles. "Classy."

"Fuck off," I choke out, my eyes watering as I turn to Dante "Seriously, Dante? Could you be any fucking cheesier?"

He turns, glaring at me. "Could you be any more of an arsehole?"

"I thought it was sexy," the woman on the stool says.

She would; she's dimpy as fuck, just how he likes them. She isn't bad looking, but she looks desperate. It pours off her in the way she's dressed, the way she has puffed her hair up until it looks like she has stuck her fingers in a few plug sockets. And her skin... My God. Do women not get that fake tan has a limit before it stops looking good? She's orange as fuck, and when she moves a little and it reflects off a certain light, it looks patchy.

"Yeah?" Dante drawls.

"Yeah, darling."

"I think you should grab your coat, then come with me," he tells her seriously.

"And why is that?"

"Look," he declares, holding his hands up. "I'm no photographer, but I can totally picture us together. Naked."

The dimwit actually picks her coat up, laughing. She leans into Dante, whispering something in his ear. His eyes light up, and when he looks back over at us, he gives us a thumb's up.

I roll my eyes, wishing they'd hurry up and fuck off. I don't even know how the fuck his pickup lines work. The man is a total goof.

"Oh, you're the reason Santa has a naughty list," he rasps when she whispers something else. He pulls her against his chest and does something that makes her moan.

"Go now! Before I kick you out," Nate barks.

Dante throws her over his shoulder and turns, walking backwards as he grins at us. "Don't be jealous."

"I seriously don't know how the fuck he does it," Nate declares once Dante has left.

"I think it's the whole cheesy shit that does it for the women," I admit, laughing.

"God, drinking used to be fun," he groans.

I chuckle because it's the same sentiment I thought earlier. "Do you reckon four hours is long enough?"

Immediately picking up on my meaning, he smirks. "Want to crash?"

"Fuck it. Let's go," I tell him, gulping back the rest of my drink. My phone begins to vibrate, and I grin when I see Danni's name across the screen. "Looks like they missed us too."

"That Danni?" he asks, as I swipe to answer.

"Don't tell me you're drunk already and need a lift home," I tease.

"Cage," she calls out, sounding frantic. I tense, freezing on the spot.

"What's going on?" I demand, and Nate goes on alert next to me.

"Cage, oh God. It's Caitlyn. She had some flowers delivered. We thought they were from you, but she freaked out over the card," she explains, breathing heavily. "We can't get her to talk to us and it's beginning to scare me. I've tried to get her to calm, to listen to me, but it's like she's not even there."

"What did the note say?" I demand, already rushing out the bar.

"That her time was up," she whispers.

"Fuck," I growl. "I'll be there in five."

I end the call, racing towards the cabin.

"What's happened? Is Danni okay?" Nate asks, following beside me.

"Yes. Caitlyn had some flowers delivered. She read the note, and from what I could make out from Danni, she collapsed then spaced out."

Fuck, I shouldn't have left her. I should have stayed closer.

When we find this guy, I'm going to kill him.

DANNI IS AT the door when I arrive, holding it open. I rush inside, finding Caitlyn on her knees, her face pale with tears streaming down her cheeks.

Fuck.

I don't greet anyone else as I kneel beside her, gripping her shoulders.

"Kitten," I murmur softly, trying to shake her out of her trance.

It's like she can't even hear me. I call her name, but she stares ahead, lost in a trance that has pulled her into a nightmare.

This has been a long time coming. I knew the day we were told about Lou's murder that she wouldn't be able to take much more. And she can't.

"Caitlyn," I yell, beginning to feel the panic rising in my chest.

She jerks back and blinks up at me. I watch as her pupils dilate then focus on me. I freeze, preparing myself. Moments later, a sob so primal tears from her chest and I feel it to my very core.

I reach for her at the same time she flings herself at me, wrapping her arms around my neck.

I run my hand down her back. "Hey, it's okay. Everything is going to be okay. Shhhh," I soothe.

"*Why?*" she chokes out. "Why is he doing this to me? I haven't done anything to him."

"Caitlyn," I whisper, my heart breaking for her.

"He's taken everything away from me. All of them, and I did nothing," she chokes out, becoming hysterical. "And now he has sent that man to kill me. What happens to Carrie then?"

"Caitlyn, baby," I murmur, feeling eyes on us.

She pulls back, her eyes red and swollen. "No! He deserves everything we have done. We are doing it to protect ourselves, to protect Carrie. But it's not going to end. He's coming, Cage. He's coming."

I tuck one hand under her legs and the other around her back and lift her in my arms. I give a chin lift to Nate before escaping into our room where we can have privacy.

Stepping into the room, the lamp in the corner is on. I make my way to the bed and lay her down before sliding in beside her.

"You need to stay strong. Just for a little longer," I demand softly, holding her close.

"I-I can't," she chokes out as she clings to my T-shirt.

"You can. You've overcome so much, baby. We need to stay strong together. You've got me now, Kitten, and I'm not going anywhere, neither is Carrie."

She begins to tremble in my arms. "I'm so scared."

"I know, but it's going to be okay."

"Cage," she pleads, and I don't know what she's pleading for, so I pull her closer and lean down to kiss her head.

She snuggles into me, and after a while, her sobs begin to slow down. Her body relaxes against me and I know she's fallen asleep.

I slowly untangle myself from her hold, placing a pillow in my place. I creep out of the room, then back down the hall to where Nate and Danni are sitting in the living area.

"Hey, is she okay?" Danni asks, straightening when she sees me.

Her eyes are red from where she has been crying. I walk over to her and give her a hug, kissing her gently on the cheek.

"She will be. She's gone to sleep now," I tell her.

"That was awful," she replies.

"What happened?" I pause, taking a look around the room. "Where's Kelly?"

I glance back towards the bedroom, wanting to get back to her, but I also need to know what happened. Danni only gave me a brief run down on the phone.

"She left when you took Caitlyn to your room to give you some privacy," she replies, before taking a breath. "We were laughing and joking around when there was a knock on the door. She took the delivery off the flower lady then came inside. We all thought they were from you, but Caitlyn questioned it. She said you knew daises were her favourite flower." She stops, inhaling as she shakes her head. "It was weird. One minute she was smiling and the next, she collapsed to her knees, but it was her expression. It was… it reminded me of the day Dad told us about Mum."

"Danni," I whisper.

She wipes under her eyes. "I read the card, Cage. Someone is after her. Why? What's happening?"

I lean over, taking her hands and giving them a squeeze. "Look, Danni, you cannot tell Laura or Dad any of this."

"I won't, I swear," she promises.

"Caitlyn's sister was murdered by her husband after she found out about his criminal activities. Caitlyn has had the information to put him behind bars for a long time but has been too scared to use it. He's a dangerous man."

"And he's the one coming for her?"

"Yes. He's hired someone to hurt her," I explain. "We've just gone to the police about it, with the information, and that's why she's been sent the note."

"And the note? It was like she knew what it was before she read it."

I sigh, running a hand along my stubble. "He's hurt her before. It was a few days after I arrived here, and she got hurt badly. Since then, he has been sending threatening notes."

"Is she going to be okay?" she asks, her lower lip trembling. "You've got to protect her, Cage."

Ah hell. I hate seeing my little sister scared.

"I will," I declare, my shoulders slumping.

I had been so concerned about my family finding out. Not because it could put them in danger, but because I didn't want them to judge Caitlyn. They love me and hate it when I do reckless shit that puts me in danger.

But this is different. I'm protecting the woman I love.

I shouldn't have worried about it, it seems, because Danni is just as worried about Caitlyn as we are, and it isn't because she has a big heart. It's because Caitlyn has managed to make them fall in love with her too.

"Are you okay?" I ask after I give her a moment to absorb everything.

"Yeah."

"Good," I tell her. "I'm going to get back to her in case she wakes up and I'm not there."

"Go," she orders.

I turn to Nate. "Will you make sure she gets home?"

"Sure," he agrees quickly.

Too quickly.

I inwardly roll my eyes. The two think I'm blind, and I'm not. I see the way they look at each other. I'm not stupid.

And I'm not naïve when it comes to Danni. She has had a crush on Nate since she was a kid and was terrible at trying to hide it. The only reason I've never mentioned anything is because Nate never showed an interest in her, not even to harmlessly flirt with her. That didn't mean there wasn't something there. I've caught him watching her when he thinks no one is looking. More than once. And I can't deny he seems different with her lately.

I just wish I knew what was going on in their heads.

At the end of the day, she is still my little sister and always will be. I don't want to see her get hurt. And I'll kill him if he does—friend or not.

Danni stands, grabbing her bag. "Will you call me tomorrow to let me know how she is?" she asks. "If she wants me to come around again, I will. I don't have work until tomorrow evening."

"Of course," I reply, leaning down to press a kiss to her cheek.

She forces a smile then heads to the door. "Take care."

"Night, guys."

Nate stops just outside the door and turns to Danni. "Go wait by my bike. I'll be there in a minute."

She glances from Nate to me, then back to Nate, probably wondering what he wants to talk about. When neither of us say anything, she huffs, stomping towards his bike. My lips twitch as she leans against it, crossing her arms.

"Be careful riding back," I warn him.

"I will," he replies. "I've bagged up the card and will send it off tomorrow. I'm going to get in touch with the florist to see if she has any details on who bought them."

"We know who sent them," I bite out.

"Yeah, but we need to get as much evidence pointing to this Kane guy as we can. Right now, he is the main threat to Caitlyn. Robin isn't going to get his hands dirty, not whilst he's hiding from the police."

I run a hand through my hair, feeling exhausted. "You're right."

"I'll drop your sister back, then I'll get a start on it. I'll call Rome and see if there is anything he can do. I think it's time we take this guy down once and for all. I know we haven't found him yet, but we will."

"Thanks, brother."

"Any time."

"Ring me late morning with what you got. I want to make sure she's gotten enough rest."

"Will do," he promises and opens his mouth like he's about to say something. I don't like the look that crosses his expression. "Night."

"Wait, what was that look for?" I ask.

He shrugs. "Everything will be okay, Cage. I swear it."

I watch them leave before shutting and locking the door. Once everything is locked up, I head back to our bedroom, finding Caitlyn in the same position I left her in. I peel off my clothes and slide in next to her, snuggling up to her warmth. Her arms lock around me and I sigh, hoping that tomorrow she will be the same Caitlyn I left before I went out tonight.

And whatever Nate is planning, I just hope he's careful.

Chapter Thirty-Seven

CAITLYN

IT HAS BEEN DAYS WITH NO word as to where Kane is or what he's doing. Days of not going outside, eating, sleeping, or talking much to anyone. I have withdrawn from everyone, too scared about what my future holds. He could show up at any moment and has already proved what he's capable of. I don't doubt his intentions. I'm not naïve enough to believe he's going to leave me alone.

I tried. I really did, but it's like the part of me that wants to answer back is closed off to the outside world.

It's killing Cage. I see it in his eyes each time we share a glance. And despite all of that, it's hard to assure him I'm okay. That I will be okay.

Danni has spent a lot of time around here, keeping me company since Cage didn't want to leave me alone. It hasn't been enough to bring me out of this funk. Not even my daughter has, who I love more than life itself.

Everything is closing in on me and I'm beginning to feel suffocated.

Danni reaches for my hand. "Come on. Let's go sit in the living room. You need to get out of this room."

"I'm tired," I moan.

"I know, but you need to. He's getting worried, and with Nate gone, he needs you to be strong a little longer."

The morning after the flowers arrived, Nate disappeared, on the hunt to find Kane with a group of men he trusts. And apart from the phone call Cage received on the evening, explaining what he was up to, no one has heard from him. It's beginning to worry me.

My hands shake as I grip her back. "Okay."

She slumps before sliding out of the bed. "Come on."

I pull myself up, my legs shaking. "God, I feel sick."

"It's because you haven't eaten. I'll make you some soup after."

"Thank you," I tell her. "And thank you for being here."

"I wouldn't be anywhere else."

We head into the living room just as Cage gets off the phone, his expression tight and filled with worry.

"Whatever happens, you have to stay strong," Danni warns me.

Tears gather in my eyes as she steers me over to the sofa. "I'm just so tired of all this crap."

"I know," she replies softly. "But you need to find the strength. Don't give them the power."

Power.

I close my eyes, her words hitting me close to the heart. Because that's what it all comes down to.

Power.

And neither Kane nor Robin has that over me. They don't get to control my life, nor do they have the right.

She's right. "They don't have power over me," I whisper.

Tears glisten in her eyes as she grips my hand tighter. "No, they don't."

"You doing okay?" Cage asks, handing me a cup of tea.

I nod, soaking in the warmth. "I'm sorry I've been out of it."

He has done everything to pull me out of this slump, but it hadn't worked.

"Never be sorry. You've had a lot thrown at you."

"Is Carrie okay?"

"She's with Hayley and is doing fine."

"Who was on the phone?"

"Nate. He's on his way," Cage announces, and I gape at him, wondering if I heard him right.

"Is he okay?" Danni asks, biting her bottom lip.

He nods, but I see him clench his jaw as he looks away. "He'll be here soon."

He's hiding something. "Cage, what is happening?"

Taking a seat next to me, he pulls me into his side. "He's going to explain everything when he gets here. He was in the car and the reception was shit. He's close though."

"You said he was going after Kane," I remind him, remembering that much over the past few days. "He's dangerous; you said so yourself. Please, has something happened?"

"Please tell me Nate is okay," Danni rushes out. "You aren't lying to us, are you?"

"Why do you care?" Cage asks her, giving her a daring look.

She shrugs, sitting back. "He's Nate."

He watches her for a moment longer before glancing down at me. "I swear he's okay, but I think it's best that Nate is here to fill you in. You'll have questions I can't answer."

The front door pushes open and Cage tenses before shooting up from the sofa.

"Nate called and said to meet here," Dante announces, scanning the room. "He's not here yet?"

"You fucking scared us," Danni snaps.

Dante takes in Danni and grimaces. "Shit, sorry."

He walks in and heads to sofa next to Danni, shoving her across until he's squeezed in next to her. She shoves at him, but he doesn't budge. "Arsehole."

He grins. "But you love me."

"Whatever!" she mutters.

He turns to me, his eyes narrowing. "Are you in there today or you still a zombie?"

"Fuck you," I croak out.

He chuckles. "So glad to have you back."

"Don't be a dick," Cage mutters.

"I'm not. I was beginning to get creeped out. You know I hate zombies."

"They aren't real," Cage snaps.

Dante points to me. "Are you sure?"

I chuckle, the first genuine one in days. "Shut up, Dante. I'm not a zombie."

"Just saying, if you had started bleeding from the eyes or starting eating brains, we wouldn't be able to recover."

"I'm sure she'd have lived," Danni mutters, rolling her eyes.

Dante grins and wraps his arm around her shoulders. "Don't be jealous, Danni. I would have mourned you if she had eaten your brain."

"God, you really worry me," Cage mutters.

Dante winks. "Glad I'm on your mind, sugarplum."

The door opens again and Nate hobbles inside, another guy next to him supporting his weight. I inhale sharply at the bruises covering his face, the blood on his shirt, and jump to my feet, along with the others.

"What the fuck? You said he was okay," Danni snaps, slapping her brother's chest.

"I'm fine," Nate tells her, warning her away when she gets too close. "But I've got a few bruised ribs."

She steps back, biting her thumbnail. "What happened to you?" she whispers.

"I'm okay," he assures her once more.

He doesn't look okay. He's clutching his ribs, bent to the side like he's favouring that side. He has cuts and bruises everywhere.

His friend lets him go, and he staggers, reaching for the doorframe to support his weight as he hisses out a breath.

Cage rushes over, helping him. "Fuck. Have you been checked over?"

"Sit him down," I order, moving a few cushions off the sofa.

Cage helps him over to the sofa and gently lowers him into the seat. "Man, you look bad."

"Do you need anything?" I ask, scanning over his injuries. He has a gash on his neck that looks like it was caused from a knife wound. It's been cleaned and a couple of butterfly stiches are on it.

He turns to me, and a smile lights up his face. "No."

"Why are you smiling?" I ask, beginning to feel creeped out.

"We got him."

"What?" I ask, getting back to my feet. A shiver rolls through me and I turn to Cage for answers.

"He got him."

"K-kane?" I ask, my attention on Nate now.

This can't be real.

I'm dreaming.

"Yes."

"No," I deny.

"Yes," Nate promises.

My knees give out and Cage dives forward, reaching for me. He supports my weight, holding me against his side. "It's okay."

"He got him," I choke out.

"How?" Dante asks. "You look like you went three rounds with Mike Tyson."

Nate groans and leans back. "I feel like it."

"Sir, I'm going to get back," the guy at the door announces.

"Thanks, Smith."

"Take care," he tells Nate before he leaves, closing the door behind him.

Danni winces and pulls back when she gets near Nate. "Why do you stink?"

"Because I was hiding in an abandoned cattle shed close by and it was like a sewer pipe had burst there."

"How did you find him?" Cage asks, completely bewildered.

Nate shrugs. "He fucked up at the florist. He left CCTV footage, so I hacked the CCTV from around the area and traced his movements. It cut off at a certain point on the CCTV, but I managed to pinpoint the general direction he went in and searched for him from there," he explains. "We nearly bypassed the cattle place, but something pulled me towards it."

"And he was there?" Cage asks.

"Not at first. We found his bed and belongings in one of the rooms upstairs. He had been there for a while because there was empty food packets and containers."

I sag against Cage. It explains why Kane looked like a homeless man when I met him if he was staying in a place like that.

"Shit, mate, why didn't you call me?" Cage demands.

"I'm glad he didn't call me. My face is too pretty to look like that," Dante declares, pointing to Nate.

Nate rolls his eyes. "Because you had Caitlyn to look out for and I wasn't one hundred percent sure it was him staying there."

"You should have called. You went rogue and could have gotten yourself killed," Cage snaps. "That wasn't your risk to take."

"Looks like he nearly did," Danni adds, still watching Nate closely.

"I'm fine," he assures us. "He came back and took me by surprise. We ended up getting into an altercation. He was skilled. One of the guys tried to intervene but…"

"But?" Cage urges.

Nate's expression falls. "He was stabbed. He's okay. He's in the hospital being looked over."

"Where you should be," Danni mutters.

"I'm honestly okay," he tells her. "The paramedics checked me over. I'm good. I'm going to go back later to check on him though. I couldn't give you this news over the phone."

"Where is he now?" I ask, my voice shaky.

I can't believe this is really happening. For the first time in days, I feel like I'm awake, like there is hope at the end of the tunnel. I know Kane isn't the end to my problems, but it removes a big part of it.

His gaze softens when he glances at me. "You're safe now. The police have him. I promise."

I drop down beside him and pull him in for a hug. "Thank you. Thank you. Thank you."

"Babe," he mutters, hissing out in pain.

I pull back, wincing. "Sorry."

"What have the police said?" Cage asks.

"He's wanted for numerous crimes. He's going away for a long time," Nate admits. "Rome met us at the cattle sheds and took him in."

"I can't believe this is happening. It's like it's not real," I whisper.

Nate rubs a hand down my back. "It's real, Caitlyn."

"What if Robin sends someone else?"

Cage shakes his head. "I don't think that will happen. Rome has slowly been destroying his business from the inside, turning his men against him. It won't be long before they turn on him."

"You can't know that," Danni argues.

Nate faces her. "He does know that. Robin lost power the minute those files arrived at their destinations. The men lost respect for him. And the few that know about Caitlyn, see her being alive as another weakness he's showing."

"But it's not like he hasn't wanted to kill me," I grumble.

"Yeah, and his failure is what's showing his weakness."

"God, this is such a mess," I mutter.

"But a mess that is slowly unravelling. We'll get him," Cage promises.

"What about Lou? Does Johnson know you've caught her killer?"

"As far as I know, yes. He should back off now."

"Thank fuck," Cage mutters.

"So, this is a win," Dante announces.

"Yeah," Nate replies, grinning.

"Then we should go out and celebrate."

I wince, taking a look at Nate. "Maybe we should wait until he's fully recovered."

"Fuck that. I need a beer," Nate grumbles.

Cage chuckles. "First round is on me."

"All my drinks are on you," Nate corrects.

Shaking his head, Cage mutters, "Whatever."

As the men go into detail about the fight, I tune out, lost in my own thoughts. He's gone. For a few days I crumbled because the fear of him coming after me, of taking me away from all whom I love, consumed me. It pulled me into a darkness that swallowed me whole, but now I'm free.

If only for a little while, I feel free.

Now all we have to do is find Robin.

Chapter Thirty-Eight

CAITLYN

I'M ON MY LAST SONG FOR THE night, and for the first time since I started the job, I don't want to get off the stage. I feel free, in love, and happy.

I have changed a lot in my time here at the resort. I have grown as a person, as a mother. I have become a girlfriend, a friend, a loved one.

I've become who I was always meant to be.

And being up here, having people cheer me on, only increases and captures that feeling more. It gives me a confidence I didn't know existed.

I feel like I'm high on life, which is a massive change to how I normally feel.

And it's because of the people who surround me, the ones who give me the strength to push forward.

I'm gutted this is my last ever set here. The band, Live Wire, who Roy has hired, are starting tomorrow, so I want to make my last night count.

I want it to be memorable.

"I'm ending the night a little differently," I breathe into the mic, before reaching for my glass of water. I take a sip, soothing my dry throat. "As many of you know, this is my last night up here for a while." I chuckle and my cheeks heat when a few members of the crowd groan. "And I wanted to use this last song and dedicate it to someone special."

I scan the crowd until I reach Cage, who is sitting at the bar with Nate on one side of him and Dante on the other. Once I have his attention, I turn back to the crowd. "This person changed my life in the best possible way. They gave me hope when I had none. They gave me a chance when I wouldn't give myself one. They gave me love when I felt unworthy of it.

"This song is for the man who captured my heart." I meet Cage's gaze, smiling wide. His eyes heat and I shiver, closing my eyes briefly. "I asked you once if this is too soon, and you answered no. I didn't believe you. But I do now. What I felt wasn't rushed, and we weren't happening too quickly. I understand it now. It was love. From the very first moment I met you, I loved you. It was love in its purest form, and although we have faced many challenges, our love hasn't changed. It hasn't diluted or gone away. It has simply blossomed like a flower on a spring morning."

I duck my head when I realise the crowd has gone silent, everyone enraptured by my words.

Tucking my hair behind my ear, I then glance up at him, my lashes fluttering. "This is for you."

I give Tom a nod to play the song, closing my eyes as I hum the intro.

380 | LISA HELEN GRAY

"How long will I love you…" I sing, letting the music flow out of me, pouring all my emotion into every word as I cover Ellie Goulding's, *How Long Will I Love You*. Each time I sing the answer, I feel it within my soul, and I lock gazes with Cage, letting him know this is for him.

Because we aren't measured by time. I will love him as long as he wants me to, for as long as I live, and for however long he stays.

I'll love him even when he doesn't want me to. Because he is the one.

He is the one I want to go to sleep with each night and wake up to every morning. He is the guy I want to share my troubles with, and all the good stuff. He is the person I want to raise my children with.

For however long I get to. Tears gather in my eyes as I begin to hum the intro once more, only this time, it's proven difficult when a lump forms in the back of my throat.

Cage stands and strolls towards me, weaving around the tables as the last words slip through my lips.

"How long will I love you? As long as stars are above you."

The silence is deafening for a moment before the crowd stands, cheering and howling.

I blush, stepping back from the mic and giving them a small wave. Cage stands near the edge of the stage, looking up at me.

"Kitten," he growls.

I kneel in front of him, running my hand down the side of his face. "I love you, Cage Carter."

"I love you too," he replies and grabs me by the hips, swinging me off the side of the stage. I laugh as he places me down on my feet. "You were amazing."

He leans down, pressing his lips to mine, and I moan into his mouth. I grip the back of his neck firmly, pulling him closer. It's delicate at first, soft, until he deepens it, cupping the back of my head. I moan at the feel of the bristles of his beard scratching against my cheek. It's a sensation I love when he kisses me.

He kisses me like it's his first time, and like it's his last. Heat rises inside me as our tongues touch, and I savour the taste of peppermint and beer.

When he pulls back, I flick my eyelids open, finding him watching me, his pupils dilating, darkening. My breath hitches as I lean up, pressing a kiss to the corner of his mouth.

"Thank you," I whisper. "For everything."

"You never have to thank me," he replies hoarsely, just as a commotion pulls his attention away. He groans and I glance over at the bar to find Dante on the bar, cheering and whistling.

"You get him, tiger," he yells.

Cage shakes his head and turns back to me, his eyes filled with so much happiness they almost glow. "I love you."

I melt against him. "I love you, too."

He turns back to the crowd and yells, "I love this woman!" at the top of his lungs.

He turns back around, the grin still on his face as he sweeps me off my feet and into arms. I squeal, laughter pouring out of me as I cuddle into his chest.

"Cage," I groan, ducking my head into his neck as he moves through the crowd.

His chest vibrates and I feel the warmth of his lips on the side of my head. "It's only fair they know I love you back."

I pull back, staring lovingly up at him. "I think kissing me like I was your air did that."

His heart pounds beneath where my hand is placed on his chest. "There is nothing I could do on this earth that could express how much I love you."

I frown. "Being with me does that. Everything you do does that."

He slides me down his body and I moan at the feel of his erection. He cups my cheeks and leans down, kissing my lips. "I love you."

"Alright, get a fucking room," Dante growls, and I pull back, feeling my cheeks heat. "Preferably one with me."

"Shut up," I scold him, yet I'm unable to keep the dopey smile off my face.

"Hey, that's no way to talk to your biggest fan," he snaps at me playfully.

"You aren't her biggest fan," Cage argues, pulling my back to his front.

Dante arches his eyebrow then turns to me. "Are you sure he was love at first sight because I can walk past you again."

I muffle my laughter as Cage clips him around the ear. "Fucking dickhead."

"Leave me," I tell Cage, laughing lightly.

I take a step forward as they bicker, leaning over the bar to wave Kelly down. She holds up finger, gesturing for me to wait as she finishes serving a customer before moving down the bar towards me.

"Hey, girlie, you were the shit up there tonight. You nearly brought me to tears on that last song. You are seriously gifted," she praises.

"Thank you," I mutter, unable to meet her gaze. I'm not used to taking compliments like that and they make me uncomfortable. "Can I have a glass of coke please?"

Nate's phone begins to ring, startling me. He grabs it off the bar, glances at me, then gets up off his stool before leaving.

Weird.

"You excited about tomorrow?" Cage asks, as Kelly comes back with my coke. I hand over the money before turning to Cage.

I arch an eyebrow at the stupid question. I'm getting my cast off and I couldn't be any happier. "I feel like I'm going to be seeing Taylor Lautner, I'm *that* excited," I answer.

Kelly chuckles behind me, and no doubt it's more over Cage's confused expression.

"Who the fuck is Taylor Lautner?" he growls, his jaw clenching.

"Jacob Black from *Twilight*," I tell him, putting him out of his misery.

His brows pinch together. "The gay one that sparkles?"

"No, dork, he's the hot werewolf with the eight pack."

"Oh, you mean the lad with the wig?" I nod and he grins. "I'm way hotter."

"Pfft, you wish, dude," Kelly sighs wistfully. "The things I would lick off that man's body."

Dante chokes on his beer before sobering, his eyes widening with mischief. "What would you lick off my body?"

She dismisses him with one look. "I'd rather lick a toilet seat," she replies.

I chuckle under my breath. He has been trying to get in her knickers ever since they met. She just isn't interested—or at least, sometimes I think she isn't. There are moments I'll catch her smiling at something he said or gazing at him like she really does want to lick him.

"Don't be like that," he playfully scolds. "Not when I feel like this is Hogwarts Express and we're going to go somewhere magical."

She snorts. "In your dreams."

"You're always in my dreams," he tells her.

Although he seems relaxed, I can see him concentrating hard on her, most likely wondering why she won't sleep with him.

Over the past few months of knowing him, he has had his fair share of women. I'm yet to see him take one of them seriously. And although he's playful with Kelly, I know it's just to tease her.

He takes a swig of his beer when we continue to wait for a comeback. She doesn't give him one, much to his dismay.

"She loves me really," he tells us, nodding as she walks away to serve another customer.

I open my mouth to tease him, but Nate pushing his way through the crowd has me tensing.

Shit!

He looks… I don't know, worried maybe? He's always brooding

and has a frowny face, but this seems like more, and I have a sinking feeling in my gut it has something to do with me and the issues going on around me.

Cage, feeling me tense, turns in the direction I'm looking. "Fuck," he grumbles.

Nate reaches us and immediately jumps in. "Has something happened?"

He glances from me to Cage. "It's happening."

Cage tenses. "What's changed?"

"Kane has been a chatty Cathy and let it slip where Robin is hiding out. Rome wants us to meet him here tomorrow around noon to go over the strategy."

"He's letting us in on it?" Cage asks, eyes widening.

"I made him promise that when he found out where that fucker is hiding, he would let me in on it. I also said you'd want to come along. You in?"

"Fuck yeah, I am," Cage growls, grinning like a fool, before it slips, and he turns to me. "Shit, you have your appointment tomorrow."

"I'll ask Roy if he can take me," I tell him, my heart racing. "But is it safe for you to go? I don't want you to get hurt."

"We'll be fine. Don't worry about us," he declares, bringing me close. "This is nearly over."

My eyes mist over. "It's nearly over."

He drops his forehead against mine. "I wish I could take you tomorrow."

"Take you where?" Kelly asks. I hadn't realised she had stepped back into the conversation. She must not have been there long because I know the others wouldn't have spoken about Robin in front of her or within hearing distance of anyone else.

I turn, forcing a smile. "Hospital. I have to get my cast removed tomorrow, but Cage has been called out on some business."

"I'll take you," she offers as she occupies herself with cleaning the bar up. "What time is your appointment?"

"Half twelve, but I can get someone else to take me. You don't need to do that."

She waves me off. "It's fine, I can take you. I don't start work until three tomorrow."

"Okay," I reply, nodding. "Thank you."

"I need to go clean up, but I'll pick you up about half eleven?"

"Yeah, that's fine."

A flicker of something passes over her expression. "Are you taking Carrie with you?"

"No, Laura is keeping her at her house until we can go pick her up," I admit.

She nods, beaming. "Just us then. We can grab lunch after."

"It's a date."

I SHOOT UP in bed, my heart racing as I fight to catch my breath. Cage stirs beside me and sits up when he realises it's me.

"Nightmare?" he asks softly.

"Yeah," I choke out.

"Come here," he orders, and I fall against his chest as he lies us back down. "What was it about this time?"

"Tomorrow," I whisper. "What do you think will happen?"

"Honestly? I'm not sure. We can only hope for the best at this point. We've come too far not to take action now."

"But what—"

"Hey," he interrupts, pressing a kiss to my lips. "We aren't going to know more until tomorrow."

"How can you be so calm?" I demand shakily. "What if it's a trap? I don't want to lose you, too."

"Nothing is going to happen to me," he swears to me. "Rome has everything under control, and even if he didn't, I can take care of myself. You have nothing to worry about. I promise."

His words don't comfort me or chase away the sick feeling I have in the pit of my stomach. They don't chase away the nightmare. "I've got a bad feeling about this, Cage," I admit, my voice trembling.

He pulls me closer. "Look, I'll promise you now, if I feel something is wrong, I will call it off or take a step back. Okay?"

"All right," I agree, not believing his words. I know him and I know he wants to get this over with.

I yawn, resting my head against his chest. He kisses the top of my head. "Goodnight, Kitten. I love you."

"I love you too," I tell him, closing my eyes.

Sleep doesn't come as easily this time. I lay there, eyes closed, until I feel Cage's breathing even out. Only then do I exhale, letting the tear slide down my cheek.

He might not be worried about tomorrow, but I am.

I can't have anything happen to him. I'd rather give myself over to Robin than let that happen.

Chapter Thirty-Nine

CAGE

MY BOOTS CRUNCH UNDER THE DRIED-out twigs as we make our way through the forest to our meeting point.

The building Robin is hiding in is a fifteen-minute walk and we're coming in from all sides.

Rome, Nate and I, along with a few others, are grouped together. The plan is to go in and take them by surprise and subdue anyone who tries to stop us. One man will be waiting at each exit point to make sure Robin doesn't get away.

I can't wait to look this guy in the eye and tell him it's over, that he will never look at or speak of Caitlyn ever again. I want to give her this, to give her the peace she has craved for so long, and to let her know she's safe.

We're close, so fucking close to ending this, yet that churning in my stomach won't go away.

I can't pinpoint what is exactly wrong or why the hairs on the nape of my neck seem to stand on end. It's there at the back of mind, nagging me. I just can't grasp it. And it's pulling me away from concentrating on the task at hand.

"You okay?" Rome whispers, coming to walk beside me.

I shrug. "Yes, and no."

"The plan is solid," he assures me.

I do think the plan is solid. He has groups of men he trusts, along with some of Nate's, and together we're going to swarm the building, which we had to memorise the plans for. It's large, but with all of us working together, we can do it.

It would have been better if we could have sent someone to scout the area, get them to let us know how many people were there. But Rome didn't want to risk tipping anyone off.

I rub the back of my neck, slowing my pace. "It's not that."

"Caitlyn?" he guesses. "Where is she today?"

"She's getting her cast off," I tell him. "But no, it's not her either."

She woke up late this morning. She was mad that I let her sleep in, but she needed the rest. I woke up a few times to find her staring up at the ceiling. The first time I spoke with her, but she didn't like that she was keeping me awake.

Always thinking of others.

After the fourth time, I didn't wake again until the morning. When I saw her sleeping soundly, I let her rest.

"Who's taking her?" he asks, pulling me from my thoughts.

"A friend of hers—Kelly."

"She should be finished soon though, right?" Nate asks, glancing at me.

I shrug. "Yeah."

"You don't have to be here," Nate suggests, coming to a stop in front of me. "You are here but aren't. We need your head in the game."

"It's not that. I just... I feel like I'm forgetting something."

"Right now?" Rome grumbles, not looking too happy before taking a step away. "Did you not turn the oven off or something."

I glare at his back, his sarcasm not appreciated. "No."

"Mate, we are going to be there soon. Just push it aside."

My eyes scrunch together as my jumbled thoughts try to straighten themselves out.

Then it hits me.

'What if it's a trap?'

Those were the words Caitlyn said to me last night, and I pushed them off as fear. I didn't stop to process what she was saying because I trusted that we had this. I was naïve to think that.

"Stop," I yell, causing the others to stop too.

"For fuck's sake, let us do our job," Rome snaps. "This is our one fucking shot at finding the bastard."

He's wrong. I don't know how I know this; I just do. "No. This has to be a trap."

"What?" Nate asks.

I run my fingers through my hair. "Last night, Caitlyn asked: what if it's a trap? And I blew it off. But this is Kane. He managed to sneak into our house, evade us for months, and go undetected whilst in the same room as Caitlyn. This is someone who has killed and would have most likely gotten away with it had it not been for that note," I tell him.

"I'm not sure what you're getting at," Rome snaps.

My eyes burn into him. "Who interviewed him or saw him after being arrested?"

"Just me, Marker and Johnson. There're others too, but we are the only ones who interviewed him."

I slam my fists against the side of my head, stepping back. "Fuck, this is a trap. She was fucking right."

"Then where are they?" Nate asks, glancing around the forest. "We're ten minutes away from the building.

"We got this information," Rome snaps. "Are you telling me I can't do my job?"

"From a psychopath who loves to play games," I growl, taking step towards him. "He told you what you wanted to hear. We all did."

"You couldn't have said this when we were going over the plan?" Nate asks, groaning.

"What's the hold up?" one of the officers asks.

"This dickhead thinks it's a trap."

I take a step towards him but Nate rushes between us, pushing me back. "Not now."

Rome runs a hand over his bald head. "Look, I'm sorry. I get you're worried. You've got a lot on the line, but we need to do this. We have no proof this is a trap."

"I know that," I bite out.

"Let's continue with the plan. If it is a trap, we're prepared. We will be extra vigilant."

"I'm right about this," I tell him, and glance down at my phone, smiling when I get a message from Caitlyn.

CAITLYN: It's off and it feels like heaven.

I pocket my phone as Rome replies. "Let's get this done."

I follow behind, keeping up with the steady pace, and ten minutes later, we come to a clearing, the old three-storey factory still and quiet. There are no cars, and there is no movement inside from what we can see through the window. It's eerily quiet.

I crouch down next to Nate, scanning the building. "This isn't right."

"Hate to say it but I think you were right," Nate suggests. "A guy like him, with enemies like his, he would have more security. There would be at least two people on those doors."

"He doesn't need much security when he owns guns," Rome

mutters. "But I have to admit, this doesn't feel right." He leans down to his comm, whispering, "Proceed with caution."

"As much as it pains me to give the guy credit, he isn't stupid. He didn't get this far up the food chain by being thick. What I don't get is why we are here."

And I don't. It's bugging me to no end.

"Let's figure that out after," Nate mutters.

"Let's clear the building."

I sigh, pushing off the ground, and race towards the back exit. I lean against the wall, listening for sounds inside, yet hear none.

Nate kneels in front of me, picking at the lock before pushing back, letting another guy rush forward to pull the door open. He goes inside first, before we hear him whisper, 'clear.'

I jerk my chin in confirmation, and Nate goes in first, me following close behind. The layout is simple as we head down a long hallway that runs along the back wall, clearing each room as we go.

"Clear," echoes through the radio.

"Clear."

"Clear."

We keep our steps light as we rush to check each room. When we push through the last door at the end, we find the floor littered with old newspapers.

I turn, slamming my hand against the wall. "Fuck!"

Nate's hand clamps down on my shoulder. "Let's see what Rome has first."

I turn, glaring at him. "He hasn't got a fucking clue himself, Nate."

"Cage," he warns.

"We were played. Kane is probably sat in that cell laughing at us."

"Mate, I'm as fucked off as you," he tells me. "You need to keep it together."

I storm out of the room, smashing the door against the wall as I go. I'll have to go back to Caitlyn and tell her I failed. She'll have to spend another day living in fear and I hate it for her. I wanted to make it right.

But I couldn't.

She left this morning with hope sparking in her eyes. And now I'll have to watch once again as it dims.

Heading outside, there are now cars out front. Rome is scanning over papers laying out on a bonnet of a truck, his radio still gripped in his hand. He slams his fist down, the metal protesting underneath. "Fuck!"

"See, you aren't the only one pissed," Nate points out.

"I still want to punch his lights out," I growl.

Nate looks at me like I'm crazy. And maybe I am. I don't care. "Let's see what he's got."

Rome turns at hearing our approach. "Don't even fucking say it," he warns me.

I hold my hands up. "Wasn't going to," I lie. "But I need to know if you have another plan."

"I fucking don't. He knew we would be here."

"Robin?" I ask, sharing a look with Nate. He shrugs. "You think he told Kane to tell us to come here?"

He points to the bonnet. "That was left in a room upstairs on a desk."

I step up to the truck and glance down at the note. The blood in my veins boils as I take a step away, needing to get in control. "Fuck."

"Thanks for giving me what I want," Nate reads out loud.

"Fuck," I roar.

"This was his plan all along. And I bet once it's done, they have a way to free Kane," Rome bites out, slamming his hand down on the car, denting it. "It was just a distraction."

"No," I whisper, staggering back.

It all makes sense.

"Cage?" Nate calls, stepping closer.

I stagger back, jerking as my phone begins to vibrate against my leg. "Because now they have what they've wanted all along."

"What?" Nate asks, eyebrows pinching together. "The information? I've got that alarmed, Cage. It's not been touched."

"No," I whisper, lifting my phone up, revealing Laura's name. "Caitlyn."

"No," he mutters, just as his phone rings.

There's only one reason why she would be ringing me.

"Hello?" I answer, gulping. I knew the second I saw her name on the screen what was coming. It was like a sixth sense. I could feel it in my gut. In the very beat of my heart.

They have Caitlyn.

They got exactly what they wanted.

"Cage? Are you with Caitlyn? She hasn't picked up Carrie yet and I'll need to be in work soon. She said she was on her way but that was over thirty minutes ago."

"No," I whisper, just as Nate's eyes widen.

"Kane's dead," he informs us.

Because they have what they wanted and are cleaning up loose ends.

"Cage," Laura calls.

I failed.

Pulling myself together, I grip the phone and answer her. "Laura, I can't explain everything right now, but I need you to do something for me."

"Has something happened?" she asks, her voice trembling when she senses my urgency.

"Laura," I plead, needing her to listen. I glance over at Rome as a growl slips through his lips. His nostrils flare as he storms forward, swiping all the paperwork off the top of the bonnet.

"What do you need me to do?" she rushes out, her voice pitching.

"I need you to call Dad. Tell him to stay there and not to answer the door to anyone. Doesn't matter if it's an officer or someone you may think you know. You do not answer to anyone but me, Nate, or Dante," I warn her. "Do you understand?"

Her voice is shaky when she answers. "Cage," she whispers.

"Laura, do you understand?"

"Yes!"

"I'll call you in a bit," I tell her. "Get Dad there."

I end the call, and head to Nate. He turns, his expression tight. "Who was that?"

"A contact I have at the station. Kane is dead. He thought we would want to know."

"We have fucking nothing now. Nothing," I roar.

"Caitlyn?"

"She hasn't picked Carrie up. She messaged Laura saying she was on her way, but never arrived."

He pales. As a family friend, he knows where Laura lives. It isn't far from the hospital Laura works at. "Shit!"

I turn to Rome, and before Nate can stop me this time, I charge at him, gripping him around the neck. He smacks my hands away before pushing me back. "They've got her. They've got Caitlyn."

"I know," he tells me, his eyes narrowed.

"Are you in on this?" I bite out, causing the others to gather around us.

"No, I'm fucking not," he spits out, his eyes glacial. "That was my guy on the inside. He said he's being moved."

"What does that mean?" I bite out.

"It means we need to know Caitlyn's last whereabouts until he can text us his location."

Nate steps away, pulling his phone out. "Darius, I need you to do another favour. I don't have my equipment with me to do it myself. It's Caitlyn, the girl I was telling you about?" He pauses, pinching the bridge of his nose. "She's gone. She was with her friend, Kelly Dean, coming back from St. Barnyards Hospital."

He rattles off more information as I stand there uselessly. I should have known he would try to get to her. Instead, I was so blinded by my need to catch Robin that I forgot to protect her.

Nate gets off the phone. "Hopefully, he finds something we've missed."

"We need to get out there and look for her," I demand.

"We need to wait. I've got people on this."

I throw him a dirty look. "Yeah, and look at where we are. It was the one thing I wanted to prevent happening," I roar.

I begin to head towards one of the cars still running with no one inside. If he isn't going to do anything, I am.

His phone blares and I keep going, only stopping when I hear him talk. "Where? Fuck!"

I slowly turn, dread filling the pit of my stomach as I take in his expression. "What?"

"We need to go. And we need to go now," he warns us.

Chapter Forty

CAITLYN

KELLY FALLS IN STEP BESIDE ME as we make our way back to the car. I have a bounce in my step as I pull my phone out, firing off a text to Cage.

It's off.

Finally, after weeks of not being able to scratch an itch, or do certain day to day chores, I'm finally free of my cast.

We get into the car and Kelly glances over at me. She has been quiet, her eyes red and puffy like she hadn't gotten any sleep.

"Did you message Cage?"

"Yeah," I reply, glancing down at the blank screen. My smile drops when I remember why he isn't the one here with me. I had been so ecstatic over my cast being removed that I forgot he will be heading into enemy territory right about now.

I close my eyes, resting my head back against the headrest. I want to be hopeful this nightmare will end today, but this has been my life for so long and Robin always manages to stay one step ahead.

They are all risking a lot to help me and Carrie. Too much. And if it doesn't work today, we need to come up with another plan, one that involves us getting away from Robin for good. Because I'm not going to keep putting those I love in danger.

"Has he messaged you back?" Kelly asks, her voice tense.

I refresh my messages as I absently reply to her. "No, not yet. I'm sure he's busy," I explain, then glance up, scanning the road. My brows pull together as I read the road sign. I'm not familiar with the area, but I know this isn't the right direction to Laura's. "Um, Kelly, do you realise you're going the wrong way?"

"There's something I need to do," she chokes out, her fingers tightening around the steering wheel.

Going on alert, I sit up straighter in my seat. "What is going on? You've been acting strange all morning. Have I said something to upset you?"

"I'm sorry," she sobs out, leaning forward.

"Sorry about what?"

"They gave me no choice."

"Kelly, you're scaring me," I admit, shaking as she pulls onto a dirt lane.

"I don't want to do this," she cries. "I really don't."

"Do what?" I yell. "Pull over, Kelly."

"I can't," she chokes out.

"Pull over."

"They have my son," she cries as the car picks up speed.

I drop back into the seat, the breath stalling in my lungs. "Who has your son?"

Tears stream down her cheeks. "I'm sorry."

"You said your ex had him."

She shakes her head, wiping under her eyes. "He's dead."

I inhale, my eyes widening. "What? You said he hurt you, that he—"

"He did. He abused me to the point I didn't know who I was anymore, and then he died. It was a sweet relief, but then his past caught up to me."

"Kelly," I plead, not understanding what is going on. "Pull over."

"I can't," she strangles out. "I have to do this. I have to get him back. He's all I have. I'm all he has, and he has to be scared."

"Kelly, what are you talking about?"

The car swerves and I cry out. "I have a plan, Caitlyn."

"What plan?"

"I have to give them you, and in return, I'll get my son."

My stomach bottoms out. I'm denying it, *want* to deny it, but the truth is right in front of me. "You are here because of Robin."

"I don't want to do this, Caitlyn. You have to believe me, but I've seen what they're capable of. What they'll do if I don't do as I'm told."

"Don't do this," I plead. "Please."

"I have a plan," she tells me, just as a police car comes into view, parked on the side of the road.

The car slows down, and I turn to her. "Kelly, you don't have to do this."

Her tear-filled gaze meets mine when she puts the car into park. "I have no choice. I really have no choice. But I won't let them hurt you, I promise."

"Hurt—"

My mind goes foggy when she pricks me with something. I look down, watching as she pulls the syringe out of my arm.

"I'm sorry," she chokes out, and pulls out another two syringes, sliding them up the sleeve of her jacket.

My head drops back, my vision blurring as I try to focus on the two men walking towards us. I can't make them out, and when I open my mouth to call out for help, nothing happens.

Kelly strolls to the front of the car, and I watch as she dives for one of the men. It's the last thing I see before everything goes black, and I'm pulled into the darkness.

My eyelashes flutter like a butterfly taking flight for the very first time. My tongue feels heavy, and my throat is dry as I try to call out.

All of it comes back to me in flashes as I struggle to sit up, disorientated. I grip onto something hard, wooden, yet something sharp smacks my hand out and I collapse to the ground.

A figure forms in front of me and I squint, trying to focus on who is there.

"I wouldn't try to move if I were you," the deep voice rumbles.

Instead of seeing two, I'm seeing one, and who I see has me pushing back against a brick wall. "You."

Detective Marker grins, kneeling in front of me. "I told you I'd be seeing you soon."

"W-where's Kelly?" I croak out.

"Being taught a lesson."

My gaze hardens on him. "Why? Why are you doing this? You are meant to protect and serve."

"Yeah? When it suits people. The majority of the time we have to deal with abuse, vandalism, being spat on and other crap."

"So, you work for a murderer instead?"

"He pays better," he spits out.

He leans down, gripping my chin in a vice grip. "Stop!"

"You should have kept your mouth shut," he bites out.

"You won't get away with this. Cage will come looking for me," I warn him. "Then your cover is blown."

The slap has my cheek smacking into the floor, and instantly, blood pools in my mouth. "He has to find you first."

Hinges creaking in the background has my entire body tensing. "Boss wants to speak to you," a voice rumbles.

Marker straightens, taking a step back, which gives me a view of the room. The guy at the door steps aside, and my eyes widen as Kelly is dragged in, battered and unconscious.

"No," I whisper.

"Mummy!" a little boy screams, and I startle, realising it came from beside me. My hands shake as I lift myself up, my heart tearing open as I watch a boy crawl out from under the old, beaten desk, rushing over to Kelly's side. "Wake up, Mummy. Wake up."

"Shut up!" Marker demands, and the boy whimpers, covering Kelly's body.

I stay tense as he leaves the room, and the guy who had helped bring Kelly in turns to look in my direction. "You're next, bitch."

I shiver as they close the door behind them, a lock latching into place. Once they are gone, I drag myself over to Kelly, still feeling the effects of whatever was in that injection.

"Hey, I'm Caitlyn," I greet the boy, keeping my voice low.

"Don't touch her," he screams.

"I just need to check her over."

Her face is a mess. There are deep wounds on her head and her entire face is covered in blood.

Her body is covered with the same bruises, and as I glance down at her hands, I notice her nails are torn and bloody.

What did they do to her?

He leans back a little and I sag when I feel her pulse against my fingers.

"Have you been naughty too?"

"Naughty?"

"They said I was here because I was naughty, and that Mummy couldn't have me back until she did as she was told."

"You aren't here because you've been naughty," I tell him, my heart breaking.

"They took me away from her, and when I cried, they got mad and said I couldn't see her because I was naughty."

I go to reach for him, but he jerks back, whimpering. "Listen to me, you have done nothing wrong. They are the bad people," I tell him, keeping my voice firm, yet soft.

"I've been good. I promise," he tells me, hugging Kelly's hand to his chest. The tears cause two streaks down his cheeks. He's dirty, and from the old bruising and new ones, he has been hurt during his time here.

"I'm not going to hurt you," I promise. "Can you tell me your name?"

"It's Ethan," he answers, his voice scratchy. "She came for me. She really came back for me like she promised."

"When did you last see her?"

His sob hits me like it's my own. "I don't know. They hurt me because she wouldn't listen to them."

"Listen to them?"

"She said she didn't want to do it."

"Do what?"

"I don't know," he cries. "But she came back for me like she promised."

"Of course she did. She loves you."

"They said she wouldn't come back to me."

I grit my teeth, fighting back the tears. This could have been Carrie.

When I first realised what Kelly had done, I couldn't believe she had betrayed me. I couldn't believe she would do it to me, that she'd hand me over to the enemy.

But Cage's words from the other day hit me.

I could blame myself.

I could blame Kelly.

Hell, I could blame my sister.

But none of us were at fault. We weren't to blame for what was happening. Courtney fell in love with the wrong person and died trying to correct a wrong.

I'm protecting my daughter. Courtney's daughter.

And Kelly… she fell in love with a monster and is now protecting her son.

The people who died along the way were murdered by one man. Maybe not all by his hand, but he was the reason.

None of those people had to die.

Now, seeing her reason for doing all of this, I can't blame her. I can't even muster any anger.

Because what she did is exactly what I would have done.

What I am, is disappointed. She could have come to any of us, and we would have helped her get Ethan back. She had to have known that.

"Ethan, your mum has been looking for you for a long time," I whisper. "She's going to be so happy when she wakes up."

"Then we can go home?"

"Yes."

He lays his head down on her chest, his body shaking with tears. "Please wake up, Mummy. Please wake up."

I stagger to my feet, the room spinning for a moment as I take a look around. The smell hits me for the first time, and I lift my arm, covering my nose in attempt to escape the odour. It smells like a sewer. I take a step further into the room and find the cause of the smell. It's a bucket in the corner behind the desk.

I glance back at Ethan, tears in my eyes. He has been kept in here this whole time.

I move past it, ignoring the flimsy blanket under the desk, and head to the window. It's covered in grime and rusted at the hinges, but the wood is breaking off, giving me a little bit of hope.

I unlatch it and grip the handle, giving it a lift, but it doesn't budge. A frustrated growl slips through as I try again. The handle snaps off into my hand and I cry out, throwing it to the floor.

I pull the sleeve of my cardigan down and use the cuffs to wipe at the window. But the grime is welded on to it.

"It doesn't open," Ethan croaks out.

I force a smile in his direction before turning back to it.

But glass does break.

I cover my entire hand with my cardigan and whack my fist against it. I cry out when I feel the glass tear into my skin, the warmth of blood rushing down my arm.

I ignore the pain and open my mouth to scream, but as I reach the window, I get a good look outside, and any hope of screaming for help evaporates.

There's nothing there.

No one is going to hear me scream. Only the people who captured me.

Fields and trees fill my vision. A scream bubbles up in my throat and I slam my hand against the window once more, ignoring the sharp shards of glass cutting into my skin.

"No!" I cry, my voice hoarse.

I turn, resting my back against the brick wall, and slide down, tucking my legs to my chest.

We aren't getting out of here. Even if I did, how would I carry Kelly and her son?

Tears fall as I grip the side of my head. "Cage," I plead. "I love you."

Chapter Forty-One

CAITLYN

IT COULD BE MINUTES, HOURS, that I have been locked in here. There's no movement from outside the door and the only sound I've heard was a car pulling up not long ago.

Kelly hasn't woken up and I'm beginning to worry. I tried shaking her, yet she laid unconscious. If it weren't for her pulse, I would assume she was dead. I dragged them behind the desk, not wanting them to be in view if Robin's men decide to come back and take their anger out on them. Ethan fell asleep cuddled up to Kelly not long ago, and as my eyes begin to droop, I know it won't be long until I lose consciousness. Whatever Kelly gave me is still swimming around through my system. Everything seems like a blur and my eyelids are heavy.

Stay awake.

I catapult up when footsteps near the door. I crawl over to the desk, blocking the view of Kelly and Ethan.

The hinges protest as the door is pushed open, revealing a bulk of a man. If I were to guess, he's in his thirties, and apart from the clenched jaw and narrowed eyes, he looks nothing like the previous man I saw.

Ethan jerks awake, whimpering, and I close my eyes. "Please don't hurt them," I plead when the guy doesn't stop.

He kneels beside the desk, his expression softening as he looks at Ethan. "Ethan, can you remember what we talked about?"

"Luke?" Ethan whispers, crawling out a little from under the desk.

"Yeah, it's me, buddy," he answers softly.

I watch him warily, my pulse racing. He doesn't seem like the others. "Who are you?"

"My name is Luke. I work for Detective Rome," he explains as he checks Kelly's pulse.

"She hasn't woken up."

"She will in an hour or two. They gave her something that knocks you out."

"I think… I think she gave that to me," I tell him. "But I wasn't out this long."

"She didn't give you the full dose," he explains, wincing in pity. "It's why she has these injuries. She tried to use it on Marker."

I close my eyes as shame hits me. She said she had a plan, and I didn't believe her. She really had tried.

"Are we leaving now?" Ethan asks, hope shining in his eyes.

"Soon, buddy," Luke promises.

"Wait, you're getting us out?"

"No, not yet. Rome has been informed you are here. I've only just found out they moved you here," he explains.

I glance from Ethan to Luke, my brows pulling together. "If you know him, why haven't you already got him out?"

"I couldn't risk my cover. I wasn't sure what he asked Kelly to do, not until after."

"He's just a boy," I tearfully rush out. "You should have saved him."

"I couldn't," he grits out. "I was never given the opportunity and I couldn't risk his safety. Once those emails were sent out, I was going to get him out, but he was moved. This is the first time I've seen him since."

Luke.

I close my eyes as it hits me where I remember the name. "You were the guy who was in love my sister."

He tenses and glances away, but I saw the pain inside of him at the mention of her.

"Yes," he replies, his voice filled with deep emotion. "Courtney found out who I was working for and promised to keep my cover a secret if I helped you all escape." He pauses and meets my gaze. "I'm so sorry I couldn't save her."

I rub at my chest, the ache there hollow. "Me too," I whisper.

"Do you remember what we talked about?" Luke asks Ethan once again.

"That when it gets loud and men are shouting, to stay on the floor and hide."

Luke ruffles his hair. "Good boy," he tells him. "Don't move until I come back for you or unless your mum says it's okay."

"She's still sleeping," he whispers, lifting his head towards the window at the sound of another car approaching.

"Fuck!"

"Wait," I rush out, gripping his wrist. "If you knew about Kelly then why didn't Rome tell us?"

"Because she was never a threat to you."

I arch an eyebrow. "I'm here because she brought me here."

"You've been through hell. I get where that anger is coming from, but whatever you think you've been through, she's been through worse."

"What?" I whisper, rearing back. His words are like a slap to the face. "I'm not angry. I'm disappointed she didn't tell us so we could help her, but that's it'. Don't assume to know me."

"Sorry," he breathes out. "It's been hard having to deal with these guys day in and day out."

"She was my friend," I tell him. "Rome could have said something. Prevented this."

"Her husband sold her before he died. Left her with debt she couldn't afford and had men from all over after her. She disappeared and I thought she managed to escape what was coming."

"Sold her?"

"Her husband had a debt. It wasn't paid before he died so it went to Kelly, who he had as collateral. She knew nothing about any of this, not until he died."

"She said he abused her."

He jerks his chin in a nod. "Probably worse," he agrees. "She disappeared but then Robin mysteriously had her son. He brought her in and told her if she wanted to see him alive again, she would do what she was asked."

"Moving her near the resort?"

He nods. "You've got to believe she didn't want to hurt you. She came back after her first shift and by then, they'd had Ethan for weeks. They couldn't hurt her, so they hurt him."

"And she came back," I guessed.

I slump against the desk, tears slipping down my cheeks.

"They gave her no choice," he warns me. "They threatened to kill Ethan if she didn't do what she did today."

"I can't talk about this. Not now," I choke out. "You need to get us out of here."

"I can't. Rome knows you are here. I think that was Robin arriving, so you need to brace yourself."

"He's going to kill me," I cry out.

"Please, don't make this harder," he pleads. "I have to get back out there before they notice."

"Then take Ethan," I plead. "He's just a boy."

He flinches. "I can't."

"Why not? You've got nothing to lose if Rome is already on the way," I snap.

"Yes, why not indeed, Luke?" Marker drawls, stepping into the room.

The gun in his hand has me pressing back against the desk. Luke quickly stands, turning to face Marker.

"Can't a guy have a little fun?"

"And what fun would that be?" Marker asks casually.

"Well, it's always fun if they think they can escape."

Marker tilts his head to the side. "You know what Robin does to those who betray him?"

Luke's body tenses, right before he flies into action, rushing forward. A scream bubbles in my throat as a deafening sound goes off in the room. I blink in a daze, my ears ringing.

My eyes widen as I see Luke stagger back, blood pouring down his leg. He reaches Marker and takes him down to the floor, landing a punch to his gut. Marker grunts, before kicking up, twisting Luke off him.

Run, my head screams.

I crawl under the table, holding my hand out for Ethan. "Come on, honey. We need to go."

"I'm not leaving Mummy," he cries.

"Please," I plead, as I hear the two men wrestling behind me. "I'll come back for your mum."

He takes my hand, giving Kelly one last look before crawling out from under the desk.

"No," Luke warns me.

I meet his gaze as he pins Marker down. "I can't risk his life," I tell him and head for the door.

I pull on Ethan's hand and together, we race towards the door, coming to a stop when the host of my nightmares stands in front of me, a gun pointed right at me.

I shove Ethan behind me, breathing deeply as I take a step back into the room.

"It's been a long time."

"Let's us go," I demand, taking another step back. "Go to your mum."

Ethan lets go of my hand and his feet slap against the floor as he reaches his mum.

A sickening crack echoes in the room and my eyes widen as I watch Marker fall to the floor, his eyes wide and unblinking.

A strangled cry slips through my lips as Luke steps forward, blood gushing from the gash on his lip and eyebrow.

"Put the gun down," he demands.

Unaffected, Robin begins to laugh. "Ah, the man who fucked my wife."

He knew?

"Put the gun down," Luke demands once again, staggering slightly.

Robin steps further into the room, his expression a mask of fury. "Sit down and wait your turn," he snaps, just as the second shot echoes around the room.

"No," I cry out, but Robin jerks his head and one of the men standing outside the room steps forward, grabbing me by the hair.

I turn to Luke as he falls to his knees, his hands clutching the wound on his stomach. There's so much blood.

So much.

A metallic smell fills the air, and I heave. He falls onto his side, coughing as his eyes widen in shock.

"No!"

"Luke," Ethan cries.

I glare at Robin. "You're a monster."

"And you still have something I want."

"I'm not giving you a thing."

He lifts the hand wielding the gun, aiming it at the desk, where Ethan is. "Are you sure about that?"

"He's just a boy," I yell, and I hear the click on the gun. "Stop! Don't. Please. Don't."

I watch in horror as his finger presses down on the trigger. I clench my eyes shut, covering my ears. He hasn't even given me time. I would give everything to save him, to stop this.

The gun blares, and I collapse into the arms of the guy pinning me in me place. Tears swarm my vision, and in that moment, I don't want to ever see again. I don't want to see tomorrow.

Let alone today.

The gurgled noise has bile rising in my throat and my eyelids fly open. I inhale sharply at the sight of Luke, his back to us, with blood pouring out of the wound.

He saved Ethan.

Nothing could have ever prepared me for this moment, not even the action movies I obsessed over.

Because this is really happening. A scream so loud tears from my throat.

I'll never forget this smell, or the sound of a man dying.

If I make it out of this, I'm never going to be the same.

None of us are.

There's an empty feeling inside of me, and I'm numb to it.

"Neil, bring her," Robin orders, and I struggle against the hold, needing to get to him.

He can't survive an injury like that. Blood gushes from the back of his neck, pouring like a fountain down his back.

No one could survive that.

Could they?

Even if someone were to arrive now, is our country even equipped to deal with a bullet wound?

A sob tears from my throat as Luke collapses to the floor. Blood still gurgles in his throat, and I scream at the sight of it pouring out of his mouth when he rolls.

Neil's body shakes with laughter as Luke's chest convulses. "Fucker had that coming."

"You bastard," I yell, struggling as he drags me out of the room.

Another guy steps up to the door. "What should I do about this body?"

Neil shrugs. "Leave him to teach the kid a lesson."

"You monster," I cry, not making it easy for him as he drags me down the hall.

We reach another door and Neil kicks it open, pushing me inside. My knees hit the floor and I cry out. My hair comes loose, and I push it back, glancing up. Robin stands above me, loosening the tie around his neck.

I grunt, wheezing as he boots me in the stomach. I didn't even see him move.

"Courtney was a screamer, too," he tells me, amusement in his tone.

I try to get to my feet, but he kicks me again, this time harder. "You are going to burn in hell."

"You'd think you'd have learned from your sister's and parents' mistakes, Caitlyn."

I push up to my knees. "You killed them."

He grins and gestures to someone behind me. I glance back too late. Neil drags me to my feet and over to the metal chair. He sits me down, tying my hands behind my back.

Robin pulls out a wooden one and it creaks as he takes a seat.

"They were going to end up dead sooner or later. They were bringing too much attention to my business."

"I'm not giving you anything. There's nothing you can do to me. Not now."

"Ah, but there is," he drawls. "Where is it?"

He's talking about the evidence.

"Why do you want it? Everyone has already seen it."

Death is the only thing I can describe staring back at me. He sits forward, clasping his hands over his suit covered legs. He narrows his eyes, the brown irises burning into me. "I killed your sister for trying to blackmail me. I killed your parents for looking into me. And I killed all those people in between for getting in the way of what I want," he bites out. "What do you think I'll do to you?"

"Nothing," I goad him, remembering Luke's words. Rome is coming. Which means Cage will be here soon. "Because it's too late."

He sits back, running a hand through his black hair. "You think it's too late?"

"Everyone who can be trusted has it," I bite out, struggling against the ties around my wrists.

He shakes his head, watching me like he pities me. "Papers can easily be forged. They can disappear. But those originals? They can't. And I want them."

"I'm not giving them to you."

"Tell me, how is Mr Carter?"

I struggle even harder, ignoring his grin. "You won't go near him."

"Or the lovely couple who own the resort? Are those papers worth their lives?"

My breath quickens as a silent scream slices through my head. "They will come for you."

"And Carrie…" he sighs, feigning boredom. "Is that brat worth keeping those papers?"

"No," I roar, and the rope tears through my wrists during my struggle. "You won't go near her."

She's safe. I have to believe once Cage figures out Robin isn't at the building they thought he was in, he will make sure Carrie is safe.

His fist connects with the side of my face, and I spit out blood, hissing out a breath. "You've made me look a fool for far too long, Caitlyn."

He swings his fist once more, and this time I brace myself, tensing as I shut my eyes. The force knocks me to the side, causing the chair to topple over with my weight, and the metal clangs against the floor.

I cry out as my cheek smacks into the floor and the binds at my wrist pull taut.

I groan, becoming aware of every bruise, every cut or ache in my body. The room begins to spin, and my vision dims as feet step in front of me.

Kneeling, Robin pulls up his sleeves, before reaching over and slapping my cheek. "Where are they?"

My lips tighten as I say nothing.

Neil, behind me, laughs, kicking the back of the chair. "I think she wants to play."

I close my eyes, silently praying.

Please, Cage, Rome.

I can't have Robin leave here. I can't have anyone else hurt because of him. I can't. And I never want my daughter to lay eyes upon him. Just the thought of him getting his hands on her has my stomach pummelling out.

"Do you know what I did to your sister?" he asks, jerking his head behind me.

The metal chair is shoved upright, and I wince as the rope cuts in deeper and tugs at my shoulders.

Another man enters the room, this one with shaggy hair and a large, sharp knife. "Is this what you wanted?"

Robin nods and takes a few steps away to retrieve it. My breath hitches as he holds it up, letting the light outside gleam on the silver. "This was the exact same knife."

Tears slip free as I struggle to keep my sobs inside. He doesn't get to see me break.

He nods like I answered. "She screamed sweet agony."

He bends down and I spit in his face. "I hate you," I bite out.

Robin steps back, pulling out a tissue to wipe his cheek, his lips tight.

"You're going to regret that," he roars, and rushing forward, stabs the knife into my thigh.

The scream comes from the pit of my stomach and my head flies back. Warmth trickles down my leg and I'm unable to hold it back.

The agony shifts when he pulls it out, and my head drops forward. Blood pours like a fountain down my leg as I struggle to keep my breathing even.

"Talk," he demands.

I tilt my head up, using the last of my energy, and narrow my gaze on him. I'm looking into the eyes of the purest evil, one without empathy or a soul.

"Get fucked."

Cage is coming for me.

He tsks, shaking his head, and leans forward. I flinch and watch as the light shines in his eyes as he grips my thigh. I cry out, gritting my teeth together, but as he presses his thumb into the wound, I howl, my stomach rolling.

"Talk," he roars, pressing further, and the sensation, the pain, it's all too much.

I can hear the blood roaring in my ears.

Taste the metallic of the blood in the air.

And the room around me spins, right before my eyes roll to the back my head and everything goes black.

Chapter Forty-Two

CAGE

"C AN YOU NOT PICK UP speed?" I grit out.

"First, you need to tell us what's going on," Nate demands.

Rome glares in Nate's direction. "You know everything that is going on."

"No, you're hiding something."

I glance at Rome from where I'm sat in the back, between the seats. His jaw clenches and he glances away.

He is hiding something.

"This involves my woman. You need to fucking tell us."

"It's Kelly," he grits out.

My brows pull together. "What? Have they found her or something?"

Nate hisses out a breath. "No, the bitch is clearly working for Robin."

I tense and turn to Rome, waiting for an answer. He doesn't make us wait. "She's as much a victim of Robin as Caitlyn is. He's had her son, and to make sure he doesn't get hurt, she's had to do what he tells her."

"Spying on Caitlyn?" I snap.

"I knew something was up with her. She has been acting shady since we first met her."

"Believe it or not," Rome bites out, "not everyone is heartless. She's done the best she could in an impossible situation."

"I don't give a fuck," I snap. "Right now, I only care about Caitlyn."

"When Luke called, he said Robin hadn't arrived and that he was on his way there. Hopefully, Robin arrives before we do because this really will be our last chance to get to him."

"But the information already got sent out," I remind him. "Why is he still after her?"

"To show power. To get the original copies," Rome answers, swinging the car around the corner. I grip onto the back of the headrests.

"He wants to destroy the originals and claim doubt about the copies we made," Nate murmurs.

"Are you sure you aren't a police officer?" Rome asks, eyeing Nate warily.

"Just good at my job."

He pulls up haphazardly into a bank of weeds, other police cars and cars doing the same.

The sky darkens with signs of a storm brewing, the July sun hidden behind the dirty black clouds as we jump out of the car.

"Gather round," Rome yells as he pulls out his tablet. "The building has four floors. It's an old office building. It has emergency exits here, here and here," he tells them, pointing to each of the locations. "The two main entrances will be heavily guarded. Teams one and two will dismantle those. Teams three and four will split up and cover the other three emergency exits."

Another guy steps forward in full uniform. "Is everyone suited up with stab proof vests?"

A chorus of 'yes' comes.

"Wait," Nate demands. "Why do I have a feeling we're about to be side-lined?"

"Because you are," Rome admits.

"Like fuck we are. My woman is in there."

"And that's exactly why I can't have you go in. Your priority will be to get to Caitlyn and that will put not only yourself in danger, but the men around you. You two can keep a look out. I have ambulances and other officers on standby ready to move in when we get a lock on everyone inside."

"You said Luke gave you the information you'll need."

"Yes, but he was only giving a guestimate. There's no saying who Robin will bring with him or who was already there." He turns back to the group. "We have three victims inside, one being a six-year-old boy. Please be on the look out and get them to safety."

"I can't just sit outside and wait," I tell him.

He glowers and steps up to me, spit flying out of his mouth when he yells. "Use your fucking head, Cage. I don't have time for this. *You* don't have time for this. They have guns. And believe it or not, charging in there will get you killed. You aren't equipped to handle gun violence. These men and I, are."

His words are a distant memory as the sound of gun fire fills the air. The wind whistles through the trees around us and a few droplets of rain land on my arm as I crouch down.

"Move out," Rome yells, before stopping and turning to us. "Don't try to be fucking heroes. We will get your woman out."

He moves before I can argue, right before a second shot goes off.

I spin around, a roar tearing from my chest. I slam my fists down on the roof of the car, kicking at the dirt beneath my feet.

I turn, facing the direction the men ran to and sigh with frustration. It's going to take five minutes to get to the office building, another four, maybe more, to get inside.

By that time, Caitlyn could have bled out.

I can't stand here feeling like a spare part.

"We going in or what?" Nate asks, reading my mind.

My shoulders drop and I jerk my chin in a nod. I grab his arm before he can take a step. "You don't need to come."

He glances up from my hand on his arm to meet my gaze. "She's family."

Yeah, she really fucking is.

We race down the lane, skipping through some overgrown bushes and trees. The leaves give us cover as we near the building. We're getting close, and the closer we get, the thicker the trees become. This place is in the middle of nowhere and the land around it goes on for miles.

The old-bricked building is crumbling in places. The roof has seen better days and the windows needed updating years ago.

"How are we going to get in?" I ask, noticing the side door still being guarded.

I scan the area, not seeing one of Rome's men in sight.

"Through that door," Nate suggests and pushes to his feet. I move out to the left, where the door being open gives me covering. My boots crunch the twigs and stones under me, but the sight of Nate distracts the guard long enough for me to slide against the side of the building, slowly making my way towards him.

The guy manning it looks up, drawing the gun in his hand. "Who are you?"

"We've come to collect a package," Nate replies, his voice deep, unnerving.

"We don't have anything being picked up, so I'll ask again: who are you?"

I give Nate a nod to let him know I'm ready.

"Your worst nightmare," Nate answers, and we both move at the same time, our movements swift, quick.

I snatch the gun, lifting it over his head as Nate moves in, slamming his fists into the guy's temples. He drops like dead weight to the ground and Nate leans over him, grabbing his hands and tying them with zip locks.

"You just happened to have them?"

He looks up, grinning. "It's all I could find in your truck."

Once tied up, Nate takes the gun apart, throwing a clip off into the bushes behind us. "Let's go."

Moving inside, we bump into Rome. His gaze narrows. "I fucking told you to stay at the cars."

"My dad could never control me either," I tell him, then push him aside as I see the barrel of a gun coming around the corner. I swing it up, ignoring the buzzing in my ears as a shot goes off. I kick the guy's legs out from under him, disorientating him before stomping down on his knee. The crunch of bone is music to my ears.

I hand Rome the gun before reaching for the zip ties Nate hands me. I tie the guy up, leaving him howling in pain, before reaching the stairs.

"We have the first and second floor covered," Rome mutters.

"Don't feel too bad," Nate teases as he runs up beside me. "We were going to do this with or without your permission."

"You're going to get yourselves killed," he growls, just as we reach the third floor.

I push open the door and immediately dodge the guy wielding a knife. I push him to the side, and he straightens in time to come face to face with Rome. His height reaches Rome's chest so it's comical to watch his head tilt back, his eyes widening as Rome swings his head back, smacking it right into his head. He staggers back before hitting the wall and falling to the floor, out cold.

Nate steps over his outstretched legs and reaches down for his wrists, tying them together.

"No," we hear screamed, and Rome's head snaps up, glancing down the hall. "Fuck!"

We take a step in the direction of the little boy's scream, but we stop as an agonizing scream flitters through the air, coming from the other side of the hallway.

My heart stops as I race towards her.

"Go to him," Nate orders. "I've got his back."

I race down the hall and just reach a door when Nate tackles me from behind, shoving me against the wall. "Do not go fucking racing in there," he hisses.

"They are hurting her," I grit out, my stomach bottoming out as she screams hoarsely.

He holds his finger up to his lips when it goes quiet. My heart stops and my legs threaten to give out.

No.

No, no, no.

I waited too long for someone like Caitlyn. I'm not going to lose her now. She has Carrie. She has me. And she now has a family.

"She's out," someone jokes, chuckling.

I grit my teeth as I tense and Nate steps away, gripping the handle. He holds his hand up, mouthing, "Quiet."

"Get the bucket," a deep voice orders.

Nate pushes the door open, keeping low. We crawl inside, keeping our backs to the wall as we around a corner.

Caitlyn is tied to a metal chair, her hair soaked and covering her face as she gasps for breath.

Blood pours from a wound on her leg, and she has cuts and bruises covering her face and body.

Scanning the room, I only see the two guys standing behind her, none of whom are Robin, who I had seen in a surveillance photo.

A whimper escapes her, and I break. Shoving past Nate, I head for the nearest guy to her, catching him by surprise as I take him to the floor. The guy's fist pummels me on the side of the head, and I lunge, grabbing his head and smacking it back against the floor. His eyes roll into the back of his head, and I rear my fist back, catching him in his temple, making sure he stays out.

I whirl around, finding Nate fighting the other guy one on one, and I quickly rush to Caitlyn, untying the ropes at her hands, when something sharp digs into the side of my neck.

"I wouldn't do that if I were you. I wasn't finished."

I turn, the knife cutting into my skin as I face him. "Robin."

"Drop the knife," Nate orders sharply, moments before something thuds to the floor.

Robin's gaze flicks to Nate, and I take the opportunity to snap my hand out, knocking the knife from his grasp.

He roars and swings his fist at me, but I roll to the side before jumping to my feet. I spin my leg out, hitting him mid-stomach, and he staggers back.

"You're going to pay for this," I growl, leaping towards him. I swing my fist back, smacking him across the jaw.

He howls and comes back at me, diving and hitting my mid-section, taking me to the floor.

"Cage," Caitlyn cries, taking me off guard.

My vision blurs, my temples pulsing as Robin manages to catch me off guard. I slam the palm of my hand against his nose. He roars as blood sprays all over my face.

I kick up, landing a blow to his face. He staggers back, his head hitting the wall as he collapses to the ground.

I crawl on all fours, coughing as I stagger my way over to Caitlyn and Nate.

"Caitlyn," I whisper, a smile tugging at my lips.

I got her.

She's safe.

It's over.

Her eyes widen, and her lips part. "Cage," she screams.

Nate looks up from inspecting her wounds and takes a step forward, horror washing over his expression.

The world around me slows to almost a pause. I slowly turn to my fate, as everything explodes into motion.

Men dash into the room, firearms up and ready.

But it's too late.

Robin uses the radiator as support to hold himself up, the gun in his other hand. He grins as I double over, clutching my stomach. My hand comes away with blood covering every inch of my skin, and I frown, mesmerised by the sight.

My lips part to scream, but no sound comes out, only a gasp of air that's pitiful. Caitlyn falls to her knees by my side, her hands pressing on the wound. I close my eyes as I struggle to catch my breath.

She's safe.

There was a time when I was younger when I wished death would take me. I wished it when my mum died because I wanted to stay with her.

I chased danger like an adrenaline junky and ended up fighting as a way to let out that anger before fighting professionally.

Now that time in my life is laughing at me.

I don't want to die, not when I have so much to live for, a family to take care of. She might not be my wife, and Carrie might not be biologically mine, but they are my family in every other sense of the word, and I don't want to leave them.

I close my eyes as Caitlyn tries to shake me awake. "Please, Cage, don't leave me."

I love you.

Even with my eyes close, everything feels like it's spinning, but her hands anchor me, the warmth, the love.

I love you.

Chapter Forty-Three

CAITLYN

N O, NO, NO, NO. THIS WASN'T meant to happen. He wasn't meant to get hurt. No one was.

Rome was meant to come in with his men and take Robin down. Not Cage. Not like this. Not because of me. I'm not worth this.

Blood rushes to my wrists as Nate unties me, reaching for me as I slide off the chair. He lifts me steadily to my feet and I whimper, the pressure in my thigh burning.

Cage.

Our gazes meet and his lips pull up into a smile, but movement from the corner of my eye has dread filling the pit of my stomach.

My eyes widen as Robin lifts his hand, aiming the gun at the love of my life. "Cage," I wail, reaching for him. Nate holds me back for a moment, but I shove him away.

I rush over as he falls to the floor, and a whimper slips free as I drop down beside him and assess his wounds. Blood spills through my fingers as I press down, crying out.

No, no, no.

Tears swarm my vision as I kneel beside him. "Please, Cage, don't leave me," I plead as Nate rushes past me with other men following him.

I ignore them, knowing they are going for Robin.

Cage's face pales as he stares up at the ceiling, not really seeing me. I press my hand down further, needing to stop the bleeding.

"Cage! No, Cage, wake up," I scream when his eyes begin to flutter shut. "No, no, no."

Cage's hand slips to his side and I watch as the life begins to drain from him.

Hands land on my shoulders, and I shove them away. "No," I cry out, terror filling my chest.

I'm not going to let them take me away from him.

"Get the medics in here now!" Nate barks, and I glance up in time to see him shove Robin at another officer. "Do not let him out of your sight."

"I'll end you all," Robin roars.

"I hope you die and go to hell," I wail.

The hands on my shoulders squeeze. "Caitlyn."

I glance up at him. "Rome?"

"Yeah, honey, it's me."

"Help him," I plead.

"Where the fuck are the medics?" Nate roars, shoving my hands out of the way so he can press down on the wound.

I clasp his hand in mine and lean over, kissing his cold lips. "Please, please, don't leave me."

I can't lose him.

Coldness seeps into my veins and I shiver as I struggle to catch my breath.

"Caitlyn, let the men take a look."

A sob wrenches from my throat as I slouch over him. I heave in a breath, the life choking out of me.

Everything is falling, spinning out around me, pain funnelling into my heart.

All it took was a second.

A second to pull a trigger.

To tear my world apart.

It isn't my life bleeding out of me, it's Cage's, yet that feeling, that lifeless feeling, grows inside of me like cancer.

"I love you," I whisper. "I love you."

For so long I have spent life in fear. He opened up my world, my heart, and I let them all in. I let him in.

And life couldn't just give me this one moment, this one thing in life that I would live the rest of my life being happier for. I don't need anything else. I just need my family. I need him.

I glance up, finding Robin, who is still being pinned down, and meet his gaze. "Why? Why would you do this?" I choke out.

Blood covers his teeth when he grins. "I always win."

"Caitlyn," Rome murmurs.

"No," I choke out, clinging to Cage. His breathing is becoming shallow.

"I've got her," Nate orders, and I feel another set of hands pulling me back.

"No," I screech, crying out when the wound on my leg tugs.

"Stop. The paramedics need to get him in the ambulance."

"No, please, I need him," I cry out before collapsing against him, my breathing heavy.

"Fuck," he hisses, his hand going to my thigh. "We need another paramedic."

"One's outside," Rome replies, and Nate sweeps me up into his arms.

I cling to his neck, crying out. "Please, I need to stay with him. He shouldn't be on his own."

"Calm down," he demands. "The paramedics are looking him over. We need to get you in the ambulance."

"I'm not leaving him," I snap.

"I know, and you aren't. But they need to work on him, Caitlyn," he tells me, his voice filled with emotion. "I need you to be strong for him."

My expression crumbles as uncontrollable sobs pull from my chest. "Why? He's gone. He's left me. He's left me."

"He's not gone," he tells me, his voice fierce, almost demanding. "He's still breathing. He's in a critical way, and that's why we need to get you both to the hospital."

My body spent of energy, I sag against him. Fresh air hits me in the face moments later, stinging the cuts and wound on my body. I hiss, clinging to Nate tighter.

Nate tenses and a shiver races up my spine. "What?" I whisper, lifting my head.

Kelly is awake, Ethan cuddled to her chest with a blanket wrapped around them both.

Her hand raises to her mouth, a choked sob slipping past her lips. "I'm so sorry. I'm so, so sorry."

"Don't speak to her," Nate snaps, heading over to the paramedic. "It's her leg."

"We need to get her to the hospital," he replies, and I cry out as he presses on the wound.

"What ambulance?" he demands, just as the sirens of one start up and pulls out onto the lane.

"Nate," I whisper, when I seem him still staring at Kelly like he's seconds away from committing murder.

I can't speak to Kelly. Not yet. She's the last thing on my mind, and until I know Cage is okay, I'm afraid that if I do, I'll say something I don't mean.

428 | LISA HELEN GRAY

"In here, sir."

"Fuck no," he roars, stepping back.

"I'm sorry?"

"I'm not putting her in this ambulance with that bitch. She's the reason she's in this mess in the first place, and why my best friend is hanging on for his life," he growls.

"Nate, it's fine," I whisper, too weak to witness another fight.

"Like fuck it is," he says to me.

"Nate, get Caitlyn in my car," Rome orders. "I'll drive."

I catch one last glance of Kelly, crumpled into the back of the ambulance, her body shaking with tears.

My heart splits in two, one part of me wanting to reach out to her, the other not having the energy.

Nate climbs into the car, keeping me in his lap as we wait for Rome to get in.

"Nate," he begins.

"Don't," Nate snaps, holding me closer.

I soak in his warmth as we ride the rest of the way in silence, both of us left to our own thoughts. We're covered in blood, and not only our own. I have mine, Kelly's, and Cage's covering me.

And as my eyes fall closed, I have to hope this is the end of it, that we no longer have to worry about Robin.

I JOLT AWAKE to the brutal sound of a gun firing. "Cage," I scream, breathing heavily.

I scan the room. I'm not tied to a chair. I'm not in that building. I'm in a hospital bed.

Roy drops the paper and rushes over to the bed, sitting beside me. "It's okay, you're safe," he assures me softly, pulling me in for a hug. "You gave us a fright."

"Where's Cage?" I ask hoarsely, willing my head to stop spinning.

"He's still in theatre. Nate will be back shortly to check up on you."

Just as I'm about to ask Roy another question, Laura and Danni come charging into the room.

"Oh my God, we came as quickly as we could," Laura gushes as tears stream down her face.

"Is he... is he okay? Dad's gone to find out what's going on. What happened?" Danni asks as she holds back her sobs. "They said he was shot but that can't be right."

"Carrie? Where's Carrie?" I ask, eyes wild as I scan the hallway behind them.

"Hayley has her," Laura explains. "Please, tell us what happened."

I close my eyes, this moment bringing back too many painful memories. I had been them once. I had been the sister who waited to hear back from a sibling, not knowing if they were going to make it.

I can't answer them. It's tearing me apart.

It's all my fault.

"We don't know, honey," Roy explains. "Caitlyn has only just woken up, so let her process everything before she answers."

"No, I need to know what happened to my brother," Danni cries, clinging to her sister.

I curl up in a ball on my side, clutching the blanket as I try to block out their cries. I let them down.

I'd caused this pain. I had ripped a family apart because of my selfish wants.

Because I thought I could love.

Now he's in theatre and I don't know if he's going to make it or not.

"Caitlyn, talk to us, please," Laura demands.

"Girls," Roy pleads.

My chest heaves as I let out the most inhumane, vicious sobs, coming from deep within me. My head constricts in pain as memories of losing my family, raising Carrie, and most of all, meeting Cage, flow through my head, breaking my heart that much more.

I clench my eyes shut tighter, trying to block them out, but then the image of him collapsing after being shot is there and I can't handle it.

"Please, Caitlyn, what happened?" Laura begs from beside me.

"It's all my fault," I choke out. "I'm the reason he could die. I shouldn't have come here. I should have stayed away from him."

My chest hurts with each breath I take, my throat raw as the tears continue to fall. I want Cage. Need him.

A hand on my back startles me. "Caitlyn."

"Nate?" I breathe out, a fresh wave of tears hitting me.

"It's not your fault, Caitlyn. Cage and I both knew who we were dealing with when we swore to protect you. We shouldn't have been in that building unprotected. That's on us, not you."

"Please, is he going to be okay?" I ask, struggling to sit up.

He helps me get into a more comfortable position before sitting back. "He's out of surgery. They said it all went well and that the next twenty-four hours will be critical. His vitals are looking good, and they are pleased with his recovery so far."

My lips part as I wipe the tears away. "Really?"

"Really," he assures me. "How are you feeling?"

"Like I've been stabbed in the leg," I tell him.

He smiles, but it doesn't reach his eyes. "That's because you have."

"You were stabbed?" Danni whispers.

"Danni," Nate murmurs but she takes a step back, shaking her head. She looks like a wild animal trapped in a corner.

"And Cage was shot?"

"Danni," he murmurs, and my heart breaks as she collapses to her knees, her chest heaving as she wails.

"I can't lose him, too. I need him."

Nate moves quickly, picking Danni up off the floor swiftly. Moving over to the stuffed comfy chair in the corner, he places her in his lap.

"He's going to be fine. He's a fighter," he assures her.

"What if he's not? What if we lose him?" she sobs.

"Hey, everything's going to be okay, baby. Just stay calm, okay? Your dad is just finishing off talking to the doctor, then he will be here in a minute to fill us in properly."

I close my eyes, blocking them all out as I lie back down. I did this to them. I caused them this pain.

"Sweetheart," Roy whispers, taking my hand.

I squeeze his hand back, letting him know I heard him but can't talk.

Not now.

Not until they can take me to Cage.

I MUST HAVE fallen asleep because when my lids flutter open, I feel like I have been asleep for hours.

I don't move, not wanting to draw attention to myself. Roy is still here, his head back as he snores lightly.

Laura isn't in the room, but Danni is, and she's asleep, curled up into Nate. He opens his eyes as if he senses me watching.

"You okay?" he whispers.

I nod, feeling my gut clench.

"How's Cage?" I croak out, my voice dry, raw.

Jim steps into the room, startling me. "He's going to be fine. I just came back to check up on you. I'm glad you're awake."

"He's okay?" I ask, and it comes out more of a plea.

"You can go see him once you feel up to it," he assures me.

"Please," I look at him pleadingly. "Can we go see him now?"

"You need some rest. The doctors are concerned with how low your blood pressure is."

"Please," I beg.

He sighs and leans down to press a kiss to my forehead. "Let me go talk to a nurse."

Laura heads inside, her shoulders slumping when she sees I'm awake. "Hey, how you feeling?"

"Sore," I answer honestly. A part of me wonders if she hates me for her brother being shot. I wouldn't blame her if she did. "I'm so sorry."

Her fingers running over my scalp feels soothing. "What for?"

"For putting your brother in danger. I never meant for him to get hurt."

"Nate filled us in, Caitlyn," she explains, pressing a kiss to my temple. "He told us everything once you passed out. None of what happened is your fault and I'm so sorry you had to go through that."

Tears blur my vision and a lump forms in my throat. "But it is my fault."

"No, it's not," she states, arching an eyebrow. "Don't make me shout at a weak person."

"Hey, the nurse is going to be in shortly to check you over, then she wants to take some bloods as a precaution. After that, she said I can wheel you down to see Cage," Jim announces, heading back inside.

"Thank you," I tell him.

"Anything for you," he declares. "I've just spoken to Hayley. She wants to know if it's okay if she brings Carrie to the hospital. She's been asking about you. Since we didn't know what we should tell her, we've been trying to hold her off as long as possible."

"Let me see Cage first, to see how he is. I need to think how I'm going to handle telling her."

"Anything you want."

I nod, then turn back to Nate, my gaze going to Danni. "How is she?"

"Tired," he murmurs, gazing tenderly down at her.

"I'm sorry," I whisper. "I never meant for any of you to be hurt. Physically or mentally."

Jim takes my hand, gently squeezing it. "She'll be okay," he promises. "She's strong."

"She's hurting because of me."

"She's hurting because she loves her brother," he assures me. "After their mum died, Danni took it the hardest because she never really fully understood it. Cage, after going through his own pain, looked out for her and together, they formed a bond that none of us could be a part of."

"Not even me," Laura whispers.

"They love you," Jim assures her.

She smiles. "I know. And I'm glad they had each other," she admits before turning to me. "She loves you too and I think today was just a little much for her."

"I love you all too," I whisper.

"Then don't worry your pretty little head about anything," Jim orders. "You are all going to be okay."

I force a smile, praying like hell he's right.

Chapter Forty-Four

CAITLYN

J IM PUSHES ME INTO CAGE'S room on the ICU ward. He's alone, the other beds empty. But I don't take much notice as Jim wheels me closer.

He's still awfully pale, and machines are hooked up everywhere.

"Oh God," I cry out, reaching for his hand.

Jim leans down, pressing a kiss to the top of my head. "I'll give you some time alone."

"Wait," I call out when he steps away. "When will he wake up?"

"He's been in and out, so hopefully soon," he tells me.

I nod, and I listen to him leave.

"I'm so sorry," I tell him.

I take in his ashen face and curl my fingers around his hand tighter.

I lift it, pressing my lips to the palm of his hand. I want to reach up and caress his face, press my lips to his, but I can't risk pulling my stitches, especially if it means they'll send me back to my room.

"Please wake up," I beg him. "I love you. I love you so goddamn much it hurts." I close my eyes. He might not be awake, but I want him to hear my voice, to know I'm here. "You have to wake up. Carrie and I won't have it any other way. And it's your fault." I force out a dry laugh. "You showed me love. You gave it to me in the purest form. You showed me what it's like to really live. Now you need to come back to me so we can keep living it."

I press my head against his hand, my chest heaving. "It killed me today, Cage. I was so scared when I realised what was happening. But I knew you'd be there. I knew you wouldn't stop looking. And if you didn't find me, I knew our daughter would be safe and loved. Because she had you." I pause, the breath stalling in my chest. "Why? Why did you go inside that building? Why would you risk your life for me?" I shake my head, lifting it to look up at his handsome face. "You nearly left me. And you would have left me not even half the person I am when I'm with you because you complete me. Cage, you complete me. Without you, I don't know who or where I'll be, so please, please wake up.

"When you pull through this, Cage Carter, you're never leaving me again. I want you for the rest of my life."

Tears fall as I cling to his hand, silently praying for him to wake up.

Because I want it all. I want the future he promised me, the love he gave me, the home he shared.

A tap on the door startles me and I jerk up, wiping at the tears. I turn, my neck stiff as I face Rome.

Anguish fills his eyes as he steps inside. He heads over to me, pulling out the chair the nurses placed next to the bed.

"How's he doing?" he asks, taking a seat.

I glance away. "I don't know. I haven't spoken to his doctor yet."

"I'm sorry about today. I never meant for this to happen."

"I know," I whisper.

"He saved you."

"What?"

He nods, glancing at Cage, still unconscious. "We had already entered the building but there were extensions we were unaware of, exits we didn't have covered. My men were searching the floors one by one. I ran into Nate and Cage. They were alert, and they fought their way to get to you. We split, and I went one way and they went the other. In the room they were holding Ethan and Kelly, the men had just been told of the breech."

"I don't understand."

He closes his eyes. "Had Cage not got to you, I wouldn't have made it. Robin would have got the call and killed you there and then. Cage distracting him gave us a chance to get to you."

"He's been my hero for a long time," I whisper. "He's always saving me. Even from myself."

"He's a good man."

"The best."

"I have something for you," he tells me, pulling out a white envelope.

"For me?" I ask, taking it. My breath hitches when I see the writing on the envelope. Tears gather in my eyes. "This is my sister's handwriting."

He nods, wincing. "Officer Luke had that in his belongings. It was brought to me not long ago."

I grip his hand. "He was—"

"He died half an hour ago."

A guttural cry slips up my throat. "He tried to help me. If I had listened instead of panicking, he might still be here."

"He was a dead man for a while. Robin knew about him the

entire time and used him to feed useless information to us. It just happened that he died today. It could have been a lot sooner."

"He seemed like a good man."

"He was, Caitlyn, and if he could, he'd tell you what I'm about to. This isn't your fault. It's Robin's. And he would die to keep you alive."

"He didn't know me."

"He doesn't need to. It's his job."

"I'm so sorry for your loss," I tell him, hating the pain in his voice.

"Thank you. I have a few things to clear up here, so if you need me, call."

"I will, thank you."

"And Caitlyn, Robin is finished. You'll never have to worry about him ever again."

I sag against the chair as he leaves, my breathing coming in fast and deep. I grip the letter in my hand, wave after wave of emotion running through me.

So many lives.

So much grief.

It's over.

Sometime later, I manage to calm myself enough to pull the letter from the envelope, my vision clouding with tears.

Dearest Caitlyn,

It feels weird writing a goodbye letter when you're a floor above me, safe and sound. But I couldn't risk taking another step with my plan without doing it. I couldn't risk something happening to me and never getting to have this final moment with you.

If you are reading this, then I'm gone, and you know all about Robin and what kind of man he is.

And I'm sorry.

I'm sorry for leaving you alone in the world with monsters. I'm sorry I couldn't show you that there is good in the world, a light beyond the darkness.

I'm sorry for bringing him into your life.

My stupidity and immaturity got you into this mess, but I hope one day you'll forgive me. Because what I'm about to tell you could make you hate me forever.

I'm the reason Mum and Dad are dead. They hired someone to look into Robin and the person found out more than they bargained for. They are all dead, but that information is still out there. No words can describe how I'm feeling or how sorry I truly am. You've lost everything because of me, but I promise to make this right, even if I die trying.

If something does happen to me, I want you to use it to get away from Robin. Go to the police. I can't say much in case this is found, but trust the person giving it to you. Know that he tried to take care of me and will take care of you.

I wish I had time to tell you all my regrets, but this would be a long-arse letter if I did. My biggest one is not giving you the life you deserve, for putting this heavy weight on your shoulders.

I pause, wiping at my cheeks so I can read the words. Reading her words is like hearing them in my head. I can picture her beautiful face and glassy eyes as she pours her heart out writing this.

I clutch at my chest as I turn the page and try to pull myself together.

By now you'll also understand why I got you to sign those papers, why I left my daughter in your care. Because although I'm hoping for the best, I can feel it in my gut that this isn't going to end well for me. I guess a part of me knows I'm not going to survive this.

But you will.

You have to. For her.

Which is why I'll leave a separate letter for her. And when the time is right, give it to her. Let her know she was loved, and she had more than one mummy.

It kills me even imagining a life without her. I want nothing more than to be the mum she deserves, to be the person she cuddles and cries to. I want to hear her first word, see her take her first step, plan her first birthday.

And if I'm not, you need to be that person for her.

You need to raise her like she is your own. I want you to protect her like your life depends on it and don't stop until you do. Because she's innocent in all of this and I'm scared he'll go after her.

I know this is a lot to ask, but you're the only person I trust in this world, the only person I could leave my child with and rest peacefully.

I want you to give her the life I can't. Spoil her on birthdays. Soothe her when she's poorly. Teach her to ride a bike. To read. Everything.

But mostly, love her. Love her for the both of us.

Be the mum that little girl needs because I can't.

And never feel guilty for being her mummy.

And no matter what happens, know I'm with you. Always. I will die for you, for her.

Please take care of her, and yourself. I love you both so much. It pains me to say goodbye, so I'm not going to. I'll see you later.

Love you more than life itself. Both of you.

Live your best lives, my dearest Caitlyn and Carrie.

Forever in my heart.

Courtney

Xx

My tears drop down on the page, smudging the ink. She knew she was going to die. She knew I'd be the one to take care of Carrie. She trusted me to stand up and be the mum she needed me to be for her daughter.

With shaking hands, I fold the paper up then pull out an envelope addressed to Carrie, marked to be opened on her eighteenth birthday. Placing it safely back into the bigger envelope, I tuck the letters to my chest.

We never got to have a funeral. We never got to say goodbye. And for years, it's what kept me from mourning her, why I couldn't let go.

This is what I needed, what Robin robbed from me.

"Don't cry, Kitten."

I inhale sharply, snapping my head up and coming face to face with the man I love.

And he's awake.

"Cage," I whisper.

"Hey," he murmurs groggily.

"I thought I lost you." I cry out as I lift myself so I can stand beside the bed. Pain radiates up my leg and my ribs. Holding my breath through the pain, I move forward so he can see my face.

"I'm here," he whispers.

"Please don't ever leave me again. I can't live without you. I don't want to live without you. I need you," I choke out. "Please don't ever put yourself in danger again."

He winces. "I'd do it again in a heartbeat."

"I'll call the nurse," I tell him, pressing the button behind his head.

"A-are you okay?" he asks, struggling to talk.

"Fine! I'm not the one who went all Bruce Willis and got shot."

His lips pull up into a lazy smile. "Bruce Willis?"

"Yeah, he is always getting shot at in *Die Hard*. Have you not seen the movie?"

"Yeah, I've seen it," he whispers.

He closes his eyes, wincing as he tries to catch his breath.

Leaning over, I press the button for the nurses' station again. *Where the fuck are they?*

"So help me God, if they don't come in to see you in a second, I'm going to throw the biggest hissy fit anyone living has ever seen."

Cage smiles at me, his eyes drooping a little. "I love you," he whispers.

His voice sounds strange, like it doesn't belong to him. Eyeing the jug of water by the side of the bed, I bite my lip. I'm not even sure if he's allowed any.

"I love you, too, baby," I tell him, leaning down to kiss his forehead. *He's awake.* "I'm going to get a nurse. They need to check you over."

"Stay," he demands softly.

"No, they need to make sure everything is okay."

"Wait," he orders, gripping the edge of the bed. His eyes close as he inhales and exhales deeply. "You hurt your leg."

"I'm fine," I lie and take a step away. I go dizzy for a moment, the sensation causing my stomach to roll. I breathe through it and take another step towards the door, moving carefully.

"Sit down now," Cage growls, and I hear the exhaustion in his voice.

"No, they're pissing me off. You're critical for the next twenty-four hours yet they ignore my calls not once, but twice. Nuh uh, no way."

Pulling the door open, I forget what I'm supposed to be doing when I hear Nate laying into Kelly. She's standing there, her shoulders slumped, letting him yell at her.

"You nearly got them killed," he roars.

"I had no choice. They were going to kill my boy," she explains, her shoulders shaking with her tears.

He snorts in disgust. "You could have come to us. We could have helped you."

"He hurt my son," she cries out.

It's too much.

All of it.

We were all victims when it came to Robin. We all had something to lose, more for some.

But it's over now.

"Stop!" I scream "Just stop!"

"Caitlyn, you shouldn't be out of your chair," Laura scolds, rushing to my side.

I meet Nate's gaze. "She did what she had to do to save her son," I tell him.

"She nearly got you killed. My best friend is in there lying in a bed with a bullet wound."

"I know," I whisper.

"I never wanted anyone to get hurt," Kelly whispers, folding into herself. "I promise, I never wanted this."

"You don't deserve our forgiveness," Nate snaps.

"I'm not asking for it," she tells him, and it comes out more like a plea.

My heart breaks for her as I take another step towards her, but I come up short when I find the nurses all sat like this is a live reality show.

"YOU!" I bark towards the nurses, who jump from being caught ogling Nate and Dante. "I've pressed that fucking call button twice in the space of fifteen minutes. My man is critical and needs assistance. I struggled through some serious fucking pain to come out here to find help, to discover you eye-fucking these pair. Get a fucking doctor to come and see him, *now*."

Laura steadies me as Danni moves forward. "He's okay?"

I give her a soft smile. "He's awake."

"Told you he's like a fucking cat with ten lives," Dante booms.

"It's nine lives, you moron," Laura mutters next to me.

"Who the fuck cares," he replies, grinning like a fool.

The nurses finally head into Cage's room, along with Danni. "Go," I tell Laura and Jim.

Laura doesn't move, conflict written all over her face. "Are you sure?"

"Yes," I whisper.

She and Jim head inside and I step over to Nate. "Can you give us a minute?"

"I'm not leaving you with her."

I place my hand on his arm. "I'll be fine. Please."

He sighs, and scowls at Kelly before heading inside with the others.

I face her, stunned by her appearance. She still looks a mess. She's battered and bruised, but it's her attire. She no longer looks like the perfect model in her tracksuit and baggy T-shirt.

Her breath hitches. "I'm so sorry," she whispers, tears falling down her cheeks.

"I know," I whisper.

Now that I'm here, now she's awake, all the questions I wanted to ask, I can't find.

"I tried. I tried so hard to make sure no one else got hurt, but he had Ethan," she chokes out. "He hurt him when I refused, and I couldn't... I couldn't..."

"It's okay."

Her expression crumbles. "No, it's not. It's really not. Years ago, I made a mistake of falling in love with the wrong person. When he showed his true colours, I was too scared to leave. I should have. If I had been stronger, we wouldn't have been here. Me and Ethan wouldn't have been pulled into his crap."

"Kelly," I murmur, reaching for her.

She pulls back. "You've done nothing but be good to me. And I'm sorry. So fucking sorry. But you have to believe me. I only took you because I thought my plan would work."

"What was your plan?" I ask.

She glances away. "A shit one clearly."

"I remember the two other syringes."

She nods, fiddling with the sleeves of her jacket. "They gave me stuff to knock you out, said the more I gave you, the longer you would be out. So, I got a hold of two more syringes. I put more into the other two." She pauses and takes a deep breath. "He wouldn't tell me where Ethan was, not until I did this. When I got out the car,

Marker gave me the location of where Ethan was being held. That's when I went for him. I tried to stab him with the needle, but he was too fast."

"And they did this as punishment?" I murmur, gesturing to her injuries.

"Yes. I remember being dragged into a room and beaten. Then waking up in the ambulance with Ethan next to me."

"Why didn't you come to me? I would have helped you," I tell her, the back of my eyes burning.

"Because I was scared that he'd know. He always seemed to know everything. I didn't have any family to turn to, or anyone to ask for help."

"You had me."

She shakes her head. "No, I didn't. Not then. And when I did get to know you, I couldn't trust you'd help me or be able to help me." She pauses, her expression filled with anguish. "He's all I have, Caitlyn. I love him more than life and if I could have traded places with him and you, I would have."

"Stop," I demand softly. "You did what you did to save your son."

"I wanted to help you too. I didn't want to lose you as a friend."

"Kelly, I forgive you. I forgave you the minute I met Ethan."

"No!" she chokes out, stepping back. "How can you forgive me? I nearly got you all killed. I might as well have shot Cage and killed Luke myself."

"Yes," I affirm. "Yeah, it's not going to be how it was between us, but we'll get there."

"They all hate me," she whispers. "And I don't blame them."

"They don't understand why you did what you did. I'll talk to them. Right now, though, you need to go home and get some rest; you look like shit," I tease.

Her chuckle ends up in a grimace. She pulls herself together before meeting my gaze. "You really are something else, Caitlyn."

"Kelly," I whisper, feeling like there's more to her words.

She shakes her head. "You know what's funny? I've wished for a friend like you for years. Every time he hurt me, I prayed to find someone like you to talk to, or just have. And when I finally find you, I do something terrible to you."

"It all worked out in the end," I tell her, then slowly pull her in for a hug, mindful of both of our injuries.

She hesitates for a moment before hugging me back. "I really am sorry, Caitlyn."

"I know," I whisper, then pull back. "Where is Ethan?"

She glances down at the floor, biting her lip. "I made him wait with Rome in the waiting room. I knew this wasn't going to go so well and didn't want him to witness any more violence."

Yeah, I get that. Poor kid has been through enough.

"Is he okay?"

"Shaken up, but he will be okay. He was asking to see you. He told me you looked after us after they knocked me out." She pauses, taking a deep breath. "He's really worried about you. I think after Luke, then them dragging you away, it's scared him."

"Will you bring him over once everyone is well enough? If you want to, that is? And tell him I'm okay and that he's brave."

I'm not even sure what her plans are now she's no longer under Robin's thumb. She could have a home to go back to.

"He would love that," she tells me, and after a moment of awkward silence, she says, "I need to get back to him."

I nod. "Okay."

She pauses before she turns, glancing at the door to Cage's room then back to me. "I know I don't deserve this, but could you keep me informed on how you both are?"

A lump forms in my throat. "Sure, same with you and Ethan."

"Bye," she whispers, and turns, heading towards the lift.

"Goodbye," I reply, but it's too late for her to hear me.

"Thank fuck that bitch has gone," Nate bites out, startling me.

"Don't," I warn.

"You can't be serious," he growls.

I turn to face him fully, catching a quick glance of Dante behind him. "Nate, have you ever loved someone so much you'd die for them? And I truly mean die for."

His gaze hardens. "What she did is different."

"No, it's not, and one day you'll understand."

"I'll never understand why she did what she did."

I pity him. "I hope there is never a day that you are in her position."

He rears back. "You can't honestly believe any of that."

"Yes," I whisper. "Because I would do the exact same for Carrie. I'd do anything for her."

"Caitlyn," he whispers, shame-faced.

"Don't. I get you're angry. I'm not telling you not to be, but don't take it out on the person who doesn't deserve it. She's alone and needs our support." When he opens his mouth to argue, I put my hand up. "Don't be an arsehole."

"Fuck," he growls, running his fingers through his hair.

"Now can you carry me back to my man," I demand, whimpering, my bravado evaporating. "Because my leg really hurts."

He sweeps me into his arms, and he grunts. "One day we are going to stop being put in this position."

I lay a kiss upon his cheek before resting my head on his chest, yawning. "But then I wouldn't get snuggles."

S TONES CRUNCH UNDER MY shoes as I walk along the stone path. I keep my head down, trying to keep myself together.

So much has happened over the four weeks since Robin kidnapped me. One being our recovering. It has taken a lot longer for Cage, but he's finally in a place where he's doing good.

We're doing good.

Carrie, not so much. She might not have understood our injuries or knew the extent of them, but she felt them like any other loved one would. For weeks now she has been having nightmares about us leaving her. She sees it in her dreams and wakes up screaming for us not to leave her.

Danni stayed with us at the cabin, not only to help with Cage but with Carrie. I think having everyone so close is helping, but I know these things take time.

I glance down at my empty hand, wondering once again if I made the right decision not to bring her, if she should be here holding my hand right now.

After the arrest of Robin Quinton, Rome carried on digging through his files and found where he buried my sister a week ago. I hadn't even known she was buried. I always assumed he covered up her death, but apparently, he paid people off to fake her cause of death.

I'm not sure if the time is right to tell Carrie. She's already going through so much and I don't want to make it worse by confusing her. She will know about Courtney, and I'll make sure she knows how much she is loved.

Cage stops me at the end of the path. The path I know my sister's grave is going to be along. Tears gather in my eyes as I cling to his jacket.

I've wanted this for so long, but now it's here, I'm scared. Scared of what it means, what it will do. Because the letter was one thing, it was a goodbye I never got, but this… this seems final, real in a way I never let myself believe before.

"We don't have to do this," Cage assures me. "We can come back."

"Do you think I'm doing the right thing in not bringing Carrie?"

He runs his hands over my cheeks, down my neck, until they rest on my shoulders. "Right now, she needs stability. She needs to see us strong. When the time is right, we will tell her together."

I press up against him, wrapping my arms around his waist. "We are going to give her the best life, just like she wanted."

"Yes, together," he promises.

"Let's go," I whisper, and reach down, taking his hand.

He links his fingers through mine and together we walk along the stoned path, before coming to a stop halfway down.

Courtney Quinton. Beloved wife and mother.

My breath hitches. She wasn't a Quinton, not at heart. She wasn't just a wife or a mother. She was a sister, a daughter, a friend, and a mentor. She was everything.

"Kitten," Cage urges when I collapse against him, sobbing into his chest.

"She's not a Quinton."

"Shush, baby. We've already got the all-clear to change the headstone."

"I feel like he's done this to continue torturing her," I choke out.

"It's over now. It's over," he assures me.

I let go and kneel on the ground, pushing away the leaves that have fallen and pulling at some of the weeds.

Cage goes to take a step back, but I grip his leg. "Please, don't leave."

"I'm not going anywhere. Just giving you some room."

I nod, and face the headstone, my gut churning once again when I see her name. "It's me," I announce quietly. "I'm sorry it took me so long." I close my eyes, her words in her letter hitting me. "I was mad at you for so long after you died. You left me, left Carrie, and I didn't know what to do." I pause, digging my fingers into the grass. "But I'm not anymore. I don't think I really was because every time I looked at Carrie, I saw you. And how could I be mad."

I smile wistfully. "You'd be so proud of the beautiful little girl she turned into. She looks so much like you, even acts like you at times."

"I can't stay long, but I'll be back. I'll always be back," I tell her. "I needed to come to thank you. You gave me the most precious gift in the world. You trusted me to care for her, to love her, to treat her as my own. And I promise you, I have. And I always will. She gave me a reason to keep fighting." I turn to look at Cage from over my shoulder and smile before turning back. "Now I have a family to keep fighting for.

"I have someone else to fight for and he's everything, Courtney. He loves her just as much as we do. He loves me. And we love him.

"I miss you. I miss you so much. I'm sorry for everything that happened. I love you."

I stand as Cage comes up behind me, wrapping his arms around my waist. "It's okay," he whispers.

I glance down at the grave, my vision blurred with tears. "I promise to change the headstone, to give you the resting place you deserve."

Cage kisses my temple. "We will."

"I'll give her everything, I promise," I whisper, and step forward, pressing my fingers to my lips before placing them on the headstone. "See you soon."

"We can come back," he promises me.

I lean up, pressing a kiss to the corner of his mouth. "I know." I kiss him again, needing him to know I'm okay. "Take me home."

CAGE

"WHERE ARE WE going?" Caitlyn whines, fiddling with the blindfold I put on her nearly thirty minutes ago.

We're nearly home, and I have a surprise for her, one I don't want her guessing before we get there.

"For a smart, woman, you should know the meaning of surprise," I tease.

When I found out we were visiting her sister's grave, I knew the day was going to be hard on her. But I also knew it would be the day for healing, for old wounds to begin to close, so I began to put my plan into action, recruiting friends and family to help whilst I recovered.

It killed me the first few weeks. I didn't have my strength back, and even now, if I overdo it, I get exhausted.

But I'm here for her. She can no longer make me stay at home whilst she goes to appointments, no longer tell me to rest when Carrie wants to play.

I'm doing better, and I need her to see that too.

Pulling up into an empty spot, I shut the engine off. I wipe my sweaty palms down my legs and face her, even though she can't see me.

"Stay there, and no touching the mask," I warn her.

Jumping out, I round the car and pull open her door. She unbuckles her belt and lets me lift her out of the car.

"Put me down. You still need to take it easy," she scolds, making me chuckle.

"I'm fine. Stop worrying."

Danni opens the door, keeping quiet as I step past her. I wink, and carry on past the others, heading for the stairs.

"Where are we?" she asks suspiciously.

I chuckle. "Wait," I warn her, before stepping into the room.

I gently place her on her feet and stand behind her. I want this to be the room she sees first. I want her to see I had been serious from the very beginning, that this had never been temporary for me.

When I first showed her around the house, she couldn't help describing how she would have stuff, but in this room, she described what she'd do if she had this space for Carrie.

So, I gave her that dream.

In the middle of the room is a single, four-poster princess bed. The frame is made out of oak and painted white. The sheets are plain pink with white throw pillows.

It has a reading area under the window that's surrounded by fairy lights. The seats are made from the same material as the bedsheet.

"Are you ready?" I whisper against her ear.

"Yes."

Removing the blindfold, I hear her sharp intake of breath and take a step to the side as she steps forward.

"When? How? What?" she asks, flabbergasted as she takes it all in.

"I wanted Carrie's room to be the first room you saw," I admit, studying her closely as she moves over to the toy box, running her finger across the *Frozen* artwork I had done on it.

She spins around, absorbing it before stopping on me. "This is… this is beautiful, Cage," she tells me, her eyes glistening. "When did you get all of this done?"

"It was the first room we did. Laura and Danni finished it off with the accessories while we were recovering. I told them what you wanted, and they made it happen."

She charges at me with force as she wraps her legs around my waist, and her arms around my neck.

"It's perfect. Just like you, Mr Carter," she whispers, emotion clogging up her throat.

"Just like you, you mean?"

She shakes her head, staring at me with so much emotion it threatens to undo me. "No, I mean *you*," she whispers, her voice choked up. "What you've done for us…" She stops, unable to speak for a moment. "You've made us a family, Cage."

"We were already a family. Now we can live in a house, just like you dreamed."

"I love you so much," she tells me, as I wipe away the tears that have slipped out.

"I love you more, Kitten," I tell her, pressing my lips to hers before pulling back. "But this isn't your only surprise."

"It's not?"

"No," I admit, pulling the blindfold back out. My hands shake with nerves.

"Are you okay?"

"Yes, but I need you to put this back on."

"Okay," she sighs. "But Cage…"

"Yeah?"

"When can we move in?"

I chuckle and lean in to kiss the tip of her nose. "Tonight."

"I can't wait to get Carrie."

"Me neither," I tell her, pressing my lips together. She doesn't need to know she's already here.

I lift her back into my arms and she sighs wistfully. "I could get used to this."

I laugh. "Always."

I pass everyone once again and meet my dad's gaze. His eyes mist over as he gives me a nod of approval.

I head out the back door and towards the path, taking her to the one place we shared that has good memories.

Coming into the clearing, I set Caitlyn down softly on her feet. Leaning in, I place my lips to hers.

Moaning, Caitlyn steps forward, her body flush against mine. I groan, kissing her back just as fiercely.

Our sex life hadn't suffered for long. One week of none and we both caved, both thankful to have that moment again.

"Caitlyn," I moan, pulling back.

My muscles ache as I uncover her eyes, letting her adjust to the light. She blinks up at the fairy lights I had placed around every tree on either side of the path. It lights up the entire place and is something I hope I don't have to fix often. But I wanted to make this special for her, for us.

Her lips part as she stares up in amazement. "Did you do all of this?"

"Yeah," I admit, hoping she likes it.

"It's beautiful," she murmurs and stares off into the water, where the moon shines down on the reservoir.

I bend down on one knee while she's distracted, and she turns, doing a double take. Her breath hitches as she places a hand to her chest.

"Cage," she whispers, her eyes once again glistening.

I pull the ring out of my back pocket and hold it up, using my free hand to reach for hers. Her chest rises and falls.

Fuck, this is harder than I thought.

I clear my throat, pulling myself together. "Caitlyn, before I met you, I thought I knew who I was. But I didn't have a clue. Not really. Because with you, I not only found the love of my life, but I found me. I'm a better person because of you.

"But that isn't why I want to spend the rest of my life with you. I love you, Caitlyn. I love everything about you. I love your laugh, even when you laugh at your own jokes. I love your smile, and the way it lights up a room.

"I love how you love our daughter. I love your strength, and I love your mind." I take a breath, my hands shaking as I slide the ring a little onto her finger. "You're the woman I want to wake up to and fall asleep with. You're the person I want share my highs and lows with, the good and the bad. The woman I want to spend the rest of my life with.

"Caitlyn Michaelson, will you do me the honour of becoming my wife, for now and forever?"

My voice cracks as I watch tears stream down her cheeks.

"Please say something. Anything. Just don't say no," I plead.

Her gaze locks on mine and in that moment, I feel like she's reaching into my soul, just like I always feel when she looks at me so deeply.

I felt like this from the first moment I met her, and I hope I feel like this the day we die.

"Yes," she chokes out, and I sway, unsure if I heard her right. She throws herself at me and I land on my back with a thud. "Yes. Yes. Yes. Yes."

She pulls back, hovering above me. Her tears splash down on my face. "I love you," I whisper.

"I love you too," she tells me, before slamming her mouth down on mine.

Fuck, she's everything I'll ever need.

"I only asked you one question, you know," I tease, pulling back a little. I never want to let her go.

"Don't be a dick," she warns, unable to keep the smile off her face.

Sitting up, I pull her onto my lap and slide the ring fully onto her ring finger. It's a simple two carat white gold ring with a sparkly princess cut diamond and a pink stone centred in the middle. Caitlyn isn't one for big gestures. She likes things simple, thoughtful, and from the heart. Which is what I have given her.

"It's stunning," she breathes, staring down at her hand.

"Yeah," I agree, staring at her beautiful face.

"Now, how about I show you how much I like it," she says seductively as she reaches for the hem of her dress.

Placing my hand on top of hers, I still her movements.

"Not so fast there, Kitten. I have another surprise."

"I thought you only had one more?" she asks, her forehead creasing.

I grin, lifting her to her feet. "I lied."

She takes my hand, pulling me against her. "Well, I have one for you too."

"If it's your mouth around my cock, it will have to wait," I tell her, although, if I didn't think our guests would coming looking for us, I'd make them wait so I could show her how much I love her.

She snorts. "No."

"What then?" I ask, wrapping my arms around her. "Because I have everything I need right here."

456 | LISA HELEN GRAY

"Yeah, you do," she murmurs, and I feel like there's a hidden meaning there. "Remember at the hospital, when the nurse called me back to my room that first night?"

My brows pull together. "Yeah, she said she needed to check you over."

"She did. My bloods came back. I have been waiting for your birthday to tell you. I wanted it to be a surprise."

I'm drawing a blank. "I'm lost, Kitten."

"I'm pregnant," she whispers.

I blink, wondering if I heard her wrong.

"What? How?" I stutter.

"Now, if you need me to tell you how babies are made, we aren't doing it right," she teases.

"Smartarse." I freeze, taking a moment to digest her words. *We're going to have a baby.* "You're really pregnant?"

She nods, beaming up at me. "Yes."

I grin and swing her up into my arms. "I fucking love you," I tell her, tears gathering in my eyes. "We are going to have another baby."

She melts into me, her smile blinding. "Yeah, we really are."

"Is it a boy or a girl?"

"We'll find out on your birthday," she replies.

A baby.

Walking back towards the house sometime later, I can't keep the grin off my face. I'm going to be a dad. Carrie is going to have a brother or sister. And the love of my life said yes.

"So, Mr Carter," Caitlyn murmurs, pulling me to a stop outside the backdoor. "Is this everything you wished for?"

I pause at her words and shake my head. I reach up, cupping her cheek. "No. I got more."

"Cage," she whispers, and leans up on her toes to kiss me.

I push open the backdoor, and inside erupts in cheers. Caitlyn pulls away, startled at first, but when she looks inside at our friends and family, she grips my arm, her smile stretching across her face.

"Congratulations!"

I glance down at her, smiling back.

Some things are better left forgotten, but this… This is a moment to treasure for the rest of our lives.

Together.

The End

Acknowledgements

This is the second edition of Better Left Forgotten so it deserved a new acknowledgement whilst keeping the memory of the people who helped bring this together the first time. You guys will always be a part of this book.

It's taken a long time—too long—but this story is something I am finally proud of. Having spent hours upon hours re-writing and editing this book, I'm ecstatic about it being complete. I never thought this day would come with my busy schedule, but it's complete.

And now I need a large drink.

Maybe two.

If this is your first-time reading BLF, I really hope you've enjoyed it and will leave a review on the correct platform.

If this isn't your first time, I really hope you enjoyed the changes made and appreciate the work put into it. I did this for you guys.

If you are giving this book a second chance, thank you for believing in me.

To Stephanie at Farrant Editing. Thank you for sticking by me when it came to this series. I know there have been a lot of changes, a lot of rearranging when it came to scenes, but you stuck with it. *You* helped me stick with it. Just when I was going to pull this completely off market, you talked me out of it. I found the motivation and time because of you. So, this book is for you, for all the hard work you put in to helping me get these all re-edited and complete.

And my kids… Thank you for listening to me and doing your online schoolwork so I could do my work. Thank you for being quiet every time I got my laptop out to work. Thank you for understanding that sometimes, I can't do something because I have to work. Thank you for not waking me up early when you knew I had worked until 6am.

Thank you for being you.

Printed in Great Britain
by Amazon

80389183R00262